I0666145

The Deadly Divine

A Trouble Thriller

Matthew Doggett

Five Brothers Publishing

Contents

Get Your Free Novella

GET YOUR FREE TROUBLE novella by heading over to Matthew DoggettAuthor.com/Trouble

Not only will you get a free Trouble story, but you'll also join my epic email list. I send regular freebies and exclusives, and only email once or twice a month.

Prologue

BETRAYAL WAS ON JOHN Virgil's mind as he sat on the low couch, dressed in an ill-fitting coat. The couch was so low, and John so slumped, his knees were nearly level with his chin.

He thought about the phone call he'd made at the gas station. Regrets swam in his head.

He finished off his second single-serving bottle of wine and leaned over, opening his legs so his modest belly wouldn't press against his thighs. With a stomach full of wine and a head full of anxiety, he didn't want to risk a vomiting episode. He reached into the bag between his feet for another small bottle. He wanted the wine to do its sweet work, to stay in his body and give him a little solace, a little comfort. He wanted it to take the edge off his regret. And his dread.

The shades were drawn over the windows in the living room, keeping out the night and obscuring them from any prying eyes. The soft lighting in the house gave it a cozy feeling that John would've enjoyed had the situation been different. As it was, he was only vaguely aware of his surroundings. He had other things on his mind.

Across the living room, near the front door of the one-story house, Shelly and Trent Waller were speaking animatedly to each other. John knew Shelly and Trent well. And that was one major regret. He'd betrayed their trust. They just didn't know it yet.

"Just relax," Trent said. "We're safe here. The only other person who knows where we are is Parall Mitchell."

"Don't say that word. Please." Shelly said.

John lowered the third bottle from his lips, stopping the glug-glug-glug sound it was making. He looked at Shelly, who glanced over her husband's shoulder at him. He still thought of them all as Paralls. Parall Shelly and Parall Trent since they shared a last name. He even thought of himself as Parall Virgil. He'd grown so used to it. Why did he want to leave in the first place? He couldn't remember. The wine burbling softly in his head kept him from thinking too hard.

"We'll stay one night," Trent said. "Mitchell said he's going to try and send help. Just one night, okay?"

The situation was wearing on all of them. Shelly and Trent, both in their late twenties, had a right to be concerned. They'd taken a big step. They all had.

Trent glanced over his shoulder at John, his eyes flitting with disapproval across the small bottle of wine in his hand. Then he turned back to his wife and nodded once. Shelly, looking up at her husband, brought a hand to her head and ran it through her short brown hair. The hand shook as she did it. Even John could see it from his position on the couch.

"Okay," she said finally,

"We'll be okay," Trent said. "We did the right thing. We're *doing* the right thing."

Shelly stepped to the front door and peered through the peephole. She fingered the deadbolt lock even though it was fully turned, seated securely in the doorjamb.

She turned back and embraced her husband for a long moment.

"You doing okay over there?" Trent asked, breaking the embrace and turning to face Virgil.

"Good as I can be," Virgil said. He held up the small wine bottle. "I missed alcohol. Probably a little too much."

Trent and Shelly each managed a small smile.

"We're going to try to get some sleep," Trent said.

Virgil nodded. "I guess Angel—uh, Shayna's still out?"

"I think so," Shelly said. "Last I checked, anyway. After we ate dinner, she passed out pretty quickly."

John Virgil nodded. He could still feel the fast food like wet cement in his gut. "I'll take the other bedroom when I'm done out here. Don't think I can sleep quite yet."

"Yeah," Trent said. "We'll see if we can. It might be tough."

The married couple said goodnight and went to the master bedroom, where they'd placed the girl. It was better that they stay with the girl. They seemed to have a connection with her.

John Virgil was not inclined to move from his spot on the couch. He was comfortable, and he also wanted to be the first to greet whoever they sent. He didn't know when they'd arrive, but it had been several hours since he'd made the call. He wondered about the "help" Mitchell was supposedly sending. He knew it wouldn't be cops.

John Virgil drank one more bottle. He'd bought two four-packs, so he was halfway done. His head was swimming, and his bladder was nearly ready to burst. After screwing the aluminum cap back on the empty bottle, he sat quietly, listening for signs that Trent and Shelly were still up and about. He heard none.

He stood up and padded to the front door. He peered out the peephole, seeing nothing but darkness beyond the pool of light in the recessed doorway. It was an isolated house, with woods all around. That was why they'd chosen it.

Slowly, he turned the deadbolt, unlocking the door. There was no knob lock.

He padded back past the living room and toward the kitchen, hanging a right at the hallway. The first door on his right was the bathroom. He stepped in and shut the door behind him.

After pissing about a gallon out, he washed his hands and stood in front of the mirror, looking down at the reflection of his hands pressed to the countertop. He'd always liked his hands. They were strong and thick-fingered, just like his father's. He looked at the ill-fitting clothes he was wearing, purchased with haste from a Goodwill in Pueblo, Colorado.

There was a noise from the hallway. Like someone tiptoeing past. Then there was a loud thump from the direction of the master bedroom, followed by a sound like a gasp.

John stood up and looked at the bathroom door, his heart suddenly thundering in his chest. Were they here already?

A muffled scream followed by another thump bristled the hair on John's neck. Surely they weren't beating them. Surely. Virgil had been promised there would be no retaliation.

But the sounds . . . Those thumps sounded like muffled gunshots. He stood paralyzed for a moment before lunging forward to lock the bathroom door. As he reached for the knob, the door crashed open, slamming into his hand and breaking two of his fingers. John pulled the hand to his chest as he backpedaled, hitting a towel rack on the wall at the back of the bathroom.

Two men in jeans and hooded sweatshirts stood in the doorway. They had cloth skull masks pulled up over the bottoms of their faces. And they both had pistols with silencers on them. He recognized both of them by their eyes.

John wailed as one man—Borden—stepped into the bathroom and pointed his gun at him. "Please! I'm the one who called!" he shouted. Borden stepped closer with the gun. John put both hands up and turned away, stepping over into the tub and yanking the shower curtain closed. He heard the man chuckle before the shower curtain was ripped open.

Borden fired three times, the bullets smashing into John's chest and pulverizing several major organs. John slid down the tiled wall and into the tub, unable to believe the pain that quickly became his entire world.

But he didn't die. Not right away. He stayed alive as his blood moved down the slope of the tub and into the drain. As each wheezing breath brought a symphony of pain.

He slumped against the outside edge of the bathtub, his left cheek pressed to the cold porcelain. The little girl—the one they called Angel—was led past the open doorway by one of the masked men. She glanced in at Virgil, her face blank.

He could feel death closing around him, enshrouding him in what felt like a blanket of ice. Despite his fear and his pain and his dread, he was quickly overwhelmed by regret. He should never have made the call. But he'd just been so scared. He'd forgotten how the world was.

As Angel turned away, prodded gently by the masked man, John Virgil took his last ragged, agonizing breath.

Chapter 1

IT HAD HAPPENED FAST. Too fast.

He should've put it together quicker than he did, but he was tired from the road and the lack of sleep. Trouble nearly dropped the Zastava M88 pistol as he pulled it out of his leather jacket pocket. His hands were numb from the long ride, as was often the case. After so many hours gripping the handlebars, the carpal tunnel in his right hand was acting up, adding pain to the numbness.

He crouched behind a bush, putting it between him and the house, as he transferred the gun to his left hand and shook out his right. It had been a long time since he'd practiced shooting with his non-dominant hand. He wasn't confident he could hit anything smaller than a barn.

And in a life-or-death situation, he wanted all the edge he could get.

They hadn't been in there long, but the muffled gunshots told him there wasn't any more time to waste. Yeah, it had happened fast. He hadn't been prepared. He'd let his guard down. Tired from the road. Not ready to rock and roll at the drop of a hat. *Stupid.*

One second, Trouble had been sitting out in the woods, watching the house. The next, an SUV was screeching up, four men jumping out, weapons held low. Four men with masks pulled up over the bottoms of their faces. Masks with grinning skeleton teeth.

Then they were through the door. Too fast and too quiet to be a forced entry. Had the door been unlocked? Did they have a key?

The first thing they'd done was turn off the front light. This wasn't their first rodeo.

The house was set far back from the road in a lot surrounded by woods. The nearest neighbor was a quarter mile away in each direction. He'd checked. In fact, he'd parked his bike near the next house down, just off the driveway in a clear patch of woods.

He was never one to go into a situation blind. But now he didn't have much of a choice. People were dying in there. They were being executed.

He had to do something.

They'd needed help, and he hadn't been quick enough to give them any.

Now the only help he could give would be vengeance. But in Trouble's book, that was better than nothing at all.

9mm pistol back in his right hand, he peered around the bush. The front door of the one-story ranch-style house was still open. Shadows moved inside.

Trouble moved, running up and putting his back to the brick wall just outside the recessed front door. Someone was coming. Heading out of the house. Voices were low inside. He heard something about brass. "Pick up your brass," maybe. They were getting ready to leave. Cleaning up. Gathering potential evidence.

Trouble heard footsteps approaching. The scuff of boot on concrete as someone stepped across the threshold. He turned, getting ready to move.

The guy who stepped out was slightly smaller than Trouble. He reacted quickly, but Trouble's right hand was already moving, swinging the butt of the pistol down and hitting the guy in the side of the head, eliciting a crunch. With his left, he gathered a fistful of black wool jacket in his hand, yanking the guy toward him just after he'd clocked him.

The guy went limp. Trouble dragged him out of view and left him lying on his back. After pulling the man's weapon out of his shoulder holster and tossing it aside, Trouble straightened and pressed on the guy's nose with the toe of his black boot. Hard. The guy didn't make a move. He wasn't faking it.

Trouble was back at the brick wall just as someone else was stepping over the threshold. There was something strange about the sound of the movement, though. The scuffing sounds were close together. Like they were taking small, hesitant steps. Maybe whoever it was had been injured.

Trouble waited, getting ready to do the same thing all over again. Hit with one hand, grab and drag with the other.

But the footsteps stopped.

Silence for a moment that seemed to stretch. Trouble held his breath.

"Dorian?" a slightly muffled man's voice called. "You good?"

Shit.

His mind raced. He didn't want to go up against three out in the open. But the recessed doorway created a kind of bottleneck. Even if all three men were standing there, they'd be stacked up behind each other. It would make shooting difficult. For them. Not for Trouble.

He could move now and take his chances, or he could retreat and try to get them in the open, as they went for the SUV.

"What's going on?" another man said. A second voice. From farther back. Still inside the house.

"Shh," came the first man's reply.

Trouble pivoted on his right foot, stepping around the corner, bringing his gun up in both hands for accurate shooting.

As he took in the scene, his heart dropped into his guts. He suddenly knew the reason for the strange, close footsteps he'd heard. The lead man was standing with a little girl in front of him. Blonde-haired and vacant-faced, dressed in a set of baggy pink pajamas with cartoon characters on them. He'd been walking her out that way, a hand on her shoulder, stepping wide so he didn't kick her feet. Something about that scene—the little girl being led out of the house like that, hand on her shoulder—stabbed a knife into Trouble's chest. He didn't know why. And he couldn't think about it now. Not unless he wanted to get killed.

There was another masked man there, standing behind the one with the girl. *Where's the third?*

All three pairs of eyes stuck on Trouble. The girl didn't seem to register the danger, but the two men did. Their eyes widened fractionally. Arm muscles twitched as they reflexively brought their guns toward him.

"Don't move," Trouble said. The lead guy already had his gun up, but he'd been pointing to his right, at the other side of the recessed entrance. He'd had a fifty-fifty chance, but luck wasn't with him. Not this day.

But Trouble knew all too well how quickly luck could turn.

The guy in the back hadn't had his gun ready. He'd brought it up only a few inches, and it was nowhere near an optimal firing position. He'd have to get it high to fire over his buddy.

"Talk low," Trouble said, looking at the lead guy. He wore a black baseball cap and a skull mask, leaving only his dark-colored eyes uncovered. "Where is the fourth man?"

"Inside," the guy said. No inflection. No fear evident in his voice.

"Move the gun down to your side. If it comes anywhere near me, I'll shoot you both."

The guy hesitated. The little girl stared up at Trouble, un-comprehending, silent, watchful. *What the fuck is going on here?* He hadn't been told anything about a kid. He hadn't been told much of anything, actually.

The third man stepped into view in the entryway of the house, some fifteen feet away. Trouble's eyes shifted over to him automatically. The lead man's gun started moving, but not down. Up. Toward Trouble.

The trigger pull weight on his M88 was about ten pounds—nearly double that of an average semiautomatic pis-tol. Since Trouble's hands were still numb, it took him a fraction longer than it normally would have to pull the heavy trigger. Luckily, the girl was small enough and the man close enough that Trouble wasn't worried about hitting her. And he didn't.

The first bullet smashed through the man's sternum two inches below the jugular notch at the base of his throat. Trou-ble was already moving to his right when he fired the second bullet at the second man. He knew the shot missed, but that wasn't his main concern. He wanted to get away from the kid so she wouldn't be caught in the crossfire.

As he ran toward the side of the house, he passed by the man he'd hit in the head. Without breaking stride, he shot the guy once in the chest. There was no longer any reason to take unnecessary risks. There was no reason to let up or go easy.

Good guys don't break into houses in the middle of the night to shoot people and kidnap little girls.

He didn't have any idea what this whole thing was about. He'd been called nearly twelve hours earlier by someone he trusted implicitly and asked to drive to this place called Mon-ument, just outside of Colorado Springs. His friend, Dylan, said he didn't have much information, but that someone close to him had called and asked for help. Dylan was on the other side of the world, but Trouble had been under ten hours away. Could he, as a personal favor to Dylan, head down and help them out?

That was all Trouble needed to hear. He'd hopped on his Triumph motorcycle and started the trek down from where he'd been outside of Billings, Montana.

Now, as he ran around the corner of the house, he wondered just what the hell he'd gotten himself into. He ducked under the windows he passed, slowing as he reached the back of the house. Three shots down. Six left in his gun. He waited at the back corner, listening hard. Would they follow him around the corner? Would they head back through the house to head him off? Or would they leave with the girl?

Trouble knew that she was the key to this whole thing. They hadn't had her when they'd gone into the house. And as far as he could tell, they weren't coming out with anything but her.

When no one followed him around the house after a few moments, he turned and made his way along the back of the structure, ducking under those windows that were obscured with shades or curtains and peeking cautiously into those that weren't.

He saw no movement and nothing of import through the two windows he looked in. Just dark rooms.

Then he heard a car door slam, followed quickly by another. An engine roared to life as Trouble sprinted along the side of the house, toward the driveway. He burst through the wall of Leyland cypress trees bordering the head of the driveway to see the SUV speeding away.

He would never make it back to his bike in time. There was no license plate on the vehicle. No identifying stickers or marks.

"Goddammit," Trouble said, huffing from his run. He could see his breath in the cold Colorado air.

"That's right, motherfucker," a man said to his left. The guy emerged from behind the end of the line of Leyland cypress trees, his gun pointed at Trouble. "God has certainly damned you."

Chapter 2

TROUBLE TURNED TO LOOK at the guy. He'd been the last to show up, taking Trouble's attention away long enough for the lead guy to make a move. Like his pals, he wore a baseball cap. It was black, but it had an image on the front. A jungle cat, black but outlined in white and turquoise. A panther. It was in mid-growl. Some sports team. Football, probably.

Between the top edge of the mask and the bottom edge of the hat, Trouble could see low-cut blond hair. The guy's eyes were hard to see under the brim. He was about six-foot. Maybe a hundred and seventy pounds.

"Who are you?" Panther said, stepping close enough for a sure thing but far enough away to keep out of reach. As someone who'd been held at gunpoint more times than he could count, Trouble always hated it when bad guys in the movies got close enough for the good guy to throw an elbow or a punch. That shit just didn't happen in real life. Not in his experience.

"I said, who the hell are you?"

"Nobody," Trouble said. He'd turned his head toward the man when he first stepped out, and he still had it turned. He didn't want to move his body. He didn't want to give Panther an excuse to shoot him. *Delaying the inevitable,* a sardonic inner voice said.

"Did Virgil call you? Or one of the Wallers?"

Trouble shook his head.

"Who else knows you're here?" Panther was getting mad. Losing patience.

"Only a couple of people," Trouble lied.

Panther flexed his jaw. Trouble could see it through the movement of the mask. Columns of vapor erupted from their mouths as they breathed.

"Alright. Drop the gun."

A sliver of hope sliced through the dread in Trouble's gut. He bent his knees, starting to kneel.

"Don't move!" Panther shouted. "Just drop the fucking gun."

"You know what kind of gun this is?" Trouble asked. "It's a Zastava M88. You ever owned one of these? They're notorious for firing when dropped. So I'll drop it if you want, but you never know where a bullet's going to go."

Panther paused, considering.

Trouble didn't know whether they fired when dropped or not. He knew that some pistols did, but he wasn't sure about this particular model. It was an obscure enough gun that he doubted Panther was familiar with the model.

"Alright, fine," the guy said. "Kneel down slowly and drop it, then."

Trouble did, his worn blue jeans tightening against his upper legs. He held the M88 out in front of him by the butt, his fingers well away from the trigger, barrel pointed down. When it came time to drop it, he held it out away from him as far as he could. Like he was scared of it. Scared to drop it near him. He focused on his peripheral vision.

The ploy had worked. Instead of putting his focus on Trouble, Panther was staring at the M88. His own pistol had drifted, and he was pointing it about halfway between the M88 and

Trouble's body. It wasn't much, but Trouble hoped it would be enough.

Trouble tossed the gun away from him, springing back the other way on taught legs, diving toward the line of bushy evergreen trees just a few feet behind him. Panther fired twice. Trouble did a rolling flip through the trees and came up on his feet. If he'd been hit, he hadn't felt it yet.

Instead of booking it toward the back of the house, he ran along the edge of the trees, toward where Panther had been on the other side. He'd taken three lunging steps when the guy burst through the greenery directly ahead, leading with his gun. Trouble lunged, grabbing the gun with his left hand, and hitting the guy with a weak right elbow. They went down, falling onto and then rolling off one of the trees.

Trouble hit the ground first, and Panther ended up on top of him. He still had a grip on the man's gun, but maybe not for long. If the guy could get his knees under him, he could exercise more leverage and with a greater range of motion. Trouble couldn't let that happen. He had to get off his back. To switch positions. In nearly every fight he'd been in, the guy who ended up on the ground was the guy who lost.

Fighting with Panther for the gun with his left hand, Trouble had his right free. The guy pushed off the ground with his left arm, raising up to try and get on his knees. Using his right arm, Trouble hit Panther on the inside of his elbow, causing his locked-out arm to collapse. In nearly the same instance, Trouble rocked his head up to meet Panther's as his upper body fell momentarily down.

The curve of Trouble's forehead smashed into the guy's nose with a crunch. The man cried out, bringing his left hand up—either to protect his face from another blow or to clutch his smashed nose. Trouble used it. He shoved the guy up with his right hand, kicking with his legs to throw his body weight into it.

They switched positions, and Trouble quickly got onto his knees, straddling the guy's hips to take his legs out of the fight. His left hand was still occupied, fighting for the gun, but his right was free. He punched down, but Panther parried it with his left hand, taking all the power out of it.

Then the man's left hand was at his neck, squeezing. Trouble tried to pull his hand off, but it was no use. He was getting weaker. The struggle for the gun was taking too much of his energy.

Trouble reached down toward the man's face to hit his broken nose or put a thumb in an eyeball. But before he could complete the move, the guy's head exploded with a bang. Blood splattered Trouble's face, causing him to flinch.

He jumped away reflexively, rapidly cooling droplets of blood on his face. Another bang sounded, and something whistled through the air next to his head. He realized Panther had been shot. By his own guy, no less. The one who had driven off in the SUV. He was leaning against a tree in the woods between the yard and the road, firing with a rifle of some kind.

Trouble scrambled through the line of trees again while more gunshots came. He was up and running toward the back of the house as soon as he got his feet under him.

He cursed himself for letting go of the gun. And for leaving his other pistol in his saddlebag.

Lots of mistakes. It was a miracle he wasn't bleeding out right now.

He rounded the back of the house and kept going, barging into the woods bordering the backyard. The gunshots had stopped, but he was sure the guy was running after him. When he made it about ten yards into the woods, he slid down behind a smoke bush shrub. Peering between its branches, he watched for the man.

In a matter of moments, he saw the guy. The barrel of his rifle appeared first at the corner of the house. Then the man holding it appeared, sweeping the yard with what looked to Trouble like an M4 or some other AR-15 variant. It was hard to tell, thanks to dark and distance.

The man, wearing a mask and a black beanie, apparently decided to cut his losses. He backed up and then disappeared.

Trouble waited to see if he would show up again. He listened hard for any movement.

After nearly two minutes, he got up and worked his way back toward the house. By the time he came to the line of trees bordering the driveway, he was sure the man had gone. Along with the little girl.

His M88 pistol was still sitting where he'd tossed it down. He grabbed it, checked the chamber and magazine, and made sure it was ready to fire. He stepped over to Panther, who, he now saw, had taken a bullet in his left cheek. It had obliterated his nose and the top of his mouth. If the shooter had waited a moment to fire, Trouble's hand might have been right there.

The guy was still breathing. Still alive. The shot had missed his brain. Blood gargled in the back of his throat as he breathed. His eyes were closed. Maybe he'd passed out from the pain or the shock.

Trouble took pity on him. He pointed his weapon at the man's head and fired one shot, right through the panther on his hat. Then he picked up the guy's pistol—which had his fingerprints all over it—and moved toward the house. He made sure the pistol's safety was on before unscrewing the suppressor and putting the gun in his left jacket pocket. He put the suppressor in his right pants pocket.

He had to assume the police were coming, but he wanted to check out the house. See if there were any other children left in there. Or anyone else alive.

All he found were three dead people. All adults. Two men and one woman. One man was in the bathroom, lying slumped in the bathtub, his unseeing eyes staring toward the open door. The other two people were in the master bedroom. The man had been shot as he slept, apparently. But the woman was on the floor. She'd jumped out of bed before she'd been killed.

There was no one else in the house.

Trouble committed what he deemed important details to memory and then left, walking back through the woods toward where he'd parked his bike.

Even though he'd taken in grotesque scenes of violence this night, the one image that kept coming back to him was of the little girl being led out by the man, a hand on her shoulder.

Before he reached his bike, he knew what he had to do.

And he knew he wouldn't stop until he did it.

Chapter 3

"I NEED YOU TO tell me everything you know about this fucking job," Trouble said as soon as Dylan picked up the phone.

Trouble got mad sometimes. He had a temper. But he didn't often get rattled. And Dylan knew him well enough to read him through his tone. So the biker wasn't surprised when there was a long moment of silence before Dylan cleared his throat. "What happened?" he asked.

Trouble took a breath. He had to remember this wasn't Dylan's fault. And the last thing he wanted was to get sloppy. "I'm on a payphone," he said. "Your end secure?"

"Of course," Dylan said.

"Good." Trouble took another deep breath as he watched a semi-truck rumble by out on I-25. He was at the side of a truck stop, talking on what was probably the last working payphone in Colorado. There were two of them affixed to the exterior brick wall of the building, near the restrooms. The other one didn't have a receiver. The metal-coated wire swung in the night breeze.

"Listen," Dylan began, "I told you everything I know when we discussed this earlier. But that doesn't mean I can't try to find out more. But whatever you can tell me about what happened will help."

"Yeah. This thing is fucked, man. I wasn't there for five minutes when an SUV full of masked assholes with guns rolled up. They didn't hesitate. They didn't knock. They didn't even break the door down. They just went right in. Next thing I know, there's gunshots going off from inside the house. All I know is that these guys are killing people in there. People you asked me to protect. So I . . ." He trailed off, not wanting to think about what he'd done.

On the ride out of Monument, he'd started considering the possibility that he'd made a mistake. What if he'd killed the good guys? What if they were just trying to save the kid from some human traffickers or something? His throat thickened. He'd killed two men outright. And it was his fault that a third died.

When it was clear he wasn't going to continue talking, Dylan spoke up. "What did you do?"

He didn't say it with judgment. It was as if he was asking Trouble what he had for lunch.

Trouble leaned forward, putting his left hand against the brick wall. His head drooped as he spoke in a near-whisper. "I waited for one of them to come out, then clocked him. But the ones inside knew something was up. So I decided on a direct confrontation. That was when I saw the kid. A little girl. They were taking her out of the house. That's what this is about, isn't it? Do you know who she is?"

"I don't know. I'll find out. But you need to tell me what happened. Will I see this on the news? Is the girl okay? Is she with you?"

"They got away with her. But three of them are dead. The fourth got away. I don't know what they're going to do with her. We need to find out where they took her. We need to find her."

"Okay," Dylan said. "I'll tell you exactly how it went down. I got a call from my ex-wife about ten minutes before I called you. She asked for help but said she couldn't tell me much about why. Just that some people were in trouble, and they needed help. She said it would be a babysitting job for a day or two at the most. Three adults. She didn't say anything about a kid."

Three adults, Trouble thought. *Nothing about a kid.* "You trust her? She wouldn't play you?"

"No way. She's my ex, but there's no way she would do anything like that. Besides, she knew it wouldn't be me who went out there. She only called me because I know people like you. And before your paranoia starts talking, let me just say it would have to be a pretty elaborate setup if this was someone coming after you."

"And what about someone playing her? I mean, how do we know that the guys retrieving the kid weren't getting her back from some kidnappers or something?"

Dylan was silent for a moment, apparently playing it out in his head. When he spoke, his voice was calm and measured. "What does your gut tell you?"

That, Trouble realized, was a good question. The whole thing had thrown him for such a loop that he hadn't had a chance to really listen to his instincts. Normally, he did it almost automatically as a part of winding down from any confrontation. But he hadn't even started winding down from the shitshow at the house yet.

A voice came on the call, telling Trouble that he needed to insert another fifty cents to extend the call. He dug his remaining two quarters out of his coin pocket and put them in.

"You still there?" he asked.

"Yeah."

Trouble sighed. "My gut tells me that the guys with masks and guns were bad. The way they killed those people . . . but then again, if I had a kid and three assholes came and kidnapped her, I might not hesitate to blow them away like that. Still . . . I don't think that was the situation. I think the people in the house were trying to protect the girl."

"You said three people in the house. Describe them to me."

Trouble did. A couple in the bedroom, late twenties. A man in the bathroom who looked to be creeping up on middle age.

"Okay. Did you happen to find anything with names on them? Driver's licenses or passports for any of them?"

"I didn't stick around for long enough. And I didn't really want to go digging around, leaving my DNA all over the place. So no, I don't have any names for you. But there was one thing. . ."

"What?"

"Well, the two in the bedroom were sleeping in their clothes. And the guy in the bathroom was fully dressed." Trouble paused, gathering his thoughts.

"Yeah?"

"Well, all their clothes were kind of . . . I don't know . . . worn. And ill-fitting. It was strange. And it didn't really even register until just now. I knew something was bothering me, but I didn't know what. Now I know it was the clothes. I mean, you'd expect one out of three to be wearing ill-fitted clothes, maybe. But all three of them?"

"Did they look like they were related?" Dylan asked.

"No. I don't think so."

There was silence on the line for a few long moments as both men mulled it over.

"All right, Terrence," Dylan said. He always used Trouble's real name. Unless he was mad at him, which wasn't often. "Let me get to work."

"How long you think you'll be? When can I call you back?"

"Give me a couple of hours," Dylan replied. "Where are you headed?"

"I don't know. I'm south of Colorado Springs right now. I was going to head down to Pueblo. Maybe get a bite when my stomach settles."

"Okay. Call me in . . . three hours. I should have something for you."

Trouble hung up. He turned toward the highway and watched as headlight beams cut the night. The flow of traffic had always mesmerized him. And he always felt his best when he was on the road, moving, the asphalt passing under him.

But on the ride down from Monument, he hadn't felt good at all. He hadn't felt the hope. The possibilities. The excitement. He hadn't felt at ease.

As he walked over to his Triumph, he hoped he could get that feeling back.

Chapter 4

THE MAN CAME THROUGH the door of the small café like a ghost. Trouble wouldn't have even noticed his entrance had it not been for the bell over the door that clanged upon opening and closing. He was so quiet and unassuming in demeanor that Trouble would've disregarded him immediately if he hadn't been here for a meeting.

The cafe was made up to look like a house. Or it had been someone's house before it was gutted and changed into the eatery it now was. There were mismatched tables and chairs, complete with mismatched tablecloths and fabric napkins in muted colors.

The man looked right at home in the place. He was wearing a raggedy blue windbreaker that was two sizes too big for him. Underneath the jacket, Trouble could see a pale green V-neck t-shirt. But his slacks and shoes seemed to complete the outfit. His brown slacks were pressed and only beginning to wrinkle, but the shoes looked like they'd been pulled out of a second-hand store's dumpster.

It wasn't hard to figure out this was the guy he was supposed to meet. Noting the guy's clothes, Trouble remembered the people in the house in Monument. It couldn't be a coincidence.

The mismatched man scanned the few faces in the place before seeing Trouble in the corner. His feverish, light-colored eyes seemed to buzz in their sockets as they stared at him.

Trouble was the only guy wearing a leather jacket in the place, which was what he'd told the woman on the phone—the intermediary. So there was no other option. No other person fit the bill. But still, the guy stood there just inside the doorway, staring at Trouble, gears turning behind his eyes.

Trouble raised a hand and waved him over. That seemed to snap the man out of it. He moved in little, sliding steps, as if it was too much work to lift his feet fully off the ground. *Arthritic steps*, Trouble thought. But the guy wasn't old. He wasn't young, either. His light brown hair was thinning, retreating up his creased forehead. He had it fairly long on top and short on the sides. It had been done up in a part on the left side, but now it was frazzled. Like the last time he'd messed with his appearance was days ago. Maybe it was.

"Hey, Mitchell?" Trouble asked as the guy approached.

He nodded. "You're Mr. Rubble? Terrence?"

"That's right. Call me Trouble. Why don't you take a seat."

The guy pulled out one of the two seats on the other side of the table and sat down. Trouble noticed a wedding band on his left hand.

"I'm a friend," Trouble said once the guy was situated. "Okay? You can relax. I'm here to help."

"Can I see some identification?" Mitchell asked. It wasn't a forceful question. He said it with regret, like he was sorry for the inconvenience.

"Sure," Trouble said as a server walked over. "Do you want anything? Coffee?"

Mitchell shook his head.

"I'll take another coffee," Trouble said to the gray-haired lady with the black apron on. "My friend is fine."

She nodded and went to fetch the coffeepot.

It was the middle of the afternoon, but Trouble had been on the road for most of the last twenty-four hours—first to Monument, and now to this little town in northern New Mexico. He'd stopped in Pueblo and ate, then he'd called Dylan. As promised, Dylan had something for him. It wasn't much, but it was something. And it led him here. Sitting with the girl's father. At least, that was the impression he'd gotten when talking to the woman who wouldn't identify herself. It wasn't Dylan's ex. It was the woman who had called Dylan's ex for help. The whole thing was very cloak-and-dagger. Trouble couldn't imagine why they were being so paranoid. But he hoped to find out.

His wallet was on the table, along with his burner phone. He pulled out his driver's license and handed it over to Mitchell. The man studied it for several long moments before handing it back to Trouble.

"Satisfied?" Trouble asked.

Mitchell nodded.

"So, are you going to tell me what this is all about?" He had to be careful. He didn't know this guy from Adam, and he wasn't about to tell him he'd killed two men the night before while trying to rescue his daughter. Plus, he wanted to get the story straight from the horse's mouth. He wasn't about to volunteer any information. Being overly cautious had served him well in the past, and he'd managed to calm his nerves on the drive down to New Mexico. Although he still felt a persistent dread in his gut. A dread he couldn't quite explain. It was always there, like an itch in the middle of his back. So close, yet so far away.

"My daughter," Mitchell said. "I need help with my daughter."

"What does she look like?" Trouble asked.

"My daughter?"

"Yes. What does your daughter look like?"

Mitchell paused, his head was tilted down, and he looked at Trouble through upturned eyes. "She's nine years old. She has blonde hair with a reddish tint. Blue eyes. Fair skin."

"So you contacted someone for help finding her, right?" he asked Mitchell. "Someone you trusted?"

"No," Mitchell said, shaking his head.

Trouble had chosen a table in the front corner of the small establishment, next to a large picture window. Mitchell kept looking out the window as if he expected to see someone he knew. There wasn't much to see out there but the small parking lot and a wooded hill across the road.

Trouble waited for more. Mitchell seemed reluctant to elucidate. "Okay. So you don't need any help finding your daughter. My mistake," Trouble said. "Sorry to waste your time. I just thought that meeting you might allow us to speak frankly. I thought you could tell me what the problem is. So I could help you."

Mitchell leaned forward, ready to speak, when the server came up with the coffeepot. He leaned back as the gray-haired woman poured Trouble a cup.

"Thank you," Trouble said.

The woman nodded once and looked at Mitchell warily. She didn't try to hide her suspicion.

When she was gone, Mitchell leaned forward again. "I don't need help *finding* my daughter," he whispered. "I already know where she is. I needed help protecting her *yesterday*, but that clearly didn't work out. And since I heard she came back this morning, I don't suppose there's any use in trying again. They probably know I helped them escape. Who knows what they'll do to me."

"Woah, slow down," Trouble said. "Helped *who* escape from *where*? Where is your daughter right now?"

Mitchell's eyes fixed on Trouble's face. "She's up there," he said, pointing a thumb back over his shoulder.

"Okay," Trouble said, looking out the window toward the road that went up into the mountains. "Let's go get her."

Mitchell scoffed and shook his head. He slumped and looked down at his hands. "They're dead, aren't they?" Mitchell asked. "My friends?"

"Who were your friends? Describe them to me."

"John Virgil. Middle-aged. Hair like mine. I mean styled in the same way. A little bit of a belly. Looks like an insurance salesman. Trent and Shelly. Younger than me. Good-looking, both of them. Married. Shelly's pretty, even with her hair cut really short. Both have sandy brown hair. Trent has the same haircut as me, too. At least, he did when I saw him last."

"Yeah," Trouble said. "Yeah, I think they're dead."

Mitchell made a pained sound and looked down at Trouble's coffee cup. He was silent for a long time. "What about the people who came and took her? What happened to them?"

"I don't know," Trouble lied. "I guess they got away."

Mitchell shook his head and moved to stand up. "You're lying. You're working with *them*, aren't you?"

Trouble reached out and grabbed his wrist. "All right, all right. Just sit down, okay? I'll tell you what happened."

Mitchell looked at the server and the other patrons.

"Don't mind them," Trouble said. "They're fine. I didn't tell anyone we'd be here, okay? Did you?"

Mitchell shook his head and sat down.

Trouble let go of his wrist and then said, "Okay. I was there, but I got there late. I didn't have enough information going in, so I sat outside to watch the house for a little while. That was when four guys with masks and weapons pulled up. They were in the house and shooting before I could make a move. When I did, three of them got killed. The fourth got away with your daughter—what's her name?"

Mitchell was staring wide-eyed at Trouble. His mouth was hanging slightly open.

"What's your daughter's name?" Trouble asked again.

"Uh—Shayna," Mitchell said. "But most people call her Angel. You said three of them got killed? How?"

Trouble shook his head, thinking how he could sidestep the question. Then something caught his eye outside. There was a gas station just north of the café on the same side of the road. To the south was a Dollar General. But across the street to the west, there was nothing but a steep hill flush with pine trees. Running along next to the road was a shallow but wide stream. And, Trouble noticed, something was moving on the hill beyond the stream. Something big.

He turned and looked out the window, half expecting to see a bear lumbering out of the woods. But he saw nothing. Whatever it was had stopped moving. And he couldn't make out much more than dark shadows under the trees.

"What are you looking at?" Mitchell asked, a hint of panic in his voice.

"Nothing. Just thought I saw some movement in the trees."

Mitchell's eyes bulged. He turned his head to the window and gazed across the street. Then he threw himself back, falling out of his chair and onto the floor.

Trouble sat there for a long moment, stunned, looking down at the cowering man on the floor. Near the back of the seating area, the waitress looked from Trouble to Mitchell and back again. Trouble just shrugged. Then he looked back out the window. There were footprints coming across the road from the trees. Boot prints, from someone who had stepped in the stream. They disappeared behind an SUV on the north side of the parking lot.

"Mitchell?" Trouble asked. "Do you drive a silver Ford SUV?"

"Yes," Mitchell said from the ground.

"Okay. Stay here." Trouble got up from the table, leaving a ten-dollar bill for the coffee.

He gathered his phone and wallet. "I'll be right back," he said. He walked out the door with one hand in his right jacket pocket, gripping his Zastava M88 pistol. It was a chilly spring day, but the sun felt nice on his face. He rounded the back of Mitchell's SUV at a casual stroll, but he saw no one.

What he did see was a small pink backpack hanging from the SUV's side mirror – the right size for a preteen girl. He looked around, glancing across a narrow swath of untended New Mexico grass at the gas station. A man stared at him from the rear window of a Jeep that was pulling away from the pumps. The guy was twisted around in the back seat, staring right at Trouble through the zip-on plastic window. His face was pale and, it seemed from a distance, scarred somehow. The latter could've been a trick of the light. He wasn't sure.

The black jeep pulled out from the gas station. As it left, Trouble caught a glimpse of two other men in the front seats. They weren't much more than pale figures. They all glanced his way before turning out of the gas station and onto the road that headed north into the mountains.

Trouble stepped over to the pink backpack. It was unzipped slightly, so he put two fingers into the gap and opened it a little more. Inside was a piece of paper. Trouble took his leather riding gloves from a jacket pocket and pulled them on before retrieving the paper. It was a note.

Don't let the fear take over your life. Don't let the world tell you how to live.

We can give her freedom. We can give her love. We can give her enlightenment.

Come home, and you can have them too.

There was nothing else in the backpack. Trouble took both items inside and found Mitchell still sitting on the floor. The staff and the three other patrons were all staring at him.

"Get him out of here," the server said from her place near the kitchen.

"Let's go," Trouble said. "You've got a lot to tell me."

Chapter 5

"THAT'S SHAYNA'S BAG!" MITCHELL said, lurching up from the floor. "Where did you find it?"

Trouble didn't answer. He stepped outside, not wanting to push the people in the café too far. He didn't want the cops showing up. Although he wasn't wanted in New Mexico, he was sure there was some sort of national database police could search to see if a perp had warrants in any other state. And he had warrants in at least two.

Trouble scanned the gas station and the Dollar General parking lot before stopping next to Mitchell's SUV. He turned around and gave the backpack to Mitchell, who dug the note out and held it in both hands, dropping the backpack to the ground.

By Trouble's count, he read it three times, each time with mounting hysteria.

As his eyes went to the top of the note for a fourth time, Trouble spoke. "Do you know anyone who drives a black Jeep?"

Mitchell didn't answer. His eyes were filling with tears. Trouble had a hard time looking at him. He could feel the desperation coming off the guy in waves. And that desperation was driven by love for his daughter. More than anything, that made Trouble uncomfortable. He knew desperation well. But seeing such pure, insanity-inducing love made him antsy. He didn't know how to deal with it. He suddenly felt like he was standing too close to a malfunctioning nuclear reactor.

"Mitchell!" he said, making the man jump. "Do you know anyone who drives a black Jeep?"

"They know it was me," he said. "They know it was my idea. Oh, Jesus God, they know."

"Talk to me, Mitch," Trouble said, realizing he was losing the guy quickly. "Who are they?"

Mitchell glanced around wildly, shaking his head. He reached down and grabbed the backpack, then started around the back of the SUV. Trouble followed.

"Where are you going?"

"I was foolish," Mitchell said. "I was foolish to think anyone could help me."

"I *can* help you. Just tell me what the hell is going on," Trouble said, suddenly feeling nauseous. As uncomfortable as it made him, he was pulled toward Mitchell's problem like a magnet. He wanted to help the guy get his daughter back. No, he suddenly *needed* to, even if he didn't understand the true source of the compulsion. The memory of Shayna and the masked man at the house flashed in his mind like a strobe.

Still shaking his head, Mitchell opened the driver's side door and slid into the seat. Trouble held the door open so he couldn't shut it. He leaned in toward the man. "If you won't let me help you, at least go to the police."

Mitchell laughed once, a harsh, humorless sound. Then he fixed his buzzing eyes on Trouble. "Just go home," he said. "Sorry to have wasted your time."

"No," Trouble said. "You wanted help, well here it is. We can figure this thing out. Believe me."

Mitchell tried to close his door, but Trouble wasn't budging. The man leaned over and popped open the glove box. He pulled a silver Smith & Wesson revolver out and shoved it into Trouble's chest. "Get away," he said, looking down at the gun.

Trouble noticed his finger wasn't on the trigger. He could easily disarm the man, but he decided against it. He stepped back, hands raised. As soon as he was clear, Mitchell slammed the door, started the engine, and pulled out of the parking lot. He turned north, heading the same way the Jeep had gone.

Trouble made a split-second decision, jogging over and mounting his Triumph, which he had backed into a parking spot out of habit. He fired it up and pulled out of the lot just as Mitchell's SUV disappeared around a bend in the road.

He pulled the throttle back with his right hand, quickly working the clutch and gearshift with his left hand and foot until he had Mitchell's SUV in view. He eased off, keeping back a safe distance. He had no idea what Mitchell might do. And if the guy was going to try to shoot him, he didn't want to give him a big target.

Trouble didn't think it was likely, though. The guy was desperate, but Trouble wasn't his enemy.

As he cruised along, Trouble took note of the changing scenery. They passed a few cabins nestled on the hillsides among the spruce, pine, and aspen trees. Most of the driveways were made of dirt or gravel. A couple of elegant-yet-rustic mansions were visible over the treetops, seeming to hold court over the winding valley from their lofty perches. A fraction of a golf course passed by on his right side as he continued following.

He had no plan. He wasn't sure what following Mitchell would do, aside from piss him off. But it was the only course of action he could think of. Whoever these people were, they were pushing Mitchell close to the edge. The fact that he'd been so quick to pull a gun on Trouble spoke volumes to the man's state of mind—even if he hadn't really intended on using the weapon.

There was no doubt that Mitchell knew he was being followed. But he didn't try to lose Trouble. Maybe he knew it wasn't possible. There was no way an SUV could go fast enough to outrun an experienced rider on a bike like Trouble's. And it wasn't like there was a sprawling city to hide in. As they got further away from the little town with the café, the fewer manmade structures were visible.

For nearly thirty minutes, Trouble followed along, doing just over fifty-five miles an hour—matching Mitchell's speed. They continued up into the mountains, gaining a few hundred feet every ten miles or so. The air grew cooler as it thinned. The smell of pine trees and damp undergrowth permeated the air.

Finally, the left blinker on the SUV engaged, followed shortly by the flare of brake lights. Trouble slowed, maintaining the gap between vehicles. The single-lane road Mitchell turned onto was unmarked and made of packed dirt. It looked as though it went up the sloping hill, but Trouble could only see the first fifty yards or so before it disappeared into the trees.

The SUV stopped as it turned off Highway 64, effectively blocking entrance. Although Trouble couldn't see Mitchell through the tinted windows, he could feel the man looking at him. But he kept going, passing by.

There was little traffic on the road, but Trouble didn't want to turn around in the middle of it. The winding road made visibility around curves impossible. So he had to travel nearly a mile before finding a gravel shoulder suitable for pulling off and turning his bike around.

When he got back to the dirt road, Mitchell's SUV was gone. Trouble turned onto the road and followed it up through the thickening afternoon shadows. The first sign he saw was a half-mile in, and only slightly disconcerting. It said, "Forgive those who trespass against us, for they shall be delivered from evil."

He wasn't sure if it was just his cynical worldview, but he thought he saw a threat in there. The second sign made him certain that he was being warned. It read, "Those with pure intentions will come to no harm here. Those without will experience the wrath of God."

Both were professionally made signs. The words weren't in marker scrawled on cardboard. They were white words on a bright red, reflective background.

He took a moment to ask himself whether his intentions were pure. *He* thought they were, but he also realized that purity of intention was subjective. Somehow, he doubted that whoever was up there would agree with him about it. *Please don't let me be misunderstood,* he thought, a tune creeping into his head. He continued on.

The next sign he came to was at a Y in the road. The left road looked less used, with wild grasses growing between wheel ruts. The right road was level, hard-packed dirt, and it looked like a continuation of the road he was on. There was also a sign there, but it was a green-and-white street sign, like those in every city in America. It said, "Discomfort Road." Trouble followed it.

He came around a bend in the road and saw that it widened about a hundred feet before a large gate. There were three men visible around the gate, and two of them were aiming rifles at Trouble. The third was walking down from the gate-house, smiling, his own semiautomatic rifle slung over his shoulder.

Trouble could see two vehicles moving up the road where it continued beyond the gate. The one in back was Mitchell's silver SUV. The other one was a black Jeep. He just caught a glimpse of them before they disappeared over the hill's crest.

Trouble looked quickly at the three men, sizing them up, assessing the threat, computing the odds of success if he had to make a move. They weren't good. They had him dead to rights. Provided, of course, they were proficient with their weapons. All three of them looked like brothers, but that was an assumption based on the way they were all dressed and their hairstyles. Each man wore a simple, dark-blue button-up shirt, black pants, and combat boots. Their hair was cut short on the sides and longer on top, with a part on the left side.

One of them was in some sort of perch on the other side of the fence that ran off into the woods in both directions. He was crouching in the perch, only his head and shoulders visible over the top of the fence. Other than where the man was crouching, the solid, rust-colored metal fence was topped with razor wire.

The other man pointing a weapon at him was standing in the middle of the road in front of the closed gate. All the men looked to be in their middle to late thirties.

Stopping about fifty feet from the metal security gate, Trouble sat on the idling bike and waited for the smiling man to get to him. He didn't try to hide his confusion.

"Hello there, neighbor," the man said. "Are you lost?"

Trouble looked around for a moment, thinking about that. "You know, I think I am," he said. "I'm looking for my friend Corman. I thought I was in the right place, but Corman wouldn't ever greet me with the business end of a gun, let alone two of them."

The man looked over his shoulder at his lookalikes. Then he turned back to Trouble. "Sorry," he said. "Can't be too careful." He signaled with his left hand, and the two men lowered their weapons. But they continued to stare at Trouble.

"Corman said he was in a resort type place," Trouble said. "Is that what this is?"

"No," the man said, still smiling.

Trouble waited for a moment to see if the guy would volunteer any information. When none was forthcoming, he asked, "Well, what is this place?"

"It's private property," the man said. "In fact, this road is a private road. We'd appreciate it if you could just turn around and head on back down. I'm sure your friend Corman is waiting for you."

Trouble returned the guy's smile. "You got some place here," he said. "What's your name?"

The man seemed to hesitate before answering. "Vogel," he said. "And you?"

"You got some place here, Vogel," he said, releasing his hand brake and guiding the bike back so he could turn around. "Some place."

As he cruised away from the gate, he looked into his side mirror. All three men were pointing their weapons at his back. Vogel's smile was gone. In its place was a look Trouble couldn't quite place. But he was certain he saw fury there. So much so that he half expected to be shot in the back. When he rounded the bend in the road, he realized he was holding his breath.

As he came to the Y in the road, he stopped and looked down the road less traveled. He thought for a long moment. About Mitchell's behavior. About the backpack and the note inside. And about the black Jeep leading Mitchell's SUV into some kind of compound.

But mostly, he thought about that little girl being led out of the house by a man with a mask and a gun.

Trouble turned right and started down the road he hadn't yet taken.

Chapter 6

THE BUMPY ROAD TROUBLE was on seemed to skirt the top portion of the mountain. Although mountain wasn't really the right word. He didn't know what factors distinguished tall hills from mountains, but he thought it would be a stretch to call this one a mountain. But that didn't mean it wasn't wide. By keeping an eye on his odometer, he determined he traveled over two miles before the road ended in a clearing.

He couldn't see the compound he assumed was some distance uphill from him. He couldn't see the fence he figured was guarding it. All he could see were trees.

And a little footpath leading away from the clearing.

There was room enough for a couple of cars to park here, and divots in the ground to suggest that happened somewhat regularly. The footpath leading up the hill at a gentle angle was well worn. Trouble looked around for cameras attached to trees. If there were any, they were well hidden.

He hadn't been followed from the gate. That much, he was sure of.

He looked at the footpath, the yellow-green grass along its edges, the blanket of fallen pine needles coating the ground on either side. He remembered Vogel's face as seen in his side mirror. There was a whole lot of wrong going on here. If this was a militia group, like he thought it was, he had to be careful.

Up here all alone like they were, it would be an easy thing to just shoot him and bury him in the woods. Only one person knew he was here, and Dylan wasn't likely to go to the police if he didn't hear from Trouble. Not for a while, anyway.

There was a gap in the trees wide enough to fit the Triumph, so Trouble eased the bike through. He was going to see what was up that path. But he didn't want to leave his bike out in the open. The footpath was calling to him in a way he didn't quite understand. But it wasn't just the path. It was everything he'd seen since Mitchell had walked into that café over an hour ago.

He found two close-growing spruce trees about fifteen yards from the edge of the clearing and parked his bike behind them. The low rumble of his engine was replaced by the occasional birdsong and the whisper of wind through the trees. He stood and listened, straining to hear the sound of an engine growing closer.

Nothing. No one was coming. Not yet.

Trouble crossed the clearing and started up the footpath, his black Doc Martens boots crunching along on the pale, rocky dirt. It was after four o'clock, and the sunlight slanted through the trees to land on his back. He could feel it getting colder as this portion of the Earth rotated away from the Sun. It would be dark in less than two hours.

He'd been walking for about ten minutes when he spotted the structure through the trees. He paused, glimpsing slivers of the brilliant white walls through thin gaps in the trees. Listening for sounds of life, he stood still for two minutes. And heard nothing but the sounds of the forest.

The structure became clear as he continued his trek up the sloping hillside. It was about the size of a two-car garage. But it wasn't purely utilitarian. The front of the rectangular structure had four white pillars – two on either side of the white marble stairs leading up to the double doors. These pillars supported the gable roof, also white.

The sunlight hitting the top of the structure made it hard to look at. He paused at the bottom of the three-step stairs and studied them. They looked like genuine marble. The shallow portico was made of the same material. The pillars were made from chalky stone, along with the rest of the structure's walls. The doors were solid finished metal, painted with some kind of glossy white coat. There were no windows in the doors or the front of the structure. *The temple*, Trouble thought. *Maybe they're not a militia group. Maybe they're a religious group.* That would explain the strange signs he saw coming up the main road.

He stepped up onto the portico and tried the door. The heavy-duty handleset didn't budge. There were two key-operated deadbolt locks, both of which he assumed were locked. He pressed his right ear to the door and listened for several long moments. At first, he thought he heard a soft rustling sound from inside, but he wasn't sure.

He walked around, seeing that there were no windows and no second door. He wondered why it was out here, so far away from anything else. It looked expensive and new. And he couldn't begin to imagine what it was for.

He looked up the hill, toward where he figured the compound would be, based on what he'd seen at the gate and how the road curved around the geographic feature.

He picked a direction and walked.

He'd been walking for fifteen minutes when the far-off sound of hammering reached him. It bounced off the trees, growing louder as he moved uphill. He considered pulling his M88 pistol out of his jacket pocket, but decided against it. He didn't plan on getting within effective pistol range, anyway. And he didn't want to give anyone an excuse to shoot him.

Trouble continued to move up toward the work sounds.

He could hear the occasional chatter of male voices, along with the whirr of an electric drill. Soon enough, he glimpsed movement through the trees. There was a small group of men constructing a fence a few hundred feet uphill from where Trouble crouched behind a tree. The fence was made from wooden posts with rust-colored metal panels affixed to them.

It was hard to see through the trees, but Trouble counted four men working on the fence, extending it through the woods. They all wore green, long-sleeve button-up shirts, brown carpenter pants, and tan work boots. All four men had their sleeves rolled up around their forearms.

Thinking he could afford to get a little closer, Trouble made sure the men weren't looking his way and moved around his tree. He crept forward to a small outcropping of gray rock and crouched behind it. A twig snapped to his left. He whipped his head that way and saw a woman in a blue shirt walking in his direction. She carried a semi-auto rifle in the patrol carry position, held diagonally across her body with the barrel pointing down.

Trouble ducked down behind the rock, his heart suddenly hammering away. She was close. Much closer than the workers. If she continued on her path, she'd pass within twenty feet of him. His mind reeled. Would she shoot on sight? He had to assume she would.

He couldn't run. She would see him if he did. And he didn't want to engage her. He had no idea if they were truly responsible for Shayna's kidnapping. Until he *knew* that they were, he couldn't make a move. And the last thing he wanted to do was get into a gunfight with people who were defending their own property. But he slipped his M88 pistol out of his pocket, anyway. He kept the safety on. For now.

Listening hard, Trouble heard the woman come closer, her feet crunching pine needles, fallen branches, and the occasional pinecone. He held his breath as she passed by, sounding much too close for comfort.

Suddenly, the crunching stopped. Trouble had to resist the urge to move, to look, to run. If she'd seen him, he'd know it soon enough.

After what seemed like minutes but was only seconds, he heard her moving again. He took a long breath when he was certain she hadn't seen him and was continuing on her way.

As soon as he was confident he could move without being seen, he crept down the hill. When the sounds of the men working were barely audible, he allowed himself to relax. And he admonished himself. If he wasn't careful, he could start a fight with people who'd had nothing to do with the three murders and the kidnapping in Colorado. If these people wanted to patrol their own private property with legal weapons, that was their right. If they wanted to build strange temples in the woods, that was also their right.

How do you know Mitchell is the victim? Trouble asked himself as he moved down the hill in the quickly fading daylight. Maybe what he'd seen in Mitchell wasn't genuine love for his daughter, but madness. Maybe he was abusive. Maybe the girl Trouble had seen in Colorado wasn't his daughter at all, but a victim of human trafficking. Maybe the guys with guns were her saviors.

That's fear talking, an inner voice said. *Something isn't right here.*

The close call he'd had with the patrol guard had rattled him more than he wanted to admit, but he was trying to be logical. He had no proof of anything. Mitchell didn't want his help. What could he do out here, besides get himself shot for trespassing?

Through the trees ahead, Trouble could see the back of the temple. He was itching to get on his bike and ride away. Regroup. Find another way to get the information he needed.

But as he approached the temple, he heard voices. Someone was there.

He slowed, realizing he still had his pistol out. After determining that the people weren't yet to the temple, he moved off to his right to come around the structure from the side. As he moved in a wide arc, he tried to make sense of what he was hearing. It was a chant of some kind, the words unrecognizable to Trouble. There was something eerie about it.

Once again, he found himself hunkering down behind a large tree, staring through the forest at a group of people working toward some purpose. The purpose of the workers up the hill, he could understand. What these others were about, he wasn't sure.

There were two people in the lead: a young boy and a woman, holding hands. The young boy looked to be eight or nine. The woman was probably in her late twenties. Both of them were wearing bright white pajamas.

Behind these two came a man and a woman in strange, colorful robes. They were the ones doing the chanting. Trouble thought they would look right at home at a hippie toga party. The man was older, his white hair cut and styled the same as every other man Trouble had seen. The woman had a pixie haircut. Trouble realized that the woman in the white pajamas also had the same haircut. As did the female guard he'd seen on patrol.

Behind these four people on the foot trail, there walked two men with blue long-sleeve shirts, black pants, and combat boots. They carried semi-automatic weapons. He was starting to see a trend. All the people carrying weapons around the place wore the same clothing: blue shirt, black pants, combat boots. It was a uniform.

From his side-on view of the temple, Trouble watched the group get all the way to the door, where their chanting stopped. The woman and young boy stepped aside while the white-haired man produced keys from somewhere in the considerable folds of his robe. He then led the four inside, leaving the security guards to stand watch at the bottom of the steps.

Less than five minutes later, the two in the colorful robes came out. The man locked the door as the woman stepped back down onto the dirt path, holding the hem of her robe up so it wouldn't get dirty.

The pair walked down the path, and Trouble expected the security guards to go with them, but they didn't. They stood there in front of the temple, showing no signs of moving.

While watching the group go up to the temple, Trouble had assumed that the security guards were escorting them there because they were outside the compound's perimeter. But now he was thinking the guards were there to make sure the woman and boy didn't run. He wondered what had happened during those three or four minutes when the four of them had been in the temple. He hadn't heard anything that would indicate violence, but that didn't mean much.

He crouched behind the tree as the woods slowly adopted night in its entirety. And he continued to crouch there while his vision adjusted to the low light. Ten minutes passed, but he couldn't see the guards. Then twenty passed. He still couldn't see them. The bright temple was barely visible as white lines behind the many trees.

He'd been holding out for his night vision to improve further, but this was as good as it was going to get. He stood up from his crouch and froze as his knees cracked, the noise seeming deafening in the quiet woods.

He heard nothing from the direction of the temple.

He moved closer, choosing each step carefully. Despite the chill night, his palms were sweaty, the M88 still held in his right hand sticking to his skin. There were occasional sounds of night animals moving around, but nothing else. No small talk from the two guards. No sniffling. No throat clearing. Nothing.

More than once as he moved toward the temple, Trouble thought about moving back and skirting the footpath to get his bike. Had he not seen the woman and boy go into the temple, he'd already be gone. But his earlier fear from the close encounter had been usurped by the terrible possibilities running through his mind. He couldn't leave now. So he kept moving slowly forward.

Finally, he could see the shapes of the two guards standing in front of the white structure. He was about thirty yards away, peering at the two men. He couldn't make out their features anymore, but he recalled them from earlier. Both in their twenties. Both well-built. Both about as tall as Trouble—around six foot. Like all the men he'd seen so far, they had the same haircut with the part on the left.

He considered how to go about what he wanted to do next. The old throw a rock trick only worked in the movies. He needed a way to sneak up and incapacitate them without killing or seriously injuring them. His first instinct was to take one hostage with his gun and make the other one drop his weapon and get on the ground. But if these two men really were part of a fanatical religious group, that was a big risk. They could be ready and willing to die for their cause at the drop of a hat. The other guard might not care that his compatriot's life was being threatened. He might just open fire, killing both Trouble and his hostage.

No, that wouldn't do. He needed another way.

A plan came to mind. Only, he had to admit, it wasn't really much of a plan. Like a lot of choices in Trouble's life, it was best summed up in two words: Fuck It. Both the drawbacks and benefits of "Fuck It" were exemplified in its lack of coherent planning. On the one hand, you didn't have to scramble and panic when your plan when to shit, because there *was* no plan. On the other hand, not having a plan was how many of his peers had ended up in jail or dead.

Trouble considered, still looking through the darkness at the guards. Both men had their weapons held at patrol ready – sometimes called sling ready. They could have them up and firing in moments. So he'd have to be fast.

He judged the distance between them to be about ten feet. He could cover ten feet quickly. A second or two, he figured. But covering the distance wouldn't really be the problem. The problem would be the time it took to put the first one down. Even if it was just a simple elbow to the head, it would give the other one time to get his gun up. A squeeze of the trigger, and no more Trouble.

Besides, the straight-on, attack like a madman idea depended on surprise. But they would surely hear him running through the woods. Even if he managed to sneak up closer, he'd still have to run a good ten or fifteen yards before getting to the first guy.

Not a great plan.

Then he remembered the swath of dirt around the temple. It was a recent build, and the freshly churned dirt around it hadn't had time to be coated with fallen pine needles, pinecones, and branches. If he were patient and careful—two things he struggled with mightily—he would be able to sneak up on the guards from around the back. He could walk through that dirt without alerting them.

Fuck it to Fuck It, Trouble thought. *Here's a plan that might actually work.* He took a moment to be proud of himself. In his middle thirties, he was finally growing up, learning to plan things. What a wild life.

He crept carefully back into the woods, moving slowly, watching out for fallen branches and pinecones. He looked back through the dark woods every few steps, making sure the guards hadn't moved. But soon enough, he was too far to see them. And he started to move around to come on the temple from behind.

When he came to the rear of the structure, he stood, listening. Still, he heard neither man talk, cough, snort, or sneeze. It was starting to freak him out. Even the most well-trained soldiers couldn't suppress the occasional fart. They couldn't keep a bug from flying up a nostril. But these two . . .

Trouble told himself they had surely made some kind of noise when he was out of hearing range. Surely. They weren't robots, after all. He hoped they weren't, anyway.

He sat down in the dirt behind the temple and pulled off his boots. He also took off his leather jacket, the zippers of which made noises when he ran. He didn't like taking off the jacket in times of danger, thinking it provided him with protection in the form of luck. It was a superstitious belief, but one he couldn't seem to dispel.

Laying his jacket over his boots, he debated putting the gun away for the assault. He quickly decided that the benefits of having it ready outweighed the drawbacks of sticking it in his waistband.

He started around the side of the structure, keeping it on his right side. It would be easier for him to throw a right elbow by coming around this side of the temple. He wasn't sure a blow with his non-dominant arm would do the trick.

As he made it about halfway down the side of the temple, he finally heard one of the men speak. "I need to use the bathroom, Parall James," the voice said.

Trouble had a moment to wonder what the hell kind of name Parall was before the guy stepped out from the front of the temple and into his line of sight. The guard took three steps before freezing and turning toward Trouble, who no doubt stood out against the white temple with his dark clothes.

"Parall James!" the man called out.

Trouble shoved off the temple wall as the man raised his gun. Had he not called out, he might've gotten the rifle up in time. But that moment of delay gave Trouble enough time to get to him. He grabbed the barrel of the AR-15 with his left hand, swinging a right elbow into the man's face. Bone crunched under the blow, and the man went down hard. Trouble let go of the rifle barrel because the weapon was attached to a strap. He kept his forward momentum going, running toward the nearby trees as gunshots sounded behind him.

He felt bullets impact the ground around him as he dodged through the trees. Without slowing, he turned a hard left, aiming to get back around the temple. The gunfire stopped and a flashlight beam lit the woods where he'd been moments earlier. He slid down behind a contour in the land, and the beam flashed past it.

"Sentinels! This is Parall James at Suzerain's pantheon. We're under attack."

Trouble could still see the flashlight beam searching the woods. If the man was talking into a radio, which is sounded like he was, then both his hands were now occupied. Realizing this, Trouble launched himself over the low contour and sprinted at the man. The flashlight beam came up and spotted him on his third stride. He'd been expecting it. He raised his pistol and fired twice, wide of the light.

Human nature took effect. Only the most grueling and horrendous training could prevent you from seeking shelter when someone was shooting at you. The flashlight beam whipped away toward the ground as Parall James turned and ran for the temple close behind him. In the frantic movements of the beam, Trouble saw that the man he'd elbowed was still down. He didn't know for how much longer.

While James ran to the front of the temple, Trouble moved around the back. He didn't stop. He barely even slowed. He wanted to get to the guy before he had a chance to calm down, to think. Plus, he figured there was a small army of heavily armed individuals gearing up to descend on the area.

He could see the illumination from the flashlight as he approached the front of the temple. Slowing, he made sure to stick to the dirt, his black socks now coated with the stuff and carrying a few hitchhiking pine needles. That the flashlight was still on was good. The smart move would've been to turn it off. But with the adrenaline and the nerves, James probably wasn't thinking clearly. It was likely the first time he'd ever been shot at.

His back to the wall, Trouble peered around the corner and saw that James was up on the small portico, his back to the doors. He had his AR-15 in one hand, his flashlight in the other. He wouldn't be able to fire the weapon effectively with one hand. But at close range it might not matter. He was turning back and forth, clearly frightened. Trouble wondered where the radio was. He'd probably dropped it.

Once again, human nature was on Trouble's side. After peeking around the wall, he concealed himself again. But he could see the man's movements thanks to the flashlight beam. It was moving back and forth every two or three seconds. Erratic movements would have been more beneficial for the man, but he was operating on what amounted to lizard-brain autopilot, oscillating between fight and flight.

Trouble waited for the beam to come near his side of the temple. As soon as it started its journey back to the other side, he moved quickly around the corner. One high step brought him onto the marble portico. Another step got him within five feet of James. And as the man turned back, Trouble had his pistol pointed at the guy's head from a distance that would make missing nearly impossible.

"Stop moving," Trouble commanded.

James stopped moving. His gun was pointed out away from the temple. It would take a half-turn to get it pointed at Trouble. But James never made that turn.

"Do you have a key?"

James shook his head. His eyes were wide, his Adam's apple bouncing under his clean-shaven chin.

"Who has the key?"

"Only Parall Salazar and Suzerain," James said, his voice shaking.

"And where are they?"

"At home. On the hilltop."

Trouble sighed. "Turn around."

"What are you going to do to me, Devil?" James said, apparently growing confident.

"Just turn around. Away from me."

James turned around. Trouble moved a step closer to him, then shot his elbow forward, hitting him in the back of the head. His skull smacked the metal door, and then he fell. Trouble caught him by the collar and eased him down so he wouldn't crack his skull on the marble. Then he moved over the prone James and looked out at the place where the other man had been lying.

He was gone.

"Shit," Trouble said. He moved back cautiously and leaned down, grabbing James's flashlight and turning it off. Then he looked at the doors to the temple. His original plan had been to try and get in there, to see what had happened to the woman and the little boy. To talk to them, if they were still alive.

That plan was no longer possible. Even if he could find a key on James, which he doubted, the other man was now out there in the woods somewhere. And more people were surely on their way.

It was time to go. Now.

Chapter 7

HE SAW THE HEADLIGHTS when he was still some thirty yards away from where his bike was parked behind the two spruce trees. There were two vehicles pulling into the small clearing, braking hard as they stopped.

Trouble had lost precious moments heading back to get his boots and jacket. He'd moved cautiously, half expecting a rain of bullets to come from somewhere in the trees. But he neither saw nor heard any evidence of the missing security guard.

He'd sprinted down the footpath a good distance before stopping to pull on his boots and then his jacket. Then he resumed his running, sticking to the path until he saw the headlights ahead. He detoured into the woods and stopped, waiting for the people to pass him by so he could get to his bike.

Five people ran past: two women and three men. As far as Trouble could tell with the limited light, they were all wearing the security guard uniforms and carrying AR-15s or M4 carbines. When they were gone, he resumed his trek down the hill. But he didn't get back onto the path. He stuck to the woods, working his way down parallel to the footpath.

The headlights on the two vehicles were still on, making it impossible for Trouble to see if anyone was left inside.

Approaching and searching the two vehicles – which he now saw were a truck and an SUV—would be impossible without significant risk. His best bet was to get on his bike and get gone as fast as he could.

He made it to the Triumph, trading the pistol in his right hand for the keys from his pocket. The motor fired up without a hitch, and he moved out from behind the two spruce trees, maneuvering toward the clearing and the road beyond.

But as he got closer to the nearest vehicle—the SUV—he noticed that the driver's door was open. It hadn't been open before. He looked around wildly, seeing a man emerge from behind a tree ahead.

He was pointing his semiautomatic rifle at Trouble's chest.

"Stop!" he shouted.

Trouble wasn't sure what to do. The man was blocking the direct route out into the clearing. The best course of action would be to run him over, but there was no way he could do that before the guy shot him. He stopped, putting his left leg down to keep the motorcycle upright.

The man had the same haircut and clothing as the other men; Trouble could see him clearly in the motorcycle's headlight. His hair was darker than Trouble's, which meant it was black. His eyes looked light from a distance, but it was hard to tell their true color. He was thin and tall, making Trouble think of Ichabod Crane.

They stared at each other for a moment. When it was clear he wasn't going to shoot right away, Trouble spoke. "What do they do in that temple? What happens to the people who go in there?"

The man didn't answer. He was having some sort of internal debate. Trouble hoped he'd come out on the right side of that debate, but there wasn't much he could do about it now. Aside from talking to the guy.

"I saw a woman and a little boy go in there. Do you know them?"

Something flickered in the man's eyes. It was pain, Trouble realized.

"You do know them, don't you? Are they your people?"

"The worthy are my people. The wretched masses, the unabashedly trying, those who know not what they do." He spoke with a deep voice that cracked on the word "people." The motorcycle's headlight reflected off a tear that ventured down from his right eye.

"I only want to help. Someone came to me for help, so that's what I'm trying to do," Trouble said.

The man blinked. Shouting came from the woods bordering the footpath. Trouble looked over a shoulder but saw no one coming into the lighted woods. Not yet.

He turned back to look at the tall man. "I need to go." He eased his motorcycle forward. The man didn't move. He was still debating himself. Only, that wasn't strictly true. He had someone else's voice in his head. The voice of the leader or leaders of his little group. That voice was battling the man's true inner voice.

The front tire of the motorcycle came within two feet of the man before he pivoted, lowering the weapon. Trouble looked up into his eyes as he eased past. More tears streaked down his lean face.

Then Trouble was leaving him behind, his engine purring as he sped down the dirt road as fast as he dared. His relief increased when he came to the Y in the road without encountering any more hostiles. And he felt even better when he turned onto US Highway 64, heading back toward the little town with the café and the gas station and the dollar store.

But he wasn't done with the place. Not yet. Not by a long shot.

***

The man heard the gunshots faintly from where he perched on the clifftop overlooking the valley. It sounded like they were coming from the other side of the hilltop.

He sniffed, a dull ache coming to his temples. He was reminded of how quickly the walls were closing in. But he still had time. Or so he told himself. As he stood up on the sandstone cliff, he stretched his thick arms to the sky and reveled in the gentle breeze stirring his pubic hair. He only felt truly free when he was completely naked. And freedom was of the utmost importance to him.

A few lights shone down in the valley below. There were half a dozen houses down there, but only three of them had lights on now. The main road used to access all the houses wound through a deeper part of the valley off to his right. The trees and hills blocked any evidence of headlights from view.

He felt like a king up here. And in a way, he was. If he had his way, he would burn all six of the visible houses down, so his view wouldn't be spoiled by the structures of man. Maybe one day soon he would make it happen. All it would take was a few words in the right ears, and his will would be done.

His feet were no longer tender, after spending so many hours without shoes or socks on. He moved quickly back from the cliffside, his calloused feet having no trouble navigating the uneven rocks. His ebony skin was ashen in the dry mountain air, but he'd come to revel in the minor discomfort. After all, he taught his people that discomfort was essential for enlightenment. For Ascension. So what was dry skin? Nothing. Less than nothing.

When his people saw him wandering around, naked and barefoot, they were reminded that he was special. That he was somehow more than human. It was a carefully constructed persona he'd spent years perfecting. And it worked.

He'd started a fire as darkness descended, but it had burned down to embers while he'd been thinking—meditating. Picking a few small twigs from a pile near the fire pit, he went about building the flames back up again.

When the flames were dancing, he turned his gaze toward the little girl who stood at the edge of the campground. She wore a simple white tunic and sandals. Her strawberry-blonde hair was straight, long, and well-cared-for. Smiling at her, he stroked his beard, which had begun to go gray. She stared at him with large blue eyes, blinking occasionally, her face impassive. He knew she hadn't moved since they'd come out here together. That was good. She was the most special of them all. He felt like he could think again, now that he had her back. She was an Angel incarnate.

The sound of footsteps coming down from the Sanctuary prompted the man to stand up, the flames warming his naked body and causing the hair on his legs to curl.

Parall Marsden stepped down onto the flat bluff he used as a campsite. She was dressed in a multicolored robe that indicated her level. Her blonde hair was cut short around an angelic face. "Suzerain," she said, a little out of breath. "Someone has attacked two of our Sentinels at your temple. We need—"

Suzerain held up a hand, silencing the woman. "What is wrong with this picture, Parall Marsden?"

A look of pure panic flicked across her face before she realized where she'd gone wrong. "I'm sorry, Suzerain," she said, bowing slightly. She straightened and then reached up, releasing the clasp at her left shoulder. The robe fell, revealing her naked body. Her nipples hardened in the cool breeze. She stepped out of the robe and slid her sandals off, standing three feet from the man.

"Why do I ask this of you?" he said.

"Because we all strive to be equal," she said, as though reciting a lesson.

"And so I ask you to speak to me as an equal. To not hide your body with clothes while mine is presented to you. But why else do I ask this?"

"Because there is no shame in nakedness," she said, eyes downcast.

"That's right," the man said, looking up into her face. He was a short man, and most of his flock towered over him. "We learn shame as we grow into these adult bodies. It's not a natural part of being human. Animals aren't ashamed of their nakedness, are they?"

"No, Suzerain," she said.

"Of course not," he said, then paused. "Now, you say someone attacked two of our Paralls at my temple? I say to you I've seen this coming. I've been given a vision. It was meant to happen. We have not captured these people—or this person—have we?"

"No," she said. "Not yet."

He nodded. "And we won't. Not yet. Do you know what it means?"

The woman smiled. "That the time is coming."

"That's right," he said, looking over at the little girl, who gazed at the two adults blankly.

He felt himself stirring, and he looked back at Parall Marsden. She looked down at his crotch, her gaze drawn by the movement there.

He stepped closer to the woman and raised one hand to touch her breasts.

"There is no shame in love," she said.

"That's right," he whispered. "We're here to love, aren't we?"

Parall Marsden shivered under his touch, a breathy "Yes" escaping her as his hand moved down her belly and between her legs.

The little girl continued to stare blankly at the two adults.

Chapter 8

TROUBLE PASSED THE SMALL town's law-enforcement station as he looked for a motel. Dalewood Sheriff's Department. There was one cruiser parked outside the small office, which was sandwiched between a barber shop and a boutique sporting goods store that advertised fishing licenses. He recalled seeing a large but battered election sign for a Sheriff's candidate named John Vegretti on the way in.

He considered briefly involving law enforcement. But it wasn't a serious consideration. He'd never been a big fan of the way police went about things. Besides, he figured there was a good reason Mitchell hadn't gone to them already. And if he had, they clearly hadn't been able to do anything for him.

As he spotted a motel near the end of the half-mile strip that was Dalewood's downtown, he wondered what, if anything, had become of Mitchell and his daughter. Shayna, he said her name was.

His nerves had calmed on the drive back to the town. He'd stopped to gas up at a service station on the north side of Dalewood. Now at the motel, he was able to convince the clerk to give him the room without an ID. It took more cash than he would've liked, but he didn't think putting the room under his own name was a good idea. He was willing to part with the greenbacks for that peace of mind.

As he pulled his limited supplies out of the two saddlebags on his Triumph, his phone started vibrating in his pants pocket. The display told him it was Dylan calling.

"Hey," he said, holding the phone to his ear with his right shoulder while he gathered up his clothes and the extra cash he pulled out of the saddlebags.

"How's everything going?" Dylan asked. "Did you meet the guy?"

"Yeah, I met him. But things aren't going too well."

"What did he say to you when you talked to him?"

"He didn't say much," Trouble said. "Just that he knew where his daughter was, but he needed help getting her. Before he could elaborate, some weird shit happened."

"What weird shit?"

Trouble told him about the man who'd been watching the diner from across the road, the backpack, and the note. Then he went through his little excursion in the woods near the temple. It took him a good ten minutes to get through it all. When he was done, he'd moved all his stuff into the motel room and removed his boots and his dirty socks. He was lounging on the bed.

"What. The. Fuck," Dylan said.

"Yeah."

"Sounds like a cult."

"Smells and tastes like one, too," Trouble said. "You're the tech guy. What did you find on Mitchell?"

"Jack shit," Dylan said. "He dropped off the map like he's Houdini. Last evidence of him being a part of society is about five years ago. He emptied his bank accounts, stopped posting on social media, and ceased having any bills in his name."

"Great," Trouble said. "Well, there's got to be some evidence of this cult, right? Can you work your magic and find out whatever you can about them? Anything at all would help."

"Yeah, of course. But whatever they put out into the world will be highly sanitized. Maybe I'll find something on some ex-members speaking out against them. Otherwise, there won't be much to go on. These groups are very clever about how they interact with the public. And since this one has been around for at least five years without making the news, I'm guessing they know what they're doing."

"Well, see what you can find. I'll do the same. I don't think they're from around here. They're still working on building a fence around their compound, so check recent land sales in the area. In the last year or two."

"Got it." Dylan paused for a moment. "What do you think happened to the woman and the boy?"

"I wish I knew. But is it ever a good thing with these groups?"

"Sometimes," Dylan said. "Sometimes these groups do lots of good. But this doesn't sound like one of them."

"No. I can tell you that right now. Whatever they're doing, it's not good."

Trouble hung up with Dylan, but he didn't put the phone down. He signed onto the motel's Wi-Fi and started his research. But he didn't have the name for the cult. And doing searches for "New Mexico Cult" or "Dalewood Cult" got him nothing.

He put it on the back burner, hoping Dylan would be able to get him some information he could use. While he waited, he decided to shower. The motel's bathroom was serviceable. The hot water worked, and there was soap and shampoo he could use. When he was done, he dried himself with one of the scratchy white towels.

When he'd pulled on new underwear and his dirty blue jeans, he checked his phone. There was a message from Dylan. It said, "The Divine Emissaries."

He had a name.

Chapter 9

TROUBLE WAS WEARING A shirt he bought at the sporting goods store. It was a white, black, and red long-sleeve plaid shirt, worn over his black t-shirt. He'd left his leather jacket back at the motel and had walked down to the sporting goods store just after ten in the morning. He had one of his two M88 pistols tucked into the back of his waistband.

He hoped that, without the leather jacket and the motor-cycle, he wouldn't be recognized when he walked into the meeting in the local church. The church was located two short blocks beyond the main strip, directly behind the block with the sheriff's station, sporting goods store, and the barbershop. The block between was occupied by a small park, in which Trouble sat and watched the church's front doors.

At first, he watched for people dressed the same as those he'd seen yesterday. The security personnel with blue shirts and black pants. The workers with green shirts and brown pants. But the people he saw walking into the church were all dressed differently. And none of them had the uniforms he was expecting.

In the end, it was the haircuts that gave them away. Two men walked in through the front doors of the Christ Commu-nity Fellowship Church just before eleven. There had been a slow trickle of people before them, but they were the ones who caught Trouble's attention. They had the same haircuts he'd seen on the security guards at the compound. The same haircut as Mitchell, in fact. Long on top and short on the sides, parted on the left.

It wasn't a dead giveaway, but coupled with the information he'd gleaned from his internet searches, it was enough.

It was Saturday, and the bright spring sun was shining on the quaint town of Dalewood, New Mexico. As Trouble stood up from the sunny park bench, he glanced at the kids enjoying the playset in the middle of the park. A man smiled as he pushed a little boy on a swing. A couple of women chatted on another park bench, glancing around regularly to make sure their children were safe. Kids screamed with joy as they slid down slides, climbed up colorful ladder rungs, and played tag.

It did little but remind him of the way the little boy looked as he walked into the temple. There was no joy on his face. No light in his eyes. He was blank, emotionless. Did that mean he was being abused? Did it mean he was walking, whether unknowingly or not, to his death? No. Not necessarily.

Most kids, in Trouble's limited experience, didn't like church or religious ceremonies. He couldn't blame them. To a child's mind, there was nothing more boring than listening to someone drone on about things you didn't understand.

But if there were terrible things going on there—if the kids were being abused in any way—Trouble was going to find out. He *had* to. He felt compelled to make sure nothing untoward was going on. He wasn't entirely sure why he felt so strongly about this. He'd never been one to let abuse slide. Even as a kid, he found himself standing up to bullies when none of his peers seemed willing.

But this was different. There was an ache deep in his chest that he couldn't place with any confidence. It had been there since encountering the little girl at the house in Monument.

Something was driving him, he just didn't know exactly what it was. But it didn't really matter. His course was laid before him. The goal was there, he just needed to figure out how to reach it.

And his first step was to attend the meeting hosted by the Divine Emissaries. He approached the church, which was made out of dark wood with a peaked red metal roof. The name of the church stood out above the door in white letters affixed to the façade. And as Trouble stepped through the doors, a woman greeted him with a smile, handing him a flyer on blue paper. As he walked into the main room, down the aisle between two columns of pews, he read the flyer. It was essentially the same thing he'd read on the Divine Emissaries website the night before. Most of it seemed pretty benign at a glance.

Trouble had gone through a several-year phase in his late teens when he was genuinely interested in religions. Every time someone handed him a flyer or pamphlet, he read the whole thing. And considering he'd spent much of his late teens either in group homes or homeless shelters, he'd been handed a lot of religious literature. He'd been ready to believe something in those days. And in fact, not much had changed. He was still ready to believe, but after so many years of not having any proof of a higher power, he'd wasn't holding out hope. The whole faith argument had never been enough for him. He wanted more.

He'd seen some wonderful things during his life, but they could all be attributed to human kindness. And if it was all a benevolent God's doing, then Trouble was happy there was such a being. But he thought it more likely that people were capable of both great goodness and astonishing evil. And he figured this group—the Divine Emissaries—was no different.

They were capable of anything. Just what exactly they were doing was the question.

Trouble selected an aisle seat on the right and sat in the uncomfortable pew. The wooden seatback pressed the gun against his lower back. There were about a dozen people sitting in the place, with more trickling in as eleven o'clock approached. He re-read the flyer, picking out the lines that seemed especially interesting.

"We do not ascribe to one religion; we are children of the universe."

"Our students include millionaires and executives, actors and musicians, engineers and psychologists."

"Change your life through our teachings and find the success you seek."

It was a mishmash of religious rhetoric and self-help jargon. Trouble figured they had a copywriter among their ranks who had crafted the narrative. It ended with a call to action to visit the church he was now sitting in. Clearly, it had worked. There were nearly twenty people sitting in the church, waiting for the meeting to commence.

If Trouble had organically come across the flyer or the website, he wouldn't have given it a second thought. Then again, he wasn't the target audience. Who was, he didn't know. Glancing around the room, he looked for commonalities among the audience. There were people from numerous backgrounds, as far as he could tell. Black, Hispanic, and white. Young, middle-aged, and old. Men and women. A couple of people were wearing expensive-looking suits or designer clothes, while others looked on the verge of homelessness.

But, by a slim margin, most of the audience members were young. Under twenty-five. What that implicated, he didn't know. Maybe young people were just more likely to be seeking out a belief system. And one that promised success as well as meaning was likely to attract a few folks.

The inflow of people seemed to stop. Trouble checked the time on his phone. Four after eleven. A man sitting in one of the two front pews turned in his seat and looked at the crowd. He stood up and smiled.

"Welcome, everyone, to the Divine Emissaries Discovery Session," he said. He was a good-looking man with a strong jaw and sandy-brown hair. In his late twenties, he dressed in understated clothes that skirted the line between luxury and utility: khaki pants, a short-sleeve collared shirt, and immaculate chukka boots. His watch glittered in the lights affixed to the wooden rafters above. He had one of those familiar faces that immediately reminded Trouble of some television actor. Hell, maybe he *was* an actor.

"My name is Bruce Thornton, and I've had the pleasure of being a Divine Emissary for several years now." He paused, gathering his thoughts. "Now, before I found this wonderful group of people, I was lost. In fact, I was more than lost. I was at rock bottom. But I couldn't even tell you what hole I was in." He smiled, his perfectly white teeth gleaming. Some of the audience chuckled. Trouble groaned inwardly.

"I discovered them at the exact right time in my life. I was reeling from a years-long drug addiction when . . ."

Bruce Thornton kept talking. Behind him, catching Trouble's eye, was a man who came through a side door beyond the pulpit. He smiled as if to apologize for his intrusion, his eyes scanning the crowd as he walked toward the pews, clearly intending to take a seat. It didn't seem as if he was looking for anyone in particular. Just seeing who was there. But when his eyes landed on Trouble, he did a double take. He didn't stop walking, but his face changed slightly.

Trouble fixed his green eyes on the man, returning his gaze. The guy recovered and then sat in the front pew—the same one Bruce Thornton had been sitting in. He moved like he was pulling something out of his pocket. A phone, Trouble guessed.

Although the man wasn't wearing a blue shirt and black pants, he was likely part of the security force. Trouble recognized him from outside the church. He was one of the guys that was heading inside while Trouble was watching from the park bench. His black hair was thick, and he looked to be in his late thirties. He had some muscle on his frame, which was why Trouble pegged him as security. That and his demeanor. He looked capable. A fighter.

". . . my confidence back," Bruce Thornton was saying as he talked animatedly from the pulpit. "I started making more money. My shyness disappeared. I found a sense of peace that I carry with me to this day. But I'm not trying to tell you it's easy. It's not. It has been the hardest thing I've ever done in my life. Even harder than quitting opioids."

Trouble's ears perked up at that. He'd been through his own battle with opioids. It was a war he'd be fighting for the rest of his life.

Bruce continued. "Becoming a Divine Emissary has been a challenge like no other. But if there's one thing I've learned in this life, it's that nothing good comes easy. So it makes sense that achieving the peace we all seek as humans would be the hardest thing of all, right?"

Some of the audience members were nodding emphatically. They were eating this up. And even though he'd only been paying limited attention to it, there was something resonating within Trouble, too. Who wouldn't want success and peace and confidence? Trouble could use more of all three.

The security guy sitting in the front pew turned in his seat and looked back at Trouble. Once again, Trouble met his gaze. He even gave him a smile. It seemed to piss the guy off. The door beyond the pulpit opened, and the blond guy from the compound's gate walked through. Vogel.

His face was impassive. Nothing like the barely cloaked fury Trouble had seen in his side mirror as he rode away from the compound entrance yesterday. Although Trouble stared, Vogel kept his eyes down, clearly pretending he didn't see the man.

He bent down and whispered in the other guy's ear while Bruce kept talking. Finally, Vogel's eyes came up and found Trouble. Without looking away, he said three words to his buddy. Although Trouble couldn't hear him, he could see clearly what Vogel said: "Yeah, that's him."

The two men stood and walked around the side of the line of pews. Vogel stopped at the one Trouble sat in. There was no one else sitting with him, so Vogel turned sideways and moved in, sitting next to Trouble. The other guy came around the back, approaching from the aisle.

"It's time for you to leave," Vogel whispered, his warm breath prompting Trouble to lean away from him.

Trouble looked at him. His straw-blond hair. His dark brown eyes. His clean-shaven cheeks. He looked for the fury he'd seen on that face yesterday, but found no trace of it. The man was good at hiding it. He wondered if that was something taught to him in the cult, or if it was something he'd learned to do long ago.

"I'm interested in becoming a Divine Ambassador," Trouble said, all innocence. "Why do I have to leave?"

Saying the wrong name had no visible effect on Vogel. "We know it was you who attacked our men last night. They both suffered concussions because of you. And although our leader teaches forgiveness, we don't want you causing trouble in here. So it's time for you to leave."

Trouble felt the other security guy's presence to his left. He also saw some heads turning toward their little group. Audience members were growing curious.

"Why would I attack your men? Why would anyone attack your people?" Trouble asked. "What are you guys doing up there in that compound?"

"We're minding our own business. Like you should. Now let's go."

"Okay," Trouble said, standing up and stepping into the aisle. "Let's go to the police. If you think it was me who attacked your guys, I think we should involve law enforcement. Get to the bottom of this thing."

Vogel said nothing. Just walked behind while the other guy walked ahead.

They stepped out onto the sidewalk. "Just go," the other guy said. "Leave us alone." He turned back to head inside, but stopped when it was clear Vogel wasn't coming.

"Go ahead, Parall Wynn," Vogel said, staring at Trouble. "I just want to have a word with this man."

"Parall Vogel," Wynn said, "I—"

Vogel turned his gaze on the man, who stopped talking. "Go back inside, Parall Wynn," Vogel said through clenched teeth.

There was some of that fury. It was surfacing. He couldn't hold it any longer. Wynn headed back through the doors, leaving Trouble and Vogel on the sidewalk. There were still children and their parents in the park. Nothing serious would happen. Not here.

"I don't know where you came from," Vogel said. "But you need to get out of this town now. Today."

"Or what?" Trouble said.

"Or I'll make you leave myself," Vogel replied, getting into Trouble's face.

"How would you do that?" Trouble said, unfazed.

Vogel was faster than Trouble expected. His right hand fastened around Trouble's neck. Trouble brought his left hand up and grabbed Vogel's neck. His right hand went around and gripped the M88 in his waistband, but he didn't pull it out. Vogel wasn't trying to choke him. Not yet. He was trying to make a point.

"This is *our* town," the man said, his face contorted, eyes burning. His grip was tightening. "And you're not going to ruin it with your fear. We will not succumb to your devilry. I won't allow it."

"Am I interrupting something?" It was a woman's voice, coming from behind Vogel.

The two men released each other quickly. Trouble discreetly covered his gun with his shirt as he looked at the woman. He'd seen her sitting inside for the meeting. She had curly brown hair pulled back into a bun. Her tanned skin glowed in the sun. Her eyes were blocked from sight by sunglasses, but she had an amused smile on her lips.

"Yes," Trouble said. "We were having an argument. Maybe you can help us? I think the Divine Emissaries is a cult. He disagrees. What do you think?"

Vogel glared at Trouble for a moment before speaking. "Heed my advice," he warned, then stormed back inside.

Trouble looked at the woman. She wore a thin gray hooded sweatshirt unzipped over a white tank top. Her blue jeans were rolled up at the cuffs over white tennis shoes.

"That looked pretty intense," she said.

"He's a pretty intense guy," Trouble said.

They looked at each other for a moment. She seemed like she wanted to ask him something, but she didn't.

"Well? What do you think?" he asked.

"About what?"

"The Divine Emissaries. Are they a cult or not?"

"Oh, right. Definitely a cult."

Trouble smiled. "Good. Well, I'm glad at least one person saw through the bullshit." He turned to leave. "Take care."

"Wait," she said, hurrying over to him. "I'd like to talk to you about them."

"The cult?"

"Yeah," she said. "They've got my sister. And I need to get her back before something terrible happens. I don't know what you did to them, but it looks like you got them rattled. So, can we talk?"

Chapter 10

SHE SAID HER NAME was Carmen. Her sister's name was Megan. There was something familiar about her, but Trouble couldn't place what exactly. Maybe she just had one of those faces.

He told her his name was Terrence, but to call him Trouble. Surprisingly, she had nothing to say to that. Unlike most people, she just nodded and took it in stride.

He agreed to sit down with her, and they walked down to Dalewood's main drag, where they found a quaint restaurant with tables and chairs that looked as if they were made from pine trees, covered with a shiny finish.

When Carmen took her sunglasses off, Trouble was struck by her emerald-green eyes. They sparkled, even in the shade of the restaurant. He thought eyes like that made his own green eyes look dull and lifeless.

Her brown hair was sprinkled with sun-kissed natural blonde highlights, indicating she spent a lot of time outside. He pegged her for an outdoorsy type. She had tanned skin, an athletic build, and an easy grace in the way she moved.

"Tell me about your sister," he said. "When did she get involved with the Divine Emissaries?"

"About five years ago," Carmen said. "But only in the last couple of years have things gotten really crazy. And just in the last year crazy enough for me to drop everything and try to come find her."

"What changed in the last year?"

"She stopped talking to me. Before, we used to talk once a month or so. But all of a sudden, she stopped taking my calls. Then her phone number was disconnected. Then I called it and someone else answered, saying they just got the number."

A kid in his late teens came up and asked them if they wanted anything to drink. It was going on eleven-thirty, and the place was starting to fill up. Trouble figured he should order something substantial because table space was about to be at a premium. After Carmen ordered a coffee, he ordered a breakfast plate along with a coffee and a water.

"Haven't had breakfast yet?" she asked, smiling slightly.

Trouble shook his head. "So when did you get into town?" he asked.

"Last night. It took me forever to even find out the group had moved down here."

"Where did they move from?"

She started to answer, then stopped, looking at Trouble with mild suspicion. "Why don't you tell me why those guys kicked you out of the meeting? Then I'll tell you what I know."

"Fair enough," he said. "A guy asked me for help yesterday, but then he got cold feet. I followed him up to their little compound and got turned away at the gate. And from what I've gathered, they had a little problem up there after I left. They thought it was me. It wasn't."

It was instinct to skip over the stuff at the house in Monument and the confrontation with the two guards last night. He wasn't about to incriminate himself to someone he'd just met.

The waiter came back with two mugs and a coffee pot, along with Trouble's water.

"What kind of trouble did they have, Trouble?" Carmen asked.

He smiled and shrugged. "I only know what the guy told me while kicking me out of that church. He said something about an attack on his people. I couldn't tell you what, when, or how."

Carmen studied him with her bright, intelligent, and mistrusting eyes. "What kind of help did the guy want? The one who got cold feet."

"He wouldn't tell me much. Something about getting his daughter back."

"What changed his mind? And why did he ask *you* for help? Why didn't he go to the police?"

Trouble shrugged again. He didn't know how much to trust this woman. For all he knew, she was a part of the organization, sent to gather information on him—or worse. They could've seen him sitting at the park and set the whole thing up on the fly. "Why haven't *you* gone to the cops?"

"I have," she said. "Before I came down. Apparently, my sister came into town to talk to the sheriff. There's not much they can do. She's not being held against her will. She wants to be there. They've gotten into her head. She thinks their leader is the messiah or the ultimate guru or some combination of the two."

Trouble nodded. "Nobody joins a cult," he said.

"Apparently, they do," Carmen said.

"It's a saying. It means that people who join cults don't join thinking it's a cult. If they did, they wouldn't join. They think it's something good. They think they're going to change the world. Or change themselves for the better. That's how these groups hook people. Did you listen to what that guy back in the church was talking about?"

"Yeah. Before I got distracted by you and those two guys. Sounded like bullshit to me."

"Sure. Because you know what it leads to. But if you never had any previous experience with the group—if your sister wasn't stuck in it—you might feel differently. You might have gone in there ready to believe that they could change your life. That they could provide spiritual guidance, a blueprint for success, and the life you've always wanted. That's the hook. The soft sell. That's how they get you in. And it takes time, effort, and work to go from that to someone like your sister, who refuses to leave. People will spend years in a group like that before they get to the point where they don't know which way is up."

Carmen nodded. "I can see that. How do you know so much about cults?"

"I stayed up late last night doing research. The question is: how do you not?"

She smiled slyly. "The truth is, I do. I've been researching groups like these for the last year. I just wanted to make sure you're on the level."

"For what? What do you think I can do to help you?" Trouble asked, getting to the meat of the thing.

Carmen had to think about that. And while she considered, Trouble's food came. He started in on the scrambled eggs as she answered.

"It looks like you have a way with people," she said. "And with a nickname like Trouble, I can only assume that you're no stranger to confrontation. I saw the look on that guy's face outside the church. He was riled up. And I figure if the guy you're talking about doesn't want your help anymore, I can use it. Specifically, you and I can figure out a way to catch them doing something illegal. Or prompt them to do something illegal. Then we can get the police involved."

Trouble sat back and looked at her, chewing. "I don't know," he said after swallowing. "It sounds like you're asking *me* to do something illegal. I can't do that."

Carmen shook her head. "Of course not. We can come up with a legal way of doing this. I'm sure of it. There's got to be some way we can find out what's going on in their compound. Surely they're doing something or other that's against New Mexico laws. We just need a way to find out what it is, document it, and bring it to the police."

Trouble considered it. But he quickly came to the conclusion that working with her would be more of a liability than anything. He wasn't about to let New Mexico laws govern his actions. He didn't yet know what he'd do to get to them—to find out what was really going on there. But if he were to work with Carmen, he'd be putting them both in danger. And if he did break the law while she was around, there was a risk she'd get picked up and spill about it. The last thing he wanted was to be in jail. That would do no one any good.

"I'm sorry," he said to her. "No."

Carmen slumped in her seat, genuine hurt in her eyes. "Why not?"

"Because that's not how I work. I'll do what I can to get your sister out, okay? But I can't work with you. It's not a good idea. For either of us."

Carmen was silent, glaring across the table as Trouble resumed eating. "Fine," she said, clearly angry. She stood up from the table, grabbing her small purse from an empty chair next to her.

As she moved toward the door, Trouble reached out and grabbed her arm. "Wait," he said. She turned to look at him, hope in her eyes. "What does your sister look like?"

"Like me," she said. "But I saw a picture on their website. It looked recent. Her hair is cut short and dyed blonde."

Trouble nodded. "And what's her last name?"

"Same as mine," Carmen said. "Marsden."

Chapter 11

HIS MEAL WAS GOOD. Eggs. Bacon. Hash browns. Coffee with enough sugar to combat the bitterness.

He went over the conversation with Carmen again, looking at all the angles, thinking about ways to help her without adopting an untenable amount of risk. He decided he'd made the right choice. But he should've at least asked her where she was staying. Or for her phone number.

The kid came back with the check, and Trouble paid cash, leaving a 20% tip on the table as he left. He wanted to get back to his motel room and put his leather jacket back on. He felt strange without it. Like he was walking around in someone else's skin. He was also tired of feeling the gun against his low back. With the jacket, he could put it in a pocket.

He stepped out onto the sidewalk and looked around, taking in his surroundings. Habit.

The main drag was on a road called Center Street. Buildings lined the street, most of them two stories. There were some made out of brick and sandstone, but most of them were wooden. There were a couple of restaurants, a store that advertised gourmet sweets, a bar, clothing shops, and a few other stores that catered mainly to tourists.

Parked vehicles bordered the two-lane street on which traffic crawled past at 25 miles per hour. There was a single stoplight at the intersection to Trouble's right. He turned that way, heading back to his motel.

But then he stopped. And turned back to look left. There was a silver SUV coming down the road. And although he couldn't see the driver clearly thanks to the reflection, he could see the man's jacket. It was a raggedy blue windbreaker.

Trouble stepped between two parked cars as Mitchell approached. He lifted a hand and signaled for him to stop. As the SUV got closer, Trouble saw Mitchell see him. The man looked even worse than he had yesterday. His face was gaunt, his eyes bulbous and insane.

He didn't stop.

Trouble turned, watching him go. But the light at the intersection was red. Mitchell was forced to stop some thirty yards away.

Trouble ran down toward him on the white line that separated the parking area from the traffic lane. He came up on the passenger side and tried the door handle. The door was locked. He was breathing heavily, still unacclimated to the relatively thin air. "Open the door," he said through the glass.

Mitchell said nothing, shook his head.

"Come on, Mitchell. I just want to talk to you. You're not the only one with kids in there, are you? What about all the other children?"

The light turned green. Mitchell's head swiveled forward. As he shifted his foot from the brake to the gas pedal, Trouble jumped up onto the running board, grabbing the roof rack with his left hand.

"Get off!" Mitchell screamed, the burst of emotion catching Trouble by surprise.

"Pull over."

Mitchell looked at the line of cars on the right. Trouble could see the gears turning. "Don't you fucking do it!" he shouted.

Mitchell shifted the wheel to the right.

Trouble grabbed the roof rack with both hands. He wrenched himself up off the running board and onto the hood a split second before the side of the SUV crashed into and scraped along the side of a Honda crossover. People on the sidewalk looked on with wide eyes as the SUV with the man on the hood pulled away from the cars and continued on down the street.

Trouble pulled the pistol out of his waistband and pointed it through the windshield at Mitchell. The man looked at the gun and then up at Trouble, a humorless smile on his face. He wasn't scared. He wasn't stopping.

Looking up at the top of the vehicle, Trouble saw that there was a sunroof there. He lunged up and smashed the butt of his pistol into the tinted glass. It cracked. A second and third hit sent glass raining down into the cab, causing Mitchell to swerve and pull off the road into a driveway. Trouble glanced around, recognizing that they were near his motel at the end of the main drag. The driveway Mitchell had pulled into belonged to a grocery store.

The SUV rocked as it came to a stop, taking up two parking spaces at the rear of the lot. Trouble was still standing on the hood, leaning up over the roof. He looked down through the broken sunroof. Mitchell looked up. He had a few minor cuts on the back of his neck from the glass.

"Are you done?" Trouble asked. "I don't understand why you wouldn't just pull over and talk to me. What's going on?"

"You can't fucking help me," Mitchell said, vibrating with anger. "No one can."

"What does that mean? How do you know I can't help you?"

"It's over," Mitchell replied, shaking his head.

"Talk to me, Mitchell. We can figure this out. You'll never know if you don't tell me what's going on."

Mitchell slumped forward over the wheel and started sobbing.

Trouble could feel eyes on him from people in the parking lot. He tried to block their view of his weapon with his body. "I'm going to get down now," he said to Mitchell. "You won't drive away, will you?"

Still sobbing, Mitchell shook his head.

"Put it in park and unlock the doors."

"It's over," Mitchell wailed as he put the vehicle in park. He hit the door unlock button, and Trouble could hear the locks disengaging.

"Okay," Trouble said. He jumped off the hood, gun still in his right hand.

As soon as his feet hit the ground, he heard the doors lock again. The transmission shifted loudly, and then the SUV was pulling away from him. He ran with it and jumped up onto the running board again, but before he could get a good grip with his free hand, Mitchell swerved. Trouble went down hard, rolling along the asphalt as Mitchell pulled back onto Center Street amid a chorus of honks from cars he cut off.

"Son of a bitch," Trouble said, pushing himself up and running toward his motel. His shirt was ripped, and he had some scrapes and bruises, but he was okay. He pulled his keys out of his pants pocket as he got to his Triumph. Pausing to put his pistol back in his waistband cost him precious seconds. He fired up the bike and pulled out of the motel parking lot, gunning it down the street to catch up with Mitchell.

He didn't know why it was so important that he stop Mitchell. Now that he had a moment to think on it, he was surprised at the man's reaction. Trouble had thought that jumping onto the car would show Mitchell how serious he was, getting him to pull over so they could talk. But then the guy swerved into a parked car. If Trouble hadn't moved when he did, he'd be dealing with two broken legs, at the very least. After that, he'd been acting on instinct.

Why was Mitchell now so willing to inflict harm when not even a day earlier he'd been asking for help? What had happened between then and now? What the hell was going through his head?

He had to stop Mitchell. The guy had answers that would help Trouble, but it was more than that. Something in the man's eyes. Something in the way he showed no fear when Trouble pointed his pistol at him.

Mitchell needed help, whether he wanted to admit it or not. But not just help making sure his daughter was safe. No, the kind of help he needed was more immediate. He needed to be saved from himself. Trouble had no idea how he would go about doing that, but he had to try.

He had to pass two cars on a double-yellow to catch up with the silver SUV. Then he hung back, much like he had yesterday, and waited to see where Mitchell was going. He had to stop sometime. Trouble would be there when he did. And he was done fucking around. He wanted some answers. Even if he had to smack the guy around a little. This thing was bigger than Mitchell.

Highway 64 wound southwest, down out of the mountains and into a high desert landscape. It took little more than twenty minutes, and then Trouble was following Mitchell into the outskirts of Taos, still on 64. They stopped at a couple of lights while heading through town, but Trouble didn't try anything. He wanted to wait it out. He'd filled his gas tank after coming back into Dalewood last night. If he was lucky, Mitchell's tank was getting low.

Soon, they were leaving Taos behind, passing through farmland. Trouble saw signs for the Rio Grande Gorge Bridge. He got a bad feeling.

When they came to an intersection, Mitchell got into the left-turn lane, which would allow him to continue on Highway 64. Trouble stuck with him, that bad feeling expanding like a balloon in his gut. As soon as he turned left onto the two-lane highway, Mitchell put the pedal to the floor. The SUV lurched, its engine climbing from a growl to a low whine. Trouble pulled the throttle back and shifted gears. A glance down at his speedometer told him he was approaching 95 miles an hour.

Mitchell swerved into the oncoming traffic lane, then braked hard and swerved back. A U-Haul truck blasted its horn as it flew past going the opposite direction. *What the fuck are you doing?* Trouble thought. *Trying to lose me?*

Once the lane was clear, Mitchell gunned it again, passing a minivan in the right lane. Trouble stuck with him, keeping a safe distance between the vehicles. Flat, sandy ground spotted with scrub brush flashed past in a blur on either side of the two-lane highway. Thin clouds hung low in the sky. Snow-tipped mountains were visible in the distance.

A sign for the Rio Grande Gorge Bridge whipped past. *Just keep driving*, Trouble thought. *Just keep on going, buddy.*

There was a semi-truck coming in the left lane, some mile or two distant. Mitchell had slowed to seventy, stuck behind a dusty pickup truck. Trouble thought he would wait for the semi to pass. But he didn't. At the last moment, the silver SUV swerved into the oncoming lane and rocketed ahead, pulling in front of the pickup moments before the honking semi passed. Trouble knew not to even try it. He stuck behind the truck, watching the SUV grow smaller as it pulled ahead. There was a line of cars behind the semi that Trouble hadn't seen before. But, he guessed, Mitchell had.

The bridge was just ahead. They were coming on it fast. But Mitchell would get there a good ten seconds before Trouble. Whether he would keep driving or not was anyone's guess, but Trouble's gut was telling him that the bridge was his final destination.

As Trouble passed the parking area for those who wanted to check out the bridge on foot, he caught a glimpse of a vehicle coming on fast behind him. It was a black Jeep.

He could see the outlines of three men inside.

Chapter 12

THE RIO GRANDE GORGE sits in a massive rift that runs the length of New Mexico. It was formed as tectonic plates shifted some twenty-nine million years ago, pulling away from each other. The river came after, flowing down the Rio Grande Rift on its way to the Gulf of Mexico, helping to create the canyon that the Rio Grande Gorge Bridge now spans.

Dark volcanic rock, red-brown gravel, and scruffy high-desert plants line the sloping edges of the gorge. Sheer cliffs face each other, still separating at a rate of one inch every forty years or so. The steel bridge itself sits some six hundred feet above the river.

As Trouble approached the chasm, he watched in horror as the silver SUV came to a screeching diagonal halt in the middle of the bridge, blocking both traffic lanes. Six sightseers on the bridge's walkways looked around in confusion as Mitchell, in his oversized blue windbreaker and black slacks, jumped out of the vehicle and sprinted to the side of the bridge.

Trouble nearly lost control of his Triumph as he came to a sliding stop, his bike inches away from hitting Mitchell's SUV. He knew what was about to happen, and all his attention had been fixed on the crazed man in the ill-fitting clothes. He heeled the kickstand down, then jumped off the bike and ran toward Mitchell, who was just pulling his left leg over the chest-high white railing that bordered the concrete walkway. His hands gripped the railing tightly, and his feet were positioned between the metal railing slats on the bottom crossbar. He faced the bridge, his back to the six-hundred-foot drop behind him.

Trouble slowed as he approached, holding his hands up in a placating gesture. Their eyes met.

"Don't come any closer!" Mitchell shouted, the wind making him sound further away than he was.

Trouble changed direction, heading to the railing about six feet from Mitchell. He wondered if he'd driven the man to this. If he'd left him alone, would things have gone this far?

Thinking on the fly, Trouble did the only thing that came to mind. He jumped up and got his right leg over the railing, then his left. He stuck the toes of his boots between the slats on the bottom crossbar, just like Mitchell had done. His hands gripped the railing for dear life.

And he immediately regretted his decision.

What the fuck am I doing? he thought, looking at all the air between him and the ground. The Rio Grande was a narrow ribbon far below. His hands immediately began to sweat. *I hate heights.*

"What the hell are you doing?" Mitchell said, looking to his left toward Trouble.

"Trying to make you see sense," Trouble said, making this up as he went along. "It's not just your life on the line here, okay? It's about more than you."

A gust of wind whipped past Trouble. His stomach lurched as he realized how easy it would be to slip and fall. It took all he had to fix his gaze on Mitchell. To not look down.

"What do you think I'm doing out here?" Mitchell said, his face screwed up in anguish and wet with tears. "This is the only way to keep her safe. *He* said so."

"This can't be the—" Trouble stopped as Mitchell turned his head away. He was looking to the right, back the way they'd come. Trouble followed his gaze and saw a man standing next to the open rear door of a black Jeep. The same black Jeep Trouble had seen in his side mirror moments earlier. The same one he'd seen at the gas station next to the café during yesterday's meeting with Mitchell.

The man was bald, and the left side of his head was ragged and splotchy with an old burn scar. His blue shirt and black pants rippled in the wind. He stared at Mitchell, his expression hard. And then he nodded.

Trouble returned his gaze to Mitchell just in time to see the color come back into the man's hands as he let go of the railing.

"No!" Trouble shouted, reaching out with one hand. But it was too late, and he was too far away. Mitchell's arms came out, making a T as he tumbled back into the chasm. His eyes were wrenched shut. He flipped around once in a slow backward somersault as he grew smaller and closer to the ground.

Trouble watched in disbelief as Mitchell's body shattered on the rocks at the edge of the river below. Someone screamed from the other side of the bridge.

He felt nauseous. He'd never liked heights. And the shock of what he'd just witnessed was combining with vertigo to make him sick. His palms were slick with sweat, even in the stiff breeze.

He turned to look at the man standing beside the Jeep. His nausea turned to icy fear as he saw the man stepping back from the open door, straightening and turning, lifting an assault rifle to his shoulder. Incredulity was Trouble's first reaction. There were witnesses everywhere. A short line of cars had stopped on each side of the bridge. The nearest of the six pedestrians was just twenty-five yards away.

But he moved through this state of unbelief quickly, his limbic cortex kicking into high gear as he ran through scenarios with the speed of lightning-fast synapses. The nearest cover was ten yards away—the SUV. Too far. He couldn't run fast enough. He wouldn't even be able to get back over the railing before the guy had a bead on him.

There was only one option.

Trouble went for his gun. But even as he took his right hand off the railing, the man was putting his finger inside the rifle's trigger guard. There wasn't enough time.

So he did the only thing he could. He ducked, getting his head down under the top of the railing. He brought his right hand up to the horizontal crossbar, back to its original position. He'd bought himself a couple of seconds, if he was lucky.

The man at the Jeep was at a shallow angle to the railing, which would force him to move to get a straight shot at Trouble without the vertical metal slats in the way.

Once again, Trouble decided to go for his gun. But as he took his right hand off the top railing, the man started firing at him. The menacing reports of the weapon filled the air. Bullets struck the railing around Trouble as he dropped his hands down, one at a time, to the vertical slats. He let his body drop, his hands stopping him as the edges of his palms hit the bottom crossbar. His legs dangled, then he lifted them to press his knees against the side of the concrete foundation, taking a minuscule amount of weight off his hands.

His head and hands were still visible to the shooter, although partially blocked by the railing and the angle. He could feel the metal vibrating through his hands as bullets struck. He could hear ricochets careening off the concrete. A spray of fragments—whether metal or concrete, he couldn't tell—bit into the right side of his face. He cried out and turned his head. He had to get lower. But the only way to do that was to shift his grip down and forward, under the bottom crossbar of the railing, to where the edge of the walkway was.

No choice. The shooter was changing angles, moving in for a better shot.

He shifted his right hand down, then his left. His arms and shoulders screamed as he lowered himself, bringing his head down below the side of the bridge. His fingers were now doing all the work, grabbing like hooks onto the gritty concrete. If he took a bullet in either hand, he would fall. There was nothing to press his knees against now. Nothing to help ease the burden resting solely on his fingers. The support structure of the bridge was several feet away; there was no way he could reach it. He couldn't even see where it began. All he knew was that the searches he made with his feet yielded nothing but air.

The shooting stopped, allowing him to hear the scrape of footsteps approaching. He was a sitting duck, now. He'd bought himself a few more seconds of life by dropping down. That was it. The shooter could simply step up to the railing and look down into Trouble's face. He wouldn't even have to fire his weapon. He could just kick at Trouble's fingers. Then there would be two shattered bodies at the bottom of the gorge.

His thoughts turned to his pistol again. There were nine bullets in the gun: eight in the magazine and one in the chamber. But to get it, he'd have to hang by one hand. His muscles were already beginning to shake. He didn't know how long he could keep this up.

But he had no choice. The gun was his only option. It was either try for the gun, hoping he could hold on, or wait to die. No choice at all.

Clenching his teeth and letting out a low grunt, he shifted his weight to his left hand, pulling himself up slightly. He brought his right hand off the ledge, reaching around to grip the pistol as the footsteps grew closer. As he brought the weapon up, he slid the safety off with his thumb.

Although he was confident that the footsteps approaching were those of the shooter, he didn't want to fire blind. It was possible the shooter had left with his buddies in the Jeep, and a good Samaritan was coming to help Trouble.

He took a breath and pulled with his left arm, grunting as he lifted himself up to look between the sidewalk and the railing. The bald man with the burn scars was close. He fired as soon as he saw Trouble's eyes come up. Trouble dropped back down as bullets impacted the sidewalk inches from his hand. He stuck the M88's barrel through the narrow gap and fired four shots in quick succession.

The rifle fire stopped.

Trouble paused, the gun still pointed over the ledge. His left hand was slipping. He couldn't hold on any longer.

He turned the gun and shoved it through the gap, dropping it onto the sidewalk. Then he gripped the bottom crossbar with his right hand and pulled himself up, using both hands this time. The scarred man was running to the Jeep, limping. A trail of blood marked his progress.

As the vehicle U-turned, Trouble pulled himself up with shaking arms. He levered himself over the railing and collapsed onto his back on the gritty sidewalk, breathing hard. He grabbed his gun and held it to his chest, raising his head to watch the Jeep recede.

Feeling eyes on him, he got up, engaged the safety, and put the gun back in his waistband. Then he stumbled over to his motorcycle. He fired it up and backed away from Mitchell's SUV to give himself room to turn around. Then he was powering down the highway, headed back toward the mountains. People sitting in or standing beside their cars watched him. Several had raised phones, clearly recording. Trouble turned his head so they couldn't get a good look at him. But it was a wasted effort. He was sure the entire confrontation had been recorded. Probably by several people.

Soon enough, the police would be after him.

Chapter 13

PARALL JENSEN COULD THINK of little else but the confrontation with the man on the motorcycle last night. He'd been trained to take action. He'd been trained to not hesitate. He'd been told – and believed – that as the time of Ascension approached, resistance from the outside world would increase. Suzerain had been right about everything else. And now that they were making final preparations for the Rapture, a mysterious man on a motorcycle was attacking them. There would be more, Suzerain warned.

But Parall Jensen hadn't been able to pull the trigger when the time came. Something inside him had been screaming. He'd felt physically sick, and the severity of the emotions that came swirling to the surface had brought tears to his eyes.

He knew it was weakness. Somewhere along the line, he'd failed the Emissaries. Maybe he wasn't meditating enough. Perhaps he wasn't studying Suzerain's teachings enough. Or he was letting fear control his higher self.

But despite his shame, he told no one else about the encounter. When the other Sentinels returned from their search, Jensen told them he'd seen no one, but had heard what sounded like a motorcycle start up down the road.

He didn't know why he lied. It was almost automatic.

Now, as he stepped out of a long, low barracks building and into the bright afternoon sunlight, he caught sight of Parall Marsden walking between the wooden mess hall and armory buildings. Despite the unflattering folds of the colorful robe she wore, Jensen felt a spike of longing for her. They'd met because of Raymond Beck, in a roundabout way. And they'd started dating, both elated to find a companion who seemed to be on the same path. But as time went on and Beck started demanding more and more of their time, things fizzled out. But Jensen's feelings clearly hadn't. Memories of her touch, the feel of her body, and the way he felt when he was around her were too strong to ignore.

Suzerain said there was no shame in love, but certain women were off-limits to everyone but him. In fact, it was rare to see Parall Marsden alone. She was most often seen following two steps behind Suzerain, when she was seen at all. Her important work kept her busy. Or that's what Jensen had been led to believe.

Marsden's dark eyes met Jensen's. She started to smile at him, making his heart swell, but then she seemed to catch herself. She looked around briefly and then continued on her way, as if she'd never seen him.

He watched her go, noting how skinny she had gotten since Suzerain took an interest in her. Just looking at her face, he could tell she'd lost weight. All the women Suzerain deemed as approaching the highest degree of salvation grew thin eventually. In fact, he encouraged every Divine Emissary to fast regularly. He said that controlling your appetite was one of the best ways to learn discipline. And above all else, discipline was needed for enlightenment. For salvation. For the Ascension.

Children especially were taught to fast. They were the key to Ascension. They would be the vessels in which the Emissaries would travel. In fact, the children were rarely seen by anyone but a few adults. They stayed in their own bunkhouses and ate separately. Most of their time was spent learning how to obtain salvation through the coming Ascension. The Seraphs, as they were called, needed to be ready to receive enlightenment soon. The time was coming.

Parall Jensen moved off through the sprawling cluster of buildings, headed for the armory so he could retrieve a weapon for his shift. As he turned onto the main footpath between two rows of single-story wooden buildings, he saw Parall Vogel coming from the direction of the Sanctuary. "Parall Jensen," Vogel said. "Come with me. I have a job for you."

Jensen nodded and changed direction, following Vogel toward the gate, where the vehicles were parked. They walked on a dirt path through the trees. A breeze stirred Jensen's black hair. He sniffed, reveling in the pine-scented air.

They came to the modest parking area and got into the same black SUV Jensen had driven down to the temple last night. Only this time, Vogel was driving. Jensen racked the front passenger seat all the way back, so his long legs weren't touching the dash. The men at the gate saw them coming and opened it. They drove through.

"Suzerain wants to see you after the ceremony," Vogel said.

Jensen kept his face impassive and nodded. "I look forward to seeing him. His presence lifts me."

"As it does us all."

They drove on in silence. Jensen always had a bad feeling around Vogel. For a long time, he thought it was residual distrust from living the isolated American lifestyle. For several weeks, when they'd first come to New Mexico, he'd managed to convince himself that he'd gotten rid of that distrust. But he now realized that he'd been fooling himself. It had always been there. He'd just gotten better at ignoring it.

What else had he gotten good at ignoring?

Jensen pushed the thought away, knowing it was his fear talking. He had much work to do. He decided, as Vogel turned the SUV onto the road to the Pantheon, that he would confess everything to Suzerain when he met him later. He would seek his counsel and do whatever he said. He knew it would take much effort. Much discomfort. But change was only possible with discomfort. With effort.

As they pulled up to the temple path and parked, Jensen felt better. He'd decided on a course of action. For now, the fearful voice inside him was quiet.

They got out of the vehicle, and Vogel told him to come to the back. He opened the hatch and revealed a clear plastic tarp, along with cleaning supplies, including a mop and a gallon jug of diluted, pale purple cleaning solution.

They carried the supplies up the path to the bright temple. There were two Sentinels standing guard with their weapons: Parall Perez and Parall Keller.

Vogel handed the supplies he was carrying to Parall Perez and produced a keyring. He unlocked the hefty metal door and opened it. Jensen wasn't sure what to expect. Not exactly. They hadn't been told specifics. Only that Suzerain was helping to prepare them for Ascension, and he needed volunteers to make the initial preparations.

But he had a feeling—coming from the same place that told him not to trust Vogel—that it would be difficult to see. And as he followed Vogel into the temple, he was proved right.

Inside was a single sunken room. Four dim lights set in the peaked ceiling provided illumination. Jensen knew they were solar-powered; he'd helped install the panels on the roof. There were three marble steps leading down to a marble floor. In the middle of the floor were two long and low pedestals: one large and one smaller. On the large pedestal, a woman with a pixie haircut lay sprawled, her arms facing up and hanging over the sides. Both her wrists had deep cuts in them. Her skin was devoid of color, of life.

On the smaller pedestal, a little boy lay on his back, eyes staring up at the ceiling. His white pajamas and slightly darker skin were coated in dry blood. The woman's right arm stuck over him on the lower pedestal. She had bled on him.

The boy's eyes moved as the two men approached. Clutched in his right hand was a bloody razor blade. He'd done the cutting. His face was blank.

Looking at him, Jensen suddenly felt dizzy. His stomach roiled, and a barely containable sense of outrage swept over him. He stopped, looking at the terrible sight ahead of him. He knew them both. The little boy, Seraph Gibbs, he knew better. He'd spent time teaching the boy, and other children his age, how to meditate on Suzerain's message, back before they'd made the move to New Mexico. Seraph Gibbs was the son of one of the women Suzerain had taken under his wing.

The woman was Parall Beil, who had been with the group since before Jensen joined.

Vogel knelt in front of the young boy, ducking his head in deference. Jensen followed suit.

Seraph Gibbs sat up, set the razor down, and then touched each man's head. Then he moved past them and outside, without a word.

Jensen stood up after Vogel and looked out the open door. The boy, who was only nine years old, stood in the sun in front of the temple, his face tilted up, bloody arms held slightly out to the side.

"What are you waiting for, Parall Jensen?" Vogel said. "Let's get to work. Go get the plastic sheeting from Parall Perez."

Jensen did as he was told. He arranged the plastic on the floor inside the doorway, then helped Vogel carry Beil's body over to it. They wrapped her up and then took her outside. Perez and Keller took her down to the SUV while Vogel watched Jensen clean the blood from the pedestals and the floor.

Seraph Gibbs sat cross-legged in the sun, his eyes closed. He was meditating. Just as Jensen had taught him.

Thoughts swirled in Jensen's head as he worked. His heart hammered. Was this what Ascension looked like? Was this what awaited them all?

He felt fear explode inside him like a fireworks display. At first, he tried to work through it using the techniques he'd learned during years as a Divine Emissary. But every time he tried to move past it or reason it away, the fear only grew. It made him sick to his stomach. And the image of Beil lying on the large pedestal, the blood drained from her body, would not leave his mind's eye.

By the time they were done, and Vogel had locked the temple up tight, Jensen decided he wouldn't seek Suzerain's council. He wouldn't tell him the truth.

He didn't know what he would do, but he knew he had to do something. What was happening here wasn't right. It was going too far.

If this was salvation, Jensen wanted no part of it.

As they walked back to the SUV, Gibbs following along behind, Jensen thought about the biker.

He'd said he wanted to help.

Chapter 14

THE NAVE WAS CROWDED with people as the sun went down outside. Jensen looked around, realizing that nearly every one of the over seven hundred members was there. The only people not in attendance were those tasked with guarding the property. Under normal circumstances, Jensen would be among the Sentinels. But his shift had been covered while he helped Vogel at the Pantheon. In three hours, when Jensen went on for the next shift, he'd take his position as a Sentinel. But for now, he was to bear witness to the very first step toward Ascension.

The Sanctuary was by far the largest building in the compound. It had been the first built, and the only one that outside workers had constructed. The rest of the compound's buildings had been built by members of the Divine Emissaries. There were plenty among their ranks with experience in building and design. But the massive Sanctuary building would've been beyond their capabilities.

The large stained-glass windows near the ceiling let colored light in. But it wasn't just pictures of saints or disciples. Featured there were pictures of holy leaders from all different religious and spiritual movements. The underlying beliefs, crafted and espoused by Suzerain, centered around the notion that there was no one true religion. And, in fact, all the different gods worshiped by the teeming masses were really the same God. And that God wasn't a deity so much as it was the combined life force of every living being ever to exist.

The Sanctuary reflected this belief. It served as a reminder that all were capable of Ascension.

When Jensen had first heard Suzerain talk, back before he was Suzerain, he had been in awe of the way the man could put into words things he always felt but could never articulate. In those days, it had been a message of peace. Of betterment. Of overcoming fear. Of reaching past your base urges to something more. Something better. And in developing a relationship with Suzerain, Jensen had grown more confident. He'd developed into what he thought was a well-rounded, happy person.

How had things changed so much? Jensen wondered now as he sang the words to a hymn about the coming Ascension. How had he not seen them changing?

Of course, he *had* seen them changing. He wasn't blind. But he'd trusted Suzerain so much—and everyone else seemed to go along—that he'd never seriously thought about what they were doing. He'd asked questions often—that was encouraged. And the answers to those questions always seemed to make sense at the time. It was only later, when he mulled them over in his mind, that the answers seemed strange or even nonsensical.

The throng of voices was loud and achingly beautiful in the acoustically designed space. A man and a woman in colorful robes faced the audience from the stage, leading them in song. Everyone was pressed up close to the raised stage; the seats had been removed from the nave for this occasion.

Most of the people in the audience, including the children, were dressed in simple white pajamas. There were a few people in their work uniforms, likely because they had come straight to the Sanctuary from their posting without having time to change.

After getting back from the Pantheon, Jensen had gone to the bunkhouse he shared with several other members and changed out of the dirty Sentinel uniform he'd been wearing. Like most others, he now wore a simple long-sleeve cotton shirt and similar pants fastened with a drawstring. He had sandals on and no socks.

As the song came to an end, Parall Marsden parted the curtains at the back of the stage and walked out in her robes, smiling. The crowd quieted as the robed singers separated to give Marsden center stage. Jensen made sure to keep his face impassive as he looked at her, feeling that familiar longing. He knew people were watching the crowd for signs of disobedience. He'd been assigned the task more than once himself, although he'd never told anyone else about it. There were hidden cameras everywhere in the sanctuary—yet another reason why outside help had been required in its construction.

As Marsden came out, a screen lowered from the ceiling in front of the dark blue curtains backing the stage. A live feed came on the screen, showing her as she settled and waited for the crowd noise to die down. She was wearing a headset microphone, and her soft voice projected from the speakers placed expertly around the space. "Hello there," she said, like greeting an old friend. Her perfect smile was three feet wide on the screen above and behind her.

A chorus of hellos answered her. The energy was electric. Everyone knew that Suzerain would come out after Parall Marsden. She always introduced him.

"I can't tell you all how excited I am," she said, shifting her gaze around to people in the crowd. "I never dreamed that I would be a part of something so wonderful. So important. So special."

She paused as heads nodded and a few people called out sounds of encouragement and agreement.

"But I have to tell you, I'm scared."

The crowd reacted negatively to this. Fear was the enemy. Fear was the biggest factor that kept you from ascending.

"It's true: I'm scared," Marsden said. "Because, as we approach the final stages of our movement—as we begin to show the world that enlightenment and true fulfillment are possible—fear will creep back into our hearts."

More low-pitched noises from the crowd. Jensen found himself shaking his head, sucked up by the crowd's energy.

"It's true. These vessels we have are only human," she said, gesturing at her body. "And humans feel fear when they do something special. Something important. But does that mean we have to let it control us?"

"No!" Jensen shouted, along with the rest of the crowd.

"No, we don't," Marsden agreed. "In fact, given all the work we've been doing to eliminate fear, we won't have any problem when the time comes. We will be able to experience Ascension and oneness without so much as a hiccup. And I'm here to tell you that Suzerain will guide us to enlightenment!"

The audience went crazy, jumping and raising their hands. Some people were crying tears of joy. Kids hugged each other and clapped solemnly.

And as the blue curtains parted at the back of the stage, the crowd noise increased. Suzerain walked out, barefoot and wearing simple white pajamas that stood out against his dark skin. He had a wireless headset on, just like the one Marsden wore. His thick, graying beard couldn't hide his beaming white smile. And his perfectly shaved ebony head shone in the stage lights. He stepped next to Marsden. The two smiled at each other. Then he kissed her on the lips.

Until that kiss, Jensen had been in a trance. He'd fallen so easily back into the old habits, the old mindset. The smile that had been plastered on his face fell as Suzerain kissed the love of Jensen's life. He quickly caught himself, forcing the smile back on.

Suzerain stepped to center stage as Marsden moved back behind the curtains. He stood with his arms held out, smiling and looking around as adoration and applause rained down on him.

After nearly a minute, the noise faded. "I love you," Suzerain said simply.

"I love you!" the crowd called.

"What is possible?" he asked.

"Everything!" came the answer.

"Are you afraid?"

"No!" half the audience answered.

"No? It's okay to be afraid. Parall Marsden is afraid. Even I'm a little afraid."

Silence swept across the crowd.

Suzerain looked around, face serious. "It's true. I'm afraid. Because I know that resistance to our peace movement is already starting. Some of you have probably heard about it . . . Two of our members were attacked last night. Did you know that?"

There was a smattering of affirmative answers, but most of the crowd was silent, eyes fixed on the short, thick-limbed man on stage.

"It's true. But I've been warning you that this would happen. I told you that, as we approached the time of Ascension, we would come under attack by those who don't understand. But this isn't a bad thing. It may *seem* like one, but it's not. In fact, it's good. That means we're doing something right!"

Cheers erupted from the crowd. Beck waited for them to die down.

"It's the same as everything else. If you want to change anything for the better, you'll have to make some people angry. And if you look at the state of the world, you'll see that most people are lost. Most people are angry . . . You know this. You've all been there before. Don't you remember how it was to be lost . . .? It wasn't a good feeling, was it? No, it wasn't. But imagine how all those lost people will feel when we show them how to be found!"

The crowd erupted again.

"But until we show them how to be found, we're going to have to take certain precautions . . ."

As Suzerain talked, Parall Rankin rushed out onto the stage, limping severely. A man in a Sentinel uniform followed, grasping at Rankin's shoulder, a frightened look on his face.

Suzerain stopped talking, apparently noticing the audience's diverted attention. He turned around and looked at the bald, scar-faced man. With only a moment's hesitation, he told the Sentinel to let Parall Rankin come on stage.

"What is it Parall?" Suzerain asked. "Are you injured?"

As if suddenly realizing what he was doing, Rankin slowed and looked at the people in the audience, every one of them staring at him.

Suzerain stepped close to the man, gripping the small headset's microphone in his fist to prevent it from picking up their conversation. Rankin had been with Suzerain from the beginning. At least, that was Jensen's understanding. He acted as a fixer. A right-hand man. There were all sorts of stories about how he got the scars on the left side of his face, some disturbing and some just sad. Most stories said he'd done it to himself to prove his loyalty to Suzerain. Maybe none of them were true. Jensen didn't know.

Rankin talked to Suzerain for a few long moments. When he was done, the bearded leader turned to face the audience, solemn. He took his hand from around the microphone, seeming to gather his thoughts.

"Parall Rankin brings more news about the resistance we face. He himself has been injured in a conflict with these . . . lost individuals. These Devils. These people who are driven by ego and toxic mentalities. Driven by darkness. They see our light and are blinded by it. They seek to put out our light only so they can get rid of their discomfort. But the only way forward is for us to shine brighter!"

And just like that, the crowd was in the palm of his hand again. Jensen doubted that Rankin's appearance on stage had been planned. But Suzerain used it to his advantage, like he used everything to his advantage.

"Parall Mitchell was one of these individuals," Suzerain continued. "Yesterday, I begged Mitchell to come back. I begged him to rejoin our efforts and work past the poisonous devilry he'd been experiencing from interacting with those who would do us harm. But he refused. The darkness was in him, and it wouldn't let go. He left this morning freely—as you are all free to leave whenever you wish—but I asked Parall Rankin to keep an eye on him.

"I don't believe Mitchell was beyond salvation. I don't believe *anyone* is beyond salvation. But he made his choice. He attacked Parall Rankin and the other Sentinels he had with him. And now Mitchell is gone. I felt a great sense of loss not long before coming out here to greet you, but I didn't know what had caused it until now. We've lost a brother. One who had been on a parallel path. So please, I ask you, let's take a moment to give thanks for his contribution to the Everything."

Jensen closed his eyes along with everyone else. The people were silent for nearly a minute before Suzerain said, "I love you."

The crowd returned the sentiment.

Rankin limped off stage, and Jensen noticed that there was a bloody bandage wrapped around the man's calf. He could just see it through the slit up the back of his pant leg.

Suzerain smiled at the audience. "Now, it's time to bring out the living embodiment of Ascension so you can see for yourself. Parall Marsden?"

The curtains parted, and Marsden led Seraph Gibbs out onto the stage. The boy had been cleaned up, his clothes changed and Beil's blood scrubbed off. His cheeks bulged as he smiled, looking around with a slightly dazed look in his eyes.

A hush fell over the crowd as everyone stared at the nine-year-old. Suzerain took his hand, letting Marsden step back. She made no move to get offstage. The bearded man got on his knees so he could be face-to-face with the child. He took both small hands in his large ones and looked deep into the boy's eyes.

"How do you feel?" he asked.

"Wonderful," the boy answered with a giggle. Their faces were close enough together that Suzerain's microphone picked up the boy's words.

"Tell me something only Parall Beil could possibly know. Show us all you're in there. Show us you can see through Seraph Gibbs's unblinded eyes. Tell us how it feels to be innocent again."

Gibbs closed his eyes. He didn't speak for several moments. The crowd was utterly silent. "When I was a little girl, I saw an angel. It came into my room and told me one day I would be part of something bigger than myself. It told me I would be accepted into a great kingdom where suffering was a thing of the past. And in so doing, I would help the world find salvation."

Suzerain turned to Marsden. "Parall, is that what Beil told you before she went to the Pantheon last night?"

Marsden's eyes were shining with tears. She nodded. "It's exactly what she told me."

People in the crowd looked at each other in amazement. Tears of joy streamed down cheeks.

"Did Beil tell you that, Seraph?" Suzerain asked the boy. "Did she tell you that story?"

Gibbs opened his eyes and shook his head. "She's with me now," he said. "I can feel her. We've become one, sharing this vessel. She speaks using my tongue."

"Everything is possible!" Suzerain cried, pulling the boy in for a hug. The crowd repeated the words in an ecstatic chant.

Suzerain stood up, lifting the boy with him. He walked down the steps from the stage and held the boy out. Several people took the child and lifted him, still chanting. Gibbs was passed all around, everyone wanting to touch him.

Jensen played along, acting like everyone else, fitting in. But he could think of nothing but the bloody mess in the temple. And the weight of Beil's dead body as he helped Vogel transfer her to the plastic sheeting. He felt sick to his stomach.

Jensen saw this for what it was: theater. Playacting. It proved nothing. But no one in the crowd seemed to see that. They no longer knew how to think. They'd lost all perspective.

Beil was dead. Her spirit wasn't inside Gibbs. She was dead and gone.

And Suzerain had killed her.

Chapter 15

BLOOD WAS GETTING INTO Trouble's right eye from the cuts on the side of his face. He pulled over at a gas station outside of Taos to deal with the injury caused by concrete fragments spraying his face when he'd been hanging off the bridge. Just as he was getting off his bike, two police cruisers screamed past on 64. Heading for the bridge, no doubt. They'd probably passed right by the Jeep with the shooter in it. Trouble hoped the guy was bleeding out from his leg wound.

Ever since watching Mitchell crash into the rocks next to the Rio Grande, he'd felt a sharp anger that wouldn't dull anytime soon. Mitchell didn't kill himself. He may have been the one to let go of the bridge railing, but that didn't mean anything. The bald guy with the scarred face had killed him. The cult had killed him. But what about his daughter? What were they doing with *her*?

He was determined to find out. She surely wasn't the only child in the place. But he needed to figure out approximately how many people had been sucked into the group. He needed to know what he was dealing with.

He grabbed some coarse paper towels from a dispenser meant for use on windshields and wiped the blood off his face. Then he went inside the station to see about some bandages and a bathroom. He tried to keep the injured side of his face pointed away from the store clerk.

The drama at the bridge had been the opposite of discreet. Before long, Trouble's face would likely be fresh in every local cop's mind. Sure, he'd been defending himself, but he'd also done it with an illegal weapon. Plus, he was surely wanted in at least two states. New Mexico would make three.

Maybe it was time to find other accommodations. Dalewood was a small town. But Trouble needed to stick close by. Where could he stay?

He wondered about the woman. Carmen. Maybe she could help. But that would mean involving her. He still didn't want to do that.

Trouble thumped a box of bandages down on the counter. "You got a bathroom I can use?"

The graying, corpulent clerk looked closely at Trouble. "You're bleeding," he said.

Trouble gestured at the box of bandages.

The guy nodded and rang him up, then gave over a key attached to a New Mexico license plate through a small hole in one corner. "Bathroom's outside."

Trouble paid and then headed to the bathroom.

The cuts were superficial. He had to dig some bits of concrete out of his skin. One small gash was about a quarter inch above his eye, just under the eyebrow. That was the one messing with his vision, thanks to the blood oozing out of it. *Could be worse*, Trouble thought. *I could be in a cult.*

He cleaned the cuts and patched up the worst ones. By the time he was done, most of them were no longer bleeding. He looked himself over in the mirror, his mind wandering. His dark brown hair was getting longer than he liked, approaching that awkward stage where he'd have to start using product to keep it off his forehead. He brushed grit out of it with his hand.

He hadn't shaved in a couple of days, and his dark stubble was slowly shifting to a full-fledged beard.

The plaid shirt he'd bought at the sporting goods store earlier had blood on it. And it was ripped from the fall he took off Mitchell's SUV back in the grocery store parking lot. He pulled it off and shoved it in the trash. He'd been wearing it during the encounter at the bridge. That meant that several people had recorded him in the shirt. Better to not take the chance. His plain black t-shirt would have to do for now.

He pulled out his phone and sat down on the single toilet, closing his eyes for a moment. He took several deep breaths and then opened his eyes to check his phone.

He had missed a call from Dylan. There was a text. It read, "Got more info on DE and their leader. Call me when you can." Underneath, there were a couple of links to news articles. He had no time to read them now. He needed to get back to Dalewood, get his few worldly possessions from his motel room, and then find somewhere else to stay. Somewhere the cops wouldn't think to look.

He suddenly wished he'd gotten Carmen Marsden's phone number. He had a feeling he was going to need a few friends before this thing was done.

***

As he pulled into the motel parking lot, Trouble had an idea about where he would stay. He thought it was the right time of year for it.

The Red Lodge motel comprised a single, long, two-story building. It had two narrow parking lots—one on each side—but no matter which one you used, you passed the office on the way in. And as Trouble passed, he saw movement beyond the wide glass windows. He watched in his left mirror as the door to the office lobby opened and a woman came out.

Carmen Marsden. Turned out he didn't need her phone number after all.

He backed into the parking spot fronting his room and turned the ignition off, leaving the keys in. He then rushed into his first-floor motel room, propping the door open so Carmen could come talk to him. The first thing he did was change out the magazine in his M88 with a full one. Then he pulled his leather jacket on, shoved his other M88 into a pocket, and gathered up his other possessions. He took a quick glance around the room to see if he was forgetting anything.

He was ready to go. Fifteen seconds flat.

One of De Niro's lines from the movie *Heat* echoed in his head, as it often did when he packed up in a hurry to ensure he wasn't arrested or killed. It was about not letting yourself get attached to anything you can't walk out on in thirty seconds flat when the heat was on.

Fifteen seconds to spare, he thought. He knew that line wasn't about objects, though. Still, it was a good thing to remember.

A moment later, Carmen Marsden stepped through the door.

"What happened?" she demanded, standing just inside the doorway.

At first, Trouble thought she was asking about his face. But he quickly realized that his right side was positioned away from her. Plus, her tone was all wrong. "What do you mean?"

"I mean, what the hell was all that with the guy in the SUV?" she said, putting her hands on her hips.

"You were watching me?" he asked, turning to face her.

If she noticed the fresh scabs and the three small bandages on his face, she made no indication. "Just tell me what happened. Was that the guy who asked for your help?"

"What all did you see?" he asked.

Her bright green eyes left Trouble for the first time since she'd stepped into the room. She looked around, considering her answer. "I lost track of you just outside of town. I wasn't willing to go ninety miles an hour to follow you."

Trouble hefted his armful of possessions—mostly clothes, but also a box of 9mm bullets. The M88 in his right jacket pocket banged against his hip with the movement. "Yeah, that was him. I was trying to get him to stop."

"So you jumped onto his car?"

Trouble shrugged. "It was an instinctual thing. Spur of the moment decision." He stepped close to her. He wanted to get outside, so he could see the heat coming around the corner. She didn't move.

"And then he swerved into the car. That was close. You're lucky you're not in the hospital."

"You don't know the half of it. Can I please get by? I need to find another place to stay." She was probably five-foot-ten or -eleven. At just over six-two, Trouble towered over most women. But not this one. She looked up into his face, determination in her eyes. He could smell her. She smelled like cinnamon.

"Did that happen when you fell off in the parking lot next door?" she asked, flicking her eyes to the right side of his face.

"No."

"How did it happen?"

"Watch the news. I gotta go. Give me your phone number. I'll be in touch."

Carmen finally turned and stepped outside. Trouble followed, pulling the door shut behind him.

"Where are you going to stay?" she asked.

"Nearby," he said, stuffing his items in his saddlebags. "Where are you staying?"

She hesitated before answering. "I have a small trailer set up in a nearby camping area."

"Good. Give me your number. Like I said, I'll be in touch. Maybe we can help each other." He stepped back over to her and pulled out his phone. She gave him her number.

"Call me now," she said.

He did.

"Good," she said, looking down at her phone. "So what changed your mind?"

Trouble fired his motorcycle up. "That guy in the SUV? He killed himself. Jumped off a bridge. But it wasn't his choice. Not really. *They* made him do it. And if that's the kind of power they hold, then I need to do whatever the hell I can to stop them. *That's* what changed my mind."

Chapter 16

SUZERAIN SAT CROSS-LEGGED IN a wide leather seat, his eyes closed. Jensen stood just inside the doorway, flanked by Vogel and a man named Fayden. He looked around the simple room, which was located at the rear of the Sanctuary building. In a regular church, it would've been the pastor's office. There was a wide picture window that looked out over the valley. It was a spectacular view, composed mostly of sprawling forest and distant mountains. There were a few houses—rustic mansions, really—peppered through the nearby forest.

Jensen knew Suzerain had a little place where he liked to commune with nature on a clifftop about fifty yards down from where they stood. No one was allowed down there except his most trusted helpers, of which Megan Marsden was one.

The bearded man sat with his back to the window. Without opening his eyes, he told his guests to sit. There were no other chairs in the room, so each man sat on pillows on the floor.

"Close your eyes," Suzerain said. "Bask in silence with me. We shall commune."

Jensen did as he was told. While in the past he would've meditated on letting go of his ego, his sense of self, or his devilry, this time he kept something very different in mind.

Something that Suzerain might have considered blasphemous had he known.

He kept repeating a name. Suzerain's real name: Raymond Beck.

His first introduction to Raymond Beck had not been in person. He'd watched a video in which Beck had shared some of his teachings. Jensen hadn't been particularly impressed. Back then, Beck had been clean-shaven and trying to cover up the fact that he was balding by wearing a ball cap all the time. But by the time Beck had come into the group in-person, Jensen's opinion had changed. He'd watched enough of the man's videos and done enough of the work with the other group members to realize it was making a difference in how he thought. How he saw himself. And how he dealt with adversity.

It had been working.

And in-person, Beck was electric. He had a calming presence that was also somehow energizing. It felt like anything was possible. Indeed, one of Beck's sayings, even back then, was "Everything is possible."

Jensen kept this in his mind, recalling how he let himself get sucked into this whole thing. When someone touched his shoulder, he flinched, looking up to see Suzerain—Beck—looking down at him.

"Parall Jensen," he said, his smile nowhere to be seen. "I'm concerned that you're succumbing to fear. Slipping back into your old ego mindset."

Jensen's heart was suddenly racing. Vogel and Fayden were staring at him from their pillows on either side. "Why do you say that, Suzerain?" he asked.

Beck knelt in front of him. "I know you, my brother. I can see you—the real you, inside. And I know you're having doubts about my leadership. About what we're doing here. I *know*."

Jensen considered his reply. He decided to be truthful. At least in part. "I've been having these . . . urges again, Suzerain. They're clouding my mind. Pulling me back into the old, bad mindset."

"These urges can't be satisfied by those on a parallel path? All you need to do is ask one of your sisters. You know there is no shame in sex."

Jensen shook his head. "It's an urge for one particular woman."

Beck sat back. "Parall Marsden," he said.

Jensen nodded.

Beck's hazel eyes peered into Jensen, seeming to pierce his façade, to see the truth underneath his lies. "Parall Marsden has moved beyond such urges, yet you would have her pulled back down, just to fulfill your own? Does that seem like a good idea to you, deep down, past your ego?"

"No, Suzerain," Jensen said. "I wouldn't have her journey corrupted. I simply tell you this so you can help me move past it."

Beck nodded. "Let me think on this for a moment. In the meantime, I have another question for you. Why did you not stop the man on the motorcycle last night?"

"What?" Jensen said, hoping his fear would read as shock and indignation. "Had I seen this man, I would've stopped him. I assure you. And although I heard a motorcycle shortly after we pulled into the clearing, I did not see one. He must have been moving through the trees next to the road while we drove in."

Beck studied him. If someone had actually seen Jensen let the biker go, his lie would make him an enemy to Beck and to the Divine Emissaries as a whole. He honestly didn't know what that would mean for him. But some of the things he'd heard made him sure it wouldn't simply mean exile. He was gambling everything on the notion that no one had seen what happened.

Finally, Beck stood up. "I believe you, Parall Jensen. But your backsliding troubles me. I'm partnering Fayden with you. I've given him a plan for you to follow for as long as I see fit. You will do everything together until I tell you otherwise. Do you understand?"

Jensen felt his heart plunge into his stomach. He should've seen this coming. It was common practice when someone was acting in ways Suzerain found troubling. Jensen kept the dismay off his face. Instead, he smiled. "Thank you, Suzerain. I will do the work. I will move past the ego to ready myself for Ascension."

"Everything is possible," Suzerain said in a flat tone. It was a dismissal.

"Everything is possible," Jensen said in unison with the other two men. The trio stood up. Jensen and Fayden walked out of the room, leaving Suzerain and Vogel.

***

Suzerain padded back to his chair after Paralls Jensen and Fayden left the room. Once he settled in, crossing his legs and draping his arms on the armrests, he looked up at Vogel. "I take it you've talked to Parall Rankin?" he asked.

"Yes," Vogel said. "What do you want me to do?"

When it was just the two of them, Vogel never spoke with the kind of deference that everyone else employed in his presence. It didn't bother Suzerain. They had an understanding. If Vogel didn't want to play the part of devoted follower, that was fine. All he needed to do was obey. If he obeyed, he got all the benefits that came along with being a part of the inner circle. And in all the years they'd known each other, Vogel had obeyed without hesitation.

"Do you know who he is?" Suzerain asked. "A brother, maybe? Or an ex-boyfriend? Ex-husband?"

Vogel ran a hand through his blond hair, swiping it back from his forehead. "His motorcycle is registered to a Scott Asheton in California. But a little digging makes me think it's been falsified somehow. Scott Asheton was a musician in the band The Stooges. He died in 2014. According to what Mitchell told us, the guy's name is Terrence Rubble."

"And what have you been able to find out about Mister Rubble?" Suzerain said.

Vogel shook his head. "Not much. No social media presence. A few misdemeanor arrests here and there. Although he does have warrants out in California and Colorado. No permanent residence. No job."

"What you're saying is you don't know who he is or why he's here."

"According to Mitchell, the Rubble guy was doing a friend a favor. Mitchell was desperate. He reached out to his sister. And his sister somehow got the Rubble guy involved. We're sure he's the same man who was at the house in Monument when Rankin was retrieving Angel."

Suzerain paused, making a fist with one hand. "What do we know about the sister? Is she here in New Mexico?"

"I don't think so," Vogel said. "I have a guy looking into it. But with Mitchell gone, the biggest threat is the Rubble guy. *If* he decides to come after us. He may not."

"I don't think there's any doubt he'll come after us," Suzerain said. "If the encounter in Monument didn't dissuade him, I doubt what happened on the bridge will. What of that incident, anyway? Should we expect a police raid anytime soon? Will Rankin's zeal be the downfall of the Divine Emissaries?"

"I doubt it. There's no way anyone saw Rankin come back here. They got away clean. Cops won't be able to get a warrant to come in here. If he'd killed Rubble, maybe. The witnesses will say they saw Mitchell kill himself because that's what happened."

"And what about the incident at Monument? Will they tie it to us?"

"Not for some time. None of the dead had records, and we still have their IDs. The police will have to identify them through dental records. And that'll take time. Right now, our biggest problem is the biker. And you're right, I don't think he'll give up even though Mitchell is dead. If what Mitchell told us can be believed, he told Rubble in no uncertain terms that he didn't want his help. But the guy still attacked the Sentinels at your temple." Vogel paused for a moment. "Uh, with Rankin injured, I'd be happy to . . . take over. To deal with Terrence Rubble."

Suzerain considered this for the better part of a minute. He closed his eyes and steepled his fingers. Vogel stood silently. "Okay. I want you to take care of this," Suzerain said, eyes still closed. Then he opened them and looked at Vogel. "Take Rankin's men and any others you choose. Do it as quietly as you can. And find out if anyone else's friends or family members have been snooping around in town. If they're here, they're a problem."

Vogel grinned. "Yes, Suzerain," he said. "Thank you."

As the blond man left the room, Beck felt the uneasy tingle fade away. Being around the man had always made him uneasy. His blond head held many secrets that Beck couldn't afford to let loose. But he was a tool. A very effective tool. And there would be no betrayal. Not from Vogel. Beck was sure of it. He just had to keep the wolves at bay for a little longer. Then he could orchestrate the Ascension.

He thought of the reaction the world would have when all was said and done. His name would be forever etched in the history books.

Beck smiled. It would be glorious.

Chapter 17

THE SECOND DRIVEWAY TROUBLE chose proved promising. It was dirt, and it wound a little way through the woods before coming to a simple metal gate. It was closed but not locked. Trouble moved through, closing it behind him.

The sun was approaching the western horizon, the heat of the day dissipating as shadows stretched and coalesced. A cool breeze stirred the pine branches, chilling the back of his neck.

There were no cars at the cabin, and there was no garage. Promising.

The structure was two stories, but the front door was located on the wraparound deck on the second floor. Trouble parked his bike around the back of the structure, under the deck and near a neat pile of firewood. Anyone coming up the driveway wouldn't see it.

He walked up the wooden deck and looked through the tall windows into a cozy living room and open kitchen beyond. There was no sign of anyone. The place was dark. Not a single light on. Nor did he see any cameras around the place.

There was a loft in the peaked roof, a steep ladder-like staircase leading up to it. He figured there was a bedroom tucked away beyond the kitchen. Probably one or two more on the first floor. He raised a fist and knocked on the door.

His hands were still stiff and sore from the ordeal at the bridge. Just thinking about hanging over the precipice got his hands and feet sweating again. And it brought back the vision of Mitchell's body crashing into the rocks beside the Rio Grande.

He thought about the look on the man's face while he waited to see if anyone was home. That wounded look on Mitchell's face had struck Trouble like a blow. It wasn't the look of a man who wanted to die. It was the look of a man who *had* to die. For his family. His daughter. Had he been trying to tell Trouble something? Had he been pleading with him to save his child from the clutches of the cult?

Yes. He had, Trouble thought. How had they made him jump? What had they told him? Whatever it was, it was a lie. That's what they did. They lied to themselves and to everyone else. That's how cults thrive. Lies upon lies upon lies. So many that the members actually start to believe them.

Trouble was no stranger to lies. He'd gotten good at lying to himself. But he was trying to put that behind him, along with the hard drugs and the self-destructive behavior. It was tough. Very tough. Honesty is never easy.

He knocked again on the door, this time hitting the wood frame with his fist instead of the glass. He knocked hard and waited. No one was home.

The door was locked, as expected. He headed back down the stairs and went around the back of the cabin. There was a door there, not far from the woodpile. It was a sturdy wooden door with six small windows in the top third. Two rows of three windows.

He grabbed a piece of firewood and used it to break the window nearest the deadbolt. After clearing the glass with it, he stood on his toes to reach his right arm through. He reached the deadbolt, but the knob was locked as well, and it was just out of reach. So he stepped on the piece of firewood, which gave him just enough height to unlock the knob.

The place smelled like a cabin should: leather and pine with a hint of wood smoke. He moved into the mudroom, looking for an alarm panel on the walls and not seeing one. Then he explored the rest of the first floor. There were two bedrooms and a den with a leather couch and a television. The place was all exposed wood slats and muted colors, with the occasional splash of dark green for variety.

It felt unused, which was exactly what he was looking for. It was probably a summer home or vacation cabin for some wealthy professionals. As fresh as spring was, he hoped no one would come to use the place for a couple of months. Even a month would be more than enough time to do what he needed to do. Hopefully.

Once he saw the empty fridge, he was sure the place wasn't in regular use. There was power, but he didn't turn on any lights. He didn't want to draw any attention. And he guessed there was probably a way for the owners to check the electricity usage from wherever they were. So he found some candles and flashlights in a kitchen cupboard and headed back downstairs. The entire second floor was surrounded by giant windows, most of which didn't have curtains. But the first floor had only a few smaller windows, all of which had curtains.

He chose the bedroom nearest the downstairs door and set up a couple of candles, ready to light when he needed them. He checked his phone and was happy to see that he had service. He wanted to check out the research Dylan had sent him. But he had something else to do first.

He went back upstairs and stepped through the front door onto the porch. He looked up toward the top of the low mountain. The place the Divine Emissaries called home. He could see a large structure up there, lights glowing through one wide window.

He wasn't sure, but he thought he could see a person standing below the large building, on top of a cliff. He went back into the house and dug around, finding a pair of binoculars in the master bedroom.

Stepping back out onto the porch, he lifted the binoculars to his eyes and shifted the focus. Sure enough, there was a man there, standing, looking out over the valley. He was a stocky and bald Black man with a bushy beard.

Even with the binoculars, it was hard to tell for sure, but Trouble thought that the man was looking directly at him. Staring.

A shiver ran up Trouble's spine. He told himself it was the breeze that had just picked up. Then he shook his head. *Don't lie to yourself.*

***

The first news article Dylan sent was over ten years old. It was a short article on a small news outlet's website. It detailed the civil case between a man named Raymond Beck and a woman named Beatrice Upton.

At the time of the article, Mrs. Upton was a newly widowed woman after her husband, Dale Upton, died while attending a retreat. Weeks before his death, the man apparently altered his will to give the bulk of his considerable fortune to Raymond Beck, who had been running the retreat.

Dale Upton was sixty-six years old when he died while doing some shamanic breathing exercises in a sweat lodge in Norfolk, Virginia. Raymond Beck had been leading the exercise and the small gathering of ten people. A criminal investigation determined that the man had died of a heart attack, probably brought on by the strenuous breathing exercises and the considerable heat in the sweat lodge. But he'd also signed a waiver on the first day of the five-day retreat.

He'd paid $12,000 to attend, and the journalist made a glib remark about Dale Upton paying for the privilege to die.

In fact, the tone of the article was clearly in favor of the widow. But the case didn't turn out in her favor. Raymond Beck had hired some good lawyers and had taken the proper precautions to prevent litigation before the retreat ever got going.

He walked away from the ordeal a millionaire, leaving the widow with a mere $500,000.

The article also mentioned that Mrs. Upton's lawyers had accused Beck of running a cult and brainwashing her husband to change his will. Turned out it was hard to prove brainwashing. Impossible, even.

Trouble had known instinctively that forming a cult was nothing you could do overnight. It took time. And the article he read was evidence that Beck had been at it for at least ten years. Certainly, some people had a knack for manipulation, but there had to be some mistakes along the way. Still, he doubted Dale Upton's death was a mistake.

He opened the other article. It was a more recent one.

Local Cult Heads West | Raleigh Sun | Rayland Burgess, Staff Writer

If you live or work in Southeast Raleigh, chances are you've driven past the New Hope Rehabilitation Center once or twice. Located on New Hope Road just south of Bluff's View Drive, the drug rehab center features a heated pool, a gym, a gourmet cafeteria, and luxurious apartments—for those who can afford the treatment.

There are nurses on call 24/7. Two medical doctors make regular stops there, and three addiction specialists are part of the salaried staff.

The place seems rather innocuous. And for those fortunate enough to convalesce on the grounds, it certainly seems like a great place to work the steps or determine the root of their addiction.

But all is not what it seems on the grounds. At least, according to accusations levied by family members of two people who received treatment at the facility.

John and Michelle Pollard, a couple known for their charitable contributions and philanthropic endeavors in Raleigh, insist that there is a cult operating on the New Hope grounds. According to the Pollards, their twenty-three-year-old son, Mark, went to New Hope for a thirty-day inpatient treatment, and never came out.

They refused to say what he was being treated for, but they admitted Mark's problem had grown severe in the months before they convinced him to get treatment. But it seems that Mark's treatment went a little too well. He decided to stay on the grounds to be a part of what he described as a "spiritual commune."

There are a number of barracks-like buildings on the property, several greenhouses, fields of crops, and one cathedral where people can practice whatever religion or spirituality they like. According to a spokesperson for New Hope Rehabilitation, these facilities are separate from the rehab facilities. This reporter took a tour of the property and got to see people working in the fields, doing yoga, meditating, cooking community meals, and doing a number of other activities.

Everyone was friendly and freely admitted that they wanted to be there.

Unfortunately, I was told Mark was in Virginia on an errand for the community. What errand, they did not and would not specify.

Although Mark insisted to his parents that it was free to stay, John and Michelle couldn't help but notice the bank account they set up for him was quickly emptying. The couple admits that they're free to visit Mark whenever they like, but they also say that he's changed.

"I don't recognize him anymore. He's not the boy I raised," Michelle Pollard says.

On the one hand, it's good that Mark has changed. He's off the drugs—every member of the commune takes a vow of sobriety before they can join. Isn't that change what people seek when they go to a drug rehab treatment program? Given relapse rates of between 40 and 50 percent among substance abuse disorders, one would be forgiven for thinking that John and Michelle Pollard should be happy that their son seems to have turned his life around.

But his life is what they're worried about.

"He seems vacant. Zombified," John Pollard says. "We just want him back."

Treating substance abuse disorders involves changing deeply rooted behaviors, which doesn't happen overnight. Some people have to re-learn how to live without drugs, which could be the case with Mark. His parents hope this is a phase and that he'll soon come to his senses.

But the Pollards aren't the only relatives concerned.

A woman who prefers not to be identified by name filed a police report that stated, in so many words, that New Hope had brainwashed her sister and forced her to give them her life savings. The woman, who we'll call Jane, went a step further.

She pointed a proverbial finger at Raymond Beck, who is purportedly a silent partner in New Hope, which now has several facilities around the country.

Jane's sister, who we'll call Jill, went in for opioid addiction treatment five years ago. Like Mark, she decided to stay, moving out of the rehab facilities and into the commune side of the property once her thirty-day stay was up. Although the two sisters talked often at first, communication soon dwindled to a trickle. After a year, Jill called Jane to ask for money. The two had an argument, and they haven't spoken since.

Soon after that call, Jane went to the police. But as is often the case with cult-like groups, there was little they could do without evidence of a crime.

Jane says she's no longer allowed on New Hope's property. Her goal now is to find others who may have evidence of criminal activity to bring to the police. So far, she hasn't had any luck. And according to recent public records, the commune may be moving.

Raymond Beck recently finished purchasing a 330-acre plot of land in New Mexico, about half an hour northeast of Taos.

Given the cost of this land, one wonders how much of Jill's and Mark Pollard's money was spent on the new digs.

Even without allegedly manipulating the commune members to empty their bank accounts, New Hope seems to be doing well. They are one of many industries making money from an opioid crisis that may not be making headlines any longer but is still going strong.

So, if you or a loved one is seeking options for substance abuse treatment, consider New Hope carefully. Their treatment program seems to work well, but, for some, it works a little too well.

***

Trouble put his phone to sleep and stretched out on the bed. He had the boxy yellow-and-black flashlight on for a little illumination. It was propped on the bed, pointing at the ceiling. He was feeling the full weight of the day's ordeal. First, the little spill off Mitchell's car, which had banged him up more than he'd initially thought. Then, the mental and physical stress of hanging off the bridge.

He thought back to the previous night's research into cults and cult tactics. From what he understood, most people were drawn to one of these cult-like groups when they were at a crossroads in their life. And having gone through the hell of heroin withdrawal in the not-too-distant past, he knew it was quite a crossroads to be at.

If you were systematically looking for new recruits for your cult, there likely wasn't a better place to look than a rehab center. And if you were looking for well-off members, then a ridiculously expensive rehab center was all the better.

People just coming off an addiction were vulnerable. They were learning to live again in the blinding light of full-bodied emotions and sharp-edged reality. And they were looking to replace the meaning they'd put—either unconsciously or consciously—into their drug use.

In a sense, drug addiction was a kind of worship. At least it had been for Trouble. Replacing it with a different kind of worship made sense. For him, it was exercise. Every day he had the chance, he would do about forty-five minutes of push-ups, single-leg squats, shoulder presses, and pull-ups. It got the endorphins flowing and kept him in shape now that he wasn't doing a physically demanding job.

He could see how people coming off a serious addiction could be attracted to the likes of a cult.

Fully clothed and boots on, Trouble reflected on this as his eyelids grew heavy. He was mentally and physically exhausted. And before he let sleep take him fully, he reached over and clicked off the flashlight, plunging the room into darkness.

Chapter 18

TROUBLE'S PHONE ALARM WENT off at two-thirty in the morning. He shut the alarm off and used the lit phone to find the flashlight. He turned it on and swung his legs over the side of the queen bed. He'd slept for a little over five hours. Plenty.

Although he'd done a cursory search of the place, he did another one, looking for supplies to use on his trip. He didn't find much of anything useful.

Moving up to the kitchen, he found a can of black beans and a can opener with the help of the flashlight. He ate half the can of protein-rich legumes and then walked outside, leaving the open can with the spoon in it on the kitchen counter. He doubted anyone would be showing up to use the house in the early morning hours. Which was part of the reason for getting up at this hour.

He collected his box of 9mm bullets and loaded an extra clip with his motorcycle gloves on. Then he left his bike where it was and started off through the woods, headed for the mountain. He'd turned off the boxy flashlight and left it next to the cabin's front door. He would make do with the flashlight built into his phone.

It took him a little under an hour to reach the base of the low mountain, and he had to walk close to another cabin—this one occupied.

Luckily, there were no fences to navigate as he made his way toward the compound. Only hills and trees and bushes.

He spent several minutes spying the best way up. Which meant he had to skirt around the cliff face to a steep hill. By the time the hill started to level off near the top, Trouble was breathing hard, his leg muscles burning.

When he'd first gone out of the cabin, the night air had been chilly. Now he'd worked up a sweat and was tempted to take his leather jacket off. Instead, he pulled out his gun and knelt next to a tree, looking ahead into the dark. His eyes had adjusted, and he could see the compound's fence about forty yards away.

Once his breathing was under control, he moved along parallel to the fence, keeping his distance. There was no way he could get over the barrier without supplies he didn't have access to. With a ladder and a heavy-duty rug or a sizeable carpet remnant, he could get over the razor wire. For now, he was betting on the fact that they hadn't yet finished the fence. And he knew that the unfinished portion of it was on the other side of the compound. He still had more walking to do.

Erring on the side of caution, he moved slowly and kept noise to a bare minimum. He didn't know how much they'd beefed up their security since the incident at the temple. Night-vision cameras were relatively cheap and easy to set up. So he kept the fence in sight, but only just so. And he tried to keep trees, bushes, boulders, and contours in the land between him and the compound.

Three times he spotted guards perched on the other side of the fence, the top halves of their bodies visible over the obstruction.

When he came to the dirt road that led to the gate, he moved further away from the compound before crossing. Then he came back to within sight of the fence and continued on. He'd been walking for nearly two hours when he found the end of the fence.

But it wasn't just a gap, like he'd seen the other night. They'd been smart. They'd taken precautions. Now, there were several coils of razor wire set up on the ground where the fence ended—two coils on the bottom and a third on top, making a pyramid. He couldn't see how far they went but assumed they filled the whole gap, no matter how long it was. Otherwise, there was no point.

Trouble sighed, thinking.

It looked like a World War I battlefield. There was no way he could pick his way through without getting caught and sliced up. But maybe this was a good thing. Maybe there was no guard posted to patrol this part of the compound this early in the morning. Maybe that was why they put the razor wire up.

He cursed himself for not getting up earlier. He should've assumed there would be something like this to contend with. He wanted to get in and out of the compound before the sun came up. Which only left him a couple of hours. Checking his phone carefully—so as not to create too much light—he saw that it was four thirty-seven. The sun would be up by seven fifteen at the latest.

He wanted to move closer, to inspect the razor wire. Maybe he could just move it using a branch. But his gut told him to stay put and watch for a while. He forced himself to listen to that instinct, hunkering down and slowing his breathing, watching and listening.

Trouble's mind was never silent for long, and his thoughts turned to what-ifs. It was easy to think that everyone in the cult was ignorant or evil. His only interactions with the Divine Emissaries thus far had been combative or low-key hostile. He'd been shot at more than once, nearly crushed by a car, and threatened with violence—if not through words, then through expressions or body language.

What if it came down to a kill-or-be-killed situation? How would he feel about killing someone who was probably a good person, deep down? Someone who'd been taken in by the cult only because they wanted to better their lives and the lives of those around them.

He still had no proof that there was anything more than a few bad actors operating within the protection of the group. He was determined to at least get Mitchell's daughter away from these people. There was no telling what they were doing to her. And he hoped getting into the compound would allow him to see what was happening behind the razor-wire-tipped walls.

He thought about the boy he'd seen the other night. For all he knew, the woman and boy who went into the temple were perfectly fine. Not a scratch on them. Maybe they had just been praying. Or meditating.

Trouble needed proof, one way or the other. Until then, he would be second-guessing his actions. He would be tiptoeing the line between inaction and outright violence.

One thing he wouldn't second guess was a confrontation with the bald guy who'd shot at him on the bridge. If he saw him—and he hoped he would—there would be no hesitation. That man needed to die on principle. Trouble didn't like it when someone tried to kill him. And if they didn't finish the job, he'd do his best to make them regret it.

Maybe he'd already bled out from the leg wound. But Trouble doubted it. That was wishful thinking. There hadn't been enough blood on the bridge for it to be a serious wound. But it sure as hell would slow the man down.

It was a start.

The sound of soft footfalls came to Trouble's ears. He refocused, putting his attention toward the compound. Someone was coming.

An armed man walked slowly by on the other side of the fence, beyond the rolls of razor wire. He stopped, turned, and walked back the other way.

Of course they're patrolling inside at night. Why wouldn't they?

When the man was gone, his footsteps no longer audible, Trouble checked his phone again. Four forty-five. Eight minutes since he'd hunkered down and started watching.

He decided to wait. To see how long it would take for another guard—or the same one—to come by. While he waited, he looked for cameras, other guards, or anything else that might alert those inside to his presence.

At four fifty-four, the same guard came back. He walked into view, took a look around, and then headed back the way he'd come. Nine minutes.

Trouble guessed that it took him about nine minutes to walk the entire unfished portion of the fence twice. A little over four minutes down, the same back. Over and over again, all night. Since Trouble was at one side of the gap, he would have nearly the full nine minutes to figure out a way over.

And he thought he had a way that would work.

As soon as the guard was well out of sight, Trouble moved down the hill, away from the fence. He found a tree that looked promising. It was a young pine tree, about twelve feet tall, with bushy green branches. Gripping its sappy trunk with both hands, he pushed and pulled on it, judging how solidly its roots were in the ground.

It should do, he thought. He rocked it back and forth, pushing and pulling, gaining momentum. The ground at his feet shifted and bulged as the roots moved. When the roots on one side came up, covered in rich loam, he pulled it back the other way. The tree pulled free of the ground.

After checking his phone, Trouble hoisted it on his shoulder and walked back up the hill with it. Given the time, the guard should've been patrolling away from this side of the gap. When it was clear that the guard wasn't around, Trouble laid the tree down carefully so the guard wouldn't see it when he came back.

While he waited, Trouble tried to clean the sap off his hands with fallen pine needles and dirt. It at least made them less sticky.

Around five thirteen, the guard came back. He walked just beyond the place where the stacked razor wire met the fence, and Trouble lost him from sight. Then he showed up a few moments later, walking back the other way.

When it was safe, Trouble hoisted the tree up again and moved up toward the fence, scanning for hostiles. He came to the place where the fence met the razor wire and laid the tree diagonally against the wire right where it met the fence. He then reached up and around the pyramid of razor wire, feeling the back of the fence. While the front was smooth metal paneling, the rear was exposed. He found a wooden crossbar to use as a handhold.

He stepped back from the fence, moving around the bottom of the tree. Being careful to avoid the sharp barbs, he grabbed the end of the wire coil and tried to drag it out of the way. No luck. It was fixed to the ground with stakes. And while he could probably pry the stakes out and then move the wire, it would take too long. He would use the tree.

If he could've moved the wire, it would've been the less risky option. Plus, he would've kicked himself if he had gone over and not checked to see if he could drag it out of the way.

Trouble moved back around the tree and up against the fence. He put his left foot against the mid-point of the trunk, testing it with his weight. The razor wire shifted and folded under the diagonal tree.

Confident that it would work, Trouble reached around the fence with his left hand, finding the crossbar again. Putting some of his weight on his left arm, he stepped both feet onto the tree. The razor wire shifted more, the top coil collapsing down into the two underneath. Carefully, he moved sideways up toward the top of the tree, gripping the edge of the fence with his right hand.

When he was confident he could completely clear the wire, he tested it with little jumps on the tree. The last thing he wanted was to slip off the tree and cut his legs up in the wire. But it acted as kind of a spring. He couldn't put all his weight on it, but he could put enough to assist his jump.

He bounced twice more and then jumped, pulling hard with his left hand and spinning his body around. He landed awkwardly on the other side, collapsing down to his butt. He'd cleared the wire and was now facing the inside of the fence.

He quickly reached up and grabbed the top of the tree, trying to pull it off and toss it down on the outside so the guard wouldn't see it. But it was no use. The branches had become snagged by the barbs, and it wouldn't move.

Trouble would have to take out the guard instead, so he wouldn't sound the alarm.

He'd been hoping to avoid confrontation, but that wasn't feasible now.

Pulling his pistol out, he looked around. About twenty yards away—over in the direction the guard would be coming, but further back from the fence line—were several adjacent piles of construction material. They looked promising.

The guard would be coming back any minute. And Trouble needed to get to him before he spotted the tree and the half-crushed coils of razor wire.

He thought about the girl. Shayna—Angel. She was in here somewhere.

Off in the distance, a twig snapped.

Time to rock and roll.

Chapter 19

THE NEATLY STACKED PILES of two-by-fours, metal sheeting, and bags of quick-mix concrete provided a convenient hiding place for Trouble as the guard approached. He crouched behind the construction materials and listened as the footfalls grew closer.

When the guard was abreast of his hiding place, he looked over the stacks of wood at the man, who walked casually ten yards away. Just a few more yards, and he'd be able to see the tree stuck in the wire.

Trouble put his pistol away and slid one of the two-by-fours off the top of the pile. It was about six feet long. Hefting it over his shoulder, he prepared to throw it like a spear; his left hand holding it up and his right hand at the back. There was no way he could sneak up on the guy. Not with all the twigs and pine needles on the ground. He'd heard the guy coming from a long way off, and that would work both ways.

He only had one shot at this.

The man was facing away from him now, although at a slight angle. He was approaching the end of the razor wire and the beginning of the fence—right where Trouble had come over. The biker waited, thinking that the man would see the tree in the wire any second. Thinking he would stop moving. It would take him a moment to register the implications of the tree stuck there. That was when Trouble would strike.

But the guard didn't stop. And he kept getting further away from Trouble, who wasn't sure he could throw the wooden board with any accuracy from this distance. The tree was right there, not five yards ahead of the man, but he hadn't noticed it yet. Or if he had, he was pretending he hadn't. Maybe he'd seen Trouble and was thinking about how best to riddle him with bullets.

Trouble looked at the ground, thinking he might be able to risk taking a few steps to get closer.

Then the guard stopped, his body tensed as he noticed the tree. He turned and reached for the radio clipped to his belt all at once.

Trouble grunted as he twisted his body, throwing the two-by-four as hard as he could—he still wasn't sure it would reach the guy. While the board was still in the air, he scrambled over the pile of wood and sprinted toward the guard.

The man had to jump back to avoid getting hit by the two-by-four, which clattered to the ground near his feet. Trouble was closing fast, and the guy still had his left hand on his radio, the other holding his weapon, which was strapped around his shoulder. He had three options: shoot, call for backup, or run.

He chose the third.

And he was fast. He took his hand off the radio and used it to hold his assault rifle away from his body so he could run. But it took him a moment to get up to full speed. A moment in which Trouble gained on him.

The fence line had been mostly cleared of trees on both sides, but there was still plenty of flora inside the compound, about fifteen yards from the fence. The guard stuck to this cleared alley, running along the fence line. It was only a matter of time before he came upon another guard. And if that happened, Trouble would have to start shooting to get out alive. His presence would be known. He wouldn't be able to find Shayna or any of the other children he was sure were in here.

The gun in his jacket pocket banged against his hip as he ran, the zipper pull tabs jingling faintly. He was so close, reaching out a hand to grab the guard. He got his middle and ring fingers into the back of the shirt collar, but the man felt it and ducked his body forward, pulling away. The movement put him off balance. He tripped on a rock half-embedded in the ground and stumbled. Trouble slammed into him, tackling him to the ground. The guard cried out as they hit.

A light came on from somewhere up ahead, the beam searching the ground just ahead of them. The guard saw it just as Trouble did, and he tried to cry out for help just as Trouble clamped a hand over his mouth.

The guard was still struggling, but he'd gone down on his gun, and Trouble wasn't about to let him get up. He snaked his left arm around the guy's neck and clamped down with his forearm and biceps. The light swept back and forth along the ground, mere feet away. Trouble could tell it was a guard in one of those perches shining the light. He couldn't see the guard, but he could see the source of the light, and it was several feet off the ground.

He had to move. Given the angle and the curvature of the fence, he figured going directly toward the fence was the best bet. He had to risk it, even though the guy was still fighting and trying to scream. He rolled to his right, onto his back, pulling the guy with him. Before the man could get his legs into the fight, Trouble hooked his own legs over. He rolled again, toward the fence, before the guy could go for his gun and get a shot off. But the man's arms were free. As Trouble rolled them over, putting the man on his face again, the guy shot his arms out, propping himself up on his elbows.

It didn't matter. As long as his arms were occupied, he couldn't go for his weapon. And he wouldn't be conscious much longer.

The beam of light touched the ground where they'd just been. They weren't quite out of view from the guard perch, but Trouble didn't want to risk rolling the man over again. Not yet. He focused his effort on his left arm around the man's neck.

With his right hand, he felt the man's mouth open and then clamp down on the meat of his middle finger. He clenched his jaw and used the pain—and the anger that came with it—to redouble his efforts. Moments later, the man's mouth relaxed, along with the rest of his body. He fell off his elbows and onto his face, unconscious.

Trouble rolled them over twice more until they were nearly touching the fence. He watched the light carefully as it searched the area. The only evidence that anything had happened was the disturbed ground. But from a distance, it wouldn't mean anything. It probably wouldn't up close, unless you knew what you were looking for.

Trouble relaxed his chokehold, but he didn't remove his right hand from the guard's mouth. Not yet.

Soon enough, the light disappeared. Trouble listened for a minute, praying he wouldn't hear footsteps.

He didn't.

He got up off the guard and took the man's gun and radio away. He pulled the gun strap over his head and positioned it so the gun was on his back, barrel pointing down. The radio, he clipped to his belt. Then he reached down, gripped the guy's ankles, and dragged him along the fence line, back the way they'd come.

He pulled him behind the piles of construction material and took off his blue shirt, setting it aside. Then he stretched the man out on his face, pulling his arms out over his head. He stacked two fifty-pound bags of concrete mix on each of the man's forearms. Then he did the same for his legs. He also put one bag on the back of his head.

He didn't want to kill the guy, but he also didn't want him up and moving. He wasn't sure if the concrete would keep him down for more than a few moments once he woke up, but it was the only thing he could think of. He didn't have anything to tie the guy up with. He'd searched the house he was squatting in but found nothing but some twine that would be easily broken.

Taking the man's blue shirt, Trouble moved off into the woods, heading toward the interior of the compound. Much of the thick underbrush in the trees had been cleared already, but not all of it. He found a juniper bush and crouched next to it as he removed the AR-15 and then his leather jacket. He pulled the blue shirt on over his t-shirt. It was a little tight, but it would do. He didn't have the same haircut as the security guards, nor was he clean-shaven, but the blue shirt would keep him from sticking out like a cardinal among crows.

He pulled his pistol out of his jacket and tucked it into his back waistband. After stashing his jacket under the juniper, he continued on his way, rifle held at patrol ready.

He'd been walking for about five minutes when he saw the first buildings.

Chapter 20

PARALL JENSEN LAID AWAKE for several hours, listening with his eyes closed to those sleeping in the barracks with him. There were nine other people in the building, all of them adults. Fayden, Jensen's new check partner, had taken an adjacent cot. It sounded as if the man was asleep.

Jensen opened his eyes and rolled onto his back. He turned his head to the left and looked over at Fayden. He was a younger man, part of the work crew. Like everyone else, he slept in simple white pajamas. He was on his side, facing Jensen, breathing deeply. His eyelids were closed over brown eyes, his brown hair falling over his smooth forehead. There was little to set Fayden apart from other men his age, aside from a quiet assurance and watchful countenance.

He was a true believer—one that had been with Suzerain since the very early days. Oddly, he was not a part of Beck's inner circle, as many of the early adopters now were. At least, not openly. It was possible—probably, even—that he was right where Suzerain wanted him, watching and listening for dissent among the workers.

Jensen watched him for a few long moments before propping himself up on his elbows and looking around at the other sleeping figures in the barracks. Only two of the cots were empty—two Sentinels out guarding the compound.

Being as quiet as possible, Jensen slipped from under his covers and stood up, his feet cold against the wood floor. He moved toward the bathrooms first, using his peripheral vision to see if anyone cocked a head to watch him. No one moved. A few people snored.

Jensen changed direction and headed out the front door, carefully lifting and replacing the simple latch that kept the door closed—there were no locks, not on these doors. Nor were there any on the bathroom doors. The only doors with locks were those on the children's barracks.

Small rocks poked his bare feet as he stepped off the simple wooden porch. He looked around at the other barracks buildings, searching for any signs of movement. He saw none. Padding around to the back, he moved on the balls of his feet, thinking the crunch of every pine needle was as loud as thunder.

Halfway down the side of the simple wooden building, Jensen stopped and got to his knees. The buildings had been constructed off the ground and had simple wooden skirts around the bottoms to obscure the stilts and plumbing. He dug his fingers into a seam between two sections of the skirting, prying one side open and reaching in to pull out a black garbage bag.

Bag in hand, he made his way out into the woods beyond the cluster of barracks buildings. He had a change of clothes inside, along with shoes he'd pilfered from Mitchell's footlocker when he'd heard what the man had done. His plan was to change clothes and then make his way to the unfinished section of the fence to escape. He would find a way to his mother's house in Alabama to regroup. Then, he could decide on a course of action. But right now, all he wanted to do was get out of this place. They still had much work to do before the Ascension, which would give him enough time to come up with some sort of plan to stop Beck.

As he moved out into the woods, he thought he saw movement up ahead. A dark shape ducking behind a tree. His first thought was a guard. Or even Fayden, who'd followed him out and somehow gotten in front of him.

He crouched, feeling overly exposed in his white pajamas. Looking toward where he thought he'd seen movement, he now only saw night and woods.

There was a scuffling sound to his right. He looked that way, but the sound was so faint that it had probably been caused by some nocturnal animal. He wanted to change, but still felt he was still too exposed to take the time. So he scanned ahead, planning to move through the trees to a particularly thick section of foliage.

As he stood, a voice spoke behind him in a harsh whisper. "Don't fucking move." It was a man's voice. Close. Not four feet behind him. Jensen froze, half out of his crouch. There was something familiar about that voice.

Then it clicked. He'd heard the voice just the other night. And he'd heard it over the purr of a motorcycle engine.

***

Trouble couldn't see the man's face, but he could tell from his demeanor that something shady was going on. He kept the assault rifle pointed at him while he thought about what to do. He'd seen the guy's white pajamas from way off and decided on instinct to approach instead of letting the man do his thing—whatever that was.

"Drop the bag. Now put your hands up and back toward me," Trouble said in a whisper. He glanced at the man's bare feet, wondering why he was running around without shoes on.

"It's you," the man said, backing up. "How did you get in here?"

"Stop moving," Trouble said. The man stopped. "Now turn around."

Before the guy got all the way around, Trouble recognized him. The first and last time he'd seen the man, their roles had been reversed; he'd had Trouble dead to rights with an assault rifle. He stared at the gangly man for a long moment, thinking over the implications. He had a soft spot for people who didn't shoot him. But now was no time to take chances. And time was wasting.

"Get on your knees," he told the man.

His facial muscles seemed to go elastic. "Are you going to kill me?"

"No," Trouble said, "not as long as you do what I say. Now get on your knees."

The man got to his knees.

"Where are the children?" Trouble asked. "Where do you keep them?"

"Who are you looking for? I can help you. Please. I'll help you if you get me out of here."

This gave Trouble pause. Had he caught the man trying to escape? It would make sense. "What's your name?"

"Parall Jensen—I mean, Jensen. Just Jensen."

"Where are the children, Jensen?"

"That way," Jensen said, pointing over toward the cluster of low buildings. There were more than two dozen that Trouble could see. "I can show you."

"Are there guards?"

"No, but the doors are locked at night. And only a couple of people have keys."

"Let me guess, you're not one of them."

Jensen shook his head.

"Are there windows?" Trouble asked.

"Yes. But they're covered with bars."

"What the fuck is this place?" Trouble whispered, more to himself than to Jensen.

"I used to think it was Heaven. Now I know it's Hell."

Trouble kept the gun pointed at Jensen, but he looked around, thinking. He needed something he could take to the authorities. Something that could blow this whole cult out of the water, allowing people to get the help they needed. To become deprogrammed. He had an idea of what could do it, but it would be hard to do if what Jensen said was true.

Finally, Trouble sighed and lowered the weapon. "Take me to where the children are," he said. "Then I'll do what I can to help you. But if you make a move, I'll put a bullet in you. Understand?"

Jensen nodded, standing up. Excitement flitted across his face, but only for a moment, before it settled into a look of fear. "This way," Jensen said, and started off.

"Wait," Trouble said. "Do you have shoes in the bag?"

Jensen stopped, half-turned. He nodded.

"What about darker clothes? I spotted you from fifty yards off with those white clothes on."

Jensen nodded again.

"Well, hurry up. And if I see anything other than clothes and shoes come out of that bag, you're done."

Once Jensen had changed into his security guard uniform, they started off again, skirting the buildings and sticking to the trees when they could. After a few minutes, Jensen crouched behind a thick pine tree and pointed. "It's those buildings. The ones offset from the rest."

The five long, low buildings looked much like the other ones, but they had bars over the windows and heavy-looking doors. Trouble thought it odd. Why would they lock the children up, but not the adults? Maybe the children weren't as easy to control. Or maybe they were special in a way Trouble didn't quite understand. They had, after all, murdered three people just to get Mitchell's daughter back. And then there was the whole thing with the boy and the woman being locked in the temple.

Trouble thought to ask Jensen about that, but he didn't want to waste any more time.

"Okay, listen to me," Trouble said. "I'm going over there to—"

The distant sound of yelling cut Trouble off. He whipped his head around, looking back toward where he'd come into the compound. The guard was awake. *Shit.*

"Oh, no," Jensen said, looking even more terrified than when he thought Trouble was going to shoot him. "This place is going to be crawling with Sentinels soon. We need to go."

He lunged up, but Trouble grabbed a handful of his shirt and pulled him back down. "You're staying here," he said.

Jensen shook his head. "I can't! I can't do—"

Trouble grabbed him by the jaw and pulled him close. "You will stay because you care about some of the people in here, don't you? They're your friends. You've grown close, haven't you?"

There was more yelling now, getting louder as it got closer.

"You're going to stay here and feed me information," Trouble continued. "Either that or I break one of your legs and leave you here to answer awkward questions from your friends. Nod if you'll stay."

Jensen's eyes were wild, rolling around in his head. Trouble thrust him against the tree, banging the back of his skull into the mottled bark. "If you don't nod, I'll take it as a no."

Jensen nodded.

Trouble let go of his jaw. "Good. You're going to save lives, Jensen. Not *just* your own."

Lights were coming on around the compound. Trouble pulled out his phone and handed it to Jensen. "Keep this. I want you to find a kid who's willing to talk, and get him or her to explain to you what's happening in here, okay? Record it. Find something that I can use to get the authorities up here. Or to at least draw media attention to this place. Do you understand?"

Jensen looked at the cellphone like he'd never seen one before.

"I know the number," Trouble said. "I'll contact you tomorrow. Just keep it on silent mode. There's nothing of mine on there. Nothing personal. And it's not locked. Got it?"

Jensen nodded.

"Good. Now, I'm sure you won't have any problems playing off your little escape attempt amid all the chaos that's about to erupt, right?"

"I—I think so."

Trouble looked over at the children's barracks one last time. Then he moved back into the woods, leaving Jensen sitting on his haunches against the tree.

Chapter 21

FLASHLIGHT BEAMS PLAYED ACROSS the trees just a few feet from where Trouble lay. Voices belonging to both men and women called out to each other, coordinating their search.

He had made his way back to the uncleared trees and underbrush without incident, making his way inside just before these people approached. He knew his jacket was about thirty yards away, hidden under a juniper bush. Once he got the jacket—his lucky jacket—he could find a way out. It wouldn't be hard to seek out one of the guard perches built on this side of the fence and use it to climb over. He guessed most of the guards would be searching. At least, he hoped that would be the case. If not, things would get messy.

Bushes rattled and branches snapped as guards moved toward his hiding place, swinging their flashlight beams through the trees. Trouble still had the assault rifle next to him, but it would be awkward to use from the ground. He'd pulled his M88 pistol out of his back waistband and had it at the ready, safety off.

He was itching to run. To scramble up off the ground and put distance between himself and these people. It wasn't logical. He knew running would only get him shot. So he stayed still, hoping they wouldn't see him under the thick bush he'd chosen as a hiding spot.

"I found something!" someone called from up ahead. The people who had been making their way toward Trouble stopped moving.

"Over here!"

The nearby searchers moved quickly out of the woods, heading away from Trouble and toward the excited voice some thirty yards away.

Trouble's stomach dropped, knowing they'd found his jacket. It was a special sort of dread, but there was no logic in it. He had always been superstitious about that jacket. It was silly, but he couldn't seem to square the circle. It was what it was. And now, he'd have to go without it. He forced all kinds of terrible thoughts out of his head with some effort.

He stayed where he was, lying on his stomach in the dirt, listening. There was some excited chatter, then there was the faint crackle of a radio. The chatter stopped as the group of four or five searchers fell silent. One of them spoke, apparently talking into the radio. Then they all moved off quickly, drawn by some information that Trouble hadn't been able to hear. It didn't matter. Now was his chance to get out of here.

He eased out of the bushes, rifle in one hand and pistol in the other. He looked around, searching through the darkness for anything that resembled a person. Satisfied, he moved toward the fence. It didn't take him long to find one of the perches—empty. It was a simple platform built on wooden stilts with a short ladder for access. There was a gap in the razor wire topping the fence, so the guard in the perch could rest his rifle on the structure.

He climbed up and stood looking over the fence. After pulling the rifle strap over his shoulder and putting the pistol back in his waistband, Trouble climbed over and lowered himself down. He dropped the last couple of feet to the ground, then moved swiftly into the woods.

When he came to the main dirt road, he moved a good distance away from the compound before crossing, just like he'd done when coming the opposite way. Then he continued his walk back down the small mountain, heading for the cabin he was borrowing.

***

Parall Dearson froze as the man moved past below. He held his breath, watching the tall man pick his way through the trees as he approached the dirt road. This was one of the assassins he'd been told about. One of the evil men trying to kill Suzerain.

Dearson sat still in the tree, holding his breath. Somehow, Parall Vogel had known that the assassin would come this way. Probably because Suzerain told him. Suzerain knew all.

As soon as someone had sounded the alarm, Dearson had been dispatched out the front gate. Vogel and three other Sentinels had followed him out, helping him pick the best tree for the job. They watched him climb up before fading into the forest on the other side of the road. He'd been up in the tree no more than ten minutes when the unbeliever walked past below.

Once Dearson was sure the man was out of earshot, he unclipped his radio, turned the volume back up, and spoke into it. "He's just moved across the road, staying parallel to the fence. You should be seeing him soon. He's wearing a blue shirt. And he's armed."

Two clicks came back on the radio in acknowledgment.

Dearson clipped the radio back to his belt and continued watching. He wasn't sure if there would be any more assassins coming this way. He just wished he could be part of the team to kill the man. But he was only seventeen. A part of him was simply happy to be of use. This was important. They had to protect Suzerain until the Ascension. It was their duty. And their reward would be eternal life.

He shifted slightly on the branch, getting comfortable. He wondered briefly if he would hear the shots when Vogel and the others killed the man.

He hoped he would.

Chapter 22

SOMETHING FELT DIFFERENT TO Trouble. He felt like someone was watching him. He felt exposed. The cool morning chill seemed to penetrate his bones. But he shrugged it off, chalking it up to the fact that he no longer had his jacket.

Still, he moved cautiously, the rifle held ready.

Shortly after he crossed the dirt road, he heard something from off in the woods to his right. He pivoted, aiming the weapon in that direction and putting his finger inside the trigger guard. There was nothing there but dark clumps of foliage obstructing tree trunks.

Maybe a deer, he thought.

He sidestepped away from the area, pointing the gun at the darkness around the trees. He didn't want to take any chances.

As he moved, he heard the occasional commotion from the compound to his left. He was still keeping fairly close to the fence, but only so he didn't get lost. He wanted to take the same route down that he'd taken up. The last thing he wanted was to wander around in the woods for hours.

He relaxed slightly when he reached the hill, making his way quickly down the steep ground with the help of trees. He nearly tumbled down twice but caught himself with branches before his momentum became too much.

When he reached the bottom of the hill, he paused, looking up into the darkness. There seemed to be echoes of his movement. Faint crunches and crackles that stopped after a moment. Maybe his passage had gotten some animals moving, and that was causing the noise.

Or maybe I'm being followed, he thought.

He peered up the hill for several long moments before moving again.

Passing the occupied cabin was easy now that he was looking out for it. The structure was still dark. Now that he no longer had his phone, he didn't know what time it was. But he figured it was approaching seven. The sun would be coming up before too long.

He trudged on, feeling cold despite his constant movement. When the cabin he was borrowing came into view, he picked up the pace. He went in through the downstairs door—the one he'd used to break in—and went directly upstairs, staying low. He crouched behind the kitchen counter and positioned the assault rifle in front of him, aimed out the wide windows in the direction he'd come.

With the lights off in the house, he could see out the windows. But the gloom under the trees was impenetrable from this distance. Still, he crouched there, waiting, watching for movement. After a minute passed, he relaxed. He was being overly paranoid. Losing his jacket had thrown him for a loop.

His knees creaked as he stood up from behind the counter. He set the rifle down, laying it on the countertop. The clock on the microwave said six fifty-one.

The half-eaten can of black beans stood nearby, the spoon still sticking out of it. Trouble wasn't hungry, but he knew he should eat. He grabbed the can of beans and headed back downstairs, stopping when he remembered the boxy yellow-and-black flashlight. He'd set it outside the front door when he left hours earlier.

Can of beans in his left hand, Trouble moved back over to the front door, opening it and stepping one foot out onto the deck as he reached down for the flashlight there. As his fingers touched the hard plastic handle, he heard the unmistakable sound of a large animal scrambling in the woods. Then there was a noise like a person tripping, the wind leaving their lungs in a rush.

Trouble's heart immediately shifted into overdrive. Adrenaline rushed into his bloodstream like lava spewing down the side of a volcano. But he remained outwardly calm. As he straightened, he glanced toward the source of the noise, making sure his face was impassive. Just a guy hearing a large animal out in the woods.

He fought the urge to turn on the flashlight. It would be the wrong move. It would kill his night vision and give whoever was out there a bright target to shoot at.

All he wanted to do was get back over to the AR-15 on the countertop some ten yards behind him.

Trouble stepped back inside, moving out of the way to shut the door. Something changed in the air. He could feel it. Like lightning striking, raising the hair on his neck. Like an audible click, signifying impending danger.

He dropped the can of beans as he dove to the floor. Before he hit the varnished wood, the glass of the front door exploded as bullets smashed into it. The air was suddenly full of the sound of gunfire. The large windows bordering the front door also exploded, raining glass down on Trouble as he crawled toward the cover of the kitchen counter.

The Zastava M88 pistol was still tucked into his back waistband, but he knew it would do no good at this distance. He moved through the glass, feeling small cuts opening in his arms with each army-crawl movement.

The gunfire continued for what seemed like a long time but was only seconds. It tapered down as he rounded the kitchen island. One person was still firing, the rounds hitting the wall high above the kitchen cabinets there. Someone else was yelling at the shooter to stop firing. Finally, the shooting ceased completely.

"He's behind the kitchen island," a man yelled from outside.

"How the hell can you tell? I can't see shit," a second man said.

"Stop fucking yelling," a third man put in.

The yelling turned to murmurs, which Trouble couldn't hear well enough to make out. He was sitting with his back to the island. He reached up and pulled the assault rifle down. The microwave, which had somehow survived the gunfire, said the time was six fifty-three.

He could tell by looking that the assault rifle had a thirty-round magazine. What he didn't know was if it was fully loaded or not. The magazine didn't have a window or witness holes to tell him. He'd pulled back the bolt slightly and felt the brass in the chamber with his finger earlier, so he knew that he had a round chambered. He assumed he had a full magazine to work with, but he didn't like having to assume.

The rifle was the civilian version of the Colt M4 Carbine. The military version was capable of fully automatic fire, whereas this one was semi-auto. It suited him just fine. He would need to conserve his ammo to get out of this alive. He slid the safety off.

He decided, as the murmuring from outside stopped, that he would act as though he only had twenty rounds in the M4. That meant he had a total of twenty-nine cartridges—twenty 5.56 NATO rounds in the M4 and nine 9mm rounds in his M88 pistol. If he ended up with more, all the better. He just hoped there weren't any less.

Trouble got into a crouch, thinking about the best way to do this. Right now, he had the high ground. But he could easily be flanked. The men outside were surely splitting up right now—one group to cover the front door and another to look for the back door. He instinctively felt that he would have a greater advantage downstairs than he would up here. He knew the layout of the home, and he could easily get out through one of the downstairs windows if he needed to.

Keeping low, he ran out from behind the kitchen island and into the short hallway that led to the stairs. No one fired at him. In fact, he heard nothing at all from outside—not even a shout.

He still held the flashlight. He had the handle pressed up against the rifle's handguard with his left hand. It was off, but he decided he might need it. The sun wouldn't be up for another fifteen or twenty minutes.

At the top of the stairs, he paused, aiming the rifle down, listening. He heard nothing, so he made his way down the wooden steps, trying to be quiet. A couple of the stairs creaked, but they weren't overly loud. He reached the dark hallway at the bottom. The two doors on the right belonged to the bedrooms. The first door on the left belonged to the den. The second doorway on the left led to the mudroom and the back door.

He didn't think it was possible that the men had gotten inside yet. He'd locked the door after coming in. Granted, all they'd have to do was reach through the broken window to unlock it, but he doubted they knew that yet.

Still, he checked the two bedrooms and the den quickly, making sure. Then he came to the mudroom doorway. Just as he was about to turn the corner to clear the room, he heard a noise from upstairs. Crunching glass.

They were in the house.

As he turned back toward the stairs, he heard the low click of the deadbolt being drawn back. They were coming in through the back door.

He moved backward into the bedroom nearest the stairs. Listening hard and keeping the M4 pointed at the doorway, he dropped the flashlight onto the bed and reached back to unlock the window. He didn't dare open the window by lifting it. Not yet. It would make too much noise.

The crunching from upstairs suddenly stopped. Trouble wasn't sure if it was because the men had stopped moving or if they had moved beyond the glass shards.

He stepped to the bedroom doorway, placing his left shoulder against the wall, and pointing the barrel out the door toward the mudroom. He made sure the barrel didn't stick out into the hallway; he didn't want anyone coming down the stairs to see it. Not that it would matter in a minute. It wouldn't be hard to tell where he was shooting from, given the muzzle flash. Still, until he started shooting, he wanted to be invisible.

Even though his heart was hammering, he forced himself to slow his breathing. He wouldn't hesitate. Not now. He'd been hesitant to kill any of the cult members at the compound, but this was different. They meant business. And Trouble couldn't hamper himself by going easy on them. He liked living too much for that.

His trigger finger rested lightly on the trigger. He'd never shot this particular weapon before, so he had no idea how light the trigger was. But he was about to find out.

A dark, head-shaped figure appeared in the mudroom doorway. Trouble pulled the trigger. The gun fired, the burning propellant lighting up the hallway for a fraction of a second. It was enough to see that his shot was on target, hitting the man just below his left eye. The thump of his body hitting the floor was quickly followed by shouting from the mudroom.

Trouble, ears ringing, moved swiftly back to the window. He opened it and shoved the screen out in quick succession. While he worked, he tried to blink away the afterimage of the muzzle flash. The photoreceptors in his eyes were still recovering from the shock of the flash, impeding his night vision. He didn't want to go blindly out the window, and he needed his night vision back to see. But, he knew, blinking wouldn't help. Not really. Only time would. Time he didn't have. So he quickly opted to stay in the room. For all he knew, someone was just outside the window, waiting for him to come out.

He turned back toward the door just as semi-auto gunfire erupted from the hallway. Bullets smashed into the doorjamb, the hallway wall, and the side wall in the bedroom—all far away from where Trouble was near the back corner. To get an angle on him, they'd have to be right next to the doorway. And if they were firing from down the hall, then he knew where they were.

The gunfire stopped as quickly as it started. Trouble had counted eleven shots. Now he could hear murmuring over the ringing in his ears. He heard a stair creak, but he kept the M4 aimed at the middle of the open doorway, prepared to shift it left or right. The window was behind him and to his left, a wall to his right. He stood about two feet away from the wall at his back.

Another stair creaked, this one about halfway down the staircase. Trouble blinked, testing his eyesight. It was coming back, the blurry splotch of darkness in the middle of his vision fading.

He glanced at the window, trying to picture where the person was on the stairs. He shifted the gun, pointing it at the wall to the left of the door. The staircase was on the other side of that wall.

He closed his eyes and fired four times at the wall, shifting the gun slightly up and to the left after each shot. He opened his eyes as he turned to the window, leaning out and sweeping from right to left. The sky was slowly brightening. He could tell by the faint glow suffusing the trees. He saw no one lying in wait for him.

There was a clatter behind him as Trouble swung one leg out the window. He glanced back to see a man fall to the hall floor just outside the bedroom door. He was convulsing, sucking in ragged breaths as he died. Blood seeped around him from a wound in his chest.

Trouble clenched his jaw as he pulled his other leg out, stepping both feet onto the window screen he'd pushed out. The window was located under the wraparound deck. Trouble's Triumph was parked ten yards to his left as he put his back to the wall next to the window. The wood pile was about five yards further on, just under the outer edge of the deck.

Trouble looked out into the trees straight ahead, seeing no movement. He looked right and then left again before moving.

There was silence from inside the house. He didn't like that. He'd killed two of them, but there were at least two left. The fact that they were quiet meant that they might be the professionals of the bunch. Or maybe they were terrified. Maybe they were running away.

Not with my luck, Trouble thought.

He moved to the back corner of the house, checked for hostiles. When he saw nothing to make him worry, he sprinted away from the house and into the surrounding trees. Once in the trees, he worked his way back toward the front of the house. There was a small hill on this side of the house, about thirty yards from the driveway. He got down on the other side of it, lying on his belly and positioning himself close to a tree for cover. Then he got the M4 situated, propping the barrel on his hand, which was resting on a length of exposed root.

Blue morning light gave everything a faint glow, allowing Trouble to see clearly all the way to the house, the front of which was a little over a hundred yards away. He wasn't straight-on to the front of the structure, but close enough.

He waited for several minutes before he saw any movement. Shadows were forming all around him when the men finally came out of the house. He assumed they'd moved out from the first-floor door, which Trouble couldn't see from his vantage point. Either that or they'd come out one of the bedroom windows.

There were three of them, and they moved in leap-frog fashion through the clearing between the house and the woods. He recognized one of them as Vogel. The man's blond hair almost glowed in the burgeoning morning light.

Trouble could've fired on them. He knew the effective range of an M4 was much further than a hundred yards and change. But he didn't have confidence in his ability to take all three men out quickly. He hadn't fired a long-range weapon in a while. And if he missed the first time, all he'd do was give away his position.

So he watched them go, heading back the way they'd come, leaving behind two dead comrades. He thought about the man he'd shot through the wall. The way he'd been convulsing after he'd fallen to the hall floor.

He was a complete stranger. And Trouble had killed him.

He didn't like it. The guy had probably been brainwashed. He'd been sucked into the cult and twisted into something wholly unrecognizable. Stripped of his humanity. His personality. And then asked to kill a perfect stranger.

As the three men disappeared from view into the woods, Trouble relaxed slightly. He shook his head, remembering the executions at the house in Colorado. He remembered how the girl looked—Shayna. The man with his gloved hand on her shoulder, leading her out. The resigned look on her face.

And suddenly, like a flash of lightning hitting him, he remembered why that scene troubled him so much. He remembered it all. And as soon as it came back into his head, he wished it had stayed away. He didn't want to remember what happened.

Some things were best left forgotten.

Chapter 23

TROUBLE WAS A PRODUCT of the California foster care system. The only memories he had of any biological parents were so ephemeral he often dismissed the quick, blurry flashes as wishful thinking. They weren't much, anyway. Just images of a smiling woman reaching toward him, speaking gibberish like people do when talking to an infant. If the memory was real, he had no idea how old he was when he'd made it—or even if it was of his real mother.

By the time he'd been old enough to get curious about his roots, he'd quickly come to the decision that he wanted nothing to do with the people or person who'd given him away. It became a defining part of his personality as he grew into adulthood, driving him to become his own man, to be the type of person who wouldn't ever put his own flesh and blood into the hellish foster care system.

At times, he entertained various reasons for his abandonment. Maybe his parents had been killed or locked up. Maybe they'd been forced to give him up for reasons completely out of their control. As he grew out of his twenties, this driving flame inside dimmed somewhat as he considered these to be likely scenarios. But he still had no interest in finding out anything about his real mother and father. And other brightly burning flames were now driving him. Besides, his experiences as a child made him who he was today. And, despite his struggles with drug use and his unorthodox lifestyle, he liked who he was.

He wanted that part of his past to stay buried.

And as long-suppressed memories came to the surface with all the subtlety of a flash flood, Trouble quickly wished that they would've stayed buried, too. He lay prone on his belly, propped up on his elbows next to the tree, reliving a particularly hellish time in his childhood. Soon, he found that he was shaking. Warm tears streamed down his face and into the beard stubble on his cheeks.

***

Eight-year-old Terrence Rubble felt the tears streak down his hairless cheeks, no doubt cutting lines through the dirt on his face. His chin quivered, but he refused to bawl. Especially in front of him—Mister Hoffman—who was waiting inside the house. Terrence already knew that he'd have to go back to live with Mister Hoffman, who forced his foster kids to call him King, and his terrible wife Queen, when no one else was around.

The man whose house Terrence had been hiding under guided him inside without touching him. His name was Hall, and he was the opposite of Mister Hoffman in every way that mattered to Terrence's still-developing mind. He was Black whereas Hoffman was white. Hall was thin and Hoffman was portly. Hall had a bushy mustache and clean-shaven cheeks while Hoffman always had a layer of stubble on his face. When he forced Terrence to hug him, that stubble always irritated his skin, like sandpaper on his cheeks. Those hugs weren't loving hugs. Even at such a young age, Terrence knew the difference.

But the most important difference of all was in the way the two men treated him. Mister Hoffman and his wife lived one block over from Mister Hall. In the few months Terrence had been living with the Hoffmans, he'd learned the layout of the neighborhood and the disposition of the neighbors living there. Mister Hall and his wife had been the first to offer Terrence some food when they'd seen him outside. The Hoffmans only fed their foster children one meal a day, and it showed.

On that first encounter with the Halls, who were retired, Terrence was wary, as he was with every adult he didn't know—and even some he did. But even then, he was developing an instinct for people. And he quickly determined that the Halls were genuinely kind. They were good people, and they came into Terrence's life at a time when he thought good people were only found on television or in the rich Los Angeles neighborhoods that always seemed so far out of reach.

As Mister Hall led Terrence around the house toward the front door, he felt the sting of betrayal. He suddenly thought he was wrong about Mister Hall. If the man was *actually* good, he would've let Terrence stay in the crawl space under the house until the police and the Hoffmans stopped searching for him. But he hadn't. He'd crawled under the house and retrieved Terrence, all the while telling him that they'd get to the bottom of what was going on at the Hoffman house.

Terrence knew that it had been his sneezing fit that had given him away, but it didn't matter. Mister Hall should've let him stay there. He could've brought him food and water. He could've told the police that he hadn't seen the boy.

But he didn't.

As they got up onto the porch, Hall stopped and squatted in front of Terrence, who quickly wiped at his eyes, smearing grime across his face.

"You just tell them the truth," Hall whispered, kind brown eyes peering at him. "The police will get you out of there. They'll tell Social Services. But you have to tell the truth. I can't do it for you, okay, Terrence?"

Terrence said nothing. Just held Hall's gaze.

The man sighed and stood up on popping knees to open the door. "Go on," he said. "They're waiting for you. Remember what I said."

Terrence trudged inside, his guts on fire and heart pounding. He knew he couldn't tell the truth. Not now and not ever. Mister Hoffman was smart and strong and ruthless. He'd watched Terrence closely after he'd first arrived at the Hoffman foster home. Waited for Terrence to make a connection with one of the other kids—a small, quiet girl named Melissa.

Then, just as Terrence had been learning the truth of what went on in the household, Mister Hoffman took him aside into a walk-in closet. The man got down on his knees in front of Terrence and spoke in a low whisper, one meaty hand gripping Terrence's left arm.

"You're a smart kid, Rubble. I can tell." His breath smelled of stale beer and old fish. "That's why I'm only going to tell you this once. If you cause any problems for us, I won't just take it out on you; I'll take it out on Melissa, too. Do you understand me? You tell anyone who asks that you like it here. That we feed you well and take good care of you. We never hit you or even touch you in a rough way. Do you get me?"

Terrence stared back into the man's yellow-tinged hazel eyes. His instincts told him to resist. To say nothing.

Hoffman's grip on his left arm tightened. "Answer me, you little fuckwit."

Terrence bit the inside of his lip to try and counter the pain in his arm. He said nothing, stared back at the man with the oily skin and the scraggly facial hair.

Suddenly, Hoffman let his arm go, smiling. He twisted his upper body around and opened the closet door. "Come on in here," he said to someone Terrence couldn't see. He didn't have to guess to know it was Melissa.

The little girl walked in, tiny hands clasped in front of her simple white dress, eyes fixed on the floor.

Hoffman shut the door behind her and immediately grabbed Melissa by the hair, wrenching her head up. She cried out, the sound sending a bolt of fury through Terrence. He jumped toward Hoffman, fists up, but he didn't get close enough to throw a punch. Hoffman shot his other hand out and grabbed Terrence by the throat.

"Do you understand me?" Hoffman yelled, twisting his fistful of Melissa's blonde hair.

"Yes!" Terrence choked out. "Yes!"

Hoffman threw Terrence backward, sending him stumbling over shoes to smack into the back wall. He released Melissa, who collapsed to her knees, sobbing. "Don't you forget it, boy," he said, standing up and walking out of the closet.

This encounter was fresh in Terrence's mind as he walked into the Halls' living room to see the Hoffmans sitting together on the couch, holding hands and looking just the right amount of worried and relieved. A uniformed police officer sat in a nearby chair; Terrence had seen his black-and-white outside.

"You had us so worried, Terry," Mrs. Hoffman said, knowing he hated being called Terry. She'd been pretty once. That was plain to see. But age and expressed cruelty had taken their toll on her. The lines on her forehead and around her mouth gave her plump face a constant frown. Her brown hair was always done up, perfectly styled. It didn't match the rest of her appearance, which Terrence thought of as "frumpy." He knew she spent lots of time and money on her hair; he'd heard the couple arguing about it more than once.

"Come here and sit with us, Son," Mr. Hoffman said, patting the couch.

Terrence stood where he was, across the coffee table from them. The police officer watched him for a moment, then stood up and guided Terrence into the nearby kitchen, away from the other adults. Once he had Terrence in one of the chairs, he sat across from him and leaned forward.

"Listen here, Terrence," the cop said. "If there's something happening at that foster home, you need to tell me about it, okay? It's important that you don't lie to me. Lying to the police can get you in a lot of trouble. So here's your chance. Just forget about them out there and tell me: do they treat you okay there?"

Melissa's screams echoed in Terrence's mind as he looked away from the policeman and toward the living room. He couldn't actually see the Hoffmans, but he could *feel* them. As if they were somehow looking through the wall at him.

"One of the other kids was being mean to me," Terrence said, looking down at his lap. He grabbed two handfuls of his worn jean shorts. "So I ran away."

"Mean how? Was this other kid hitting you? What exactly happened?"

Terrence kicked his feet, which didn't touch the floor. He shook his head. "He didn't hit me. Just called me names. So I ran away."

The cop sighed. "Listen, kid, those nice people out there—the Halls—they think that something else is going on over there. They say that you're not getting enough to eat. And that they've seen bruises on you. But I can't do much unless you tell me what's really going on. You've got to tell me."

Terrence thought of the bruise that had formed on his upper arm after the encounter with Hoffman in the walk-in closet. Mister Hall had probably seen it when Terrence was over, before it healed.

This time, Terrence forced himself to look up into the policeman's broad face. "They feed us three meals a day. I'm just hungry a lot. And I have bruises sometimes, but only because I play rough in the park and on the playground. Not because of anything the Hoffmans do."

The cop gazed at him for a long moment. Then he shook his head and stood up. "Alright. Let's go back out there."

Terrence left with the Hoffmans and walked back to their house, where they met a social worker. Terrence had to go over it all again with the woman, saying the same things he said to the policeman, just in a different way.

Eventually, after interviewing a few of the kids, the woman left.

Terrence thought about running again—for good this time—but he was worried about what would happen to Melissa. He went up to the room she shared with another girl, thinking they could play Go Fish or some other game to take their minds off what was surely coming. But when he walked into her room, he saw that the Hoffmans were already in there.

Mr. Hoffman was sitting on one of the twin beds. He had Melissa in his lap, one arm wrapped around her chest, pinning her to him. She looked at Terrence as he walked into the room, a blank resignation on her face.

Sitting on the twin bed opposite was Mrs. Hoffman. "Here's Trash now," she said with a sneer. She'd started calling him Trash shortly after he arrived, since his last name was Rubble. She clearly thought it was clever. "Come here, Trash."

He made no move toward her.

"You're only making things worse on Melissa here," Mr. Hoffman said, petting the little girl's blonde hair with his free hand.

Terrence was vibrating with dread as he stepped toward Mrs. Hoffman. She stood up from the bed and grabbed him, spinning him around to face back toward the door. Her nails dug into the skin of his shoulders as she held him in place.

"What did I say would happen if you caused problems for us, Rubble?" Mr. Hoffman asked, still petting Melissa.

"I didn't!" Terrence said. "I didn't tell them anything!"

"You *ran away*," the man shouted. "You're fucking with our money when you bring the government around, Rubble. I told you not to do that."

Mr. Hoffman stood up from the bed and set Melissa down in front of him. He had one hand on her shoulder as they stood there. Terrence looked into Melissa's eyes. She returned his gaze, but the girl he'd come to know and care for wasn't there. She'd retreated back inside somewhere as a self-defense mechanism.

"You're going to listen to it all, Rubble," the man said. "It's your fault. This is what happens when you run away. When you cause *trouble*."

He led the girl out of the room, one hand on her shoulder. They went into an adjacent bathroom and shut the door. Then the screaming started. And it continued for several minutes. Terrence tried to break free, but Mrs. Hoffman held tight, eventually putting him in a headlock when he wouldn't calm down.

When Melissa's screams reached a crescendo, Terrence puked. Some of the vomit got onto Mrs. Hoffman's arm, which sent her into a rage. She slapped him several times and then kicked him, sending him head-first into a wall.

Everything went black.

When he awoke on the bedroom floor sometime later, the only screams he heard were echoes in his own head.

Melissa wasn't the same after that. She stopped speaking, and that blank look never left her face—at least in the week he stuck around. Convinced it would be better for everyone if he was gone, Terrence left the Hoffman house for good. He lived on the streets for several weeks before being picked up by police for shoplifting food. The first of many stints in juvenile detention centers followed.

He never saw Melissa again. And he never went back to the Hoffman house. He heard they'd been arrested for child abuse, but by that time, Terrence had become Trouble, and he was busy forgetting about that chapter in his life. But the guilt he felt never left. It stayed there, expertly buried as deep as it would go. He'd had to bury it in order to survive. To go on living. To keep from falling into the same pit Melissa fell into.

But it was bound to come back up at some point. Nothing stays buried forever.

And as Trouble lay prone in a Northern New Mexico forest, he relived those days from over twenty years ago. And he suddenly realized *why* he would keep trying to help the children in the compound. There was no doubt in his mind. He would get them out of there.

Or he would die trying.

Chapter 24

Trouble rode past the dirt road that led to the compound, thankful that Vogel and the other men hadn't done anything to his bike. If they had gone out the same way they'd come in, they wouldn't have seen it, anyway.

He turned his head, looking up into the trees and seeing nothing. Not that he'd really expected to see anything. He wanted nothing more than to get a new burner phone and find another place to lie low. His tactics hadn't changed. The fact that a hit squad had tried to kill him pissed him off, but he was still facing the same problem. How to get as many people out of the cult as possible with minimal bloodshed. If these people could just take some time—if they could just step away and see what had been done to them—then they could snap out of it.

At the very least, he needed to get the kids out. When it came down to it, the adults could do whatever they wanted to themselves. If they believed they would dance in the center of a star with God himself only after committing ritual suicide, then he could be convinced to let them. But not the kids. They couldn't decide a thing like that for themselves. Not at such a young age.

Of course, there was the problem of Vogel and the bald man. As far as Trouble was concerned, they needed to die.

But it wasn't his main priority. They would be a bonus. And the same went for the leader, Raymond Beck.

He'd had to leave the M4 behind since he couldn't very well wear it into town. He didn't want to draw that kind of attention. He'd hidden the rifle in the woods near the road, where he could get to it if he really needed it.

He had found a backpack in the house, which he now wore, although the straps felt weird without a layer of leather between them and his t-shirt. He had one M88 tucked into his back waistband and the other in the backpack.

He had taken a few minutes to apply bandages to his forearms from the box he'd bought earlier. The cuts he'd suffered while crawling through the broken glass weren't deep, but they were numerous. With his leather jacket gone, he didn't have any long-sleeve shirts to cover up the bandages. He'd just have to hope that people wouldn't notice as he did his shopping. He had no idea how long it would take for the police to find out about the shootout. The nearest house was over a mile away, but sound seemed to carry in the mountains.

He had to make this quick.

It was approaching eight thirty when he rolled into Dalewood and stopped at the grocery store next to the Red Lodge motel he'd stayed at. He hadn't passed any police cars going the opposite direction, which he took as a good sign. As he walked inside, he tucked the gun deeper into his back waistband, hoping that his shirt was loose enough to cover the bulge. He added something to his mental shopping list: a new jacket. A temporary jacket, to cover up his wounds and keep him warm in the mornings and evenings. Just until he got his jacket back from the cult. When he left with the leather, he'd also be leaving with the children, and as many adults as he could convince.

How he would do all these things was something he hadn't figured out yet. But he had at least one person who could help him. And she was easy on the eyes, which was a nice bonus. The only problem was, he hadn't memorized Carmen Marsden's cellphone number. When she'd given it to him the day before, he'd put it into his phone. And he'd given said phone to Jensen.

But he knew she was staying in a pull-behind trailer of some kind—he remembered that much. So he'd just have to search nearby campsites after he did his shopping.

The Rainbow Market was more than just a grocery store, which allowed Trouble to get all the things he needed in one stop. The place not only carried overpriced groceries, but they also sold camping supplies, fishing gear, and some hunting supplies. He walked out after ten minutes with a prepaid cellphone, a black hooded sweatshirt, and a fifty-round box of 9mm cartridges.

He pulled the sweatshirt on and put the other two purchases in his backpack. Then he rode over to the park across from the Christ Community Fellowship Church. A couple of early risers—a mother and her young daughter—were the only two people in the park. Although there were a couple of cars in the church parking lot, there wasn't much activity that he could see.

He parked his bike, sat on a park bench, and went about setting up the phone. He wanted to pull up a map of all the campsites or RV parks in the area so he could start his search for Carmen Marsden. And although he doubted Jensen would've worked so quickly, he wanted to send the man a text so he could call Trouble whenever he'd gotten the footage.

An interview with a child would give Trouble all he needed to involve the authorities. That, he hoped, would be enough to get the ball rolling. He just hoped Jensen could find one kid who was brave enough to talk. One kid who was brave like Trouble *hadn't* been when he was a child.

Chapter 25

THERE WAS NO ONE outside Suzerain's bungalow, which was an oddity in itself. But Vogel was too worked up to fully register the lack of any guards. He'd just seen two of his men brutally murdered by Terrence Rubble, and he'd been boiling with rage ever since. He'd come straight back with the two surviving men and made a beeline for Beck.

He barged through the front door, stopping cold as he saw Beck in the middle of snorting a line of white powder from the glass coffee table flanked by two plush couches. Suzerain straightened up, his eyes red and alight with anger. He was on his feet in a moment, barreling toward Vogel, small metal straw still in his hand.

"What the fuck are you doing, barging in here like that?" he said, snarling. He grabbed Vogel by the neck with one thick hand. He was strong. And even though Vogel had a good twenty pounds and four inches on the man, he was unsure of the outcome were there to be a fight.

But he knew better than to resist. It would do nothing good for him. "I'm sorry, Suzerain," he rasped out. He looked down into the smaller man's icy eyes, hoping to convey not only fear and sorrow, but to try and get Suzerain to remember who he was. They had an agreement, after all. Vogel didn't care if he was doing drugs. He wasn't here to follow the man. He was here to serve, and to take advantage of all that came along with it.

Beck let him go with a shove. He turned around and went back over to the coffee table. "Lock the fucking door," he said, getting back down on his knees.

As Vogel turned to engage the deadbolt, he heard the snorting sound of Beck finishing the line of coke. He then stepped over behind one of the leather couches, looking down at the man. There was a sandwich bag half-filled with white powder sitting just outside a gilded wooden box. The box's lid was open, allowing Vogel to see an array of different drugs—some in pill form, some in powder, and some in liquid.

He was careful not to keep his gaze on the box for long. Instead, he looked at Beck, who seemed to be collecting himself as he wiped up powder residue with his finger and then stuck the digit in his mouth, rubbing it along his gums.

"I need help every now and again," Beck said, his benevolent voice back in place. "The demands put on me to lead this flock can be wearying. So I . . . indulge from time to time. And lately, with the problems we've been having . . . with the agents of darkness gathering . . ." he trailed off, looked up at Vogel. "What's so important you couldn't knock?"

Vogel swallowed, his hands clasped in front of him. "Where are your guards, Suzerain?"

"*My* guards are *mine* to do with as I please. Or have you forgotten who's in charge here?"

Vogel was stalling, and he knew it. "I apologize. I . . . we followed the man, Rubble, to where he was staying. And we engaged him there—"

"And he got away," Suzerain interjected. "How fucking hard is it to kill one man?"

"He took two of ours out," Vogel said. "Paralls Hogue and Bynam."

Suzerain waved this off with a dismissive hand before grabbing the bag and dumping more powder out onto the table. He shook his head and laughed without humor as he formed a line with a razor.

Vogel stood silently for several long moments before speaking again. "I just thought you should know."

"I want temple production sped up," Beck said without looking up. "It was a mistake putting the first one outside the walls. I want them built inside the walls. Wherever there is space. And I want them built with whatever supplies will allow us to do it quickly. I want them done within a week."

"A week?" Vogel said. "That's not my area, but I don't think we can build them in a week."

Now Beck looked up. "We can if we have people working around the clock. Take people off of agricultural duty. Take people from wherever you can get them. We need to ascend sooner than I thought. We need to do it soon."

Vogel thought of arguing, but quickly decided not to. It wasn't his responsibility. The construction would fall under Parall Chapa's purview. *He* could argue with Suzerain. If he dared.

A knock came at the front door, and a male voice called from outside. "Suzerain? It's Parall Lundy."

Beck quickly snorted the line he'd been forming and then put the cocaine back in the box. He wiped the table off and put the box underneath. "Unlock it. Let them in," he said.

Vogel did as he was told. He stood aside as Parall Lundy, one of Beck's personal guards, led in a group of three young women, all dressed in simple white robes. They were no older than twenty, and they were all beautiful.

Lundy glanced uneasily at Vogel before addressing Beck. "Anything else, Suzerain?"

"That will be all, Parall Lundy. Thank you." As Suzerain spoke, he smiled at the girls, who smiled back shyly.

Lundy stepped out, leaving the door open, presumably for Vogel to follow him out. But Vogel didn't. He looked at Beck, his eyebrows raised. After a moment, Beck caught the look. He nodded. "When you're done, find out what Rubble did while he was in here. Find out if he talked to anyone. If so, I want to know who and I want to know exactly what was said."

Vogel smiled. "Yes, Suzerain," he said. But his mind was already on other things.

There was nothing like a reward for doing the dirty work. For being part of the Inner Circle. It would help him forget about the fiasco at the house in the woods, at least for a little while. He stepped around to look at the three girls. Two of them looked him in the eye, but the third, a brunette, didn't. He could tell she was nervous. She was a young thing—maybe eighteen.

He reached out and took her by the hand, leading her out and up to his own small bungalow—another Inner Circle perk. She didn't say a word as they went. She knew the drill. All the women did. Especially all the young ones. Besides, he liked it when he could tell they didn't want it. It made the taking that much sweeter.

Chapter 26

AFTER CHECKING TWO CAMPSITES and coming up empty, Trouble thought he should call Dylan. His friend was probably wondering where he was by now. He'd probably called or texted the phone Trouble had given Jensen. He also thought it likely that Dylan could help him contact Carmen Marsden.

The whole idea of getting evidence of criminal activity had come from Carmen, and he was becoming increasingly unsure whether it was the right tactic. As he rode around outside Dalewood to the first two campsites, hazy memories of glanced news stories and documentaries came to mind. Didn't bad things happen when cults were forced into a corner? He thought about the atrocity in Waco in the mid-nineties. He tried to recall what little he knew about the Jonestown Massacre, in which cult leader Jim Jones commanded over 900 people—men, women, and children—to drink poison Flavor Aid in the largest mass suicide in modern history. Hadn't they been under siege by concerned family members and reporters?

He knew Dylan well, and he knew his friend had probably been spending any spare time he had looking into cults and the Divine Emissaries in particular. He wanted to bounce ideas off both Dylan and Carmen.

Trouble parked his bike in an empty pull-in campsite and turned off the engine. He dialed Dylan from memory and put the phone to his ear, pacing next to the wooden picnic table and adjacent fire pit. It was getting warm, but Trouble didn't want to take his sweatshirt off; he didn't want anyone to see the crisscrossing bandages on the backs of his forearms.

"Hello?" Dylan said, wary.

"It's me."

"Been trying to call you."

"Yeah, I figured," Trouble said. "I gave my phone to the guy from the cult who didn't kill me."

There was a pause from the other end of the line, giving Trouble time to realize what he'd just said. *Maybe I'm more affected by this thing than I thought.*

"Well, I'd be surprised if you gave it to a guy from the cult who *did* kill you," Dylan said finally.

Trouble smiled, then explained about running into Jensen on his way out from the ordeal at the temple. Then he had to explain the ordeal at the temple. Then he had to tell Dylan about everything else that had gone down since they'd last talked. The only thing he left out was the memory that had surfaced from his time with the Hoffmans as a kid.

"Christ, man," Dylan said when he was finished. "Are you alright?"

No. Not really, Trouble thought. "Yeah. A few cuts and scratches, but I'm good."

"Well, I didn't want to say anything until you were done, but I saw a couple of news stories about what went down on the Rio Grande Gorge Bridge. I'm kind of surprised you're not in jail right now. But I'm even more surprised you're not dead. They got some good footage of you."

"I'm guessing the guy who was shooting at me—did you see him in the footage? Bald guy?"

"Yep. The people filming got clear footage of him, too. I don't know if they're brave or just dumb, but there's some excellent footage from multiple angles."

"Right. Well, I'm guessing that guy was there in Monument. The one who got away with the girl after blowing his own guy's face off while trying to shoot me. That's twice he's nearly killed me. I'm lucky he's a terrible shot. Anyway, I think he's holding a grudge for me killing his friends and all."

"Pfftt," Dylan scoffed. "Some people. Just get over it already!"

Trouble smiled again. Dylan had always been good at lightening the mood. He seemed to have a sixth sense for when Trouble needed to get out of the darkness in his own head. "Anyway, that's what I'm up against. I messaged that guy Jensen earlier from this new phone. Hopefully he gets back to me soon."

"So if you get footage of a kid from the cult, you're going to take it to the cops?" Dylan asked. "Won't they, like, I don't know, arrest you?"

"Maybe. But I'm thinking of a way that I won't have to take it myself. I may have a friend here. That's kind of what I wanted to talk to you about. Her phone number was in the phone I gave to Jensen. I was hoping you could contact her. Maybe through social media?"

"What's her name?"

"Carmen Marsden. She says her sister, Megan Marsden, is in the cult. She's trying to get her out."

"What does she look like?"

"Outdoorsy. Brown-blonde hair. Green eyes. Early thirties."

"I'll look into it. But listen, I've been doing some research and I'm not so sure the cops showing up and trying to force their way in is the best idea."

"Yeah," Trouble said. "I wanted to talk to you about that. But I'd rather do it with Carmen around, too. Just check her out and get back to me soon, would you?"

"I'm on it."

"And Dylan?"

"Yeah?"

"Tell me there's a good way to take down a cult like this."

Dylan sighed. "There is no good way. Not that I've found. I'll keep looking, though. You know I will."

***

Dylan called Trouble back just under two hours later.

Trouble was still sitting at the same campground. He'd decided to limit his visibility by staying put until Dylan got back to him. It was a sparsely populated campground, anyway. And it was a nice day to be sitting out in the woods, smelling the pine trees and listening to the birds. After a night of stress and gunfire, it helped calm Trouble.

"She seems legit," Dylan said. "Everything I found on her reads like a normal woman, trying to live her life. Posts outlining her worries about her sister go back several years."

Trouble hadn't asked Dylan to see if she was legit, but he didn't need to. It was just the way the guy was. Thorough. He wanted to make sure Carmen Marsden wasn't working for the cult as some kind of spy. And, it seemed, she wasn't.

"I contacted her through Messenger," Dylan continued. "She won't give me her phone number, though. She's insisting I give her yours. She said she already gave it to you once."

"You couldn't find her phone number?" Trouble asked, surprised.

"Oh, no. I found it. Easy. But I figure you might want to play this one a little differently. A softer touch."

"I thought you'd lost a step there for a second," Trouble joked. "No, you're right. Go ahead and give her my number. Tell her to call as soon as possible. Once I meet up with her, I'll call you and we'll hash this thing out."

"Fuckin' A," Dylan said, and hung up.

Two minutes later, Trouble's phone rang. "Hey," he said, answering.

"Trouble?" Carmen Marsden said. "Is that you?"

"It's me."

"When did we last see each other?" she asked.

"Really? A test?"

"You wouldn't believe the night I had. Just answer the question, please."

I bet it pales in comparison to my night, Trouble thought. "The Red Lodge Motel," he said. "Outside my room. You gave me your phone number, and I put it in my phone. But then I had to give that phone to someone else."

There was a momentary pause. "So, someone else has my phone number?"

"Relax, Carmen. I don't know what happened to you last night, but it had nothing to do with your phone number, okay? This was in the early morning hours. Besides, I didn't even put your name in with the number. Just the letter C."

Carmen didn't answer, but he could hear her breathing. She still sounded agitated.

"Listen," Trouble said. "I have a plan to try and get some people out of there. But I want to talk it over first. Can we meet?"

Chapter 27

CARMEN WAS STAYING IN a KOA Campground some ten miles north of Dalewood, out past the cult compound and about six miles further from the place Trouble had stayed the night before. When he'd gone past the driveway to the place, all was quiet. Granted, the house was set a good way back from the road, but he still would've expected to see a police car blocking entrance if the authorities had been alerted to the gunfight. Apparently, they hadn't been.

Carmen's camper was white with Scamp stenciled on the side in beige lettering. It was set up at the rear of the campground, facing a wall of trees on one side. There was a neighbor on the other side of the pull-through campsite, but their RV was quiet. Carmen's dark green, mid-size truck was parked just in front of her trailer, although disconnected from it.

As Trouble pulled up, he saw her sitting on the picnic table in the swath of grass between her trailer and the woods bordering the campground. She was wearing tight jeans, hiking shoes, and a plush blue pullover sweater. Her shoulder-length hair was styled in two Dutch braids. She stood up and waited while Trouble turned around and backed his Triumph in on a patch of dirt next to the back of the trailer.

He stepped over to her, taking in his surroundings before settling his attention on her. She was biting a lip, her eyes were wide, and her hands clutched at each other.

"Tell me what happened," Trouble said.

Carmen told him. She'd been settling in for the night, making dinner and thinking about going up to the campground's showers instead of using the small one in her trailer, when a bang came from her front door. She'd been cutting vegetables at the time, so she moved toward the door, kitchen knife in hand. When she opened the door, there was no one there. She thought maybe a bird had hit the trailer, but there was no stunned animal on the ground.

Then she heard the rattling of a piece of paper on the other side of the door. She stepped down and swung the door closed to see a note stuck there with duct tape. "Go home Devil," it said.

"They somehow found out about me. Found out where I'm staying, even," she said, pacing as she told Trouble.

"Did anything else happen after that?" he asked.

She froze, looking at him. Then, without a word, she stepped over and yanked open the trailer door, disappearing inside. When she came out, she held a mess of papers, each with duct tape on the top, and each with the same three words on it. "I finally went to sleep. And when I woke up, these were all over my door."

"Why didn't you move?" Trouble asked.

"I thought about it, but I didn't want to give them the satisfaction. They're trying to intimidate me."

"It looks like it's working," Trouble said. "I think we should move you."

"You don't think they'd actually do anything to me, do you?"

Trouble looked her dead in the eye. "Yes. I know they would."

Carmen's mouth moved, but she said nothing. She didn't realize how far these people were willing to go. He could've told her, back when they'd first met, but he wasn't in the habit of telling perfect strangers about the gunfights he got into. Especially not when those gunfights ended with people dead.

Once again, he was reminded of how different his lifestyle was from that of most of the American population. Confrontation was common. Most of the time, it wasn't life or death. At least, that had been the case up until recently for Trouble. Still, he knew that most people—normal people—didn't get into many fights. And they certainly weren't in kill-or-be-killed situations on a regular basis.

He could see Carmen trying to wrap her mind around it. He could guess what she was thinking. What if they'd come back during the night and did something to her? The trailer door wasn't exactly a hefty barrier. What if her stubbornness had gotten her killed?

Trouble glanced around for the second time, looking for anyone who might be watching them. He saw some kids playing at the distant playground he'd passed on the way in. He saw a man with a belly that was too big for his t-shirt stepping back into an RV. Otherwise, nothing.

"Listen," he said, reaching out and grabbing her busy hands, stilling them. "I'm going to help you. I think I have a way to end this. To get your sister and whoever else out. But I need your help. You said you've been studying this cult stuff for a year, right? I don't have time to study for a year. I need your advice."

Carmen's eyelids relaxed a little as she looked into Trouble's face. Her hands gripped his tightly, her skin warm and smooth. "Okay," she said, nodding. "Okay."

"Good," Trouble said. "Now, are you going to be able to focus here, or should we move you first, then talk?"

"I think I can focus here." She seemed to be getting her fear under control. Trouble had given her hope and, with it, something to focus on. That helped.

"I doubt they'll come during the daylight hours," he said. *But if they do, I'll be ready*, he thought, but didn't say. He let go of her hands and smiled. "Have you had lunch yet? I'm starving."

***

Trouble offered to help make the sandwiches, but Carmen wasn't having it. It was a good thing, really. He was just being polite. He wanted to keep watch. After putting his backpack down and pulling the pistol out of his waistband, he sat in the trailer at a little booth directly across from the open door. Carmen glanced at the pistol on the table but said nothing.

While she worked and Trouble watched, he told her his plan. By the time he was done, Carmen sat across from him at the table. They each had an untouched wheat bread sandwich in front of them, with baby carrots and uncooked broccoli florets as sides.

Trouble picked up his sandwich and started chowing down; the last thing he'd eaten was half a can of cold black beans in the early morning hours. The sandwich was good, with lettuce, tomato, cheese, and some kind of lunchmeat he couldn't place.

"What's to stop the guards from refusing entry?" she asked.

Trouble swallowed his mouthful of food before answering. "If I get what I need, they won't have a choice. The police will have a warrant. What I want to know is, do you think that showing up like that will push them over the edge? Will they start killing themselves? That's what happened in Jonestown, right? And Waco?"

Carmen shook her head. "There were so many events—years and years of events—leading up to what happened in Jonestown. Jim Jones had tested his people so many times before that, giving them drinks and then telling them it was poison when it wasn't, just to see what they'd do. So by the time the actual suicide came around, half of them thought it was just another test."

"Man. That's insane," Trouble said.

Carmen nodded. "And the Branch Davidians in Waco didn't kill themselves. At least not all of them. There's still some controversy over what happened. The authorities accidentally lit the place on fire with their smoke bombs or something. The people inside burned up or killed themselves before they could burn alive."

"Right. But the whole thing started because the authorities came knocking, right? They wanted to see the children. To make sure there wasn't child abuse going on?"

"They were accused of child abuse by ex-members, yes. But they were also suspected of stockpiling illegal weapons."

It wasn't hard to see the parallels between that situation and this one. Mitchell had started the ball rolling, all because he wanted his daughter back. Maybe he knew that there was a big risk in going to the authorities. Maybe that's why he sought out the help of someone like Trouble. Someone who was comfortable operating outside the law.

"That's kind of how the Jim Jones thing got started, too," Carmen said. "Relatives of cult members got together with some ex-members and started putting pressure on politicians to do something. That's generally how these things go. Same thing happened with the NXIVM cult here recently."

Trouble shook his head. He hadn't heard of the "Nexium" cult. "Did they kill themselves, too?"

Carmen shook her head. "No. That was more of a self-help thing that turned into a sex cult. They got the leader without any death, thank goodness."

"How many cults are there?" Trouble asked before taking the last bite of his sandwich.

"Way more than you'd think," she answered. "American religious laws are pretty lax. It's easy to form a religious group. I mean, look at Scientology. Certain Mormon sects. You could even say that our two political parties are becoming opposing cults."

Trouble didn't answer. He turned his head and looked out the open door at the gently swaying branches, most of them with new leaves.

"But to answer your question, I don't know," Carmen said. "We'd need to gauge their mindset to know what they would do if police with a search warrant showed up at the place. Really, we'd need to gauge the leader's mindset."

"Raymond Beck."

Carmen nodded. "Do you think your inside man will be able to do that?"

"I don't know. Maybe. He'll definitely be able to tell us more about the vibe in there than we already know." Trouble pulled out his phone, checking to see if there was anything from Jensen. There wasn't. He picked up a baby carrot and snapped it in half with his teeth. "So we wait to hear from him," he said.

"I guess there's not much else we can do," Carmen said.

"Well, we can move you while we wait. Do you know of any other sites around?"

Carmen shook her head.

"Well, I do," he said, smiling. "I visited a couple of them this morning, looking for you."

Carmen smiled weakly. She hadn't touched her sandwich yet.

"You going to eat that?" Trouble asked, smiling, doing his best to lift the mood.

"Yes," she said. "But it won't be an impressive showing like yours. You ate that thing in four bites!"

"Like I said, I was hungry." Trouble bit into a broccoli floret.

Chapter 28

How did I get here? Jensen thought. *How was I okay with people killing themselves and transferring their spirits into children? How did I not see this for what it really is?*

He was working hard to clear a piece of ground for a new building. His check partner, Fayden, worked nearby, helping others to clear a tree stump. The springtime sun shined down on the workers, making them sweat. But most of them had grown used to the endless hours of labor. Being a Sentinel was a somewhat sought-after position because it didn't involve much manual labor. Just long hours on your feet. But, it seemed, Jensen had been demoted. They no longer trusted him to guard the compound.

He thought about the cellphone, buried in the ground underneath the back corner of the barracks. The compound was on high alert after the recent confrontations. Jensen would have to move carefully. The biker wanted a kid's testimony, but Jensen thought that his own might work. What he'd seen in the Temple would surely be enough to get the attention of any law enforcement agency, wouldn't it?

He told himself to be patient. To work hard. To fit in. Don't give Fayden cause for suspicion.

He immersed himself in his work. But as he did, he went over his journey. He went over what had brought him here, trying to identify the tactics Beck and the others had used to turn him into a mindless follower.

This was his resistance. His revenge. It was all he could do now, but soon enough he would take action. And he would end this madness.

***

The first time Jensen saw Raymond Beck in person was at the end of his stay at the New Hope Rehabilitation Center in Huntsville, Alabama. During what the facility called therapy sessions, he and the others had watched videos of Beck. But until that time, when they'd be leaving the next day, they hadn't seen him in the flesh.

The small group of six, who were about to be done with their thirty-day stay, was in one of the meeting rooms. A wall of windows looked out on the lush grass and towering oak trees that dotted the property. The brightly painted walls and the sunlight streaming through the windows gave the place a cheery atmosphere. But the group was weighed down with unease. They'd just been sitting in a circle on pillows, discussing this unease with the help of their therapy leader, a graying woman named Silverberg. They were all afraid of relapsing when they left the safety and comfort of the New Hope facilities.

Jensen had just finished sharing his fears when the door to the room opened, and in walked Raymond Beck. Jensen hadn't realized it until that moment, but Beck had become a kind of celebrity in his mind. All the staff members talked about him with such awe. But Beck himself never seemed braggadocios. In his videos, he never really talked about himself. It was always about how he could help those who were watching the videos.

So by the time he walked in, Jensen found that he was a little nervous to meet the man. This was a surprise, after all. The staff hadn't told them Beck would be coming. At the time, Jensen thought it had been a genuine surprise, even to Silverberg. But upon looking back, he suspected it had been orchestrated.

"Don't get up," Beck said, smiling, white teeth and wide eyes brilliant in his dark-skinned face. He wore a ragged black Baltimore Orioles baseball cap, and he had a few days' beard growth on his jaw. His facial hair wasn't yet graying; it was dark brown. He wore a simple baby blue collared shirt, blue jeans, and sandals without socks.

"Mister Beck!" Silverberg said. "Isn't this a nice surprise."

"I don't mean to interrupt," Beck said. "I was in the area and just wanted to say a quick thank you. You have all taken a big step coming here. I really hope that New Hope has been just what you needed. I have confidence that each and every one of you will keep doing the work you've learned here. If you do the work, you'll stay off the drugs."

"That's very nice of you," Silverberg said. "Thank you."

A murmuring of thank yous came from the group, Jensen included; he wasn't the only one star-struck.

"Anyway, sorry to interrupt," Beck said, then turned to go.

"Actually," Silverberg said, "we were just sharing our feelings about getting back out into the world. Would you care to sit down with us for a few minutes?"

Beck stopped, half-turned with his hand on the doorknob. "I do have a few minutes," he said. "You sure you all don't mind?"

The group answered that they didn't mind. This time with a little more enthusiasm.

Beck grabbed a pillow from the large wire basket against one wall while the circle widened to include him. He sat across from Jensen and slightly to his left. As he got situated, he smiled around, looking like an excited child. "You're Derek, right?" he said, speaking to a man on Jensen's left.

Derek cleared his throat. "Uh, yeah. How did you know that?"

"Oh, I make it a point to know the names of all the people who come through my rehab centers."

"Don't you have like six of these?" Jensen asked. He'd done his research before coming here.

Beck turned his attention to Jensen. "You're Jack, right?"

Jensen nodded.

"You're right, Jack. There are a total of six New Hope Rehab centers around the country."

"And you know the names of all the people who go through all of them?"

Beck nodded, still smiling. "It's important. I became an investor in this space because I wanted to change lives. So it's not a chore for me. I like to know the names of people whose lives I've helped to change."

"He's being modest," Silverberg put in. "He also has a two hundred IQ."

Beck seemed to blush, ducking his head to hide his face with the brim of his ball cap. "Well, that just makes it easier to memorize names," he said, speaking to his lap.

This earned him a few chuckles from the small group.

"But I'm not here to talk about me," he continued. "Heck, I didn't even know I'd be here to talk at all. But since I am here, let's keep the discussion going. This is important. I'm guessing some of you are nervous about leaving?"

"Yes, we are," a woman sitting next to Silverberg said. "We're afraid of relapsing. Falling into old habits."

"Well, that's pretty normal. And it's good that you're worried about that. It's a good kind of fear. Some fear can take over and start to run our lives. That's the kind of fear that leads to drug or alcohol addiction. But it sounds like you all are in a good spot. It sounds like the program has worked. Although you should definitely keep practicing what you've learned here."

"Do you have any other advice for us?" Derek asked. "Any way to keep us from falling into old habits after a month or a year or even ten years?"

Beck winced. "That's tough . . . I guess, my advice would be to get comfortable being uncomfortable. You've already gone through some severe discomfort by quitting whatever you were doing. But that's exactly when we tend to get complacent, thinking the worst is over. If you *really* want to change your life, thirty days in a rehab center—even the best one in the world—isn't going to do it. You have to take that discomfort with you. You have to do the work to recognize good fear over bad." Beck paused, looking around, seemingly unsure. "In fact, this is a conversation I've had with a lot of people who go through the centers. And I've started a little experimental program for those who really want to change their lives . . ."

He trailed off, but no one else spoke. They were all ears.

"I'm sorry," Beck said. "I shouldn't have said anything. It's kind of a new program, and we only have limited spots available. Plus, it's in North Carolina." He chuckled. "Still, I suggest attending our outpatient programs right here in Huntsville. I'm sure Mrs. Silverberg has told you all about them."

Indeed, she had. They'd received an exit packet the day before, and the first piece of literature in the packet was all about the meetings held every weekday, once in the morning and once in the evening. She and other employees had also reminded them about it several times, saying things like, "I hope to see you at our weekly meetings! Even if it's just once or twice a week, it will help you keep on top of the work."

"If you've ever been to an AA or an NA meeting," Beck continued, "you know how dreary they can be. I've designed the New Hope meetings to be the antithesis of that. It's not just sitting around and feeling sorry for ourselves. I know that's not how all Anonymous meetings go, but it seems they can easily devolve into that. Anyway, I hope you all come. We do charge a small fee just to keep the lights on and the leaders paid. But you can always choose a monthly subscription instead of paying per visit. It saves you money and encourages you to attend more meetings!" Beck paused again, smiling at the group. "Anyway, that's my pitch. Who's going to come to at least one meeting this week?"

The question caught Jensen off guard. He hadn't decided whether he was going to come. He hadn't even decided whether he was going to stay in Huntsville. He'd come to Alabama from Ohio because his mom lived in Huntsville and because he knew he needed to get away from the dealers and users he'd been hanging with in the Buckeye State.

He instinctively looked around as four of the others raised their hands. Seeing that the majority of them were going to come, he felt compelled to raise his hand. The only person who didn't was a kid named Bryce who clearly didn't want to be there.

It was a little thing, asking the group outright who was going to come. Looking back, Jensen realized it was indicative of how the cult worked. You went along because everyone else did. That meeting was a kind of first audition. They didn't want people like Bryce in the cult. People who were stubbornly individualistic. But those who would raise their hands to fit in with the majority were welcome. And certainly those who bought into everything hook, line, and sinker were more than welcome.

But that wasn't totally fair, Jensen realized as he worked with a shovel under the New Mexico sun. They'd all wanted nothing more than to live better lives and to stay off drugs or alcohol. And New Hope offered them the chance to do that. Was that so wrong?

Bryce had probably gotten out of rehab and relapsed immediately. Maybe he'd even overdosed and died. Was that a better fate than joining a group that you thought could help you overcome the biggest mistake of your life?

Surely there was a happy medium somewhere in there. But that was easy to say in hindsight. Jensen had done what he'd done and there was no changing that now. What he did from here on was most important. He had to keep others from dying, like Beil had.

Who knows what Beck would do with the children once all the adults were gone? Nothing good. He was sure of that much.

He'd stayed in Huntsville and started attending the New Hope meetings, where he'd met Megan Marsden. She started attending the meetings about a month after Jensen did—she'd gone through the thirty-day program, too. They hit it off immediately and started dating.

They were offered part-time jobs working on the New Hope grounds. After they started dating, they were attending meetings only two or three times a week; they wanted nothing more than to be alone with each other. But other people from New Hope—employees and fellow attendees—started applying gentle pressure to the couple, urging them to come to meetings five days a week. When that didn't seem to work, Beck himself had contacted both of them separately.

Jensen remembered how he felt when he realized it was Beck texting him, asking for a phone call. It was strange. Almost like it was his father calling. Or what Jensen guessed that would feel like; his father had been out of the picture for nearly twenty years. Jensen felt at once excited and scared, like he'd done something to disappoint Beck. But when they spoke on the phone, Beck used a gentle touch to urge Jensen fully into the arms of New Hope. So gentle, in fact, that Jensen had thought it was his own idea by the time the call ended. When he'd talked to Megan about it that night, she said she'd received a call from Beck, too. They agreed to attend more meetings. At least they'd be doing it together.

Then, after about six months of attending meetings five days a week, they were invited to live in the commune in Raleigh. They jumped at the opportunity.

By that time, they were both blind to what was really happening. The "work" that they had to do in the name of conquering their addiction slowly morphed into something unrecognizable. Instead of addiction, they were working to conquer their fear. And then their ego.

They were told to cut toxic people out of their lives. In other words, people who disagreed with the path they were taking. Those who questioned the increasingly demanding "requests" made by Raymond Beck and New Hope.

In the weeks before they made the move to Raleigh, both Megan and Jensen were being harangued by their respective family members and friends, begged not to move to North Carolina. They were spending every waking moment at the New Hope facility. And somewhere along the line, they'd been convinced to "volunteer" their time to the cause in exchange for meals on the grounds and just enough money for gas to get to and from the facility.

Their family members couldn't understand how important this was. They were helping people. They had a *purpose*. What had once been an empty life, filled with the oscillation between getting high and searching for the next fix, was now full of meaningful work. Beck was a truly great man. He had a mission to change the world, and they were a big part of it. What they were doing was more than just helping people get clean. That was only a piece of it. They were leading by example. Showing that people could live fulfilled lives without the emptiness of pure consumerism. Without the anguish of being controlled by their ego. Without debilitating fear making them lash out at their brothers and sisters.

They were given rooms on the Huntsville grounds—separate rooms—so they wouldn't have to deal with their toxic family members before the move. But even before this separation, they hardly found time for each other. All their time was given to Beck, who was in direct contact with them through phone calls, video calls, and text messages, or indirectly through other New Hope employees or volunteers. They'd been too tired for sex most of the time anyway, but that temptation was taken away when they started sleeping at the facility. By the time they moved to Raleigh, Raymond Beck had set his sights on Megan, and Jensen hardly saw her at all.

It was exciting at first. The man himself thought she was doing good work. Megan was happy, so Jensen was happy. But as time went by and it became clear their relationship would no longer be an intimate one, Jensen started having trouble with jealousy. But if he'd learned anything, it was that he could work through all of his issues with Beck's teachings.

He sought Beck's help. Together, they worked at eliminating Jensen's jealousy, which was really just another form of life-killing fear. After much work, he'd managed to deal with the feelings he'd been having, eliminating them altogether. Or so he thought at the time.

But now that he was seeing things clearly, awoken to the truth by a dead woman named Beil, he knew that what he felt was true love for Megan. And it wasn't going anywhere. It had been there inside him, smoldering, all this time.

And he was determined to use it. That love would keep his vision clear and his mission firmly in mind. It would be his fuel. And that was good, because the tasks to come would surely be the hardest of his life. A hundred times harder than getting off opioids. But he knew, in the end, it would be worth it.

Chapter 29

IT WAS LATE AFTERNOON by the time Trouble got Carmen Marsden settled into another campsite. The campground was on the other side of Dalewood from the KOA, and he didn't want to risk riding through town again on his bike, so he rode with Carmen. But he rode in the trailer because he also didn't want to risk someone from the cult seeing him riding in the truck with her. If the cult learned they were working together, it would do nothing but put Carmen in more danger than she already was. He sweet-talked the old woman running the KOA to let him park his bike there for a few hours.

He still hadn't heard from Jensen by the time they were finished, so they sat across from each other at the picnic table and talked. Carmen told him about her job ghostwriting whitepapers and technical texts for the medical industry. It was a remote job, which explained the trailer. She had a condo back in Nashville, where she'd been living for many years, after moving out of Huntsville, Alabama for college.

Trouble remarked on her lack of a Southern accent, and she told him about how she'd grown up in the Pacific Northwest before her parents moved her and her sister to Huntsville during high school.

She seemed to understand while Trouble told her about his drifter lifestyle. Although her home base was in Nashville, she'd been traveling the country, living out of her trailer for about three years. It wasn't a strange concept to her, like it was to so many people. Although she did wonder aloud how he could get by with only a couple of saddlebags.

"I read a book once about a guy who travels around with only a passport, a bank card, and a toothbrush," he told her. "When he needs a change of clothes, he buys new ones and tosses the old ones. At least I'm not *that* bad."

Carmen laughed. "No, I guess not. But it sounds like you two would be good traveling partners."

Trouble shook his head. "I don't think so. That guy's always getting into seriously messed-up situations. Besides, he's a fictional character."

She smirked at him. "And this situation isn't seriously messed up? I mean, I can't even believe it half the time. It sounds like something out of a movie. Or at least something that happens to other people."

Trouble couldn't deny that.

Their conversation turned to other things. She told him about how she liked to hike and camp, but mostly she liked rock climbing. He didn't understand how people did that. He told her about his fear of heights, and she poked fun at him. It felt good.

Carmen asked questions about Trouble's past, half of which he skirted. He didn't know why. Maybe because he liked Carmen, and he wasn't proud of some of the things he'd done—things he'd had to do.

His mind kept wandering to the memory that had surfaced that morning. Kept hearing Melissa's screams as Mr. Hoffman worked her over in the adjacent room. Kept feeling the fear and anger he felt while it was happening. The feelings were even more vivid than the images conjured in his mind's eye.

He certainly couldn't tell Carmen about that, even if she seemed to know something was bothering him. He could tell she wanted to ask, but she didn't. He liked her for that.

What would she think of him if she knew what a coward he'd been when it mattered most? What would she think if she knew that was when he'd started running from his problems? But it was, simultaneously, the reason he seemed to seek out trouble. As if everything he'd been doing since running away from the Hoffman house was an attempt to make up for what he'd failed to do then. Every person he tried to help was a subconscious stand-in for Melissa. Every wrong in the world a reminder of the one wrong he should've made right.

He knew instinctively, like it was a truth he'd carried all his life, that he could save a thousand little girls from harm, and it still wouldn't stop this compulsion. Because none of them would ever be Melissa. Nothing he did would ever turn the clock back or change what he'd failed to do all those years ago.

That was why he couldn't stop running. Couldn't stop fighting.

Ultimately, he figured it was a good thing. It gave him a kind of mission in life. A purpose. But he didn't like the feeling he had inside. He didn't like knowing it would never go away.

***

"Well," Trouble said, checking his phone and seeing nothing from Jensen, "can I get a ride?"

The sun was setting, the little campground smelling like charcoal and meat as the few other campers and RVers cooked their dinner.

"Where are you going to stay?" Carmen asked. Trouble hadn't told her everything that had happened to him. He only told her, in passing, that the place he'd been staying the night before was no longer an option.

"I think I saw some small cabins at the KOA," he said. "You can drop me off there. If that same lady is working, I think I can convince her to not take my ID for a cabin. If that doesn't work, I'll find something."

Carmen glanced around at the darkening trees. Trouble could tell that she was reliving what had happened the night before. He didn't think it likely anyone from the cult had followed them here, but he also had no idea how they'd found her in the first place. She said she hadn't posted anything online about where she was staying.

She turned back to Trouble and was just about to say something when Trouble's phone vibrated on the picnic table. It was a message, not a call. He picked it up and looked at it. "Shit," he said.

"What?"

"I told my buddy Dylan—the one who messaged you my number—that I'd call him when I met up with you. We were going to hash out a plan of attack. I forgot." The truth was, he'd been distracted. Besides, there wasn't much of anything they could do until he heard back from Jensen.

Trouble picked up the phone and texted Dylan, replying to his question asking if everything was okay.

All good. With C now. Still waiting on info. Call you later.

He looked back up at Carmen. "So, how about that ride?"

Carmen grimaced. "I have a spare tent and a sleeping bag," she said, pulling on her left thumb with her right hand. "You could stay here."

Trouble knew she wanted him around just in case something did happen, but she was too proud to say it. He looked into her brilliant green eyes, thinking about the mechanics of security. She took it as reluctance.

"I mean – if you want. I know it won't be the most comfortable thing, but I only have the one bed in the trailer and I—"

Trouble put a hand up. "No, it's not that. I'm thinking it's hard to make any quick moves from inside a tent, but I can just sleep out on this picnic table. It doesn't look like it'll rain tonight."

"But then someone could just come up to you and . . ." she trailed off.

"I don't think I'll be sleeping much," Trouble said.

"How about this," Carmen said. "The floor in the trailer is carpeted. You can sleep in there. That way, you can actually get some sleep and I won't have to worry about someone sneaking up and hurting you while you're sleeping outside on the table. And if someone tries to get into the trailer, you'll be right there."

Trouble raised an eyebrow. "You're comfortable with that? You hardly know me."

"After spending most of the day with you, I know you well enough to see that you have a good heart. Even if you don't want to tell me much about yourself, I can still tell. I'm a good judge of character."

Trouble thought about his bike. He'd told the lady it would only be a couple of hours. But that wasn't reason enough to leave Carmen alone when she clearly wanted someone around. Besides, it would save him some money and some effort. Maybe he could actually get a good night's sleep. "Okay," he said. "I'll sleep on your floor. But only if you make me another one of those delicious sandwiches."

Carmen smiled, clearly relieved.

***

She didn't make him another sandwich. Instead, they made soft tacos together. Carmen browned and seasoned the meat while Trouble chopped veggies. The kitchen was cramped, so they ended up shoulder to shoulder as they prepared the meal. Trouble wasn't sure if it was his imagination or not, but he thought Carmen leaned into him a little more than was necessary given the available space. Or maybe it was wishful thinking. Either way, he certainly wasn't complaining.

They chatted as they worked, and Trouble was happy to get Carmen laughing a few times. She had a fantastic laugh. It was warm and full of joy, and hearing the sound made him feel like he'd done something right for a change.

As they set the table, he noticed her hands. They were strong hands, clearly well-used, but quite feminine at the same time. He figured rock climbers had to have strong hands. They probably had to have strong everything.

They ate inside, the door closed and locked now that it was full dark.

Carmen drank an IPA with dinner. She offered Trouble one, but he passed. He wanted a clear head.

When it came time for bed, Trouble stepped out of the trailer and stood looking at the dark woods, waiting for Carmen to get changed and do her bedtime ritual. There was a bathroom in the trailer, but it was barely big enough to stand in, and he didn't want to force her to change into her nightwear in the tiny space.

She opened the door and leaned out to tell Trouble she was done. She was wearing little red shorts that Trouble thought were underwear at first. She had a sleeveless white t-shirt on with—Trouble couldn't help but notice—no bra on underneath. As he stepped into the trailer and she walked left to where the bed was, he caught himself watching her and looked away. *Okay, maybe I won't get any sleep after all,* he thought as he dug his toothbrush and toothpaste out of the backpack he'd taken from the cabin.

Once he was done brushing his teeth, he sat down at the table and pulled his boots off, setting them aside. Carmen was in bed, propped up on two pillows with the covers pulled up, looking at her phone. There was a little light on above her head, casting a comforting yellow glow. There was no door separating the "bedroom" from the rest of the trailer. Except for the bathroom, it was all one open space.

He pulled off the hooded sweatshirt he'd bought at the general store and then his t-shirt; he never could sleep with a shirt on. Taking the M88 pistol out of his back waistband, he set it on the table and then went about pulling the sleeping bag out of its carry bag and positioning it on the floor. The kitchen had linoleum, so the only place with carpeting was a six-foot stretch of hallway leading to the bed.

Trouble paused and looked up at Carmen. "What happens if you need to go to the bathroom?" he asked. "You'll have to step over me."

She turned her attention away from her phone, looking at Trouble on all fours on the floor. "I didn't think about that," she said. She bit her lip, as if it was a particularly hard math problem that needed to be solved.

"You can just wake me—"

"Why don't you just sleep in the bed with me?" Carmen blurted out, cutting Trouble off.

Trouble straightened, standing on his knees to look at her with a furrowed brow. He wasn't sure he'd heard her right. The bed was a full, barely big enough for two—especially when one of them was Trouble's size.

"Uh . . ." Trouble began. But before he could accept, Carmen threw the covers off, got out of the bed, and pulled Trouble into a kiss. He was pleasantly surprised, and it took him a moment to process this development. Once he did, he wrapped his arms around her back and pulled her closer. The kiss grew in intensity until they had to come up for air.

"Didn't see that coming," Trouble said.

Carmen rolled her eyes in mock frustration. "Men are so dense."

Then they were kissing again. And then they were in the bed.

There wasn't much sleeping. Not at first. Not for a good, long time.

Chapter 30

TROUBLE'S PHONE BUZZED JUST as he was approaching the precipice of deep sleep. The short vibration indicated a message, not a call. He opened his sleep-heavy eyes and looked through the gloom, trying to remember where he'd set his phone. It was still in his pants pocket, he realized.

Carmen had fallen asleep with her head on his chest, his left arm wrapped around her. As he extricated the limb, she opened her eyes and rolled over, freeing his arm. "What is it?"

"My phone," Trouble said, leaning over the edge of the bed to grab his pants. He pulled the phone out and looked at it. There was a voice memo from a number he recognized. *His* number. *Jensen*. Before he could swipe up to unlock the screen, another voice memo came through.

"It's Jensen," he said. "The guy I gave my phone to."

Carmen sat up and turned on the overhead light. She looked at the phone expectantly and pulled the blankets to her chest; it was chilly in the trailer.

Trouble had forgotten that voice memos were a thing in every major messaging app. You could hold down a little button right next to where you would enter text for a regular text message. While holding it down, you could speak, recording your voice. Once it was done recording, you had the option to send it or delete it, like a regular text message.

The first message Jensen sent was nearly ten minutes long. The second was less than a minute.

Trouble selected the first message, hitting the play button and then turning the phone's volume all the way up.

"My name is Jack Michael Jensen, and I'm a member of the Divine Emissaries cult." Jensen was whispering, but his voice was easy enough to understand. Trouble wondered where he was in the compound. What little place had he gone off to in order to record these messages? "And that's what this is. Make no mistake. This is a cult. And if things are allowed to continue without interference, there will be many, many deaths in the coming weeks. So this message is for the police or the FBI or whoever handles these sorts of things. Please, help us. If you don't, Raymond Beck will send us to our deaths."

Carmen grabbed Trouble's arm as she listened, no doubt thinking about her sister.

Jensen went on to describe what he'd seen in what he called the Pantheon—the white temple. The woman named Diane Beil had died, her wrists slit, as far as he could tell, by a little boy named Samuel Gibbs.

"It's crazy, I know," Jensen said as a preface for why this had happened. "You won't understand. If you haven't been in here, you won't understand. But it didn't start out this way. It was a long road to get here. Beck's teachings slowly morphed over time, gradually leading us to these beliefs. *Giving* us these beliefs. Like a frog who gets boiled to death in slowly heated water.

"He's a master manipulator. There's even a control room in the Sanctuary—our church—with a bank of monitors. I've seen it. I've been back there, watching those monitors, looking for any evidence of dissent among our people. He says it's like a parent watching his children. Sometimes the children don't know what they need, but the parent does. But it's all bullshit. I don't know how I put up with it for so long. It wasn't always like this. I swear it wasn't."

He went on to explain that the Ascension was all about the children. Seraphs, they were called. They would be the vessels in which all the souls traveled to Eternity. To Nirvana. Their innocence was essential to the plan. Each child would carry multiple souls to the cult's version of heaven. But to do that, specific rituals had to be followed. And while the specifics of these rituals were known to only a chosen few, Jensen surmised that part of it involved the children killing the adults. Assisting them in their suicide, so their souls could transfer and once again become innocent by shedding their contaminated adult bodies and minds.

"Beil was the first to go," Jensen said. "She was a test. Beck wanted to see how we all reacted to it. I can see that now. And everyone was enthralled. They're actually impatient to get this done. If you listen to what Beck says about the outside world . . . he makes it seem like we're the only chance left for humanity. That if we don't show the rest of the world the way, then everyone is doomed to an apocalyptic hellscape. Hell on Earth, essentially. So *we* have to make the sacrifice. We have to do this for the eight billion souls on Earth. Seven hundred in exchange for eight billion. And if *we* do it, they won't have to die to Ascend. If enough of us do it, then it will gather some kind of spiritual energy or something that will show the world the error of their ways . . . When enough of us Ascend in the children's bodies, all will become clear to the world. It sounds like nonsense when I say it. When Beck talks about it, it makes perfect sense. That's his power. And he must be—"

Jensen's breath caught. For a moment, Trouble thought that he'd nearly been discovered by another cult member. But after ten seconds of silence, Jensen spoke again, his voice tight with emotion.

"I just realized I don't know how the children will Ascend. I don't know if they'll have to die, like the adults. Christ, I don't know! This is why he needs to be stopped. You need to come here and stop him. Come and find Biel's body. I can show you where it's buried. Then you'll see that what I say is true. I don't care what I have to do. Not anymore. I'll testify to everything I've seen here. I'll do whatever it takes. Just help me stop this insanity!"

That was the end of the first message.

"I—I can't believe this," Carmen said. "I can't believe that Megan would go along with this. It's the craziest thing I've ever heard."

Trouble looked at her for a moment, thinking about the little he knew of other cults. It all sounded just as crazy to him. Just as unfathomable.

He returned his attention to the phone and pressed the play button on the second and last message Jensen sent.

"I don't know how Beck will react to police showing up. Things have been crazy around here. He has us building almost non-stop. I think he's trying to speed up the process. You have him spooked. I can't speak to his mindset."

Trouble knew Jensen was talking directly to him in this message. *You have him spooked.*

"I don't know that we have any other choice but to involve the police," Carmen said. "What else can we do?"

Trouble shook his head. He didn't know. "I think it's time I call Dylan," he said.

***

"I got in there once. I can do it again." Trouble held the phone in his hand out in front of his chest as he spoke, pacing back and forth in the trailer. He'd put his clothes back on, including his sweatshirt. Carmen had also gotten dressed, sitting on the edge of her bed in jeans and a sweater.

"And what would you do when you got in there?" Dylan said, his voice coming clearly through the phone speaker so both Trouble and Carmen could hear.

"Get to Beck," Trouble said. "No more Beck, no more cult."

"That's not the way it works," Dylan said. "These people have been living his teachings for years. The outside world is just a memory. Their most important relationship is with him. So if you take him away, you make him a martyr. They'll do whatever they can to kill you and then fulfill his teachings, so they can join him in the afterlife – whatever their version of the afterlife is."

"Okay," Trouble said. "So I'll get to him and make him see the error of his ways. Make him tell his people to stop."

"Even if you could get to Beck—which I find highly unlikely, given the amount of manpower he has at his disposal—he wouldn't relent. He wouldn't do what you asked."

There was something in Dylan's voice that caught Trouble's attention. "How do you know that?" he asked. "Have you learned more about him?"

"I have," Dylan said. "The guy is a wacko. But he's a *smart* wacko. Like, really smart."

"Anything we can use to our advantage?" Trouble asked.

Dylan was silent for a moment. "I don't think so. He's a master manipulator. I don't think it was an accident that he got involved in addiction treatment centers. I think he's been planning this. Designing it so he could live as a king. There have been numerous allegations of sexual assault over the years. But he's managed to quell them, either settling out of court with NDAs or using his resources to attack the women who refused to settle. At least one woman has accused him of intimidation tactics. Threats of violence. The whole nine yards."

"So he's a scumbag," Trouble said. "We already knew that. Anyone who orders the death of innocent people is a piece of shit in my book."

"No," Dylan said, "what I'm trying to tell you is the walls are starting to close in. His lawyers are doing all they can, but if he doesn't face the music soon, he's going to have multiple law enforcement agencies out looking for him. If he could, he'd live up in that compound forever, doing whatever he wants to the poor women he's manipulated into following him. But his past transgressions are coming back to haunt him, and he knows it. I think he's trying to go out with a bang.

"Some of his earliest videos—stuff that has long since been taken down—are very telling. He talks about how the world will know his name. How he's destined to change the world. There's some dark shit in these videos. He's *angry* in them, mentioning all the people who've doubted him. They were recorded back before he really learned how to manipulate people. Most of them are from fifteen years ago. I'm honestly surprised I found them."

Trouble looked at Carmen. She gazed back, a forlorn look on her face. He figured they were thinking the same thing: how do you deal with a hostage taker who has hundreds of willing hostages?

"You still there?" Dylan asked.

"We're here," Trouble answered.

"Okay." Dylan sighed. "The only possible chance I see is a massive and surprising show of force. It would have to be enough to really scare Beck into surrendering. And also not allow him to give instructions to his people. We've got to take lessons from Jonestown and assume that he already has a

Plan B in place. Some way for his followers to kill themselves quickly and within a matter of hours once he gives the word."

"So we need the police," Trouble said, sitting down heavily next to Carmen and grabbing her hand.

"I think that's the only way. With what you have, it should be enough to get their attention. But you have to make them understand what's likely to happen if they don't take him by surprise. If they just roll up there with a few uniformed officers and a warrant, who knows what Beck will do."

"Yeah," Trouble said.

"But you have an inside man. Use that to your full advantage. Get him to describe the place in detail. Everything he can think of about the setup, schedule, armed guards—everything. With his information, the cops or the Feds or whoever should be able to get a team in there to take Beck by surprise. Enough people to prevent the worst from happening. That's the only way I see this going down with a minimum of bloodshed."

"What do you think, Carmen?" Trouble asked.

She hesitated, gripping Trouble's hand tightly. "I think Dylan's right. I think this is the best way to go. We need to involve the authorities."

Trouble nodded. "Okay," he said. "Might as well start with the local police station. They may already have some insights on the group. Besides, it's their jurisdiction, as far as I know. They'll have to be the ones to involve the Feds. I doubt they have the resources or manpower for this kind of operation."

He looked at the time in the top right corner of his phone. It was approaching three in the morning. "I need some decent sleep before this whole thing starts. I doubt there's anyone at the police station right now, anyway. Better to start in the morning."

"Okay," Dylan said. "Keep me apprised." He paused. "Do you think they'll arrest you on sight? For the thing on the bridge?"

"I guess we'll find out."

Chapter 31

As THEY DROVE INTO town from the campsite, they passed an election sign that Trouble had seen before. He hadn't given it a lot of thought until now. In large red letters over a white background, it read: "Re-Elect John Vegretti for Sheriff." Along the bottom of the leaning sign, it said, "Honesty, Integrity, and Experience."

It wasn't the only sign he'd seen on the side of the road since he'd come to Dalewood. He'd seen several more, not all of them with John Vegretti's name on them. Someone named Charles Dillard was also running for sheriff. He wondered if the election was already done or if it was yet to come. Given all the signs, he figured it was coming soon.

He wasn't too fond of law enforcement officers in general, but he'd had some serious problems with bent sheriffs. His guts tensed as Carmen pulled up in front of the sheriff's station, parking next to a cruiser in one of the diagonal spots provided.

He'd been riding with one of his pistols held between his legs, which he now tucked into his backpack before stepping out of the truck. The morning was bright and chilly. A slowly evaporating coating of dew covered everything. Even the roads had wet spots on them where the sun hadn't yet reached.

Trouble and Carmen met on the sidewalk in front of the truck and shared a look. Carmen looked worried. Despite his own feelings, Trouble smiled. He was trying to be reassuring. He didn't think she bought it.

Trouble stepped up to the small sheriff's station and opened the glass door for Carmen, stepping into the warm foyer behind her. The sun was shining through the wide windows at their backs, making the man at the desk squint as he greeted them.

"Morning. How can I help you?" He was dressed in a tan uniform shirt, with a star on the left side of his chest and a gold nameplate on the right. The star said Deputy Sheriff on it, along with the name of the county they were in. The deputy had a naturally serious face, with wide, dark eyes, thin lips, and the taut skin of a wiry man still a decade away from middle age.

"Morning, Deputy Prado," Trouble said, reading the nameplate. "We'd like to report a crime to your sheriff."

Prado smiled briefly and shook his buzz-cut head. "I'm afraid that's not how this works. You can report the crime to me. I'll be sure the sheriff hears about it."

"He's going to want to hear about it," Carmen said. "From us. Believe me."

"What is this regarding?"

"You know that cult living in the mountains not far from here?" Trouble said. "They're killing people in there."

This got the deputy's attention. His dark eyebrows came up, as the eyes underneath grew lively. "You have proof of this?"

"We've got a person inside who's willing to testify to what he's seen," Trouble said. "So unless you want a mass suicide on your hands, it's time to get your sheriff."

***

Sheriff Vegretti had brown skin and a large frame. His black hair was graying at the temples, and his clean-shaven face was thick and heavy above the tightly buttoned collar of his crisp tan shirt. He smelled of deodorant and shoe polish.

The man sat across from Trouble and Carmen in a small conference room. He probably weighed a good two hundred and forty pounds. But he wasn't intimidating. At least, not as they sat in the conference room. Trouble had no doubt that the man could use his appearance and stature to his advantage when he wanted. At the moment, he seemed like a jovial-but-wise uncle.

"Congratulations," Trouble said as they got situated.

"For what?" Vegretti asked.

"The election. I saw your signs."

The Sheriff smiled and nodded. "Thank you, but that's not for another month."

"Well, good luck, then," Trouble said.

"What happened to your face, Mister . . . ?"

Trouble had already told him his name was Terrence. Now the guy was fishing for his last name. "Just Terrence is fine," he said. "I took a little spill into a tree in the middle of the night. A branch came this close to poking my damn eye out." Trouble held his thumb and index finger close together, illustrating as he spoke.

Vegretti made a pained face and sucked his teeth in consternation.

Trouble had been searching for signs that the deputy or the sheriff recognized him from the videos shot on the bridge two days ago. He knew it had happened in a different jurisdiction, but local news was local news. If they didn't recognize him, all the better. But even if they did, it wouldn't change anything about what he had to do. In fact, it might even make things easier. He could tell them the story about the bald guy trying to kill him on the bridge. Just more evidence the Divine Emissaries needed to be stopped.

"My deputy told me about what you said. About the . . . people up there on the mountain. The Divine Emissaries. I'm sure you know this is a serious allegation. And it can open up a whole can of worms. I need to be absolutely sure that the information you have is legitimate. So why don't you start from the beginning? Start with how you came to be here in our little town. And how you know the person who's making these accusations."

"We have a recording you should hear," Trouble said. "I think that's the most important thing. Once you hear it, we'll answer whatever questions you want. It's a recording made by a man inside the compound who wants out. He knows what's going on in there, and he says people will die if we don't do something."

Vegretti studied Trouble and Carmen for a long moment. "Okay," he said, clasping his hands together on the table. "Play me the recording."

Trouble brought out his phone and hit play.

Ten minutes later, the three of them sat in silence. Jensen's heartfelt plea for help stopping the insanity seemed to bounce around the room like an undying echo.

"Wow," Vegretti said, shaking his head. "I've had a bad feeling about that group since they came up here, but I never imagined this."

Trouble nodded, leaning forward over the table. "She's been on this cult's trail for a while," he said, gesturing at Carmen. "She has also been studying other similar groups. She can tell you—"

"Why have you been following this group?" Vegretti interrupted. "In fact, why don't you tell me how you two know each other and how you got to know the man inside the compound?"

Trouble looked over at Carmen, who started by telling about her sister. She and Trouble had gone over this after getting a few more hours of sleep. In an effort to keep Trouble from being arrested, Carmen had volunteered to lie for him. She was prepared to say that he traveled with her to Dalewood, and he'd been staying with her the entire time.

Trouble was reluctant to accept, knowing it could land her in hot water, but she insisted. Eventually, he relented, and they got their stories straight.

When it came to the part about how they got to know Jensen, Trouble took over.

"I wanted to go check out the compound. Just to see what we were dealing with. And I came across a small building. Jensen called it the Pantheon in the recording. There was no one there when I first found it, but people showed up soon after. I hid in the woods nearby and watched them. I saw the woman and the little boy go in there. Beil and Gibbs. Once they were in, two guards were posted out front."

This was where things got a little complicated. He'd have to skirt the truth. "I had a bad feeling," Trouble said. "So I tried to get into the building. And in the process, I had a little scuffle with the guards. I couldn't get into the temple, and I knew backup was coming. So I left. But on my way out, I ran into Jensen. He was part of the backup group. I could tell he didn't want to be there, so I gave him my cellphone and told him how he could help us bring down the cult."

It was easier this way. Easier to compress the real story, leaving out the part about him breaking into the compound and the ensuing gunfight at the cabin.

Vegretti peered at them, brown eyes moving smoothly back and forth over their faces. "Quite the adventure," he said finally.

"We discussed this in detail," Carmen said, "and we think the only way to prevent a bunch of deaths is to take them by surprise. Get inside with a force big enough to take Beck and make sure the people under his thumb don't do anything rash. Jensen can help get a SWAT team or two inside. Or whatever the FBI equivalent of a SWAT team is."

"Hmm," the sheriff said. "Mmm." He looked toward the conference room door and gestured with his right hand. Trouble looked that way, seeing Prado come through the door, his gun drawn but pointed at the floor.

"Oh, no," Trouble muttered.

"What's going on?" Carmen asked.

Prado stepped over next to Trouble, leaving a few feet between them.

"I'm going to handle this situation," Vegretti said, speaking to Carmen. "I give you my word on that. I'm going to handle it. I have a relationship with those people. I know Beck. So I'll get to the bottom of this. But I can't let *him* walk out of here." The Sheriff indicated Trouble with his chin. "He was involved in what the kids call a viral incident on the Rio Grande Gorge Bridge."

"No," Carmen said, shaking her head and standing up. "No. No, please. You've got to listen to me. You'll get people killed if you go up there and talk to him about this. Believe me."

"Stand up and place your hands behind your back," Prado said to Trouble.

"This is a mistake," Trouble said. "I mean, arrest me. I don't care. But you can't go up there and talk to them. You need to think this through. You need to call in help!"

Prado grabbed him by the arm and tried jerking him up from the chair. Trouble yanked his arm away.

Vegretti stood, suddenly becoming a much larger presence in the room. "Don't fight him," he warned.

Trouble stood up, putting his hands behind his back as he pleaded with Vegretti. "They aren't messing around up there. A woman is dead! They tried to kill me, okay? *They tried to kill me.* And I know they've killed others. I've *seen* it."

Vegretti rolled his eyes, clearly not believing Trouble. "Do you know Beck? Have you ever met him? Someone is messing with you. Maybe because you've been messing with them. But I told you, I have a relationship with these people. You think I would welcome them into my county without getting to know them? Every time I've been up there, they've received me with open arms. They let me walk around and talk to whoever I want. They're a little strange, sure, but this is America, dammit. You don't get harassed for your beliefs in this country. Bad things happen when the government starts sticking its nose where it doesn't belong."

Cold steel touched Trouble's wrist as Prado cuffed him.

The vision of Mitchell's daughter—Shayna—came rushing into Trouble's head. And with it, the flood of memories from his childhood. His heart seemed to twist in his chest. He couldn't let this happen again. He couldn't just sit in a jail cell while that girl, and dozens of others like her, died. Even if Jensen didn't know what would become of the kids after all the adults were dead, Trouble knew. They would be killed. He was sure of it.

As his mind raced, he tried to think of something, anything. And the words came out of his mouth just as soon as they entered his mind. "Let us go with you," he said. "Let us go up there with you and talk to them. Otherwise, we release the recording to the news outlets. Your town will be swarming with reporters, and the Feds will come swooping in. It's a bad look for you. Might hurt your re-election chances next month."

This seemed to give Vegretti pause. His eyes narrowed as he stared at Trouble, who returned his gaze.

It was a last-ditch effort. A Hail Mary. Trouble knew that getting the media involved would only put more pressure on Beck. He would surely do something drastic. But maybe, if Trouble could get into the compound, he could do *something*. It wasn't a plan by any means, but it was all he could come up with.

The sheriff started shaking his head, but Carmen jumped in, clearly seeing a chance. "He's not kidding. We will do it. But if you let us go up there with you, I can talk to my sister. I need to know she's okay. And if she says everything is fine, then we'll gladly turn around and go. If they're willing to welcome you with open arms like you say, then it shouldn't be a problem."

There was silence in the conference room. Prado had cuffed both Trouble's wrists, but he wasn't making any moves to take him out of the room. He was waiting for a signal from his boss.

"I've already sent a copy to a buddy of mine," Trouble said. "Told him to send it by noon if he doesn't hear from us."

Vegretti's face was dark with anger, but that anger broke as a slow smile crept across his face. "You two drive a hard bargain," he said.

With those words, Trouble knew he'd bought the bluff.

"But Prado is coming with us," Vegretti continued, looking at Trouble. "And you're staying in cuffs."

"Fine," Trouble said. "Fine."

As Vegretti told Prado to call another deputy in from patrol, the reality of what they'd just done dawned on Trouble. Carmen was going to come with him, and he didn't want her anywhere near that place. But maybe he was being unfair. Even chauvinistic. Her sister was in there, after all.

Besides, there was no way Beck would be stupid enough to do something right in front of two cops. Would he?

Chapter 32

THEY ALL RODE UP to the compound together in Vegretti's work SUV. Prado sat in the back with Trouble, while Carmen rode up front with Vegretti. Carmen had collected Trouble's phone off the table in the conference room. While they waited for the other deputy to get back and man the shop, he asked her to text Jensen with a heads-up. She did, but Trouble had no idea whether he would get it in time; he doubted Jensen was carrying the phone around with him. And even if he did see the message, there wasn't much he could do about it.

As they came to the fork in the road, left leading to the temple and right leading to the compound, they were stopped by armed guards who came out of the woods. They'd beefed up their security.

Trouble didn't recognize any of the guards. Vegretti rolled down his window to talk to one of them, a wide guy with a craggy face and a no-bullshit demeanor.

"Here to see Beck," Vegretti said.

"He's not taking any visitors," the guard said. "I'm going to need you to turn around now."

Vegretti scoffed. "Well, hold on now. You tell him it's Sheriff Vegretti here to see him. He told me I could stop by anytime."

The guard glanced in at the passengers, his gaze resting on Trouble longer than the others. Then he stepped off the road and unclipped a radio from his belt. He spoke into it, listened, and then spoke into it again before signaling them to head on up.

When they came to the gate, they were stopped again. Several guards were posted there, but none were pointing their guns at the vehicle. Once again, Vegretti talked to a guard Trouble didn't recognize. The guy told them to wait.

After five minutes, Vegretti called to the guy, impatient. The man told them to wait. He didn't provide further explanation.

As the minutes ticked by, the feeling in Trouble's gut grew steadily worse. He shifted in his seat, adjusting his cuffed hands so he wasn't pressing them against the seatback.

Vegretti was also getting restless. He kept glancing in the rearview mirror, looking at Trouble and making impatient noises.

Finally, after nearly fifteen minutes, the gate opened, and the guard waved them in. Some fifty feet ahead of them, idling in the road, was a truck with an open bed. Four guards with guns sat in the truck bed, all of them looking back at the sheriff's cruiser.

As they drove in, the truck moved, leading the way. Trouble looked to his right, seeing that another truck with armed men in the back was bumping toward them, coming out of a narrow alley between trees. As soon as the SUV passed, the second truck pulled out behind them and tailed them.

"What the hell is this shit?" Vegretti grumbled as he noticed the vehicle.

"I'm guessing this isn't the normal reception?" Trouble asked.

Vegretti glanced at him in the mirror but said nothing.

Trouble looked out the window as they drove. There were fields of sprouting crops lining the main road, along with domed greenhouses and shacks which he assumed contained farming supplies. Off in the distance to his left, he could see a cluster of long, low buildings that looked like barracks. He was sure they were the same ones he'd seen the night he broke in.

He saw no people working in the fields or greenhouses, which he thought was strange. That bad feeling clamped harder on his guts.

They came to a massive building that was the only evidence of modern construction in the place. It was three stories tall and featured a triple-segmented slanted roof to deal with snowfall. The smooth concrete façade and the unadorned main entrance spoke to the straightforward construction. The only testament to the building's importance was its size. It loomed over the landscape, imposing and utilitarian. There was a large awning over the front doors, similar to that of a mid-range hotel.

The road continued past the building's entrance, over to a collection of cottages—a few smaller ones placed up the hill from a larger one. But the lead truck turned off the main road to a pull off under the peaked aluminum awning at the front of the building. One of the men in the back of the truck signaled for Vegretti to follow. He did, pulling up under the awning. Brake lights flared, and they stopped in front of the building.

One of the men from the lead truck jumped out of the bed. He swung his semiautomatic rifle over his shoulder by its strap as he approached Vegretti's window. "This is it. Suzerain's inside," he told the sheriff through the cracked window.

"You two stay here," Vegretti said, talking to Trouble and Prado. "Miss Marsden and I will go in."

"No way," Trouble said. "That wasn't the deal. Prado, you stay. I'm going."

"Who the hell do you think you're—"

A knock on the window cut Prado's words off. It was the same guard, addressing the sheriff. "Bring everyone. Let's go."

Vegretti grumbled a command as he shut the vehicle off and got out. Trouble reached awkwardly with his cuffed hands and opened his door. The four of them gathered in front of the heavy metal doors at the building's entrance. The armed men from the two trucks got out, along with the drivers. Trouble immediately recognized the man who'd been driving the lead truck. Vogel. They shared a look, and the blond man grinned as he walked up to them.

"Hello again, Sheriff," Vogel said, stepping up to shake Vegretti's hand. He did the same with Prado, who was sticking close to Trouble. "And who are these two?"

"Where's my sister?" Carmen said, ignoring Vogel's question.

"Who's that?" Vogel asked.

"Megan Marsden. Where is she?"

"Oh, I see the resemblance now. She's inside. Shall we go?"

Vogel led the way, pulling open the lefthand door. The four followed him in. They, in turn, were followed by all the other security officers who had been in the trucks.

They passed into an anteroom with a set of wooden doors straight ahead and two other doors off to the sides. They continued straight toward the wooden doors, which were propped open. Above the doors, there was a sentence in large letters: "Choose salvation over fear."

They entered the nave to find it about half-full of people, most of them in white pajamas. There was a central aisle that bisected the large room, chairs on each side. A large stage occupied the front of the space. The ceiling was high, with a series of stained-glass windows near the top directly over the stage. There were also regular windows flanking the sides of the room near the ceiling.

Men, women, and children sat in the chairs, spread out among every row, as if to give the illusion of a full house. They stared silently as the group moved down toward the stage.

"Megan!" Carmen called out, breaking off from the group and running up on stage. Megan Marsden smiled and hugged her sister tightly. Then Carmen started talking, asking questions, but Trouble couldn't make out exactly what she was saying. Besides, his attention was focused on Raymond Beck, who stood near the sisters, looking out at the crowd with a smile on his face. Like most everyone else, he wore simple white cotton clothes.

"Let's welcome our visitors," Beck said as the trio reached the stairs.

"Welcome!" the crowd said, in almost perfect unison. It sent chills up Trouble's spine as he scanned the audience for Jensen. He didn't see the man.

The armed guards that had followed them inside were spreading out through the audience. Some of them stood to the sides, while others sat down in seats, rifles propped on their legs.

The high windows let plenty of sunlight in, but there were still lights on, providing even illumination throughout the wide auditorium.

Beck moved to shake Vegretti's hand. "What can we do for you today?" he asked. "This is a bit of a strange visit, isn't it?" As Beck asked this, he glanced past the sheriff and looked at Trouble, whose hands were still fixed behind his back.

"It's a little embarrassing," Vegretti said, suddenly reverting back to his wise-uncle demeanor. "They think that someone has . . . committed suicide in here. They think—"

"No!" Trouble yelled. "This isn't right."

Everyone stopped and looked at him.

"Let us talk to these people alone," he said, turning to Beck but still shouting so everyone could hear him. "Let the sheriff talk to some of these people alone."

"We're a family here," Beck said, demeanor unchanged. "You're welcome to ask any questions you like. We will answer truthfully."

Trouble looked to the sheriff, who returned his gaze with a furrowed brow.

"Does anyone have anything to say to the good sheriff?" Beck called out to the audience.

One young woman stood up immediately, raising her hand.

"Yes, Andi Brightman? What would you like to ask?" Beck said.

"Someone's been trespassing on our property. Assaulting our people," Andi Brightman said, looking directly at Trouble. "Are you going to find out who it is?"

Vegretti followed her gaze, looking at Trouble before he answered. "This is the first time I'm hearing about it. I'll certainly look into it. I'll need the specifics from those assaulted to conduct a thorough investigation."

"Thank you," Andi Brightman said, sitting down again.

No one else raised a hand or stood up.

"Anyone else?" Beck asked.

No response.

"Well, I thought this might be the case," Vegretti said.

"You've got to be kidding me!" Trouble said, rounding on the sheriff until Prado pulled him back. "That's it? That's all you're going to do? Are you fucking *blind*? This isn't even all the people. There's supposed to be seven hundred. Where are the rest of them? And don't you see the armed guards sitting around? Don't you know that these people are too damn scared to speak the truth in front of *him*?" Trouble stuck his chin toward Beck since he couldn't point with a hand.

"We have nothing to hide," Megan Marsden said, stepping away from Carmen. "Our people are free to leave whenever they want. Isn't that right?"

A chorus of assent came from the crowd.

"What about Diane Beil?" Trouble asked. "Was she free to leave? Where is she? I'd like to talk to her."

Trouble was careful to watch Beck as he said the woman's name. A momentary cloud of dark emotion—fear or anger—passed over the man's face. Trouble saw it, and Beck knew he saw it. But his soft smile was there again quickly.

"Diane Beil is just fine," Beck said. "If you want to see her, you absolutely can. I can take you all to see her. How about that?"

Trouble narrowed his eyes. His gut was screaming. This was a trick. A lie. Nothing good could come of this visit. Nothing.

"I think that's a fine idea," Vegretti said. "But after we make sure she's okay, I'd still like to talk to some of these people in private, if that's alright?"

"Of course," Beck said. "Of course. If it will help put these ridiculous allegations to bed, I'm happy to oblige. I'll lead the way."

Beck stepped down off the stage and started up toward the doors. "I'll be back in just a few minutes, and we'll continue the lesson," he said to the people.

"Sorry for the inconvenience, people," Vegretti said.

Trouble shook his head as Prado walked with him up the aisle, one hand on his upper left arm. A glance back revealed that Carmen and Megan were coming, along with Vogel and the other armed guards.

Beck stood aside and waited until everyone got outside. Then he spoke to the guards. "Thank you for your vigilance, but I can take it from here," he said. "Vogel, you can join us."

The group of seven walked up the road toward the cottages, leaving behind the armed security guards. Beck and Vogel were in the lead, followed by Vegretti, Trouble and Prado, and then the two sisters.

They split from the road and walked down a paved path, moving past the smaller cottages and toward the larger one. Beyond the large cottage, Trouble could see the cliff's edge. This whole side of the property backed up to a long cliff—the same one he'd seen from the cabin through the binoculars he'd found there. There was no fencing of any kind. No barriers to keep kids from falling off the edge. *Strange*, he thought.

Off to his right, directly down from the church, there was a flat clifftop area with a stone fire pit and a couple of camp chairs.

When they reached the cottage, Beck led the way inside while Vogel stood by the doorway, seeing everyone in. They milled in a mid-sized living room. There were couches and a glass-topped coffee table to the left, and a dining table to the right. The kitchen was ahead, along with a hallway that led to at least two other rooms.

Vogel closed the door and stood with his back to it.

"Where's Beil?" Trouble asked.

"She's in the bedroom. Hasn't been feeling well, so I've been looking after her," Beck said. "Megan, why don't you and your sister sit down and catch up? I'm sure she has some questions for you."

"That's a good idea," Megan said. Carmen nodded in agreement, sharing a quick look with Trouble before they sat down on one of the couches.

"You gentlemen, follow me," Beck said, walking down the hallway. After taking a few strides, he stopped and turned, looking back as if he'd forgotten something. "Vogel?" he called, then turned to the sheriff. "I'm sorry, you can go ahead in. Last door on the right. I'll be right with you."

Vegretti walked ahead, and Prado shoved Trouble along. The door was closed, and as they approached it, Trouble had to consider that he'd been lied to. If Beil was in there—and if she could prove she was Beil with some kind of identification—then he'd have to assume that everything Jensen told him was a lie. But even if that was the case, some members of the cult still had blood on their hands. And they still needed to be stopped.

Vegretti opened the door and stepped into a bedroom. He moved to the left, toward the bed, allowing Trouble and Prado to enter. Trouble found himself near a window in the wall opposite the door. A window that looked out toward the church and the adjacent clifftop area.

He took this in automatically in a second, then turned his attention to the figure lying in the bed.

It was a little boy.

"What the hell is this?" Vegretti grumbled, then started to turn around, presumably to tell Beck they were in the wrong room.

He never got the chance.

The gunshot was booming in the small space, making Trouble flinch as the sheriff's brains splattered all over the white bedspread.

Beck stood in the doorway with a pistol in his hand and an insane look on his face. He was quickly shifting the barrel toward Prado, who cried out in surprise as he went for his gun.

Trouble ducked as Beck fired again. He felt chunks of warm wetness splatter his back as Prado's head flew apart. Before the deputy's body hit the ground, Trouble was throwing himself at the window, breaking the glass with his right shoulder.

A third gunshot sounded as Trouble tumbled out the window, landing hard on his bound arms amid the tinkle of shattered glass. He heard a crunch and felt a sharp pain in his left hand and wrist with the impact. He rolled over quickly and stumbled to his feet, jumping around the corner of the structure as Beck fired a fourth shot. The bullet missed him by inches.

Chapter 33

"GET HIM!" BECK YELLED at Vogel, who stood in the hallway.

Vogel hadn't known what was about to go down. Beck had simply come back down the hallway while the three men were filing into the room and ordered Vogel to give him his gun, which he'd done without hesitation. "Watch them," Beck had whispered, gesturing at the women on the couch before turning around.

Then there were gunshots. Four total. And the sound of glass breaking.

"He went out the window! Get him!" Beck yelled, holding the pistol out for Vogel to take. From his angle in the hallway, he couldn't see much. Only part of a body on the floor; one of the cops. And the pool of blood spreading underneath.

Vogel grinned widely as he took the gun and sprinted to the front door. Parall Marsden's sister was screaming, standing next to the couch while Marsden gripped her arm to keep her from moving toward the bedroom. Beck would have to deal with her. Vogel expected it wouldn't be difficult.

As he rounded the building, Vogel saw the Sentinels they'd left behind up at the Sanctuary. The gunshots had drawn them, and they were running over toward Beck's cottage. Vogel pulled up his radio. "Create a perimeter around the cottage," he said. "But do *not* enter unless Suzerain or I say so, copy?"

Several of the men nodded or gave a thumbs-up as they ran.

Vogel clipped the radio back to his belt and stalked down the side of the house, scanning the thin smattering of trees for signs of movement. The ground behind the cottage sloped down for about thirty yards before coming to the cliff's edge. The cliff created a natural barrier on this portion of the property for about half a mile. It was no accident that Beck's cottage and the Sanctuary were built nearby; the view of the valley was spectacular.

Stopping outside the window, Vogel glanced in at the bodies. Both the cops were down, and they weren't getting up. It was the smart move, taking them out first. They were the ones with guns, after all. And free use of their hands. The biker, Terrence Rubble, was a pain in the ass, but his hands were cuffed behind his back, and he was surely wounded after crashing through the window and onto the ground.

It was just a matter of finding him and killing him. Easy.

Before heading away from the window, Vogel saw that the bloody bed was unmade. From the way the blood and brain matter were splattered across the bedspread, it looked like someone had been sleeping in there when the killing had happened. Someone small. He figured it was Angel. She was never very far from Beck. Or perhaps Seraph Gibbs. Ever since the ritual in the temple, Beck had kept the little boy close.

Vogel glanced quickly around the back corner of the house, then moved out after seeing nothing. He stalked along the back wall and peered around the corner, seeing two Sentinels moving toward him from the front. The woods were thin here, and he looked through the trees up the modest hill that flanked the small collection of cottages. Nothing.

Surely he hadn't tried to climb down the cliff. He wouldn't be so stupid. Not without the use of his hands.

Still, Vogel moved to the cliff's edge and peered over. It was a good hundred-foot drop to the treetops below. The area directly below the sanctuary building, where Beck liked to go, was even higher.

Vogel saw no sign of Rubble's body at the bottom of the cliff. But, given the trees down there, he wouldn't necessarily see any evidence.

He studied the contours of the rocky tan-colored cliff below him, trying to imagine whether it would be possible for the man to climb down. Maybe if he'd managed to get his hands in front of him, it would be possible. The cliffside wasn't completely flat, and there were several outcroppings he couldn't see past. Rubble could be clinging for dear life under one of them.

A smear of red caught Vogel's eye on a rock about ten feet down and six feet to the left of where he was standing. He edged closer to the drop-off and squinted. Was it blood? It was hard to tell from this distance.

He brought his pistol out and fired a few shots down at the cliffside, kicking up dirt and rock fragments. The whine of a ricochet faded out and was replaced by silence as Vogel stood there, leaning out, watching and listening.

Nothing.

***

Trouble tried pulling himself in closer to the cliff wall. He could feel the impact of bullets through the rock as someone fired on the outcropping above him.

He'd managed to pull his cuffed hands in front of him, one leg at a time, before deciding that climbing down the cliff was the only option. He knew they would be looking, so he'd found a little divot under an outcropping just big enough for him to squeeze into horizontally. He had to press his hands against the top and his back against the bottom of the depression so his upper body wouldn't slide out. He had his right leg extended, pressing against the edge of the hollow to help him stay in place. His other leg was jammed awkwardly into the small space.

After only three shots, the firing stopped. Dirt and rock chips tumbled off the outcropping above him, sailing down into the trees below. He forced himself not to look down.

It's just a lucky guess, he told himself. *They don't know where you are.*

He'd broken or dislocated his left thumb when landing on his hands outside the window, and he'd also taken several cuts on the back of his neck and head. He had no idea how bad they were because he couldn't see them and, with his hands busy preventing him from falling to his death, he couldn't reach back and feel them, either. But the back of his shirt and hoodie seemed to be getting wetter with every passing minute.

Despite his predicament, Trouble could think of little else than Carmen Marsden. And of Shayna Mitchell. He refused to look down at the drop below, but when he closed his eyes, all he could see was Melissa being led out of the bedroom by Mister Hoffman all those years ago. Only the face on Melissa's body was Shayna's face.

He breathed in deeply. *Get it together. Focus on not falling off the goddamn cliff.*

His shoulders and right leg were already screaming. He couldn't hold the position for much longer. He'd have to make a move.

***

"What happened?" someone said from behind him.

Vogel turned. It was one of the Sentinels he'd seen coming down the side of the house. "They tried to kill Suzerain. One of them got away. The one in the black hoodie and jeans. Go along the cliff that way and see if you can find him. Suzerain wants him alive."

The young man nodded vehemently and ran up the hill along the cliff's edge, carrying his rifle in front of him. Vogel hoped he hadn't just made a big mistake. But telling the guy they'd tried to kill Suzerain seemed like the only option. And the thing about wanting him alive was all Vogel. He wanted to deal with Rubble himself.

He turned and jogged back up to the house, seeing that a crowd was gathering in front of Beck's cottage. They were held back by the Sentinels, but many of the women were crying, and most of the men looked ill.

Vogel moved into the house through the front door and found that Parall Marsden's sister was unconscious on the couch. Marsden herself was nowhere to be seen. Neither was Beck.

He moved further into the house, to the back bedroom opposite the one with the two dead bodies. Beck was leaning back on the bed, a ragged circle of blood on his white shirt at the stomach. Parall Marsden was on her knees in front of him, her hands stained with red as she prodded and poked at Beck's stomach.

"What the hell happened?" Vogel asked. "Are you okay?"

Beck looked up at him. "They shot me," he said, eyes wide. "They shot me, so you killed them. They came to assassinate me. They're messengers of fear. Of evil."

Vogel's mind reeled. Could he have missed something? Beck was fine when he'd left the house mere minutes ago. Then it clicked. Beck and Vogel both had the same idea, but Beck was taking it a step further. He was ever the showman, and he knew there was a crowd gathering out there. He knew exactly how to manipulate them. Vogel had to admire his audacity.

Marsden finished putting the blood on—blood sourced from one of the dead cops, no doubt—and looked up into her leader's face. "I think that's good," she said.

Beck nodded and stood up. "Stay here," he said to them. "Tie the woman up. She may be useful yet."

Marsden winced, then nodded.

"I couldn't find him," Beck blurted out. "But I have men looking for him."

"I know," Beck said, moving past. "I know."

Vogel followed Beck, watching as the man clutched his stomach and affected a limp. He opened the door and stepped outside to gasps of surprise and cries of disbelief.

"They've sent their Devils to kill me," Beck cried, stumbling toward the crowd of perhaps a hundred. "They've tried to assassinate me, but I'm not afraid. I'm not afraid, because I know the power we have. The power of the *collective*!"

He moved up to a group of hysterical followers, reaching one bloody hand out to grab a woman's arm. "Lay your hands on me!" he said. "Lay your hands on me, and we can heal my fatal wound."

He pulled the woman's hand, placing it over the one he still held over the fake wound. Then others joined in, jostling forward to place their hands around Beck's stomach. Soon,

Vogel lost sight of the short man as people surrounded him, placing hands on any part of him they could reach.

As the crowd writhed and cried and whimpered, Vogel saw a familiar bald head moving toward him, skirting the crowd. It was Rankin, who wasn't supposed to be up and around. He limped as he walked toward Beck's house, using a cane the Emissaries doctor had given him. His face was uglier than usual. Those features not permanently set in a rictus by the scars on his face were scrunched with anger and worry.

He gazed into the crowd, trying to see what was happening. When it didn't seem worth wading in, he turned toward the house and locked eyes with Vogel.

He limped into the house. "What happened? What's going on?"

Vogel put his hands up in a placating gesture. "Relax, Rankin, it's under control. Suzerain's going to be fine. We've taken care of the problem. Our people will find the last one."

"*What* problem? What 'last one'? All I'm hearing on the radio is there was an assassination attempt. Is that true?"

"It's true, but like I said, he's fine. He'll be fine. Have faith."

"I *do* have faith," Rankin said, getting within inches of Vogel's face. "But it's my job to *protect* him, dammit. It's my *duty*."

"Well, there are many of us who are tasked with doing the same thing," Vogel said, fighting to keep his anger in check. "Go look in the back bedroom. See how we did."

Rankin glared at him for a moment, then limped past and down the hall. Vogel paused for a beat and then followed, looking over the man's shoulder as he surveyed the two dead cops.

Parall Marsden was in the bedroom across the hall, talking to someone. Vogel turned around and found her still on her knees, looking under the bed. From the sounds of it, she was coaxing a child out. And sure enough, Seraph Gibbs crawled out from under the bed, dried blood splashed across his face. Vogel realized it had been Gibbs in the bed when Suzerain had done the shooting.

Marsden pulled the child into a hug, whispering sweet words into his ear, telling him everything was going to be okay.

"*You* did this?" Rankin asked, pulling Vogel's attention back.

Vogel almost said no, but then he remembered what Suzerain had told him. *They shot me, so you killed them.* The implications of taking the blame for killing two cops suddenly became clear. Suzerain was surely telling all the people outside how it had gone down. That one of the cops shot him, and then Vogel took them out.

"Yes," Vogel said. "I killed them." He'd always known how this would end. He'd always known that it wasn't going to be a long life. The things he'd done—the things being with Beck had allowed him to do—weren't the kind you walked away from. So what was adding two Podunk cops to the body count? After the other killings, the statutory rape, the kidnappings, and the intimidation threats, it didn't seem like such a big deal.

Rankin moved back down the hallway and looked down at Parall Marsden's sister, who was still passed out on the couch. Vogel followed again, remembering that he needed to tie her up. Only now did he notice the syringe on the coffee table. Beck had enough drugs in the house to kill a dozen members of the Collective, so he wasn't surprised they'd given her something to put her to sleep.

Rankin spit into the unconscious woman's face. Then, apparently thinking this wasn't enough, he dropped his cane and wrapped both hands around her throat. Vogel kicked the man in his wounded leg, causing him to cry out and clutch the leg, releasing the woman. "Don't do that," Vogel told him. "Suzerain wants her alive."

Beck suddenly came back in through the front door, followed by three Sentinels. He was beaming. "Our power is plain to see, now," he said, lifting his bloody white shirt to reveal a hairy yet unmarred stomach. "We've healed me. But this transgression cannot go unpunished. I've ordered the buses to be loaded up as quickly as possible. And anyone who has been trained to fire a weapon will be given one from the armory."

"What's the plan, Suzerain?" Rankin asked.

"We're going to make them all listen," Beck said. "We're going to show them all."

Chapter 34

THE FRONT DOOR TO the barracks swung open, revealing the Sentinel who had been "protecting" them. Jensen didn't know her well, but, like most everyone in the cult, he knew her last name: Vicars.

"Okay, let's go!" Vicars shouted. "Everyone on the buses!"

Jensen looked around at the crowded interior as people stood up and began to file out, their faces tinged with worry. Although the simple wooden structure was designed for twelve, there were nearly three times that many in here now. They'd all been working on building the new temples when they'd suddenly been corralled into the barracks and told only that the compound was under threat. That was nearly half an hour ago if Jensen had to guess; he had no way to tell. There were no clocks in the building, and the members were forbidden from wearing watches.

Jensen looked around for signs of reticence on the people's faces. A glance told him that he was the only one questioning just what the hell was happening.

"Let's go, Parall Jensen," Fayden, his check partner, said.

Jensen filed out into the center aisle between the cots and shuffled forward. When they got outside, he saw that there were several Sentinels corralling the crowd to a line of yellow school buses waiting on the road about forty yards distant.

There were similar lines snaking from the other barracks buildings.

Jensen looked back over his shoulder, down the side of the building. The phone was there, buried next to one of the exposed posts. If he could get to it, he could tell the biker what was happening. Or call the police. But he couldn't get to it. There was no way. He would be seen.

Besides, he had no idea what was really happening. They'd heard muffled gunshots while inside the barracks. Now they were being loaded onto buses. They hadn't been on the buses since coming to New Mexico from North Carolina. So maybe this was a good thing. Maybe the gunshots meant Beck was dead, and they were being taken off the premises, to somewhere safe.

Jensen knew this was nothing more than wishful thinking. The looks on the Sentinels' faces told him that much. He didn't know where they were going, but he had a bad feeling about it. And that feeling only intensified as he got onto the old school bus and saw that the people already sitting down had semiautomatic rifles held in their hands, barrels pointed up at the ceiling. Each unoccupied seat had two rifles propped on it.

Fayden maneuvered ahead of Jensen, and he sat down first, taking both rifles and holding them between his legs. "Sit down," he said to Jensen.

Jensen did as he was told, his mind racing, heart beating a frantic tattoo in his chest.

He noticed there were no children on the bus. He hadn't seen any children getting on any of the buses. And he remembered from the trip to New Mexico that they only had six buses, which only accommodated about half the total population of the Divine Emissaries. Wherever they were going, the buses would have to come back and pick up the other people, including the children.

But the guns made him feel ill. Why were they being armed? What were they going to do?

He didn't know. He clamped his hands together and closed his eyes. And for the first time since he was a kid, Jack Jensen asked God for help.

***

Trouble pressed up against the rock divot with his right hand and right leg, creating just enough leverage to keep from sliding out. He gritted his teeth as he pulled with his left hand, searing pain shooting through his broken thumb. The cuff on his left hand was tearing into his skin, but it wasn't doing much else.

He stopped pulling with the hand and inspected the cuff. It wasn't going to work. The cuffs had been fastened around the smallest part of his wrists. And he didn't think his thumb had broken in the right place to get it out of the way. Even if it had dislocated at the base, which it clearly hadn't, he doubted he'd be able to slip it through the cuff. His hands were too big.

Hollywood's full of shit, he thought, breathing heavily as the pain subsided to a stabbing throb. He was hoping to try a climb down the cliff, but that was no longer an option. It wouldn't be possible with his hands cuffed together. The only thing he could do was go back up.

He pressed harder with his right foot, shifting his back into a position where he felt stable enough to take his hands away. He eased off with his right hand, little by little. Before he could stop himself, he glanced over his right side, down the sheer cliff face. His stomach roiled, and he shut his eyes. *Stupid. Stupid.*

He felt along the top of the divot and found the ledge he'd used to get inside. He gripped it with the fingers of both hands. Then he took his hands down again and dragged his fingers along his jeans, wiping the sweat away.

Once he had a solid hold on the ledge with all eight fingers, he stopped pressing with his right leg, bringing it down to search for a foothold. He found one, tested it, and then put part of his weight on it, shifting the rest of his body out of the divot and turning so he was facing the cliff. He put his left foot on the foothold, then searched for another with his right, finding one after a long moment. Then he worked his fingers along the ledge until it ended. This was the hard part.

About two feet above the ledge, there was a bulbous out-cropping of rock the size of a bowling ball. He'd have to jump his hands up to it, stretching his body to its full length. Then he could bring his legs up higher and kind of worm his way up the same way he'd come down.

He hadn't heard anyone above him for a while. That didn't mean there wasn't someone there, waiting. But he had no choice. If he climbed up only to get shot in the head, so be it. It was better than waiting to fall off the damn cliff. He *hated* heights.

He shifted his feet in their tiny footholds, pressing his toes all the way to the tips of his boots. Then he took a deep breath and jumped his hands up to the outcropping. His right foot slipped off the toehold just as he jumped, but he managed to grab hold of the outcropping with his hands, his left thumb shooting pain as it banged into the rock. He scrambled with his right foot, looking for purchase and not finding any. His left leg was now stretched too far out to be of much use, and his sweaty hands were slipping off the rock.

Come on, come on, he thought, *how did you do this before?*

He doubled his efforts with his hands, hoping he had enough purchase to pull his legs further up. His right knee banged into a sharp edge, and he remembered. He felt with his knee, sticking it on a ledge and then using that leverage to jump his hands up over the outcropping. He breathed a sigh of relief, feeling more secure now.

The rest of the way up was slightly slanted, making the going easier. He pulled his head up over the cliff's edge and looked around for anyone. He saw the house through the smattering of pine trees. Off to his left, the church loomed. To his right, the cliff sloped upwards along a hill. There was nothing but trees up the hill, as far as he could see. That would be the way to go, he figured.

Movement caught his eye, and he ducked his head under the edge. Someone in a blue shirt—one of the security people—had come around the corner of the house. Trouble listened as the faint crunching of footsteps grew louder. He looked back down the cliff, considering. But he knew he didn't have the energy to climb back down again. If he did, he wouldn't make it back up. All he could do was sit there, clinging to the cliff face, hoping the guard didn't come close enough to see him.

The crunching footsteps drew closer and stopped. Trouble felt an itch at the back of his head, picturing the guard seeing him, taking aim. He waited for a bullet to blast him away.

But there was no gunshot. Only the resumption of footsteps, this time moving away. Trouble took a deep breath and lifted his head over the edge. He saw the guard heading away, presumably making a circle around the cottage.

When the guard was out of sight, Trouble pulled himself up the rest of the way, rolling onto his back on the rocky, pine-needled ground. He got up and jogged up the hill, away from the house and the church and, hopefully, the people who wanted him dead.

Chapter 35

ON THE TRIP FROM North Carolina, Beck had used a radio system to preach to all the passengers from his place on the lead bus. Vogel wasn't clear on how the tech people did it, but he remembered it being the longest trip of his life. It had taken over thirty hours, and Beck preached for about twenty-five of them.

And when the buses went back to collect the others, Beck went with them. And he preached to the next group.

Now, the tech people were busy setting it up so Beck could preach to the buses from his cottage. In recent months, he'd taken to staying in his cottage and preaching to the daily gatherings in the Sanctuary from the third bedroom, which had the radio equipment inside. So the infrastructure was already there, and the tech people left after testing to make sure everything was working.

Once they were gone, it was only Rankin, Vogel, Beck, and the two Marsden sisters left in the cottage. Gibbs was in the back bedroom—the one without the dead bodies in it. Carmen Marsden was awake but groggy. Her sister sat with her on one couch. Beck was across from them on the other couch, chopping up his third line of cocaine. It had been less than an hour since Beck had killed the two police officers. But every minute that passed seemed to increase his frantic behavior.

The smiling, benevolent Beck was gone. He had left along with the other followers after the "healing" charade. Now, it was the drug-addled and impatient Beck who was in charge.

"Have they found the man? Rubble?" Beck asked for the fourth time.

"They haven't," Vogel said. "He may have taken a fall off the cliff."

"If he fell off the cliff, I want his body found!" Beck snapped, then leaned down to snort the line of white powder.

Rankin stood to one side, looking sheepishly at his master. Beck had usually been good about not showing Rankin this side of him. The man had a knack for knowing what people needed to see from him, and Rankin was one who needed to believe the man was more than human. That was clearly out the window now. Vogel knew it was the beginning of the end. And he was itching to go to town and have some fun. He wanted nothing more than to lead the troops into battle. In all the excitement, he'd nearly forgotten about Rubble. It didn't matter. He was probably dead anyway.

There was a knock at the door, and Vogel quickly answered it.

"Who is it?" Beck called.

It was Angel, summoned by Beck and escorted by a Sentinel. Vogel thanked the guard and grabbed the little blonde girl by the hand, pulling her inside.

"Angel!" Beck said, opening his arms wide. "Come here, my sweet girl. Come here."

The girl walked stiffly over, her face blank as Beck wrapped her in a hug and started whispering in her ear. Beck's behavior with the girl gave Vogel the creeps. He'd never seen anything to suggest the man was a pedophile, but his relationship with her and a few other children wasn't normal. And the girl was clearly checked out. Probably better for her. Maybe she knew what was coming.

"Take your clothes off," Beck said suddenly. He was still holding the girl, but he was talking to Megan Marsden. "You too," he said to her sister.

Megan stood up and started to disrobe. It seemed to take Carmen a moment to realize what was happening. The dazed look left her face, and she reached out with bound hands to stop her sister. "What are you doing?!" she cried.

Megan smiled at her sister. "It's okay," she said, as if that explained it all.

Beck watched, still clutching Angel to his chest, as Megan disrobed.

We don't have time for this shit, Vogel thought.

"Now you," Beck said to Carmen.

"No."

Fury spread over Beck's face. "Take your fucking clothes off, now!"

"Suzerain," Vogel said, stepping forward. "The buses are loaded. Your people are awaiting orders. We only have so much time until they send more people to stop you."

Beck seemed to consider this, his wits coming back to him. "You're right," he said, tossing Angel onto the couch next to him and standing up. "You're right."

"I'm happy to take the people into town," Vogel said. "While you stay here and oversee the children."

"Right," Beck said. "Yes. You take them into town and await my orders. I don't want you doing anything until I say so, okay?"

"Of course, Suzerain," Vogel said.

"Rankin, you stay here. Gather all the adults who are left here and get them in the Sanctuary."

"Yes, Suzerain," Rankin said, clearly happy now that his precious leader was back. "What should I do with the children?"

"Keep the children in their buildings for now."

"Yes, Suzerain," Rankin said before leaving by the front door. Vogel could hear him barking orders at the guards outside.

"Marsden, put your clothes back on. I want you to prepare the children for Ascension. We'll have to do it all together in the Sanctuary. There's no time left now."

Megan Marsden looked momentarily confused, but she nodded and said yes, then began pulling her colorful robes back on.

It's really happening, Vogel thought. *Holy shit, these people are actually going to go through with it.* He'd heard Beck talk about "pulling a Jonestown" a time or two over the years—usually when he was drugged out of his mind. Vogel hadn't even been aware that they had the supplies to do it. But it really didn't surprise him. The idea that they would kill themselves piecemeal never really made sense to him. It would give people too much time to think.

As Vogel walked out of the cottage, he felt the giddy stirrings of excitement in his gut. He wasn't going to kill himself. No way. Not unless he got cornered by the cops. Even then, he'd take as many of them out as he could.

No, he was going to have a whole lot of fun. And who knows? Maybe he could slip away in all the chaos. It seemed that the opportunity was presenting itself. And if Vogel was nothing else, he was a man who recognized an opportunity when he saw one.

***

Trouble hid next to a fallen tree as two armed men moved past in the forest fifteen yards away.

"I've already been over here twice. He's not here," one of the guards was saying.

"Do you think the guy doesn't have legs?" the second one said. "He wasn't here when you were here before. That doesn't mean he isn't here now."

"Well, I don't see him. Do you?"

"No, I don't fucking see him. But we've got to keep looking."

The first guard grumbled as they moved away through the thickening trees.

Trouble could see the fence about two hundred feet distant. It ran right up to the edge of the cliff. He'd always had a decent sense of direction, so he knew approximately where he was in relation to the buildings he'd seen on the way into the compound earlier. And he knew that was where he needed to go. The first order of business was to get the cuffs off. But if he could find a weapon before then, all the better.

He was pretty sure Prado hadn't double-locked the handcuffs when he'd put them on back at the station. At the time, he thought they were only going to need to transport Trouble to the holding cell inside the station. And when it was clear they were all going up to Dalewood, it apparently hadn't occurred to him to engage the double-locking mechanism.

This meant Trouble could conceivably find a thin shim, a bobby pin, or a paper clip and get out of the cuffs. He wasn't totally sure the handcuffs weren't double-locked, but the only way to find out without a makeshift key was to tighten the cuffs on his wrists. If they were able to tighten, it meant the double-lock mechanism wasn't engaged. But they were already tight, and he didn't want to risk cutting off his circulation if he was wrong.

Experience and a lifetime's worth of shit luck had taken its toll on Trouble. And he'd started carrying a handcuff key on his keyring many years ago. But Prado had emptied his pockets back at the station. Even his attempts to counter his shit luck were often thwarted. Such was his life. But ruminating on it would do no good.

He moved cautiously through the woods, the sun high above, burning away the morning chill as noon approached. The cuts on the back of his head and neck weren't bleeding badly any longer. He could tell because each movement of his head resulted in dry blood cracking, pulling the fine hairs on his neck.

When he finally sighted evidence of human activity in a large field, he picked a spot amid some dense bushes and watched the cleared area carefully. There were tools lying around, as if suddenly discarded. Wheelbarrows, shovels, picks, and axes. The ground was all torn up. It was clear the people who'd been working in the area had been clearing it of the few trees and the many rocks there. For what specific purpose wasn't immediately evident. Maybe a new crop field. Maybe a new structure.

After a minute of watching and listening, Trouble moved from his concealment and jogged into the clearing. He swiped up an ax and continued into the woods on the other side. If his sense of direction was accurate, he was heading toward the cluster of buildings he'd seen earlier. He was hoping to find a tool shed so he could get the damn cuffs off.

His left thumb throbbed with his heartbeat. It was swollen and discolored. He tried to ignore it, tried to use the pain for clarity of thought. But it wasn't working well. Images of Melissa, Shayna, and Carmen flashed through his head as he moved. He clenched his jaw and fought back the swell of emotions. Fought back the feeling that he was a helpless kid again, up against people so ruthless it was hard to grasp.

He *wasn't* a kid anymore. And he'd experienced people ten times worse than the Hoffmans. He'd fought some of those people, and he'd won. But that didn't seem to count for anything. All the experience he'd gathered over time, and the toughness that came along with it, seemed to melt away. He found himself right back there, back at the first truly blatant encounter with the evil this world had to offer. He hadn't fought. He'd been too scared. Too overwhelmed. Too chickenshit to fight. So he ran away.

Despite the fact he knew he wouldn't run away from this fight, he still felt like a coward. Like that's who he was, deep down. And he hated that feeling. He hated it more than he hated heights. More than he hated the pain of his broken thumb. He hated it more than he hated the man who'd ordered the execution of three people in a house in Monument. Three people who were just trying to do the right thing. It was no wonder he'd pushed the memory into a deep, dark recess in his mind. He wished it had stayed there. Wished he wasn't feeling like he was. Incompetent. Small. Scared.

He glimpsed the straight lines of a roof through the trees, just over a small rise. He slowed down, approaching the rise with a thudding heart. Sweat was springing up under his hoodie.

The cluster of low wooden buildings was nearly two hundred yards away. He didn't see any movement, so he crept in, crouching and carrying the axe on his right side.

As he got closer, he could see people milling about beyond the buildings, all of them in blue shirts and black pants. None of them were close, and they weren't looking in his direction. They were all gathered near a couple of long, yellow school buses parked on a dirt road. As he moved, changing direction to get a better view, he saw that there were six buses. And from what he could tell, they were all full.

Where the hell are you going? he thought, wondering if Carmen and Shayna were on one of the buses.

As he watched, a familiar figure came striding up to the lead bus. Vogel. His blond hair glinted in the sun as he exchanged a few words with the small group of security officers. He carried a semiautomatic rifle on a strap over his shoulder and a heavy-looking canvas bag in his left hand. The small group dispersed, one of them following Vogel onto the lead bus, while the other five moved down to the other buses, each boarding one.

The lead bus shuddered slightly as the driver put it in gear. It moved slowly, and the other buses followed suit.

Trouble's throat thickened. He had no idea who was on the buses or where they were going. But there was nothing he could do to stop them. Nothing at all. Maybe they were going to another location to kill themselves. Maybe the drivers were going to find a cliff to drive off. Or maybe they'd come to their senses and were going back home.

"Fuck," Trouble whispered, unsure what to do. Surely they couldn't all be on those buses. That wasn't possible. But maybe some other buses had already left.

As the buses disappeared into the trees, Trouble checked his surroundings and moved out toward the buildings. The place was suddenly silent, and he felt that there wasn't anyone in the barracks. He ran to the nearest building and squatted beside it. He listened, leaning against the wood to feel for vibrations from inside. Nothing. Empty.

As he moved up to the front corner, he stopped and gazed in a window, seeing nothing but cots. He checked to make sure no one was around, then moved to the front door, opening it awkwardly with the fingers of his left hand. Stepping into the gloom, the first thing that hit him was the ripe smell. It was fresh, like a crowd of sweaty people had just been sitting inside. He closed the door behind him and surveyed the interior, his eyes adjusting slowly.

There were fifteen cots on each side of the building, all of them made-up but wrinkled, like they'd been sat on after being made. Thirty footlockers lined the central walkway—one for each cot. They were simple wooden things, like the kind Trouble had seen in movies about the army. He lifted the lid on the first footlocker and looked inside, seeing only clothes. He closed the lid gently, trying not to make much noise. The next one contained the same. And the next.

After four lockers, he gave up and turned his attention to the rear of the building. There was a small closet, next to which was a recessed door to what he assumed was a bathroom.

He opened the closet door and found lightbulbs, a fire extinguisher, and a small toolbox, all placed under a tankless water heater. Excitement fluttered in his chest. He turned and dropped the ax on the nearest cot, then stepped back to the closet. As he grabbed the toolbox and set it on the cot next to the ax, the sound of a toilet flushing came from beyond the closed door. Trouble looked over his shoulder at the door, mind reeling.

As the door opened, Trouble grabbed the ax and spun to face a man with a semiautomatic rifle.

Chapter 36

THE MAN STARED AT Trouble for a long moment, seemingly frozen in place. He was Black, with close-cropped hair parted on the left. His brown eyes were wide in his twenty-something face. The rifle—a civilian M4 like the one Trouble had pilfered less than two days ago—was held diagonally across his body with the barrel pointed at the floor.

Trouble held the ax in both still-bound hands, his broken thumb sticking out in a perpetual thumbs-up. He tried to get a feel for what this man was thinking, just by looking into his eyes. He opened his mouth to speak. "Listen—"

The man moved, stepping backward into the bathroom and bringing the gun up. But Trouble was already moving. He swung the base of the ax out, smacking it into the rifle barrel and knocking it aside, buying him enough time to close in.

The bathroom contained two narrow stall toilets, one urinal, and a sink—all on the right side. There were three shower stalls on the left. The floor was tile, sloped slightly to a drain in the middle. The man was directly over this central drain when Trouble jabbed him hard in the sternum with the ax handle. He stumbled back and hit the wall, which was made of finished wood. He tried to raise his gun again, but Trouble was on him, holding him back with the ax handle.

Turned slightly sideways, Trouble tried to protect himself from a knee to the crotch while still creating a solid base to keep the guy from moving. He angled the ax blade so it was pointing at the guy's neck.

"Just stop fighting and I won't hurt you," Trouble said, grunting. "But if you move your arms, I'll have no choice but to jam this blade into your neck."

The man said nothing, but he stopped fighting, and he kept his hands on the gun, which was pressed against his body.

"I'm trying to help your people," Trouble said.

"You're trying to kill Suzerain," the man said through clamped teeth.

"That's bullshit," Trouble said. "All we wanted to do was make sure everyone was okay. Beck's the one who killed those cops out of nowhere."

The man shook his head as if trying to clear a nightmare. "You're lying. That's all you people do. Lie because you're scared. You let fear run your whole lives."

The pure, undiluted childhood fear reared its head inside Trouble. He could feel it trying to drain his strength. His resolve.

Apparently, so could the man, because he managed to push off the wall a few inches before Trouble slammed him back against it.

"Don't you see what he's doing to you?" Trouble asked, a pleading note in his voice. "He's going to have you kill yourselves. Don't you see that? You're going to let that happen?"

The man almost laughed. "You call it suicide now, but just wait and see. It'll be your salvation—if you're smart enough to accept it. We must do it, so the rest of the world doesn't have to."

"Man, he's really done a number on you people, hasn't he?" Trouble said.

"He's done nothing but reveal the truth. I'm not under some spell. I'm not dazed. The wool hasn't been pulled over my eyes. I believe in this with all my heart. I know it's true. *I know it.*"

"And you're willing to die for it," Trouble said. It wasn't a question.

"Not just willing. Eager."

"Damn," Trouble said. He pulled the ax quickly away from the man, then whipped the handle into the side of the guy's head. He stumbled, falling into one of the shower stalls, pulling the curtain with him as he tried and failed to keep his feet. Trouble stepped over him and slammed the ax handle into his head twice more, knocking him out. He then unclipped the radio and the rifle, leaving the ax on the floor while he went back into the main room. When he came back for the ax, he pressed a boot into the man's crotch with increasing pressure to make sure he wasn't faking.

Back in the main room, he checked the M4's chamber to ensure it had a round ready to go. Then he slid the safety off and set it close at hand next to the toolbox. The toolbox contained a small assortment of typical tools. Near the bottom, he found a small packet of rectangular razor blades. After extracting one from the package, he grabbed a pair of pliers and gripped the thin part of the blade with the pliers. He then pressed the blade against the floor at an angle, putting his weight into it to bend the metal lengthwise down the middle. The blade snapped, leaving him with half the thin metal in the pliers.

The metal was still too wide to be an effective shim, so he adjusted it in the pliers with his left hand. He did the same thing again, pressing the piece of metal against the floor, angling the pliers down to try and snap the remaining part of the blade in half lengthwise. This time, the blade bent but did not snap. He had to turn the pliers over and bend the blade back the other way. He repeated this until, after several minutes, the blade finally gave way, and he was able to separate the two thin pieces of metal.

Grabbing one of the pieces between his right thumb and forefinger, Trouble sat on the cot and studied the left hand-cuff where the ratchet went into the housing. The cuffs were already tight, but he had to risk tightening them a little more for the shim to work. He'd have to press the shim and the adjustable part of the cuff down at the same time. This would allow him to get the thin piece of metal between the teeth on the ratchet and the corresponding teeth inside the cuff housing.

After pulling the cuff up slightly on his wrist to create a little room for it to tighten, he inserted the shim. When he pushed it as far as he could, he adjusted his grip to include the adjustable ratchet of the cuff. He applied pressure slowly at first, so as not to break the shim. Both pieces of metal moved inward, clicking once, twice, and then three times. The metal pressed tight around the thinnest part of his wrist. Holding the shim in place with his thumb, he pulled on the adjustable ratchet with his fingers. It opened easily, and his left hand was free.

Trouble allowed himself a smile before going to work on the right cuff. But since his left thumb was out of commission, he found himself struggling with the operation. It took him twice as long to get free of the right cuff, but he did it.

He put the cuffs in his back pocket and picked up the gun. Then he moved carefully into the bathroom to find that the man was still unconscious in the shower stall. He looked around briefly, thinking. He set the gun down and pulled the man over to the single sink in the room. Then he cuffed his hands together around the pipe under the sink.

That done, Trouble shut the bathroom door and stepped out into the main room. He went through four of the footlockers before he found black jeans and a blue shirt that would fit him. He changed quickly, shoving his old clothes into the footlocker. Now, if he was spotted from a distance, the spotter might not think anything of it. That was his hope, anyway.

He left the ax where it was, but picked up the radio and clipped it to his belt. He hadn't heard a peep from it yet, but figured it could still come in handy.

He moved to the front door, carrying the rifle with the safety off and his right index finger resting on the housing above the trigger guard. He opened the door and peered outside, wondering where everyone was.

His best guess was the church. But his first priority was getting Carmen to safety. And that meant going back to Beck's house to see if she was still there. And still alive.

He hoped to God she was.

Chapter 37

"THEY HAVE TRIED TO kill me because they know the power of salvation we hold!"

Beck's voice came over the speakers in the bus as the vehicle turned onto the paved road, heading toward Dalewood. Jensen could see the two buses ahead on the road, driving slightly under the speed limit.

"But I say to you, brothers and sisters, that we must show them we cannot be intimidated! We need time to prepare for Ascension, and your job is to give us that time. I ask this of you only because I know you are more than capable. I've chosen each and every one of you for this task because I know you have it in you to carry this burden. But it's not a burden you will carry for long. This, I promise you. Soon, we will all Ascend. We will show the world that they, too, can come."

The mood on the bus was strange. Some people, a minority, were calling out in assent to the things Beck was saying. Most everyone else on the bus was silent. No one dared question their mission, which hadn't yet been spelled out for them. But the presence of the guns and the fact that there had been an assassination attempt on Beck left little to the imagination.

Jensen thought he sensed trepidation. He *hoped* he did.

"I am not angry," Beck said over the speakers. "I couldn't be angry with anyone so lost as the people who ordered my death. No, I couldn't. But I am disappointed. My heart is heavy, but my hand has been forced. And the only way to ensure that the Ascension happens as planned is to show the people who would have me killed that we will not be stopped! There will be no hell on Earth—because we won't allow it to happen. We will complete our mission. We will complete it because you are divine soldiers. And by fighting this battle, you will ensure that we win the war."

This is insane, Jensen thought as Beck continued talking. *There's no way these people will kill in cold blood. No way. Suicide's one thing, but this . . .*

He knew he had to do something, but he wasn't sure what. And as they grew closer to Dalewood, the fear grew until it was a force, sitting on his chest, making it hard to breathe. His hands shook, and he felt a sudden urge to use the bathroom. Fear sweat sprang up on his skin, his armpits growing suddenly wet.

They came into Dalewood along the main drag. It was about lunchtime, and there were people on the sidewalks, heading to lunch or doing their shopping. Many of them glanced up at the caravan of school buses, probably wondering who they were and where they were going.

They passed the sheriff's station, with two marked cruisers parked out front.

Jensen looked out the front windshield and saw the lead bus pull diagonally across the street, blocking both traffic lanes. The penultimate bus stopped, followed by Jensen's. A glance back revealed a look at the other buses. The last one pulled across the street, just like the first.

The driver's portable radio crackled, and Jensen listened hard, trying to hear the words over the deafening sound of blood rushing in his ears and Beck's incessant preaching. He couldn't make out what was said.

Beck suddenly stopped talking through the speakers. There was silence, save for the honking of a car horn from up ahead. Jensen looked out the window. There was a young couple walking on the sidewalk with an infant in a stroller. They looked at the buses with open curiosity.

"Now is the time," Beck said, his disembodied voice sounding suddenly like God to Jensen. That was the power he held. "Get off the bus and gather the people into the street and wait for my command. Those who fight you will have to die, I'm afraid. We cannot save their souls. This is the most important thing you've ever done in your life. And if you're scared, it's only because you've slipped back into your old, toxic way of thinking. Be not scared, for I am with you. This is the only way."

Several people on Jensen's bus stood up and started off.

"Let's go, Jensen," Fayden said, pushing from the window seat.

Jensen seemed to be operating on autopilot. A terrible calm had come over him. As if his fear had reached a crescendo and his brain had shut off all but its most basic functions to preserve itself. He stood up and joined the others in the aisle as they all filed off the bus. As the people in town saw the passengers get off the six buses, all of them armed with military-style weapons, they screamed. And they ran for their lives.

***

Vogel was among the first passengers off the lead bus. He'd been unsure whether the cultists would go along with the plan. But he shouldn't have been worried. Beck had been manipulating them for years. This was the culmination of a lot of work, and they would do whatever Beck asked. Sure, there would be a couple of do-gooders who would protest, but they would be easily silenced.

The two drivers who were honking at the bus for blocking traffic suddenly stopped as Vogel raised the rifle and aimed it toward them. The driver of the closest vehicle reversed, backing his Chevy truck into the sedan behind him.

Vogel smiled as people began screaming. He moved quickly, running back along the line of buses and shouting for the Emissaries to take hostages. He slowed as he came to the sheriff's station, keeping close to the wall so he wouldn't be seen from inside.

He paused fifteen feet from the door, raising his M4, sliding the safety off, and waiting.

He didn't have to wait long.

The glass-and-metal door to the sheriff's station swung open, and a man in a tan-and-brown uniform stepped out, confusion written all over his face. He seemed to sense Vogel, turning toward him even as he reached for his holstered sidearm.

Vogel pulled the trigger twice in quick succession. Two holes appeared in the man's chest in a tight grouping, one slightly higher than the other. He stumbled, shock overcoming confusion on his paling features.

Vogel was moving even before the deputy finally fell backward on the sidewalk and convulsed in his death throes. The blond man pivoted as he came to the sheriff's station door. He couldn't see well because of the sunlight reflecting off the glass, but he saw a blur of movement and fired five times, shattering the glass door.

He stepped over the dead deputy and looked inside, seeing no one. Then he yanked the door open with one hand, smacking it into the dead deputy's shoulder as it completed its arc. Moving over crunching glass, Vogel stepped into the station and moved swiftly to the desk, aiming the gun over and down.

A second deputy, grizzled and gray-haired, lay on the floor, struggling to pull his gun out. He had a bullet wound in his left arm and one on the left side of his neck. Vogel put two more bullets in him, both in the head. The man's hand went limp, and his gun clattered to the linoleum floor.

Vogel quickly cleared the rest of the station before heading back outside. He'd heard a couple of gunshots and some more screaming as he took the deputies out, but as he came out of the sheriff's station, the town was eerily silent. He was impressed with how well the Emissaries had done. They had people gathered in small groups in the street and on the sidewalks. The civilians sat, crying and pleading as their captors—most of them in white pajamas or blue-and-black outfits—aimed their weapons down at them.

Doors to the various shops and restaurants were opening, Emissaries escorting people out to join the other civilians.

"Good," Vogel said as he walked. "Suzerain is so proud of you all. Make sure they don't move. If they move, shoot them."

A woman in white pajamas was waving to Vogel from down the street. She had a concerned look on her face, so Vogel double-timed it down. She was in front of a little Italian restaurant, holding her rifle with one hand.

"What is it?" he asked.

The woman gestured inside, then led the way through the wooden door.

Several Emissaries stood inside the small one-room restaurant, pointing their weapons at a middle-aged man kneeling on the floor. Nearby, an Emissary Vogel recognized lay dead on the ground with two gunshot wounds in his chest.

"He killed him," the woman from outside said, gesturing at the kneeling man. One of the Emissaries standing guard held up a revolver in explanation.

"What should we do? He killed one of ours?" the woman asked.

Vogel raised his rifle and shot the man between the eyes, the inside of his skull splashing against a maroon tablecloth behind him.

"Help clear these buildings," Vogel said. "Get everyone else out into the street. And be careful."

The Emissaries looked at Vogel with wide eyes and gaping mouths. He ignored them and walked back outside. If they didn't see this for what it was, that was on them. He wasn't about to delude himself. It was all or nothing now.

As he glanced around outside, he realized that these scattered groups of hostages wouldn't do. He looked around and saw Jensen standing there next to Fayden. Jensen had no gun, and Fayden carried two. They were just standing around like a couple of statues.

"Hey!" Vogel yelled. "What the fuck are you doing? Why aren't you helping?"

Fayden looked from Jensen to Vogel. "He's checked out. Useless."

Vogel sighed. "Well, you're not useless. Let's get all the hostages over on this side of the street. Put them all on the sidewalk here. The buses will make a nice barrier. We can keep an eye on them all easily that way. Until we hear from Suzerain."

Fayden nodded and went to it, going from group to group on the street beyond the buses and getting everyone to move.

Vogel stood aside and watched, paying close attention to the civilian girls. He made a mental note of a couple who looked like they were in their late teens or early twenties. Just how he liked them.

After fifteen minutes, they'd gathered up all the hostages and had them sitting on the sidewalk, facing out. Vogel wasn't about to count them all, but he figured there were over two hundred of them. Most were adults, because it was a school day, but there were a few infants and toddlers, still too young for school.

He then started to put his plan into place. He stepped behind the nearest bus, unclipped his radio, and brought it up to his mouth. He pretended to have a conversation with Beck, whispering into the radio and then listening, purely for the benefit of any Emissaries around.

After a few minutes, he went back around and moved down the line of captors, talking to only the Sentinels who had radios. "I just spoke to Suzerain," he said to each one. "He says our normal radio channel is compromised. He wants us to switch to six."

That done, he grabbed a couple of guys he trusted and told them to turn the radios off in the buses. He didn't know what Beck had planned, but he needed time to have his fun and prepare for a swift exit. He wasn't going to be interrupted by Beck's self-important bullshit. And by cutting off communication from the compound, he hoped he'd buy himself the time he needed.

Once he was sure the bus radios were off, he walked along the crowd again and eyed a pretty dark-haired girl who looked about eighteen. "You," he said, pointing at her, "come with me."

The girl's big eyes widened, and she looked to her left at the young man beside her. *Boyfriend?* Vogel thought. *Oh, this will be good.*

"Stand up right the fuck now," Vogel said. The people around the girl diverted their eyes. Many of them were sobbing.

The boyfriend's eyes grew hard, and he stood up. "No," he said.

Vogel laughed maniacally, putting his left hand to his belly as he turned his face to the sky. He stopped laughing abruptly and waded into the crowd. People scrambled out of his way as he gripped the young man with the high-and-tight haircut by the front of his collared shirt and pulled him out. The girl screamed as Vogel tripped her boyfriend, sending him sprawling into the street. The boy landed on his hands and knees in the gap between the curb and the nearby bus. Vogel was on him before he could even turn around, slamming the butt of his gun into the back of his head.

The boy went down, and Vogel kicked him in the side of the head, snapping his skull sideways and splitting the skin over his cheekbone.

"Stop! Stop!" the girl shouted. "I'll go with you, just please, stop!" Tears streamed down her pretty young face. That was good. That was just how Vogel liked them.

He stepped away from the young man and grabbed the girl by the wrist, leading her down the edge of the sidewalk as she sobbed and the faces of the captured followed hesitantly.

Vogel led her into an antique furniture store. On the way, they passed Jensen, still standing like a statue. Vogel didn't notice as he passed, but Jensen's head moved. His gaze followed Vogel and the girl until they disappeared inside the store. And it wasn't the blank face of a man who was checked out. It was the face of a man who was unspeakably angry.

Chapter 38

TROUBLE MOVED FROM BUILDING to building, listening first and then looking through the windows to make sure they weren't occupied. Most of them were the same, with thirty cots and thirty footlockers. But as he came toward the end of the main rows, he found several smaller buildings with only twelve cots each. There was more room between cots and there were even some personal effects on the walls, which was something he hadn't seen in any of the other buildings.

He peeked around the corner of the last building and saw that it wasn't really the last. There were five more buildings, all in a row, some fifty yards away. As he looked at the nearest of the three buildings, he noted the bars on the windows. Jensen had said the children were kept in those buildings. He'd seen them at night and only briefly, but Trouble was now sure they were the same ones. And if the children were still in there . . .

He looked left and right, seeing no one around. He sprinted across the fifty yards, breathing hard and thumb throbbing as he came to a crouch under a barred window. There was a man's voice coming from inside. It was muffled, but Trouble was sure it was Raymond Beck's voice. It sounded like a recording. He raised up and looked inside but saw nothing but blackness. It took him a moment to realize the window was blacked out from the inside.

He moved to the next window, but it was blacked out, too. Besides the recorded or transmitted voice from inside, he could sense that the building was occupied. There wasn't talking or movement, but the silence underneath the muffled voice was not empty. It was a full silence. There were people in there. Probably children.

He moved to the front door, pausing to look down the dirt path that led away from the buildings. He could see the top of the church building just barely through the trees. It was down a gentle slope and perhaps a quarter of a mile distant.

Turning his attention back to the heavy wooden door, Trouble clutched the handle awkwardly with the fingers of his left hand; he didn't want to take his right hand away from the rifle grip and the trigger.

The doorknob wouldn't turn. It was locked.

Trouble cursed under his breath and looked around again. He thought about going to find Beck and Carmen, hoping they weren't on one of the buses. But what if they were? What if they were gone, but the kids were still here? And what if they were in danger? No, he needed to get into one of these buildings to see what was going on.

But he didn't have a set of lock picks. He couldn't kick through the heavy door. And he wouldn't risk trying to shoot the door open.

But there was one thing he could do that might just work.

He could knock.

***

As far as he could tell, there wasn't a peephole or any other way to look outside to see who was at the door. So he knocked, using his left hand and wincing as the movement jostled his broken thumb.

"Suzerain wants the children now," he said, just above his normal talking voice. It was a gamble.

And as moments passed, Trouble thought it wasn't going to pay off.

Then he heard movement from the other side of the door. He heard a key slide into the lock from the inside, then the sound of the heavy deadbolt disengaging. The knob turned. The door would open inward. He took a step back. As soon as the door was open an inch, he kicked with his right foot, putting all his two hundred and ten pounds behind it.

The heavy wooden door slammed into the woman opening it, throwing her onto her back into the dark room. Trouble stepped up and pointed the rifle at the woman, but he couldn't hold his gaze on her. He looked around the room, unable to help himself.

"What the fuck?" he said in an awed whisper.

There was a projector in the middle of the dark room, pointed up at the ceiling. The slightly distorted image of a speaking Raymond Beck was there, his voice coming out of speakers in the middle of the floor next to the projector.

There were thirty kids in the room, each of them lying on a cot, their heads tilted up with pillows and their eyes fixed on the moving image on the ceiling. Most of them were under twelve, and they wore the same white pajamas most of the adults wore—including the woman on the floor.

She was moving, backing away.

"Don't move," Trouble said, returning his attention to her. She did as she was told.

Trouble studied her for a moment. She had a scrunched-up face and short, wavy brown hair. She looked to be in her late thirties.

Although his eyes were fixed on her, he was listening to the Raymond Beck recording.

"You will get to be with your parents again. You will get to play and eat what you want and go to bed whenever you want. No more school. No more work. Won't that be great? But the only way to do this is to listen to me. To do what I say. Or you can listen to adults in colorful robes. They speak for me. If you do this, you will be rewarded. And soon. Very soon."

Beck droned on, moving from bribes to threats, speaking about how any form of disobedience would mean their parents would be hurt.

Trouble clenched his jaw and backed up, shutting the door behind him without turning around. With the door closed, the only light in the room came from the projector, but Trouble found a switch by the door and flipped it on. Several of the children looked over at him, squinting against the illumination. The rest of them kept staring up at the ceiling, even though the projected image had been severely diluted by the light.

Fumbling behind him, Trouble felt to see if the key was still in the interior lock. It was. He gripped it between the knuckles of his middle and index fingers, turning it to lock the deadbolt. Then he stepped back over to the woman. "How long have you been doing this?" he said, gesturing with his chin to the projector and speakers.

The woman pressed her lips together and shook her head, much like a child who doesn't want to talk. Trouble felt the rage building inside. Seeing the blank expressions on the children's faces pushed him to the edge, and he teetered there. He itched to kill the woman. To end the life of someone who would willingly do this to kids. To take away their autonomy, their individualism. To take away their future.

"How long?" he growled, pressing the gun stock hard into his shoulder.

The woman shook her head again. She crawled backward along the floor, getting close to the projector and the two small black speakers there. Trouble felt himself going over the edge. He moved with her, fighting an internal battle, trying to remember that she'd been manipulated in much the same way the children had. He shouted and stepped forward, kicking out with his right foot.

The speaker he kicked smashed into the projector, sending them clattering along the floor. The speaker stopped working, leaving only the other one to emit Beck's voice. But Trouble stepped up and smashed that one with his heel, snuffing out the cult leader's words.

Some of the kids were curling into defensive positions on their cots, hugging their legs to their chests. The others just stared blankly. Trouble spun to face the woman, who was getting up off the floor. He pushed her back down with his boot. "Don't fucking move!"

He looked around, breathing hard, wondering what to do. His eyes dragged across a shelf in the back wall of the room. The shelf was wooden, but there was a see-through metal grate hanging partially open, a disengaged padlock hanging from the hasp. Lined up on the metal shelves were large bottles of medication. He couldn't see what they were from this distance, but he had a pretty good idea.

"Get on your knees," he told the woman, taking his boot from her chest. "Crawl to the back of the room."

She made no move, so Trouble leaned down and pressed the barrel to her left knee. "Do it."

"Okay, okay," she said, talking for the first time since he'd come in.

She got on her hands and knees and crawled to the back. Trouble told her to stop next to the drug cabinet.

"What is all this?" he demanded. "You drug them every day?"

The woman didn't answer. Just cowered on the floor, her eyes cast down.

Trouble read the labels on the large bottles. The bottles were the kind pharmacists had on their shelves. The kind of containers that came directly from the drug companies. There were no little orange bottles with white caps. No prescriptions with names on them.

Trouble yanked the lockable grate open all the way and swept a shelf off with the barrel of the gun, knocking the bottles down onto the woman's head in a rattle of pills on plastic.

"What the fuck is this?" he shouted.

When he got no answer, he moved across the aisle and threw open the closet door there. His anger had taken over, and he didn't even know what he was looking for. He just knew he had to do something, otherwise he'd end up killing the woman groveling on the floor amid the pill bottles. And as much as his anger wanted him to do just that, he knew it wasn't right.

Looking in the closet underneath the tankless water heater, a solution presented itself. There were several sets of flex cuffs in there, made of thick black zip ties. He knew they were used on unruly children, but he tried not to dwell on this. He grabbed a pair and stepped back over to the woman.

He forced her into the bathroom at the back of the building, then cuffed her to the sink pipe, much like he'd cuffed the man in the adult barracks. He moved back out into the main room and looked at the children, his anger waning from a boil to a steady sizzle.

"Don't do anything that man says," he said. "Just stay here and don't do anything."

It was no use, but he'd had to say something. There would be a long road ahead for these kids, provided Trouble could get them out of here alive. But a long road was better than no road at all.

He moved to the door and unlocked it, extracting the key afterward. Then he peered out of the building, seeing no one. He stepped out, locked the door from the outside, and then moved off toward the church building.

It was time to end this. Or give his life trying.

Chapter 39

"This isn't right," Jensen said softly, looking at the recently closed door to the antique furniture store. Ever since getting on the bus, he felt like he'd been slipping ever deeper into a nightmare. Even his movements, as sluggish as his thoughts, added to the unreality of the situation. But the blatant violence Vogel had inflicted on the young man did something to awaken him. And then the look on the girl's face as Vogel led her into the furniture store did the rest.

He was swiftly waking from his daze. But he was still in the nightmare. There was still a large group of people being held hostage by what Jensen had thought of as his family. Not anymore. He couldn't do it. Couldn't stand by and let Vogel have his way with the girl. Couldn't let Beck order the mass murder of all these people.

Even a week ago, Jensen would've laughed at the possibility of Suzerain ordering the deaths of one person, let alone two hundred. Now he knew anything was possible. Anything at all.

He knew that these weren't all the people from town. Not even close. They were just the ones who'd been unlucky enough to be eating lunch or shopping when the buses came rolling in. There were others, calling 911 right now. But Jensen couldn't wait. He'd heard the gunshots from across the street when they'd first arrived. From the sheriff's station. Help would be too long in coming.

And if he didn't do anything to try and stop this insanity, he would be just as guilty as his former family members. His former Paralls—those traveling a parallel path.

No longer were their paths parallel.

They were about to collide.

"This isn't right," he said as he turned, his voice rising.

A petite redheaded woman Jensen knew well was nearby. She looked up from the hostages at Jensen, brows knitting together.

"Jessica," he said, approaching her, "you know this isn't right. This isn't why we joined this group. Not even close. You know it. I know you do."

"Shut up, Jensen," Fayden warned, rushing over from where he'd been standing near the beaten kid.

Everyone within hearing distance was looking at Jensen. The hostages with hope in their eyes, the Emissaries with a mix of anger and confusion.

"Nothing good will come of this," Jensen said, ignoring Fayden. "You all know it in your hearts. This is not the way to salvation. This is not how we become better."

"I said shut *up*," Fayden said, reversing his weapon and slamming the butt into Jensen's stomach. The other gun, held on a strap over his shoulder, fell to the crook of his arm with the movement.

Jensen doubled over in pain, taking a single breath before screaming at the ground, "This isn't right!"

Fayden kneed him in the face, sending him crashing onto his back and falling off the sidewalk into the gutter. Blood poured out of his nose.

"Think back to the people you were," Jensen called out from the ground, his voice nasally as he held one hand to his nose.

"Would you ever have held a gun on innocent people? Would you?"

Fayden stepped forward to deliver another blow, but Jessica called out, "He's had enough, Fayden! Let him be."

Fayden looked around at the other Emissaries, reading their expressions. He hesitated.

"We're not supposed to kill," Jensen continued, nearly crying now. "Even babies understand that. We're not supposed to kill another human. And that's just what he's going to ask of you. You can't do it. You know it's wrong. You can feel it like I can. I know it. This is *wrong*!"

The Emissaries seemed to be getting uncomfortable. They could no longer look their captives in the face. They were glancing at each other, trying to see what the crowd would do. It was the same thing they'd been doing ever since being assimilated into the cult. Peer pressure kept the whole thing together. Fear of going against the grain. A product of human evolution, deep-seated and difficult to ignore. Essential for a functioning civilization. For protection against being cast out into the cold, dark, predator-filled night. But maybe it would work against the cult this time. Maybe.

"These people have done nothing to deserve this," Jensen called out, still from the ground. "They are completely innocent. They had nothing to do with the attempt on Suzerain's life. Nothing! Please, just search your heart. Search it and—"

Jensen's face blew apart with the sound of a gunshot. His left eye and nose were replaced with a gory, gaping hole. His mouth moved up and down, his right eye wide. Then he laid his head back down, gently, as if going to sleep in the gutter. And in a way, he was.

Vogel stood ten yards away, just outside the antique furniture store. His M4 was pressed to his shoulder, finger on the trigger. His face was twisted in naked fury as he stared down at Jensen's body. He looked up at Fayden and opened his mouth to chastise the man. But before he could get a word out, another gunshot rang out.

Blood sprayed up in a pink mist as Vogel went down on the sidewalk.

Fayden pivoted, raising his gun up to point it at the shooter. But Jessica was ready for it. She moved to point her gun at Fayden, getting the barrel lined up on him before he could get his sighted.

"Drop the guns," she told him. He still had the second one hanging off his left arm, which had hampered his ability to get the other one up on time. He dropped both guns.

"Now get lost," Jessica said.

Fayden looked around, then turned and bolted between two buses.

Jessica then turned her attention back to her fellow Emissaries, who looked on with mounting confusion. "Do what you want," she shouted. "Go back to the compound or go somewhere else. I don't care. But Jensen was right. We have to let these people go. You all know we do."

No one moved for a long moment. The hostages were completely silent. They seemed to be holding their breath.

"I'm going back to the compound," Jessica announced. "Anyone else want to come?"

"Me," a man nearby said. "I'm coming."

"Good. Get on the bus."

"Me too," a woman said.

The sound of a distant bus engine roaring to life caught Jessica's attention, and she looked toward the lead bus, even though she could only see the back right corner of it. She realized that Vogel was no longer lying where he'd fallen. There was a small pool of blood on the sidewalk, but no other sign of him.

The lead bus moved, the portion of it she could see disappearing as the vehicle lumbered away, down the mountain, toward Taos. It didn't matter. She looked at the as-yet-undecided Emissaries.

"Who else is coming?" she shouted.

She got a couple of scattered commitments. Then the tide broke, and everyone started loading up onto the buses. A few men got Jensen's body loaded into the back of one of the buses on Jessica's suggestion.

A few of the hostages ran away the first chance they had. The others stayed still, like deer frozen in headlights. But when the buses were all loaded up and rolling, looking for a place to turn around so they could head back home, Jessica looked out the window and saw the young girl Vogel had dragged into the furniture store. She was running toward her boyfriend, who was being helped along by a couple of good Samaritans.

A shudder ran through Jessica as she thought about that. She knew Vogel hadn't been alone with her long enough to do anything, but that wasn't the point. The point was, Jessica knew what had been happening and had done nothing to stop it.

Only Jensen had. And he'd paid for it with his life.

Chapter 40

THERE WERE TWO PEOPLE going in and out of the large church building, unloading cardboard boxes from a truck and bringing them inside. Trouble watched from the tree line, wondering what was in the boxes.

It didn't matter.

What mattered was finding Carmen and Mitchell's daughter.

As he stood from his crouch, he slid the M4's safety off. Then, as soon as a man grabbed a box from the truck bed and turned to bring it inside, Trouble ran. He closed the distance fast, getting to within thirty yards of the entrance before one of the men stepped back through the propped-open door. Trouble slowed, pointing his gun at the man. But the guy saw him and ducked back inside before Trouble could tell him to get on the ground.

Shit.

The door was still propped open, but he couldn't see inside from his angle. He quickly changed direction, putting the truck between him and the door. He moved in a half-crouch, pointing the rifle at the doorway, just over the top of the truck bed.

The two men who'd been unloading boxes were wearing the same black-and-blue security clothing that Trouble was wearing. But his attempt at disguise clearly hadn't worked. They hadn't been carrying weapons while moving the boxes, but he had to assume they'd left them inside.

Trouble reached the truck and moved toward its front to get a better angle on the doorway. He saw movement from inside and dropped down just as gunshots rang out. Bullets punched into the opposite side of the truck. Glass shattered as bullets passed through both front windows. Trouble crouched next to the front driver's side wheel. This made it so they couldn't shoot at his legs, and it also put the engine block between him and the shooter.

As soon as the firing stopped, he got onto his side on the ground, sticking his upper body beyond the wheel and aiming under the truck at the doorway. He fired four shots, moving the barrel after each one to increase his chances of hitting someone, even if he couldn't see them in the gloom.

Trouble heard a gasp of pain. He got to his feet again and fired over the truck's hood, then he took cover and waited a few seconds. No one returned fire.

He moved quickly to the back of the truck and circled around it to the open door, keeping the barrel trained on the doorway. As he reached it, he peered quickly inside, seeing a dead man on the floor of the wood-paneled anteroom. He had a bullet hole in his lower leg and another in his chest. The wooden doors leading to the nave were closed, but he could hear a tumult from beyond them. Trouble glanced up at the words, "Choose salvation over fear." He could hear fear in the voices from inside the nave. Men and women shouting. They were coming close.

Ducking into the anteroom, Trouble picked up the man's M4 rifle with the fingers of his left hand and stepped back out. He kicked the hinged metal doorstop up and swung the metal door closed on the man he'd just killed. He propped his M4 against the wall next to the door and turned his attention to the other gun. After extracting the magazine, he shoved the pilfered gun through the two metal door handles on the heavy double doors. He angled the weapon down so it wouldn't fall out easily when jostled. Then he put the thirty-round magazine in his left pants pocket. It barely fit, sticking out awkwardly.

He was sure there was a back or side door in there, but it didn't matter. He just needed some time. He had an idea that Carmen was still with Beck. Maybe they were both in the church. If that was the case, he wouldn't be able to get to them. Not through the front door. But he didn't think that's where they were. Beck was busy orchestrating the grand demise. He'd want to do it from his home. Until he was ready for one final show.

As for Shayna, Trouble didn't know where she was. Maybe back with the other children. If so, she was safe. For now.

He grabbed his rifle and ran past Vegretti's cruiser, which hadn't been moved, to the front corner of the church. He peeked around the corner with one eye, looking toward the group of cottages. Several people with guns were running toward him, while others stood guard in front of Beck's house.

He stepped out from the corner and raised his gun, firing toward the people running at the church. He didn't hit any of them. He didn't want to. All he wanted was for them to hit the dirt, which they did.

Spinning around, Trouble ran back to Vegretti's SUV and looked in through the front window. No keys.

The metal church doors behind him were banging against the M4 rifle. People were shouting from within.

He moved on to the truck and peered through the shattered passenger window. The keys were in the ignition.

Please work, he thought, glancing at the bullet holes in the front quarter panel. He ran to the back and glanced into the bed. There were four more boxes in the back of the truck—two smaller and two larger. He grabbed one of the smaller boxes from the bed, setting his gun down and ripping one of the cardboard flaps open with his right hand.

There were a dozen small plastic bottles inside. But they weren't like the ones he'd seen in the children's barracks. These were simple brown plastic bottles with white labels and white safety lids. He picked one up and read it.

Pentobarbital sodium. 25 Grams.

There was an expiration date on it, and a description of the contents, which said the drug was a white powder.

He wasn't familiar with pentobarbital, but it didn't take much imagination to determine its use.

Trouble glanced up at the far corner of the church. It wouldn't be long before the people he'd shot at figured out he wasn't there any longer. They probably already had.

He tossed the bottle back in the box and pulled one of the larger boxes over, ripping it open and gazing inside. It was filled with chocolate pudding cups.

The only thing missing was spoons, and the men had probably unloaded a box of plastic ones before Trouble got to them.

Drugs, pudding, and spoons. All you needed to make a last meal for the true believers. If this stuff had been here the whole time, Beck must have known it might come to this. Maybe he wanted it to. He sure as hell wasn't planning on leaving this life alone. He wanted company.

Trouble picked up his gun and hurried to the driver's side door, wrenching it open and sitting in broken glass. He set the rifle on the dash and turned the engine over. It started, but there was a strange smell and a loud whistling sound coming from under the hood.

As he put the truck into reverse, movement caught his eye up ahead. There was a woman at the corner of the building, sighting down on him with her rifle.

Trouble ducked as he hit the gas. The truck lurched backward as bullet holes peppered the windshield, tiny glass shards pelting him as he looked at the right side mirror to see where he was going. The truck bumped off the dirt road, and Trouble turned the wheel using the ball of his left hand, whipping the front of the vehicle around. The violent movement sent the M4 sliding off the dash toward him, and he stopped it from hitting him in the face with his right hand. He tossed it onto the bench seat beside him.

He slammed the gearshift into drive and hit the gas, still steering with the four fingers of his left hand as he got a firm hold on the rifle with his right. He steered in a wide circle in front of the church, dodging a few trees as he went. With his right hand, he set the M4's barrel on the passenger window frame and laid down covering fire, mostly aiming for the sheriff's cruiser. Four Emissaries took cover as bullets struck nearby.

He bumped back onto the dirt road beyond the church and continued toward the paved path that led to the group of cottages. With the nearest hostiles safely behind him, he laid the gun on the bench seat next to him again and pulled the seatbelt on. The whistling sound from under the hood had faded to a low hiss.

As he passed the cottages, he glanced down between them, catching a glimpse of Beck's cottage. There were five buildings total—four smaller ones bunched close together in a square and then Beck's larger one in the back, some twenty-five yards behind them. The guards outside Beck's house were tracking him. With the guards there, he felt certain Beck was still inside.

When he could no longer see Beck's house—blocked from sight by two of the other, closer cottages—Trouble turned right, heading down toward the cluster of houses. When he came abreast of a near cottage, he stopped the truck. The house was to his right, between him and the people at the church. The second house in line also prevented those guarding Beck's cottage from getting a direct line of sight on him. Still, he didn't have much time.

He popped the magazine out of the M4 and tossed it down beside him. He had lost count of his shots, but he knew he'd been approaching thirty. He pulled the other magazine—the one he'd taken from the pilfered gun—out of his pocket and inserted it into the M4. He figured he had at least twenty rounds in the magazine, but there was no way to tell for sure. There was no window, nor any notches, to tell how full it was. But he could tell just by its weight in his hand that it contained more rounds than the mag he'd just removed.

He took a deep breath, looking through the cracked and holey windshield. *If they're shooting at you, they're fair game*, he told himself. His logical mind told him to take it easy on these people. These guards. They'd been manipulated. Brainwashed.

But his instincts told him something else entirely. His instincts said that if he went easy on them, he was effectively killing every single one of them. Because, chances are, he would die. If it was a matter of saving all those kids, and all those people in the church, then he had no choice. There was no one else coming to end this. Not in time.

It was up to him.

And that meant he couldn't pull his punches.

He wrenched his eyes shut, trying to clear his head of the memories clouding it. Shayna. Melissa. Screams and fear and running away. That feeling of cowardice.

He opened his eyes and rocked back and forth in the seat, a yell starting deep in his throat. He punched the steering wheel with his left hand, the jarring pain in his swollen and discolored thumb giving him a clarity of purpose.

As his yell came to a crescendo, he took his foot off the brake and jammed it on the gas. And as he cleared the second building, bringing Beck's cottage into view, he propped the barrel of the M4 on the dashboard and put his finger inside the trigger guard.

Chapter 41

THE GUNFIRE STARTED TO his right and behind him, rounds clanging into the truck as Trouble realized someone had snuck up to the cottage he'd just passed and was now firing from it. There was nothing he could do about it but duck slightly in his seat.

Four guards—all men—were in front of Beck's cabin, and Trouble was speeding toward them at around forty miles an hour. He fired out the windshield as the truck bumped over rough ground. One of the men went down and another ran away, but the other two kept firing at him, putting holes in the hood and the windshield.

A sharp pain erupted in his right upper arm. He felt a spray of warm liquid hit the right side of his face. He'd been shot.

He kept firing.

Another of the men tripped and fell, but he was up again and running as Trouble closed the distance, aiming for the short staircase. The remaining man dove out of the way as the truck's front left tire hit the staircase at an angle. Trouble let go of the M4 as the front of the vehicle bumped savagely up, smashing through a wooden beam and half of the railing enclosing the small porch. Airbags deployed. Trouble was whipped against his seatbelt and the airbag as the truck slammed into the wall to the right of the front door. The windshield and the top of the truck smashed inward as the wall buckled and fell onto the vehicle.

Then it was over. The truck wasn't moving anymore.

The dented roof where the windshield met the metal was two inches from Trouble's head. He could see nothing but debris out the front of the truck. Pain seemed all-encompassing.

He looked for the M4 in the passenger footwell, knowing he had to move quickly. The passenger airbag had deployed, and it was already deflating. Still, he moved it to look for the gun. It wasn't there. He looked on the bench seat. Not there, either. Then he realized it had somehow ended up in his lap, barrel pointing toward the driver's side door.

As he reached for his seatbelt, he sensed movement to his left. He looked that way and realized that he was looking directly into Beck's living room. The bald guy with the scars on the left side of his face was standing next to one of the black couches. There was glass and rubble around his feet, but he seemed unharmed. And he was pointing a pistol at Trouble's head.

"You killed Mitchell," Trouble said. "And you tried to kill me." As he spoke, he moved his right hand slowly, trying not to move his upper arm at all. He found what he was looking for with his fingers.

The bald man smirked with the undamaged side of his face as he braced his arms for the shot. His finger whitened on the trigger.

Trouble pulled the trigger on the M4, shooting once through the door even as he ducked down to his right.

The bald guy fired a split-second after, the bullet smashing into the headrest where Trouble's head had been. It was a reactionary shot, which was exactly what Trouble had wanted. He knew there was no way he could've hit the man through the door. Not even close. But it had thrown him off. Scared him.

Trouble had barely controlled the gun because of the recoil from the shot, but he managed to keep hold of it. He pulled the stock to his shoulder, but he stayed down. The bald man fired again and again as he moved deeper into the house. The shots were designed to give him time to move, so they weren't the most accurate. Still, they both came close.

Trouble sat up, sticking the barrel out the window and leaning to look for the man. He didn't see him. He'd probably ducked into one of the back rooms.

Trouble unlatched his seatbelt and levered himself up into the window, keeping the barrel trained on the hallway. Now that he had a better view of the house, he noticed that the side door from the kitchen was open.

He pulled his legs out of the truck, swiveling and then hopping down onto the small pile of debris. There was no sign of the man. But there was noise coming from outside. Trouble turned around and aimed the barrel at the front door, which was just a few feet from where he'd run the truck into the house.

The door opened slowly, just a few inches. The barrel of a gun poked through the gap.

Trouble fired twice, directly at the door. The sound of a body falling outside was all he needed to hear. He stepped forward and slammed the door shut with his left foot, then locked it before stepping aside, just in case someone else was out there and they wanted to fire through the door.

The truck had come through the dining room wall, slamming into, and making a mess of, the table and chairs there. The broken furniture was pressed up against the marble countertop separating the kitchen from the dining area.

Trouble listened for movement in the house, but heard none. He was starting to think that he'd been wrong. Carmen and Shayna hadn't been here.

But that open kitchen door made him think.

He stepped to the curtained window in the front wall of the living room and peered out. He didn't see anyone. Just the other cottages and the footpath between them.

Turning around, he moved cautiously toward the kitchen and the hallway beyond. He glanced out the door, looking toward the church. And he saw them.

Beck. Shayna. Carmen. Carmen's sister. They were hustling toward the back of the church. Shayna had her arms wrapped around Beck's neck, and he was holding her to him with his left arm. She looked back toward the house. Toward Trouble. In Beck's right hand, he held a pistol on Carmen, making her move ahead of him. Carmen's sister, Megan, was carrying the little boy who'd been in the bedroom when Beck had killed Vegretti and Prado.

There were several security guards escorting them to the building. Including the bald guy.

Suddenly, Carmen turned around and yelled toward the house. She yelled a single word. A name. "Dylan."

Trouble understood immediately.

He cleared the rest of the house quickly, finding no one alive. He took the pistols off both the dead cops, putting one in his back waistband and one in his front. Then he stepped over next to the broken window, trying not to slip in the blood on the hardwood floor. He knew there were rifles pointed at the house. Surely centered on the kitchen door. Maybe the place was surrounded.

He gazed out the window at a shallow angle from where he was with his back to the wall, looking down toward the cliff. He didn't see anyone. He took a moment to inspect the wound on his right upper arm. It wasn't terrible. There was a chunk of flesh missing about the size and length of his pinky finger.

He turned and leaned to look out the window toward the church. He didn't see anyone. The group had disappeared around the building, probably going in through a back door.

He knelt next to Prado, the smell of evacuated bowels and coagulating blood rich in his nostrils. He fished the man's phone out of his pocket and tried to unlock it. It said his face wasn't recognized and asked for a pin instead.

He wasn't about to guess the pin, and Prado's face was half gone. So he moved over to Vegretti. The Sheriff's phone had a small circle on the back for fingerprint reading. Trouble lifted the dead man's index finger and pressed it against the circle. The phone unlocked.

Trouble dialed Dylan's number. His friend answered on the second ring.

"Hello?"

"It's me," Trouble said.

"Oh, Christ man. You okay?"

"I'm good. A little busy. You got something for me?" Trouble asked.

"Yeah. I've been trying to get ahold of you and Carmen. You guys aren't answering. I was worried something had happened."

"It's still happening. Beck's got Carmen. So unless you have something that might help me, I gotta go."

"Fuck," Dylan said, breathlessly. "I just might have something. Maybe."

Chapter 42

IT TOOK DYLAN LESS than a minute to describe what he had found. During that time, Trouble moved around the house, checking out every window, his confusion growing as the seconds ticked by.

"Send it," he said when Dylan had finished rushing through his explanation. "Send it to my email—the new one—right now. I don't know if it's enough, but it's worth a shot. I—" Trouble paused, stopping himself from saying goodbye. "Do you know what pentobarbital sodium is?"

There was silence for a beat before Dylan answered. "It's a barbiturate. Used in low doses as a sedative and for anxiety."

"And in high doses?"

"In high doses, it causes respiratory arrest. It's used for assisted suicide in some places."

"That's what I thought," Trouble said. "Okay, I really gotta go. If you don't hear from me in the next couple of hours, know I'm still mad about you stealing my girlfriend after we first met."

"I'll tell my wife you said hi," Dylan said, a somber smile in his voice. "Be careful."

Trouble moved out of the back bedroom and into the kitchen, looking out the open door toward the church. He still saw no movement. It worried him more than if he'd seen a dozen guys waiting for him. He navigated into the phone's settings and found the screen lock options, then selected the option to keep the phone awake for thirty minutes before locking.

He then pulled up an internet browser and logged into his email account, seeing that there was one new email from Dylan with a video file attached. He stuck the phone in his back pocket and then stepped toward the front door. It had been nearly five minutes since he'd seen the group disappear around the church. He thought about the bottles of pentobarbital and the pudding cups and knew he was quickly running out of time.

There was no one attacking him right now because Beck was rushing to make his final mark on the world. He knew he was going down, and he was determined to take as many people with him as he could. Or maybe he actually believed the shit he was peddling. Maybe he'd been peddling it for so long it was indistinguishable from reality.

Trouble stepped to the kitchen door, feeling a warm afternoon breeze against his skin. And as he stepped out onto the first of three concrete steps leading out the door, he half-expected a hail of gunfire to greet him.

***

"They're coming back," Rankin said to Beck. "I finally got ahold of someone, and they're coming back."

They were in the Sanctuary's control room, and Beck had been looking at the bank of monitors, taking in the different angles of the milling crowd in the nave. But with these words from Rankin, he snapped up, his mind reeling as his thoughts seemed to lurch and stutter in his head. "Coming back?" he shouted. "I didn't tell them to come back. What the fuck are they doing? Tell them to turn around. To go back into town and . . ." he trailed off, thinking what to do. He'd wanted a show of force, but after he'd lost radio contact with the buses, he'd known something was wrong. Now they were coming back. They had failed him.

"They say they're almost back," Rankin said.

Beck turned and looked at the back of the room, where Megan Marsden stood holding hands with Gibbs on one side and Angel on the other. Her sister was whispering fiercely into her ear, but the blank look on Megan's face, and her unwavering gaze glued to him, told Beck all he needed to know. She was his, and she always would be. *Until death do us part,* he thought. *Which will be very, very soon indeed.*

He'd never feared death. Not since he was a child. What he feared was obscurity and, as an extension, losing. He was too smart to lose. Much too smart for someone like Carmen Marsden or Terrence Rubble to beat. He had always known he'd leave his mark on the world, and he'd had a hell of a lot of fun in the process. But the time was drawing near. He was going to win. He *always* won.

"What do you want me to do?" Rankin asked, ever the faithful sycophant.

"Just get them back here," Beck said. "And where the fuck are the children?"

As if on cue, the bank of monitors showed the children being led inside by several adults. Some of them were so drugged they had to be carried. But they were here. That was the most important part.

He turned his attention to a screen that showed a shallow angle of the stage at the front of the nave. A group of adults was working like a factory line at several long folding tables. Four of them were unboxing the barbiturates and the pudding, then handing the items off to another four, who were working with plastic spoons to make room for the pentobarbital. They had an empty box nearby where they dumped the unneeded pudding. They then stirred the drugs in, left the spoon in, and set the pudding cups aside on a table, where four more adults grabbed two or three at a time, handing them out to the crowd.

Beck had given explicit instructions to ensure that no one ate the pudding until it was time. He wanted to savor the moment. The feeling of holding so many lives in his hands was a hundred times better than the high he got from cocaine. They knew what was coming. They *knew* they would all die, but they were still willing to do it because *he* said so. Well, at least the adults knew. The kids were too drugged to know much of anything. They would do whatever the adults told them.

It was the culmination of twenty years of work in perfecting his manipulation tactics, even going so far as to completely change the way he talked. He'd hoped for at least another year, but that had been wishful thinking. His team of lawyers could only hold off the lawsuits and squash the news stories for so long. And his team of assassins, his Deadly Divine, could only fake so many suicides before people started to get suspicious.

"Make sure all the exits are guarded by at least three Sentinels," Beck said. "But make sure they all get their pudding, too. We don't want to leave anyone out. And when the others get here in the buses, bring them directly in."

Rankin nodded and left the room. The two Sentinels standing guard outside the door glanced in at their leader as the scarred man left.

The kids had to go first, he knew. That way, if the adults got cold feet, they wouldn't have anything left to live for. At that point, dying was better than living with the knowledge that you killed your own kid. But Beck would be the one to feed the poisoned pudding to Angel. He would die with her in his arms. And who knows? Maybe they would travel to the afterlife together.

He turned and gazed at the little girl. His obsession with her hadn't started off as such. It was another of his little tests in the early days of the cult. He'd chosen her for no other reason than she was stunningly beautiful, with large eyes and hair the color of golden silk. He'd wanted to see if her parents would willingly part with her, allowing her to spend most of her time with Beck. And they had. That was when he knew that the possibilities were endless. He'd been sleeping with many of the women before then, but kids were different. If a parent was willing to give their child over to be raised by others, it was a sign of absolute faith.

But since then, he'd grown attached to the girl. She was like his own little living doll. And while he had never been attracted to children—he thought pedophiles to be the lowest of the low—he found that his love for the sweet, innocent child was much stronger than any physical attraction he felt for any woman or man. It was a pure love. And it would remain so until the end.

Sudden shouting came from out in the hall. Beck spun around and looked at the door. "He's coming!" someone outside shouted.

Rubble, Beck thought. "Someone fucking kill him already!"

Resonant gunfire erupted from nearby in the building.

Chapter 43

SHARDS OF SHATTERED GLASS fell at Trouble's feet as he stepped back from the window, bullets speeding out just inches in front of his face. He'd come upon the wide window at the back of the building while looking for a way inside. To his left, a series of rocky outcroppings like large steps led down to a natural clifftop platform with a fire ring and two chairs. His right arm, still stinging from the flesh wound, rested lightly against the concrete building as he waited for the gunfire to stop.

He considered running across or trying to crawl under the window—there was a few feet of clearance between the bottom of the picture window and the ground. There had to be a back door somewhere over there, on the other side of the building. But if there were people guarding the windows, there sure as hell would be people guarding the doors.

Running across wasn't a great idea. He could lay down some covering fire, but he'd never been a fast sprinter. And he'd never met anyone who could outrun a bullet. Crawling would put him in a vulnerable position. And he'd have to move over the broken glass, which would slice up his hands and knees—and it would make noise.

His mind seemed to get stuck in a loop, going over those two options again and again. Run or crawl? Run or crawl?

Then a voice inside seemed to make a decision. *Run*, it said. But it wasn't talking about running across the window, getting to the other side of the building. No, it was talking about a different kind of running. *Run, run, run away.*

Trouble backed away from the window before he knew what he was doing. *There's no way inside*, the voice said. *No way you can win. All you'll do is die. They've got every entrance covered. You can't do anything for her. You can't save her. But you can save yourself.*

He shook his head, swallowing hard. He rounded the corner of the building, glancing at the cottages off to his right. The voice told him to try the truck he'd crashed into Beck's house. Maybe it would still work. Maybe he could use it to run, run, run away.

He felt suddenly small. Defenseless, despite the three guns he had on his person. Years of hard-fought experience and the confidence that came with it seemed to melt away like morning fog under a warm sun. He was all pain and fear, and he started off toward the crashed truck, thinking of nothing but getting away from that fear, that pain.

He glanced over his shoulder as he moved with quick little steps across the distance. And as he came within fifteen yards of the cottage, the distant hiss of hydraulic brakes made him jump like he'd been struck in the back.

Up near the church, on the road, a faded yellow school bus was coming to a stop. He could see the front half of another one behind it, the back half obscured by the church.

Trouble kept moving, knowing he had to get out of the open so the people on the buses wouldn't see him. He looked at the truck in the front wall of the cottage. His feet seemed to want to take him that way. He could climb through the broken back window and get into the front seat. Then he could back out and drive out of this place. If these people wanted to die, they had a right, didn't they?

Then he thought about the buses. One of those would be his best bet. When he'd first got into the truck, after it had been shot, it was making strange noises. Crashing it through the front of a building certainly wouldn't have helped. But a bus—a bus was big and powerful and high off the ground.

Trouble changed direction and headed away from Beck's house and toward the four cottages arranged in a square with the footpath between them. He came to the corner of the back cottage nearest the church and peered around it. There were people filing off the two buses. Some of them were dressed like him, in black jeans and blue shirts. Others wore white pajamas. A few of them had green shirts and tan pants—the work uniform. The mood among them seemed strange. Subdued. They had no weapons—at least none he could see.

They were all headed for the church.

He ran back to the other side of the building, turning the corner and starting up the footpath between the two pairs of cottages. He could wait for the bus to empty and then take it, driving out of this place.

The first bus to arrive was empty by the time Trouble came up to it. He looked down the road and counted five buses. People were still disembarking from the last two in line, but there was a large crowd in front of the church doors—people waiting to go inside. He could see a couple of armed guards outside the front doors, looking around and occasionally scanning the crowd.

Crouching, he stepped up into the bus, seeing that the keys were in the ignition. As he got up next to the seat, he glanced back into the vehicle. There were guns propped in nearly every seat. Some were piled in the aisle at the very back. He wondered what the hell they had gone and done. It didn't smell like gunpowder, so maybe they hadn't used the guns. Hopefully.

He looked out the side windows at the milling crowd in front of the church. Blue and white and green shirts. The two guards were the only ones with visible guns.

I can get in, he thought, turning to step off the bus without really thinking about it.

Then he stopped at the top of the steps, that voice in his head—that childish voice that was somehow unaltered yet completely changed by the passage of years—screamed with fear and desperation for him to stop. To run. To save himself.

Trouble looked at the keys in the bus's ignition. The voices warred inside his head. The fear was winning out. It was the louder of the two voices.

Trouble clenched the M4 in his hands and shut his eyes, willing both voices to stop, clearing his head. He listened to his gut.

Despite his spotty education, Terrence Rubble had taken it upon himself to gain knowledge in any manner he could. And one of the things he'd been partial to as a moody teenager was poetry. One particular line from one particular poem rang out as he stood in the bus, eyes wrenched shut. *I am large, I contain multitudes.*

Whitman had it right. The trick was learning to use those multitudes to your advantage.

He opened his eyes and set the M4 aside, lying it on the first seat behind the driver's. Using spit and the sleeve of his shirt, he wiped the blood off his face as best he could. There wasn't much he could do about the bloody wound on his right upper arm.

The voices in his head still warred, but there was always some kind of voice droning on in there. He concentrated not on the words of fear and their associated feelings. Instead, he reached deeper and found the place inside that knew what he had to do. That place wasn't always easily accessible. And it was easy to forget it was there, especially when panic was going strong. But he concentrated on it as he stepped off the bus.

As he moved around the front of the bus, heading to the other side to join the crowd with as little exposure as possible, he pulled Vegretti's phone out of his back pocket. It was still unlocked, and he tapped it a couple of times to reset the thirty-minute timer. He put it back in his pocket and then pulled out one of the pistols he'd taken from the two dead cops.

It was a Glock 22. He released the magazine and checked the witness holes, seeing that there were fifteen rounds there. He put the magazine back in and checked the chamber. There was a round inside. Sixteen 40-caliber rounds.

He repeated the process on the other gun, which was also a Glock 22. It had sixteen rounds, as well. Trouble was familiar with Glocks, so he knew they didn't have a manual safety like some other semi-automatic pistols. There were two internal safeties and a trigger safety that would prevent a Glock from firing when dropped or fumbled. He knew he'd have to hold the Glock properly and squeeze the trigger deliberately in order to shoot.

Both guns were ready to fire.

With the pistols back in his waistband and covered by his shirt, Trouble moved along to the back of the second bus, where he turned the corner and moved into the slowly dwindling crowd. He slouched, sinking his six-foot-two-inch frame down and hanging his head. A woman next to him glanced into his face and then looked away, seemingly disinterested. The two guards on either side of the open double doors seemed to be looking past the crowd, possibly thinking an attack would come from beyond the buses or from either side of the large building.

He was twelve feet from the door, his heart beating so hard he thought it should be audible to anyone near him. Using his peripheral vision, he stayed vigilant, waiting for someone to recognize him and scream out.

He was ten feet from the door, near the back of the crowd.

The guard to his left scanned the crowd, his gaze flicking across Trouble.

He was eight feet from the door, the back of Vegretti's SUV a few feet to his left.

The crowd murmured. Feet shuffled.

Fear swelled in Trouble. That voice was screaming for him to turn around and run. It was too late for that. He was going to get inside. He was going—

Out of his peripheral vision, Trouble saw the guard to his left jerk violently as he recognized Trouble and went to raise his gun in the same instance.

"It's him!" the man shouted.

Trouble dropped into a crouch and pulled the Glock 22 from his front waistband in one swift movement. Then he lunged out of the crouch, leading with his left shoulder and slamming into the man in front of him, who flew forward and crashed into a woman before they both went tumbling into the guard.

The small crowd around him erupted in chaos as some people screamed and ran forward while others looked around, their reaction delayed by confusion or slow synapses.

Trouble went back into a crouch after slamming into the man, knowing he'd bought only seconds. He moved a few feet to his right, using the roiling crowd for cover before popping up and aiming at the other guard. The man had his gun up, but it was pointed in the wrong direction. His eyes went wide, and he shifted, swinging his gun toward Trouble.

Trouble fired his weapon from his tiptoes over the heads of those still trying to get inside. The guard slammed back against the propped-open door and then fell from view, leaving a gory red smear on the door.

Everyone was screaming or shouting now. One man in white pajamas dove at Trouble, trying to tackle him to the ground. Trouble dodged him and elbowed the man in the side of the head before turning his attention back to the other guard. But the man was gone. There were people running everywhere now, and Trouble ran forward, shoving through the throng of panicked people and into the anteroom. A woman leaped at him, dragging her nails across his face before he sent her crashing into the ground with a shove.

A man came at him, but Trouble pointed the pistol at him, and the guy turned around quickly.

He could see into the nave through the open wooden doors, but the doorway was packed with people trying to get inside the large room while others tried to get out to join the fight.

There was a smaller door to his left, in the corner of the room. People were pouring through into some kind of hallway that looked as if it skirted the nave. He ran to the door and ducked into the hall.

Chapter 44

"No, no, no!" Beck shouted at the bank of monitors in the building's control room.

Chaos had erupted in the nave following the gunshot from the front of the building. The Sentinels in the large room had all rushed toward the main doors, but there was a mad scramble of people from the buses trying to get in, creating a bottleneck. Elsewhere in the large room, people huddled among the seats. Children stared blank-eyed toward the tumult, while adults cowered in fear and confusion. Many of those who'd already received their deadly pudding had cast their cups aside to grab children or loved ones, ready for action.

Someone had radioed that Rubble was trying to get in through the front, but Beck couldn't see him on any of the monitors. The two main purposes of the cameras in the building were to record his speeches and to look for signs of individuality among his flock. Dissent started small, he knew. And using the hidden cameras to sniff out unease or doubt had also added to his carefully cultivated prophetical mystique. When he called those people in to meet with him, somehow knowing that they were having what Beck called "toxic thoughts," they were in awe of his powers, whether they openly admitted it or not.

When designing the place, he hadn't considered the fact that one person could thwart his plans. He'd thought his biggest threat would come from the government, in the form of a standoff, which would've given him plenty of time to order the deaths of the seven-hundred-and-change.

This lack of foresight meant he had no cameras in the anteroom or the adjacent hallway that led from the small anteroom to the backstage area, where only a handful of people were supposed to go. He was blind. And if Rubble was smart, he would use that hallway to get to the back.

But it didn't matter how smart Rubble was. Beck knew he was smarter. He could see into the nave, and he knew that it was the one place Rubble wasn't. It was also where he needed to be to give his final speech. Surely the guards could protect him that long. And if not, he'd have plenty of human shields at his disposal.

Beck spun from the monitors, running to grab a headset from a small rack on the wall. As he put the earpiece in and clipped the transmitter to the back of his white pants, his gaze swept the room, landing on Megan Marsden. She stood against the wall next to the door, still holding hands with Angel and Gibbs. Her sister was standing nearby, her eyes fixed on the monitors. Next to her stood a Sentinel, pointing a weapon at the woman; Beck had called him in shortly after the first gunshots came from the back of the building, several minutes ago now.

"Stay here," he told Megan, moving forward and holding out his hands.

Marsden let go of the children and raised her hands to touch Beck's.

"This is it," he said. "It's what we've been waiting for. But I need you back here to manage the audio. There's no one else.

They won't be able to hear me if we don't have the PA system working."

Megan nodded, smiling, tears in her eyes. "But when the time comes . . ."

"I'll make sure someone brings you a pudding," Beck said. "As soon as I eat mine, you can eat yours back here. We'll Ascend together, even if we're not in the same room."

"Megan, don't listen to him!" Carmen shouted, moving toward them, ruining the moment.

Beck spun, backhanding her. Carmen's head whipped sideways, and she stumbled back against the wall. Beck moved after her, punching her with a closed right fist, knocking her down. He kicked her twice while she was on the ground, eliciting pained cries. Then he grabbed her by the hair and dragged her up.

"You're coming with me," he said. "And so are you two." He pointed at the children.

Carmen was much taller than him, so Beck had to shift his grip to the back of her hair, pushing her ahead of him. The two children looked up at Megan. Beck paused at the door and looked over, impatient. Megan gazed at him with wide eyes and a slack mouth. She seemed to snap out of it when she saw he was looking at her.

"Go on," she said to the children. A tear rolled down her cheek.

Beck thought maybe he'd gone too far with her sister. It didn't matter. Not now. She would do what he said. There was nothing else she could do. He had her firmly in his grasp. As he moved out the door, shoving Carmen ahead of him, he growled at the guard inside the room to follow in case Carmen tried anything. As he passed the two guards stationed outside the door, he told them to stay there and protect the room until they heard him give the signal.

"We don't have our desserts," one of the men, Reyes, said.

"I'll have Rankin bring some for all of you," Beck said. "Don't worry. We'll all Ascend together. The Devils won't win."

The group of three adults and two children moved out the door and to the right, around a curve in the hallway. They moved through another set of doors and into the backstage area. The curtains blocked their view into the nave, but Beck could hear people shouting in there, still trying to sort through the chaos at the main doors.

He threw Carmen down onto the floor and told the guard to kill her if she moved. Then, like flipping a switch, he transformed from the furious and desperate savage into the serene patriarch and prophet. He grabbed Gibb's hand with his left and Angel's with his right. And they walked out onto the stage.

Chapter 45

TROUBLE SHOUTED FOR PEOPLE to get down on the ground. Some of them did, others just ran away. He had tried to hold the other pistol in his left hand, to cover both directions as he moved down the hall, but his thumb was broken in such a way that he couldn't exert enough force to hold the weapon. The pain had been immense as he tried to grip the gun, so he quickly gave up. Still, he took shuffling sideways steps, whipping the gun back and forth as he moved down the hallway, ready for hostiles to come from either direction.

The hall was curved, following the shape of the oblong nave. Blue-and-gray industrial carpeting coated the floor, and there was a large mural on the wall across from him, depicting Beck in a Christlike pose as he floated up toward a too-bright corona. There were smaller figures painted below Beck in the mural, arms stretched up toward the man as they, too, floated up.

"Move," Trouble said to a woman on the ground. "Move to your right." She whimpered and shifted across the hall, giving Trouble room to get past. There were about a dozen people crouching in the hallway. He told them not to get up. "Stay put and you'll be fine. You'll all be fine."

As he rounded the curve, he saw a small set of carpeted stairs leading up to a pale blue metal door. He glanced back one more time, then hustled along the hallway, coming to the stairs. There was a vertical rectangular window in the door, but he couldn't see through it from where he was.

Climbing the stairs, he braced his gun hand with his left as best he could. As he came to the penultimate stair, bullets blasted through the window. Trouble ducked and dove forward, banging into the door and sending a fresh bolt of pain through his right arm and shoulder. He twisted and reached up and shot blindly through the window four times.

He heard footsteps fading away on the other side of the door. They sounded strange to him. Almost too heavy.

Trouble glanced behind him at the three-quarters of the hall he could see. Some of the people were still there, face down on the floor, hands over their heads. Others had run away in the opposite direction.

He got to his knees, making sure to stay below the window as he reached out and turned the knob with the fingers of his left hand, pulling the door open a few inches. More gunfire came from the other side, denting the door and punching into the wall next to the staircase.

The shooter had changed positions after the first barrage and was now firing from a different angle. Trouble stood up, staying on the hinge side of the door. The door swung shut, and the firing stopped. He stepped back on the landing as far as he could, his back to the stairs. Pointing the gun and taking little sideways steps, he gradually brought more and more of the space on the other side of the door into view through the window.

There was movement.

Trouble fired and continued firing as he stepped around the window in an arc. He shot five bullets, which made a total of ten shots with the gun. And as he lunged forward and yanked the door open, he knew he had six shots left.

There was a T intersection about ten feet from the door. Trouble had seen movement on the right side of the inter- section—and that was where the shots had come from—but he couldn't discount a hostile on the left side, too. He moved cautiously forward, his gun pointed slightly right of center, his eyes softly unfocused, primed to sense any movement, any shadow. He couldn't hear for shit, thanks to all the gunshots, so sight was his only viable option.

And there it was. Movement on the right. A faint shadow stretching into the intersection as someone moved forward. Trouble swung his gun that way, leaning forward and slightly to his left, using his height to his advantage. He saw the barrel of the M4 rifle first, sliding up to the corner of the hall. He leaned a little more as the person came a little closer, sliding the barrel around the corner but not yet seeing Trouble. Then there was a right shoulder in view. Trouble fired at the sliver of body part he could see. He stepped forward with his right foot and fired twice more as he brought more body into view. The first bullet missed. The second two pulverized blood and muscle and vital organs. The man dropped to the ground, falling into full view.

It was the bald guy with the scars on his head. He was still alive, but fading fast. His eyes gazed up at Trouble, then swiveled away, fixing on something at the other side of the hallway—the left side of the T intersection.

Trouble pivoted, stepping closer to the right wall to get a better angle on the left side of the intersecting hallway. He saw what the scarred guy was looking at. A man with a gun, pointing it directly at Trouble. He had him dead to rights. Trouble waited for the bullets to fly in the second it took him to get his own gun fixed on the man. But they didn't fly. And in that second, Trouble was able to read the man's body language and the look on his face.

He was not much more than a kid. Eighteen or nineteen. His face was screwed up with fear. The M4 he held was shaking.

"You can just go," Trouble said in a loud whisper, looking into the kid's eyes. "Just go. I won't shoot you. I promise you that. Just put the gun down and go."

The kid's eyes moved down to Rankin. "Don't do that," Trouble said, tightening his grip on the trigger, feeling the trigger safety start to disengage.

"I believe it," the kid managed, looking back at Trouble. "I do."

"Believe whatever you want, kid," Trouble said. "But when you start killing innocent people over those beliefs, it's time to examine them pretty fucking closely."

"You're the one killing innocent people!" the kid shouted, strings of saliva falling from his mouth.

Trouble shook his head. "Anyone I've killed tried to kill me first. This all started when your bald pal here killed three people and took Mitchell's little girl. You think that's right? You think that's fair? Is that how you want the world to work?"

"Parall Mitchell was taken by darkness," the kid said. "Suzerain said so. He told us all."

Trouble breathed deeply. He didn't have time for a theological discussion. "Listen, kid. I'm giving you a chance to walk away. If you're going to stand by your beliefs, fine. Do what you gotta do. But it looks to me like your beliefs are shaking about as bad as that gun. Now look at my gun. Do you see it shaking?"

"No," the kid said.

"Right. So beliefs aside, who do you think will walk away from this confrontation? You or me?"

The kid didn't answer.

"Who do you think will walk away?" Trouble asked again, this time with force.

The kid lowered the M4 in answer, his cheeks wet with tears.

"Good," Trouble said. "Now put it down."

The kid did.

"Where's the control room?" Trouble asked.

"That way, I think," the kid said, pointing past the bald guy on the floor.

"Okay," Trouble said. "Get gone."

The kid moved past Trouble and headed down the hallway toward the shot-up door, head hanging low.

Trouble looked down at the scarred man. He was clearly dead, his eyes fixed on the place where the kid had been. Trouble leaned down and grabbed the M4 the man had dropped, leaving the Glock 22 with three rounds left in it. He thought about taking the kid's rifle, but he didn't know if it was even loaded or if it fired at all. He knew this one fired.

He didn't know how many rounds were left in it, so he stepped over and removed the magazine from the kid's rifle, sticking it in his left pocket as far as it would go. He glanced up, seeing there was a single office door there. He moved swiftly through the door, seeing that it was a small office with filing cabinets and a large safe. There were two desks there, both with closed laptops sitting in the middle of them, along with other normal office stuff. Two identical office chairs were pushed up against the desks. The kind with wheels on the bottom and built-in lumbar support. He thought this was probably where the cult kept track of all the money and property they took from their followers.

He moved out of the room and back toward the bald guy. Stepping over the dead man, he headed down the hall toward a set of double doors.

Chapter 46

THE DOUBLE DOORS WERE much the same as the single one Trouble had come through at the end of the curved hallway. They were metal, painted pale blue, and had vertical rectangular windows in them. But, unlike the other door, he couldn't see through these windows. There was something smeared on the other side of them, obscuring his view. It took him a moment to realize that it was pudding.

Best guess, someone had heard the shots during the little firefight just passed and wanted to hedge their bets. They smeared pudding on both windows so Trouble, if he survived, wouldn't be able to see through them.

But that also meant that anyone on the other side couldn't see what was happening on *this* side.

There were push bars on this side of the doors. Trouble stepped to the side of the hallway, his back to the wall. He held the M4 by the grip with the fingers of his left hand while he reached his right hand out and gently compressed the push bar, checking to see if the door was locked.

It wasn't.

He looked around, thinking. There were a couple of possibilities. One was that no one was waiting on the other side of the doors. That seemed overly optimistic and not at all plausible given Trouble's experience. Another possibility was that there were several guys waiting for him. A firing squad's worth of people, just waiting for one of the doors to open. While more likely than the first possibility, still not as likely as the third.

He guessed there were a couple of guys over there. Two. Maybe three. Still, three guys with M4 rifles was three too many.

But when had they put the pudding up on the windows? Had it been after Trouble had shot the bald guy? Or before?

If it had been after, they would have no way of knowing who was alive. Maybe they would hesitate for a split second to see who came through the door before they started working their trigger fingers like kids playing a video game.

But a split second wouldn't be enough. Not if there were three of them. Or even two. One guy might be doable. Maybe.

Trouble looked back at the dead guy on the floor. He went over what he'd seen in the office. And he came up with a plan. It was better than nothing. By about one percent.

***

Getting the stubby three-drawer filing cabinet onto the office chair had been the difficult part. But it hadn't taken him more than two minutes. Before that, he'd dragged the dead man out of the way to give him some room.

Now, he held the top of the black filing cabinet with his left hand, keeping it steady so it wouldn't fall over. The seat of the ergonomic office chair wasn't exactly the most level of surfaces.

He had the cabinet turned sideways in the seat, so the drawers were facing right. This allowed Trouble to rest the barrel of the M4 on the middle drawer's handle. It kept wanting to slip off, but with a little sideways pressure, he was able to keep it on the handle.

He took a breath and then started rolling the chair across the thin commercial carpeting, picking up speed as he passed the dead man pressed up against the wall. The pool of blood on the carpet gummed up the wheels briefly, making Trouble push a little harder. Since the M4 was on the right side of the cabinet, he aimed for the right-side door. He wanted to be able to keep the cabinet, with its reams of paper inside, between him and any shooters. But he also wanted to be able to swivel the chair around to aim. Going for the right-side door would allow him to do this while limiting the chances of taking a bullet from the right.

The side of the cabinet slammed into the push bar on the door with a loud metal crash. The cabinet wanted to tip back toward Trouble, but he kept it steady with his left hand, his damaged thumb screaming the whole time as it bounced around uselessly.

Then the door was swinging open, crashing against the wall, revealing the straight hallway ahead. And the two men kneeling in the middle of it.

They fired. Trouble pulled his head down and fired back, swiveling the chair to the right as bullets punched into the metal. A hole appeared on the back side of the cabinet as a bullet made it through, missing Trouble's left arm by less than an inch.

The man on the right went down, two of Trouble's bullets hitting home. But the man on the left was still firing. More holes appeared on the back side of the metal cabinet. He felt something hit him in the chest.

With a final shove, he let go of the cabinet, sending it toward the second man. But it veered off quickly and then toppled over. Trouble had known it would.

He moved quickly after letting go of the cabinet, stepping left and dropping to his knee, waiting for the cabinet to fall. When it did, he had a clean shot, and he took it, hitting the man in the head.

He checked his chest for a bullet wound, but only found a sore spot on his right pectoral muscle. He'd been shot, but the filing cabinet and the paperwork inside had bled off most of the projectile's inertia, saving his life. He turned his attention to the hall.

There were doors on both sides of the hallway, all of them closed. Trouble got quickly to his feet and looked for signs that would tell him where the control room was. Jensen had told him about it in his recording, saying how Beck used it to spy on people.

There were no signs indicating what was behind any of the doors. But there was a single pudding cup next to the nearest door on the right. Its top was off and there was a white spoon sticking out of it.

Trouble walked up and pressed his ear to the door, listening and trying to calm his breathing. He heard someone talking in there. It was Beck. But his voice wasn't full and resonant, like he was in there himself. It sounded like a recording.

Trouble reached down and tried the doorknob. It was un-locked. He turned it slowly, then shouldered the door open, sweeping the room with his M4.

Carmen's sister, Megan, jumped and turned around from where she stood at a soundboard next to a bank of monitors. She raised her hands, nothing in them. But there was a pud-ding cup nearby, sitting on a desk.

Trouble lowered his weapon and stepped inside, closing the door behind him. There was no lock on the door, which he thought was unfortunate.

"How do you put a video on the screen?" Trouble asked, looking at the monitors. The nave was full of people sitting and listening to Beck.

Megan just stared at him.

"Where's your sister?" he asked. "Is she still alive?"

There was a flicker of something in Megan's eyes. Something like shame, maybe.

"She's alive?" he said.

Megan nodded.

"You're going to let her die with all these other people?" he asked, gesturing at the monitors. "With these children?"

"You only see it as death," she said, not meeting his gaze. "It's the next stage in our evolution. It's Ascension."

"No, it's bullshit is what it is. You want to kill yourself, fine. Do it. But don't make these kids do it with you. Don't let them kill your sister. She doesn't want to Ascend. And if these kids were capable of making their own decisions, I'm guessing they wouldn't want to, either."

Beck was still talking on the stage, his voice coming from speakers next to the soundboard. There were people on the stage behind him, working at tables. Trouble looked closer and saw that they were putting the pentobarbital into the pudding. Other people were passing them out. Judging by the remaining boxes, they were almost done.

"We're leaving our egos behind," Beck said, standing and holding the hands of two children—Gibbs and Shayna. "We're ridding ourselves of our toxic minds. Of all those things that keep us from finding true peace. True enlightenment."

The sight of Beck holding the little girl's hand sent a stab of near-debilitating pain through Trouble's heart.

He set the gun down and pulled the phone out of his back pocket. He opened the appropriate app and pulled up the video Dylan had sent.

"Hook this up and play it," he said, presenting the phone to her. "Then let everyone make their own decisions."

"What is that?" she asked.

There was a frozen image of Raymond Beck underneath the white play button on the phone screen. But he looked younger. He still had some hair on his head, and his beard wasn't much more than a few days' growth. It only had little patches of gray in it.

"This is Beck. This is who he *really* is," Trouble said.

Megan's eyes flicked up to Trouble's face.

"What did he do?" Trouble asked, reading something in the woman's expression. "You've seen the real him today, haven't you?"

Megan shook her head.

Beck seemed to be winding up the talk. Trouble glanced at the shot of the stage. Of Beck, kneeling down next to the children. "Everyone gather your final treat," he said. "This is it. It's time. We will all Ascend together." A man brought three pudding cups up and handed them to Beck, who then handed one each to the children.

"Look at this!" Trouble said, grabbing Megan by the arm. "Those kids are going to die if you don't do something!" His instinct was to find the stage entrance and put a bullet between Beck's eyes. But he knew that it wouldn't stop many of the people. Maybe some of them wouldn't eat the pudding, but most of them would. They would want to follow their martyr to the next life.

"Pray with me one last time," Beck said.

A look of determination came over Megan Marsden's face, and she grabbed the phone from Trouble. She sat down at a computer and found a USB cable, plugging it into the PC and then the smaller end into the phone.

Then she did something on the computer, transferring the file. After a few seconds, she pulled the video up on the computer. She clicked a few more times and then pressed play.

Trouble looked up at the bank of monitors, seeing the heads lift in the auditorium as the audience looked up at the screen above the stage. Suddenly, Beck's voice from the recording was competing with Beck's voice from his microphone.

He looked up, confused, and quickly turned around, seeing himself on the screen. His eyes went wide.

"No!" he shouted, dropping his pudding cup and standing. "Turn this off!"

"Can you shut off his microphone?" Trouble asked.

Megan looked at him briefly, then nodded and moved over to the soundboard. "This is false! It's the work of the Dark Ones!" He was frantic. Panicking. "This is—" She hit a button to mute his mic, cutting his words off.

Trouble guessed the cameras weren't designed to pick up audio. Or if they were, it was muted from the control panel. He turned to the computer screen to watch the video. He hadn't actually seen it. All he knew was what Dylan had told him.

Beck was clearly intoxicated in the recording. He was wearing a striped, blue-and-white collared shirt and sitting on a couch in a dimly lit room, talking to someone off-screen. The recording was clearly being done surreptitiously. The camera was at a strange angle, as if it were hidden among items on a side table. Despite this, the quality was good and the sound clear. You could tell it was Beck. No doubt.

". . . ate it all up. Like I was holding out a dish of catnip to a bunch of cats. They couldn't get enough of it." Beck was grinning, his speech slightly slurred and his eyelids heavy as he sat on the couch however many years ago the video had been taken. There was laughter off-screen. A single person. A man, guffawing at the remark about the cats.

"But how did you get that guy to stop smoking?" the man said from off-screen after his laughter died down. There was something vaguely familiar about the voice.

"The smoking thing?" Beck said with a wave of a hand. "That's really just the power of suggestion. I brought him into that back room for what, thirty minutes? Meanwhile, everyone out in the meeting room is doing the exercises I gave them, right?"

"Yeah," the other man said.

"So in the room, I hypnotize the guy, right? It took me a long time to learn to hypnotize people, but even longer to learn how to pick the people to hypnotize. You see, it doesn't work on everyone. You can't just pick some asshole from a crowd and hypnotize him. Not unless you get lucky. But there are certain people, certain personality types, that take well to it. And that guy's one of them."

"So you just hypnotized him and that's it? He doesn't want to smoke anymore?"

Trouble glanced at the bank of monitors while he listened to the recording. Beck was in the audience now, walking around, gesturing wildly and clearly yelling. About half of the audience was watching him, the other half was looking at the screen.

On the recording, Beck giggled and shook his head, eyes closed. "No, man! The hypnotizing is part of the suggestion. I put him in a relaxed state, right? That's really all hypnotizing is. People let their guard down and they become susceptible to certain suggestions. You can't make someone do something they don't want to do, though. But I already knew the guy wanted to quit smoking. So after maybe twenty minutes of keeping this guy in a relaxed state and spouting gibberish, I—"

"Wait, you were making it up while you were talking to him? Just off-the-cuff stuff?"

"Oh, yeah. It doesn't really matter what you say. I mean, it *kind of* does. You can't get super weird, or you'll bring the person out of it. But I mostly talked about him quitting smoking. Positive reinforcement bullshit, right? Affirmations? All that hippie nonsense? But when I brought him out and stood him in front of the crowd, you remember what I asked him?"

"Yeah. You asked him if he craved cigarettes anymore. He said no."

"Then I asked him if he'd ever smoke again, remember? I told him to really search, deep down, and see if he'd ever touch a cigarette. What did he say?"

"He said no way."

"Right," Beck said, grinning again. "I mean, what the fuck else would he say, with all those people watching? And even if he left after that meeting and lit up, do you think he'd admit it to anyone else? Fuck no. No way. Because he said it in front of all those people. Because he wanted to please me. And because peer pressure is a powerful fucking thing. But that's what I mean by picking people to hypnotize. That guy has the perfect personality for that kind of thing. He's the type to go along to get along, you know? Most of the people who stay on at the facilities after their rehab stint are like that. They're fucking sheeple. It's almost too easy."

The other guy was laughing again. "Oh, man. Oh, man. That's fucking priceless."

The camera lost focus on Beck for a moment as someone passed in front of it and then sat down on the couch next to the short Black man. Trouble immediately recognized him. It was Vogel. He wore a plaid button-up shirt and blue jeans.

"So what's your plan?" Vogel asked. "Now that you have these people in the palm of your hand, what are you going to do?"

"I'm going to live the life I've always wanted. I'm going to fuck every woman I want. I'm going to make people listen to me. Really listen. I've got some great fucking ideas in my head." He tapped his temple. "And I finally have the audience I deserve. And you're going to come along with me. You'll get my sloppy seconds." Beck laughed at this, and so did Vogel.

"That Marsden chick," Vogel said, then whistled. "She fine as fuck."

"She's mine," Beck said, suddenly serious. "It took months of careful work to get her away from that dipshit boyfriend of hers. The fuck is his name? Jason? Jayden?"

"Jensen."

"Fuck him. Little bitch. Let his girl just slip through his hands like that. He didn't deserve her."

"I'll sort him out if you need me to," Vogel said, with a little too much enthusiasm.

"Nah. He's under my thumb. He doesn't even know which way is up."

Trouble looked over at Megan Marsden. Her mouth was hanging open, her face ashen. She looked like a woman who just got the news her lover had died. And, in a way, he thought that was accurate.

The two men on the screen fell into a short silence before Beck spoke again. "With all the money we're getting from these people, I've started looking for our own little place. Some land where we can build our own little community and be left alone. We can't go on like this at the facilities. It's too much work for me. Too much travel. I need them all in one place. That way, we can control everything."

"Makes sense to me," Vogel said, leaning forward and grabbing a liquor bottle from a table in front of the couch.

"They won't all come," Beck said, "but that's okay. Those who do come will be in it for the long haul. That's what we want. But I'll try and work my magic so I can get the biggest cash cows to come with us, to keep giving us their money or sell their properties or whatever. Right now, I just need you to keep doing what you're doing. That bitch Padilla's trying to organize some ex-members against me. Keep focusing on her and anyone who even thinks about joining her witch hunt. But be careful. Do what you have to do, but I don't want to hear about it, and I don't want it coming back to bite us in the ass."

Vogel nodded. "You got it."

Beck put his head back on the couch and closed his eyes. After a moment, Vogel looked over, directly into the camera, smiling slightly.

That was the end of the video.

Trouble looked back at the bank of monitors. His heart lurched when he couldn't immediately find Beck.

"Where'd he go?" he said, moving closer to study each monitor.

Many of the audience members were crying. Others were looking around confused, dazed. Most of them had discarded their pudding cups. As he scanned the crowd, Trouble saw a couple of people trying to eat their pudding, but those around them wrestling with them, trying to stop them. But he didn't see Beck.

And he didn't see Shayna, either.

"Oh, no," he said, bringing his rifle up and running for the door.

Chapter 47

HE MOVED INTO THE hall without stopping, stepping over the two men he'd shot while getting to the control room. There was a set of wooden double doors ahead and to the right. One of the doors was open.

Cautiously, Trouble moved up to the open door and peered inside from behind the M4. He was looking into the backstage area. There was a guard there, and he raised his rifle when he saw Trouble.

"Don't!" Trouble said, getting ready to fire.

The guy hesitated. Then he threw the rifle down and put his hands up.

"Where's Beck? Which way did he go?"

"To your left," the guy said. "Toward the back door."

"Who was with him?"

"The little girl, Angel. And the woman. Parall Marsden's sister."

Trouble ran down the hall, turning a corner and seeing exterior doors to his left. He paused and took the magazine out of the M4, then replaced it with the one he'd taken from the kid's gun earlier.

He pushed through the door, using his left hip on the push bar. The afternoon sun streamed down, making him squint. He swept from right to left with the rifle but saw no one.

The door was in the back right corner of the building if you were looking at it head-on. So Trouble turned left and headed toward the rear.

He saw them as soon as he cleared the corner of the building.

Beck had Carmen's hair in his left fist, a gun jammed into her low back with his right hand. He was forcing her down a series of wide rock shelves toward a relatively flat clifftop area. At first, Trouble didn't see the girl, but as Carmen turned slightly to move down a rocky step, he saw that Shayna was in Carmen's arms.

Beck glanced over his shoulder and saw Trouble. He yanked on Carmen's hair while spinning himself around, getting her in front of him as a human shield.

Trouble's vision narrowed at the scene, blood rushing loudly in his ears. He felt suddenly sick. Nauseous. Palms sweaty. Sweat stinging his eyes. The symphony of pain in his body that adrenaline had previously dulled now took precedence.

They were about thirty yards away and about twelve feet below Trouble. Even if he'd been supremely confident in his abilities with an M4, he wouldn't have taken the shot. Not even when Beck had been behind them. It would've been too risky.

But now it seemed impossible to even think clearly about any way to dispose of Beck. To get Carmen and Shayna away from him. It was as if the analytical functions of his brain were stuck in a rut. The M4 was heavy in his hands. Mental paralysis took hold.

"Don't come closer!" Beck yelled. "I'll shoot them both! Don't think one bullet won't go right through her. It will!"

Carmen looked up at Trouble, her head stuck in an awkward position because Beck had her by the hair. Her mouth was partially open, but she had a determined look on her face. Shayna, cradled in Carmen's arms, was silently crying, her face screwed up with fear.

Trouble dropped the M4 and held his hands out. He felt small again. Weak. He was suddenly a helpless child, watching Mr. Hoffman lead Melissa out of the bedroom. The terrible screams would come next. He couldn't take the screams. Not again.

Beck maneuvered carefully down the last step and onto the clifftop. It was an area about twenty feet deep and fifteen wide. There was a makeshift fire pit near the middle, and a couple of camp chairs set about. Beck backed into one of the camp chairs and kicked it in frustration. It tumbled back and slid off the edge, dropping to the ground far below.

Run, that voice in Trouble's head said again. *Run, run, run away. Live to fight another day.*

He knew it was a facet of himself—that was clear—but a facet from a different time. When he'd been a child, abused and threatened and beaten. It was a piece of himself he'd managed to tuck away as childhood was forced from him. When he'd started living on the streets. He'd done it to survive—tucked that voice away. That fear. Because living in fear—living with a voice like that constantly in his ear—would've been tantamount to wearing a sign on his chest that said he was terrified, vulnerable, and easily manipulated. That fear would've been sniffed out and exploited. And, he realized, he'd still been manipulated, taken advantage of, *used*. He shuddered to think what it would've been like if he'd let that voice drive back then. He probably wouldn't have survived.

But all the while, he was learning to cultivate another voice. One not based in fear, but in savagery and confidence.

"Get away, Rubble!" Beck called. "Get away or we all die."

Trouble took a step back, terror ripping at his insides.

Rubble. Something in him latched onto that one word. His name. One given him by parents he'd never known in any meaningful way. Nothing more than a handful of foggy memories of his mother. Memories that may well have been made up. Gleaned from television shows or movies or even from a fantasy of how he thought people with real mothers lived.

Rubble.

His last name was fitting. A legacy handed down along with a life of living among the rubble. A life of hardship and fear and scar tissue.

Strange, that fear was supposed to keep you alive. It was a survival mechanism, as old as humankind. But too much fear was just the opposite. Too much fear would get you killed. Somehow, Trouble had realized this as a kid. As he'd been bounced around between the street and foster homes and juvenile detention centers. He'd gone to school on occasion, which was where he'd earned the nickname he now wore with a certain amount of pride.

Trouble.

That was his true name. It wasn't one he'd given himself, but it was one he fit into like it was a piece of expertly tailored clothing. And it had come at the perfect time, he now realized as he looked down at Beck and Carmen and Shayna.

Because it was what he'd been searching for. It was indicative of what he had to be to survive. It wasn't the child cowering as adults threatened and cajoled. It wasn't the kid on the playground who looked away when the bullies were at work on the weak and defenseless.

Trouble was something else altogether. It was what Terrence Rubble had been searching for. More than a persona. An identity.

He *was* trouble. Because trouble wasn't fear. Trouble wasn't second-guessing. It wasn't running away when you were supposed to stand and fight. Trouble made *other* people scared. Trouble brought out the true cowardice in tormentors.

The man called Trouble dropped his hands to his sides and took a step forward.

His fear wasn't gone. Nothing was ever that simple. He moved with an effort, fighting against that voice, remembering who he was now. Who he'd become. The type of person he was. More than the sum of his parts. More than even the multitudes he contained.

More than fear or bravery or confidence. More than any one thing. Just like Beck was more than a cult leader. He was a human. But a human who was no more than the sum of his parts.

"Don't!" Beck yelled, eyes rolling like those of a cornered animal.

Trouble stepped down, getting closer, staring at Carmen. She seemed to nod with her eyes, and he realized that she'd known what had to happen the entire time. She'd been trying to communicate it to Trouble, waiting for him to catch on. The determined look on her face wasn't a brave face at all. It wasn't a façade. It was the look of a woman who was ready to deal with a bad situation. Ready to do what was right, even if it got her killed.

Trouble had a moment to admire her for it. He'd been so wrapped up in his own fear, he couldn't see what was right in front of him. Couldn't see that Beck had cornered himself for a reason. He could've easily gone to one of the buses out front and tried to run. But he didn't.

He was determined to die. And he wanted company.

But he was also scared.

Killing yourself with a barbiturate was a very different thing than putting a bullet into your brain or jumping off a cliff.

So he was hesitating.

Trouble stepped down to the next rocky shelf. He was fifteen yards away now. He shifted his gaze from Carmen to Beck.

The cult leader was near the edge of the cliff. He could take a big step backward and fall. And if his grip on Carmen was sure, he could take her with him.

Trouble knew Carmen wouldn't keep hold of Shayna if that's how things went down. It would be the logical thing to do. To drop the girl. A few scrapes and bruises from hitting the ground would be a small price to pay for staying alive.

But if she dropped the girl too soon, Beck might shoot. He still had the pistol at Carmen's back. At least that's how it looked to Trouble from where he was.

As Trouble stepped down once more, leaving only one more wide, rocky shelf between him and the clifftop, Beck suddenly stopped fidgeting. He didn't yell for Trouble to stop. He just gazed over Carmen's shoulder, his eyes growing hard.

Trouble cocked his right elbow slightly, getting his hand in position to pull out the Glock 22 still tucked in his back waistband. While he did this, he stared into Beck's eyes, waiting for what he knew was coming.

Every narcissist he'd ever met had insisted on having the last word. It was a compulsion. And Beck was no different.

"You just killed these two—"

Beck stopped mid-sentence as Carmen tossed Shayna away from her. In the same instance, she kicked her right foot backward, trying to hit Beck. She managed a glancing blow on his shin, but it wasn't enough to send him over the edge.

Trouble reached up and gripped the Glock in his right hand, pulling it out as Carmen's weak kick landed. He was still pulling it up when Beck yanked Carmen's head back and twisted, sweeping her legs out from under her and sending her over the side of the cliff.

Before Beck was even through with this movement, he was pointing the gun at Trouble with his right hand. His body was twisted to the right, but he was aiming under his left arm, which had just released Carmen's hair. He fired just as Trouble squeezed the Glock's trigger.

Beck's bullet missed.

Trouble's didn't.

It struck the man in the gut, causing him to stagger backward half a step. Crouching and gripping his stomach with both hands—gun still in his right—he raised his head and looked up at Trouble. His eyes were wide and feverish with pain that was just beginning to set in.

Trouble wasted no time. He moved forward and shot Beck again, this time in the upper chest. The man crumpled and fell, his butt striking the edge of the cliff and causing him to flip back into thin air toward the trees and the ground below.

Trouble tossed the gun down and ran to the cliff's edge, looking down at the spot where Carmen had gone over. She was there, clinging to the cliff, looking up.

Trouble got onto his belly and extended his hand toward her. She shook her head. "I got this," she said. "Easier for me to climb up myself. Check on the girl."

He looked into her stunning eyes for a moment, remembering their time together yesterday. Recalling how she'd told him about her favorite pastime: rock climbing. He'd noticed it in her hands. They were beautiful, strong hands.

Getting to his feet, Trouble moved over to Shayna, who was curled up on the ground, whimpering. He picked her up and hugged her to him. She gripped him tight around the neck.

"You're okay," he said. "You're okay." He almost added "Melissa" at the end, but stopped himself. This wasn't Melissa. There was no changing the past. Only learning from it. Taking what you could and moving on, leaving the rest where it belonged, far behind you.

Carmen came up over the cliff with practiced ease. Standing there, she looked at Trouble and took a deep breath. "Wow," she said.

"Can you step away from the cliff?" Trouble said. "You're making me nervous."

She smiled and stepped toward him. "You don't like heights?"

"I hate heights," Trouble said.

Chapter 48

"I'M GUESSING VOGEL RECORDED it as an insurance policy of some kind." Dylan's voice came over the phone from half a world away, talking about the recording he'd found. The recording that had kept many people from killing themselves. "But it looks like he got in too deep to ever use it. Beck probably had plenty of dirt on him, as well."

Trouble nodded, phone to his ear. "Yeah." He was standing outside the KOA campground office next to his motorcycle. In the adjacent spot, Carmen Marsden and Shayna Mitchell sat in a truck they'd borrowed from the Emissaries compound. Trouble glanced in at them. The girl was clearly traumatized. She hadn't wanted to let go of Trouble at all when they were getting in the truck. Now she was pressed up against Carmen, who was playing gently with the girl's golden hair.

"So where did you find it?" Trouble asked, turning away.

"I figured there had to be something like that around," Dylan said. "So I started looking into the names you told me about. Marsden. Jensen. Vogel. Mitchell. Most people just keep their digital dirty laundry in some kind of cloud-storage service. It's not that hard to get to if you know what you're doing. The hard part is sorting through all the innocuous stuff until you find something good."

"Well, that was pretty fucking good," Trouble said. "I can't thank you enough."

"So everyone's alive? I mean . . . everyone who didn't try to kill you."

Trouble hesitated. "Not everyone. There was a handful of people who ate the pudding, anyway. I guess they couldn't take the lie. Or they didn't believe the recording. But the kids are all alive. Still, it's going to be a long road back for everyone in there. Most of them gave everything to Beck. They don't have jobs, property, or even any savings."

"It's messed up. But it's better than dying."

"Yeah. It is."

"What about the Jensen guy?" Dylan asked.

"He died. Some woman told me what happened. He essentially talked everyone out of mass murder in Dalewood. But Vogel shot him for it. Then someone shot Vogel, but they didn't kill him. He stole one of the buses and ran."

"Oh, damn. Okay, no need to ask. I'm on it."

"Thanks, Dylan," Trouble said. "I heard he went south, so that's where I'm headed. I gotta get out of here before the Feds show up, anyway. But I can't risk going back through Dalewood. So I have to go north for a while before turning south again. I'll contact you from a burner as soon as possible."

"Got it," Dylan said. "Ride safe."

Trouble took the phone from his ear and pressed the red end button on the screen. Then he stepped back over to the truck and opened the passenger side door. Carmen and Shayna looked at him. He handed the phone back to Carmen. "Thanks."

Carmen nodded in response. "You're really going? Right now?" she asked.

Trouble nodded. "I decided a long time ago I'm not going to jail for doing the right thing."

"You think you'd go to jail? You saved hundreds of lives."

Trouble studied her face. "You know I would. At least until everything was sorted out. More likely for several years. You don't kill people and walk away clean, even if your intentions are good. Not with my background, you don't."

Carmen nodded. She looked about as sad as he felt. Even if he felt like he could stick around, it wouldn't work out between them. He knew that much.

"Besides," Trouble said. "I have some unfinished business with Vogel. He doesn't get to walk away from this thing."

"What about after that?" she asked. "Maybe we can meet up somewhere. You have my number now."

Trouble smiled and looked down at his left forearm, where she'd written her phone number in large letters with a marker found in the truck's glove compartment. "Yeah, maybe," he said. "But after Vogel, I have to pay a visit to some people in California. If they're still there."

"Friends?"

"No. Not friends. A couple of foster parents I haven't seen in many, many years."

Epilogue

BRANDON WADE VOGEL WAS settling into his motel room in Bisbee, Arizona. He'd been on the run non-stop for over twenty-four hours. He'd ditched the school bus outside of Taos and had taken a small veterinarian clinic hostage, forcing the vet to clean and stitch his wound up. It was a through-and-through in his left trapezius muscle. Shrugging or turning his head or even moving his left arm caused a sharp pain in the area.

After stealing the vet's sedan, he'd made it to Albuquerque without incident, stealing another car from outside a movie theater. He'd also been hitting ATMs, withdrawing as much money as he could from the accounts he'd been steadily feeding since joining up with Beck.

Tomorrow, he'd cross the border into Mexico and lose himself in the vast country. He just had to get a few traveler's checks and then he'd be on his way.

He was sitting on the motel room bed, flipping through channels to find something good before he opened his bag of McDonald's to chow down. It was not quite six o'clock in the evening, but Vogel hadn't slept much. He was planning to be asleep by eight.

There was a knock at his door, startling him. He winced as he looked to his left, wondering who would be knocking. He'd paid extra so he wouldn't have to show an ID. And he registered under a fake name. He grabbed his pistol and stood up.

It was a woman. He could see her through the peephole. She stood fidgeting on the sidewalk, Vogel's stolen SUV visible behind her.

"What do you want?" Vogel asked through the door.

"Jamie?" the woman said. "That you?"

"No Jamie here. You got the wrong room."

"Oh, okay. Sorry," she said, then moved away from the door, down the sidewalk.

Vogel stayed at the door for a few long moments, staring out, watching for movement in the fading sunlight. He saw nothing of interest, but he moved over to the window, anyway, parting the curtains and peering out. He kept his gun in his right hand, down out of view.

As he was about to step away from the window and eat his meal, a figure stepped into view, not four feet away on the other side of the glass. It was Terrence Rubble, wearing a new-looking leather jacket and a cockeyed smile. He was pointing a pistol through the window. "I thought it was you," he said. "But I had to make sure."

Fear blossomed in Vogel's chest. He straightened, dropping the curtain as he stepped away and raised his pistol. There was the crack of a gunshot. Glass broke and the curtains twitched as a bullet came through from the other side, striking Vogel in the neck. He stumbled and fell back, hitting the bed and then sliding to the floor. He dropped his gun and brought both hands to his neck as blood poured out from the wound.

The sound of more glass breaking seemed to come from far away. The curtains moved. Rubble reached through a large hole he'd made in the broken window and parted the curtains with his left hand, the thumb of which was splinted. He still had his gun up, but he didn't fire when he saw Vogel.

They both knew he would be dead soon.

Vogel couldn't breathe. Panic crowded in and continued to grow as things began to fade away. The front of his shirt was soaked with blood.

Darkness settled on him gradually as he grew colder and colder. Rubble was just a shadowy figure that turned and walked away from the motel room window.

Death came for Vogel. It was anything but peaceful.

***

Trouble looked into his side mirror as he rode away from the motel. The woman he'd paid to knock on Vogel's door was gazing at him. There were a couple of other people stepping out of their rooms, seeing what all the fuss was about. As he came to the motel entrance, he saw the woman disappear, ducking back behind the building. She wouldn't be around to talk to the police. He'd paid her extra for that.

He turned out of the parking lot and cruised along, taking a moment to pull a pair of sunglasses out of an inside jacket pocket. The desert sun was low, shining in his face. The jacket was a little stiff, but after being without his old leather for a few days, it felt good.

He wondered if he would eventually develop a superstition like the one he'd held for his old jacket—the one still in the Divine Emissaries compound somewhere. He doubted it. Life was full of phases. Things changed. You were supposed to learn. To grow.

That was okay.

He turned left onto Bisbee Road, which was the main thoroughfare. In half a mile, he would turn onto Center Avenue. Center would turn into School Terrace Road, which skirted the small desert town and led directly to Highway 92, which he would follow south and then west.

He thought about fear and its power. That was one thing Beck had been right about. Fear can corrupt. It can kill. The thing was, Beck hadn't been addressing fear in his flock. He'd been exploiting it.

Trouble considered the road ahead as he shifted gears, picking up speed. The sound of sirens was faint behind him, coming from the other side of town. The sun was setting, burgeoning oranges and pinks adding their brilliance to the western horizon.

He smiled. He wasn't afraid.

He knew exactly who he was.

He was *Trouble*.

***

I hope you enjoyed *The Deadly Divine*. It was certainly fun to write. Read on for an excerpt from the next standalone book in the series, *Dead Man's Hatch*. But before you do that, please take a moment to review this book. It's impossible to overstate how much reviews help indie authors like me. Plus, it only takes a minute or two.

Thanks for reading. And don't forget to snag your free *Trouble* novella at MatthewDoggettAuthor.com/Trouble

Now, here's a sample of *Dead Man's Hatch*. . .

Dead Man's Hatch Sample

TROUBLE GRINNED AT THE man sitting in the wheelchair. The night pressed in close, and the bustle of the city was a constant hum of engines, conversations in Spanish, and honking horns. But the man's music floated over it all, momentarily calming Trouble's anxiety.

The man's calloused, brown fingers pressed against the ukulele's strings at the neck while he strummed a rhythm at the body of the small instrument. His grin, underneath a bushy gray and black mustache, revealed his few remaining teeth. His eyes were smiling as his head bobbed to the beat. He was into the music. He was in the zone. And Trouble could feel it coming off the guy. It was contagious, addictive.

Despite his unease, Trouble grinned. He tapped the toe of one heavy Doc Martens boot against the concrete at the corner of Mariano Escobedo and Calle Mariano Matamoros in downtown Monterrey, Mexico. He had his hands tucked into the pockets of his black leather jacket, despite the temperate night. None of the pedestrians who walked by on the busy sidewalk stopped, making it a show for one. Trouble was peripherally aware of these other people, that awareness a process that ran on its own without any effort on his part. Like breathing.

When the man's song was over, the flow necessarily broken, Trouble dug into his pocket and pulled out a one hundred peso note—about five American dollars—and stepped forward. There was an upturned blue-and-gray baseball cap sitting on the guy's lap, inches from where both legs ended at the knees. Trouble went to put the bill in the cap, but the man shook his head, still grinning. He pointed down the street and said something about a park.

Trouble knew little Spanish, but after a minute of back and forth, he confirmed that the man wanted help getting to the Macroplaza, the large park just down the road. Trouble wheeled him down the gently sloping sidewalk, past one side of the large congressional building for the state of Nuevo Leon. The dark concrete-and-glass building certainly wasn't as large as the skyscrapers jutting out of other parts of the city, but it was taller than the nearby buildings.

The journey to the park took about five minutes, during which the old man chatted in Spanish, his escort catching only every third or fourth word. Trouble had to resist glancing over his shoulder every few steps. His gut told him that the unassuming middle-aged Hispanic man in the plaid shirt, jeans, and cowboy boots would be there, pretending not to follow. He missed his motorcycle. And his guns. He felt trapped without the former and naked without the latter.

The man thanked him when their journey was finished. Trouble gave him the hundred-peso note anyway and left him in a prime spot at the edge of a walkway in the middle of the beautiful park. When he heard the sweet sound of the ukulele, Trouble turned and saw that the old guy already had an audience of two; a young couple holding hands.

Trouble smiled as he crossed the street, leaving the park. He strained to hear the instrument over the city sounds. He thought he could still hear it when a van came to a screeching halt beside him. He thought he could still hear it over the masked man with the gun in his hand, commanding him to get in the van. And when the unassuming man in the jeans, the plaid shirt, and the cowboy boots came out of nowhere and hit Trouble in the back of the head with something hard, the music seemed to get louder. Then he was face down in the van and the only sound was that of the engine and the heavy breathing of several men.

One man pulled zip-ties tight around his wrists and ankles while another man pressed his head to the floor with his knee. When his limbs were bound, they flipped him over and started rummaging through his pockets. Trouble looked with open curiosity at them, his gaze settling on the only man without a mask—the one who'd hit him.

"Do I look like I'm worth money?" Trouble asked him, his head feeling funny from the blow, the full pain of it not yet apparent.

The unassuming man smiled. He had the face of a kindly uncle or a caring teacher. "It's not money we're after," he said in excellent English.

"What are you after?" Trouble asked.

"You."

***

The Trouble continues in *Dead Man's Hatch*. Look for it on Amazon and in Kindle Unlimited in the Spring of 2023!

Also By

The Trouble Series - Gritty Crime Novels

- Too Much Trouble - Available on Amazon (Free on Kindle Unlimited)

- The Death Dealers - Available on Amazon (Free on Kindle Unlimited)

- Trouble (A Novella) - Available for free at MatthewDoggettAuthor.com/Trouble

- Dead Man's Hatch (Spring 2023)

The Undead Trilogy

A ZOMBIE APOCALYPSE LIKE you've never experienced. Discover how much fun — and how gory — the end of the world can be.

- The Rise of the Vampire Merek - An Undead Prequel - Available Exclusively at MatthewDoggettAuthor.com (For Free!)

- Undead Annihilation - Book 1 - Available on Amazon (Free on Kindle Unlimited)

- Undead Assimilation - Book 2 - Available on Amazon (Free on Kindle Unlimited)

- Undead Extermination - Book 3 - Available on Amazon (Free on Kindle Unlimited)

About the Author

When Matthew Doggett isn't writing novels about unlikely heroes and apocalyptic hellscapes, he's writing podcast episodes about terrifying creatures and heroes who stare into the black void of nothingness. You can find his short stories featured on the Dr. NoSleep podcast, the SCP Experience podcast, and the Crime Hub podcast. He is currently bouncing around the United States, looking for the next isolated cabin in which to write for a month or two. Connect with him through his author page at Facebook.com/MatthewDoggettAuthor or simply email him at Contact@MatthewDoggettAuthor.com.